Praise for Benjamin
debut novel C

"This funny novel of furniture moving gone awry is a magical realism quest for modern times. Parzybok's touching story explores the aimlessness of our culture, a society of jobs instead of callings, replete with opportunities and choices but without the philosophies and vocations we need to make meaningful decisions."
—Josh Cook, Porter Square Books, Cambridge, MA
An Indie Next List Pick

"Parzybok's colorful characters, striking humor, and eccentric magical realism offer up an adventuresome read."
—Christian Crider, Inkwood Books, Tampa, FL
Selected twice as An Indie Next Reading Group List Pick

"Simply one of the best, most enjoyable, and most original books I've read in a very, very long time. This novel about a fantastic orange couch is a lyrical story of a heroic quest undertaken by flawed but intrinsically good people. Humorous and glorious, celebratory of the sacred thing that lies inside each (OK, most) of us—I'm recommending *Couch* to everyone!"
—Beth Simpson, Cornerstone Books, Salem, MA

"Hundreds of writers have slavishly imitated—or outright ripped off—Tolkien in ways that connoisseurs of other genres would consider shameless. What Parzybok has done here in adapting the same old song to a world more familiar to the reader is to revive the genre and make it relevant again."—*The Stranger*

"Delightfully lighthearted writing. . . . Occasionally laugh-out-loud funny, the enthusiastic prose carries readers through sporadic dark moments . . . Parzybok's quirky humor recalls the flaws and successes of early Douglas Adams."—*Publishers Weekly*

SHERWOOD NATION

SHERWOOD NATION

a novel by

Benjamin Parzybok

Small Beer Press
Easthampton, MA

Small Beer Press
150 Pleasant Street #306
Easthampton, MA 01027
smallbeerpress.com
weightlessbooks.com
info@smallbeerpress.com

Distributed to the trade by Consortium.
Parzybok, Benjamin, author.
  Sherwood Nation / Benjamin Parzybok.
     pages cm
  Summary: "In Portland, Oregon, water rations are down to one gallon per person per day. Even as water is declared a communal right, hoarding and riots persist. A young water activist nicknamed Maid Marian rides her swelling popularity in opposition to the city government and becomes an icon to a city in need. Even as she and her compatriots build a new community, they make powerful enemies in the city government and the National Guard. Their idealistic dream is quickly caught up in a brutal fight for survival. This is a love story, a war story, a grand social experiment, a treatise on government, on freedom and necessity, on individualism and community"-- Provided by publisher.
  ISBN 978-1-61873-086-2 (paperback) -- ISBN 978-1-61873-087-9 (ebook)
  I. Title.
  PS3616.A788S54 2014
  813'.6--dc23
                         2014018642

First Edition 1 2 3 4 5 6 7 8 9 0

Text set in 11 pt Minion.
Printed on 30% PCR recycled 50# Natures Natural paper by the Maple Press in York, PA.
Cover art by Andi Watson (andiwatson.info).

PREFACE

How it happened:

It happened slowly. The fishermen called the rogue and unpredictable changes at sea *El Pescadero*. Winds came from differing directions, currents looped back on themselves, temperatures fluctuated. It wasn't seasonal like El Niño, though at first everyone thought it was. It didn't go away. Governments fought bitterly about whose fault was whose, and who ought to do what about it.

Along with *El Pescadero* came an increase in oceanic salinity. There were lots of theories there. When you swam in the ocean, the new buoyancy was subtle, but pleasurable.

The bone-dry summers of the west lingered deeper and deeper into winter. Everyone could see that the snow pack was melting. When was the snow pack not melting? All you had to do was look up at any of the balding mountains.

Then the great Deschutes River, elegant and fast, a river which cut across the Oregon desert like a streak of lightning across a dull gray sky, dried up in a single summer.

The farms that depended upon it followed suit. There were strikes and protests. Blood was spilled. Then, quickly, other rivers diminished.

Finally, the greatest of them all, the Columbia River, its sources choked in mud, leaked its deathsong through the gorge, and became only a scaly alligator skin of memory. In its wake, valleys turned to deserts, fertile farms to dust, and the great migration East began.

As the hordes of Droudies poured into the Midwest and Eastern United States and the last of the surface water seeped deep into the ground, anger over the millions of incoming refugees escalated. Finally, borders along the Rocky Mountains were sealed to Westerners and a meager aid strategy was conceived by the bankrupt government for the many millions abandoned to their dry fates out west.

THE DROUGHT

It was morning and the power was not yet on. Zach and Renee lay in the heat of the bed listening to the city wake outside the building's windows.

"We should learn how to rain-dance," Renee said. They were new to the relationship, and she could feel his hesitance to speak, the tentativeness to him, as if she were some toothy, unpredictable animal he'd invited into his house. She pressed her lips into his shoulder and wanted to bite him there. His skin left a taste of salt on her lips.

"Why don't you?" Zach said.

"Nah."

Zach stared at the ceiling, and she stared at him, with his short-cropped head and monkish demeanor, as if he lived his life in servitude to some greater thing, the identity of which she had yet to figure out. "I'm thinking of turning to crime instead."

"You'd be good at it," he said. He was never sure how serious she was. He made two pistols of his hands and *pow-pow*ed the ceiling. "But you'd need a mask and a horse, obviously."

"Mm, spurs."

An eerie *clop clop clop* sounded through the open window and they looked at each other in amazement.

"A horse!" she said. "You're a conjurer!"

But instead it was a big moose that stumbled along the dusty street, its skin tight over its ribs. Its head jerked left and right in anxious, almost animatronic movements.

"Oh no," Renee said, "I fucking hate this. Josh saw a bear two days ago—I told you?"

They watched it continue down the street until a shot rang out. The moose's body jerked and sidestepped strangely and then there was another shot.

"That's a whole shit ton of extra food rations if they can store it," Zach said as they watched men close in on it. "God knows how they'll store it." The moose stumbled again on a third shot but continued on. "They've got to get a straight shot in."

"I can't watch," Renee said. She climbed back in bed and spoke to Zach's shirtless back as he watched the moose fall and the hunters try to drag the animal to the side of the road. "Hunters in the streets."

"Dying of thirst has got to be worse," Zach said.

"What's happening? Tell me what's happening."

"They can't lift it, one of its legs is kicking."

"My coworker had to kill his dog," Zach said. He's a total mess about it."

"Seriously? No."

"He was a big dog. He drank over twenty units a day and was getting aggressive about his share."

"I don't buy it," Renee said. "The moose maybe, but not your own dog. Next is your neighbor, then your children and your wife. It's like a spider that cuts her own webbing."

"You think I'm in danger, as his coworker?"

"Oh, you're in danger alright."

Zach turned and looked at her and she winked at him. She was naked with the sheet pulled to the top of her thighs. She had unraveled her braids for him the night before, and her hair spilled across her arms and his pillow.

"You're not watching anymore?" she said.

"No." He pulled his gallon off the dresser and poured them each a unit, a little less than half a cup. He handed her one and sat on the edge of the bed, placing one hand on her thigh, the heat of it warming his hand through the sheet. He stared into the shallow cup of water and thought of the moose's stutter-step as it was shot, and wondered if he would know when he was the moose—the animal too lost and thirsty for reason, stumbling toward annihilation.

He was still thirsty after he'd finished. Renee stared into her cup as if awaiting a divination there. It was an effort not to refill his. Rations were two unit gallons per day. His measure of making it: if at the end of the day he had a few units of savings leftover.

He watched her sit up in bed. She divvied her hair into two halves and proceeded to rework each half into long, black braids. He was so taken with her. He wished the job of braiding would never end, so he could keep on watching.

"Come back in here," she said when she'd finished.

"I've got to work," he said, but made no movement toward it. He was one of the few people he knew who had a job.

"Nah. When the power goes on, we can pretend then. We can go about the day. Until then, let's be here."

He stood over the bed indecisively for a moment until she got a crab-claw hold on his wrist and pulled him back in. There was a struggle with the sheet as she worked at getting it flattened out and repositioned over them just so and he held still and grinned as she worried it. When it was finally to her liking, they lay side by side, the sheet pulled to their chins, and were quiet.

He found her hand under the covers. Next to him was the girl who'd served him coffee at the café down the block for over a year, the one he'd thought about at work, at night, in bed. The one he never got it together enough to approach for more than a cup of coffee. The girl he'd listened to as she talked to customers, weaving in eloquent yarns that inevitably turned to history: the collapse of the Bronze Age, the Mongol empire, the Polish peasant revolt, the Mayan uprising against the Spanish, and with each story he overheard he felt himself able to say less to her, his tongue tangled with awe.

Then two weeks ago the café was shut down and she walked home with him on her last day. At his door, he'd said, "I'd like it if you'd come inside." He still winced at the blunt, sad honesty of the line. She'd smiled as if it were really that easy and said sure.

She unfolded the corner of the sheet and reached to the bedside table next to her. "I have wet wipes!" she said. She handed him one and took one for herself. Then she submerged under the sheet with it, and he could feel the wet, cleansing and titillating trail she made with it down his chest, and then further. He reached for any part of her, first the back of her neck, then her arm, later her thigh when that surfaced from under the sheet, and then between.

When they finished she squeezed his hand tight and they were silent. After a while she said, "We're going to do a robbery. Josh and I and a couple others."

"Black Bloc Josh? From the rezoning riot?" he said. He let go of her hand and crossed his arms over his chest. Josh had been a regular at the café, who with a few others had held regular meetings in which they bitched overmuch about the state of the world, with no small amount of bravado. He sat near them once, listening in, watching Renee among the group. They all seemed hardened. Two men and two women, dirty and browned by sun, lean and fierce-looking. In his mind they were like a tribe of warriors; the men were real men and next to them, Zach felt like a boy. He wasn't sure what they'd been before: wilderness guides maybe, or labor organizers, or electricians. They certainly hadn't been ad writers. If he were to be honest, he realized he'd hoped never to hear of them again.

"A truck," she said. "We won't take a lot—it's a message."

"Renee—please." He turned and propped himself up on one elbow. "A message?" It was hard to keep the disdain out of his voice.

"It's not an official distribution truck. They're driving them up into the West Hills and we followed one. We want people to know what they're doing."

"I can help you guys send a message. Patel & Grummus is the city's ad firm. I talk to the mayor all the time."

Renee shrugged and smiled and then pulled him to her. "Don't worry, Zach."

With his lips pressed against her neck, their bodies fitting together like two hands clasped, he did just that: worry.

At the doorway to his building, she kissed him goodbye. It was an easy thing, a simple thing. Like husband and wife do, each headed off for their jobs. Him to his, her to the meeting of the water activists.

"Listen, don't," Zach said once more.

"I'll bring you a gallon," she said.

"I don't care about that."

She smiled roguishly and patted his cheek. "Don't you worry about me. I'm invincible," she said and flexed her bicep for him. "Go ahead, feel it."

He did so and nodded glumly. "Impressive. Back in one piece," he said, "or else."

On her bike, though, she felt vulnerable. She rode hard to her apartment. The streets had begun to be unpredictable—moose, yes, but the desperation had led to a steady uptick of violence. She asked herself if she were really going to go through with this, and each time some inner voice, of some stronger substance, piped up that she was.

A few weeks previously she and Josh had tailed the trucks heading into the wealthy West Hills neighborhood. They'd watched as the trucks pulled into the driveways of palatial houses. Drivers handdelivering gallon after gallon of water. Inside, she'd imagined an opulent matron bathing in a fountain. The image of it needled her for days.

Nearly a year ago, when the tap dried up and water service ceased, the city council created the Portland Water Act, declaring water to be a city-owned resource of which every citizen would get equal distribution. But as far as she could tell, while the rich swam in their fountains, kids in Northeast Portland wandered about in a dehydrated daze, the last of the city's trees died, and moose committed suicide.

Bea was asleep. She edged her roommate's door open and stared in, trying to decide whether to tell her where she was going. Bea looked peaceful in sleep, issuing a soft snore, a sort of gorilla-hum. Her brownish-red hair curled in a knotted mass around her face and her big feet hung over the end of the bed, uncovered. Though it was warm enough, Renee slipped in and quietly tucked the sheet over them.

In her room Renee sat on her bed and rotated her metal unit gallon in her hands, letting the water slosh about inside. She had a little time to kill, but it was the sort of time that could not be used. Time that sent an incapaciting buzz through one's brain, keeping her from performing simple tasks. There was less than a quart left in the container. She took a swig and then confirmed the amount on the digital readout: 6.4 units remained, out of the forty. The city issued the unit gallons, which measured a gallon into forty smaller units, under the premise: *That which is measured, improves.* The expression was affixed to the side via a cheerful green sticker, with a tired-looking smiley face at the end of it. She felt she remembered Zach had had a hand in the campaign.

She wished she could tell her parents. But even if she could find a way to get a call through to the other side of the Rocky Mountains, to whatever humble abode they might be residing in, eking out some living or scraping by on savings in order to buy their daily allotment of alcohol, she thought she knew exactly how the conversation might go:

"Hi Mom, it's Renee."

"Oh!" There would be the sound of a long exhale of smoke, as if her mother had inhaled a dragon's lungful of tobacco before answering the phone. "Renee."

A silence would persist for a few seconds as both considered what they might have to tell each other.

"I went to a water activists meeting, really cool people. We're going to do an action today to make a statement about water issues. I'm going to help stop a contraband truck."

"What?" her mother would say, the English deeply accented by her native Spanish. "What about your degree?"

Her mother always brought up her degree, as if it were a panacea for everything that irked her about her daughter's personality. Renee was the only one in the family to receive one. But to her mother's horror, she'd graduated with a degree in history, or as she'd once called it: *a degree in the dead.*

Then, as she tried to make the water activists sound compelling for her mother, the words would get a little lost in her mouth. The making of her own life interesting to her mother was a task she'd had very little luck with throughout her childhood. The more she explained, the more preposterous it would sound. A noise or two might issue from her mother, indicating her continued, but mostly bored, presence on the end of the line. Renee could see her: in her gray sweatsuit, the phone squeezed between her shoulder and ear, a glass of gin in one hand while with the other she pried off chips of paint from the wall with a long thumbnail. In the background, the dramatic monotony of Mexican telenovelas. And then her mother would say, by way of ending the conversation: Your father will want to know.

Her father, Renee thought, *would* want to know. She would love to tell him, but there was the difficulty of encountering him in a moment of coherence. When Renee's mother yelled for her father, down several flights of stairs, he would pick up his phone off the table saw, where it sat in a pile of sawdust and red wine splatter. Her parents undertook their lives on different floors of the house, him in the basement, her on the second floor, each speaking their own accents, Mexican and Polish, each living partly in the worlds from which they'd come, meeting only rarely in the middle for meals or to exit the house, or most rarely of all, when a sudden berserk passion flared up between them. Around her father were hundreds of dark, metal-worn tools, the signs of a constant, if somewhat ineffectual, tinkerer. In polar opposition to the woman two floors above, he would answer boisterously, sounding thrilled to hear from her, his words slushing from his mouth with great speed, sentences released in one order and then swallowed back and thrust out in a different order. He would listen to her deeply for a minute or two, then list back to her the details, asking questions that she'd answered, as if the conversation were going in reverse. It would make him happy, and then angry on her behalf, and then happy all over again, and then, inevitably, he would gather himself up, swell his lungs for delivery of a monstrous speech about his own comparable moment.

Her father had been a whistleblower. He had outed the Roswell Basin aquifer contamination. This was something he had done, the moment his life had ascended to, and the moment from which his life declined since. She'd listened to this same heady story a hundred times, thrilled, as a child, when the hero in the story, her father, fought and prevailed. He'd gone on the news, he'd testified to Congress, he was backed by scientists, and he'd won. Yet somehow it had ruined him, as if he'd mastered some great game that no one else knew how to play. What was left for him afterwards? What compared to the heroic moment he'd had? He glimpsed, for a moment, ascending permanently out of mediocrity. For the first time he believed in the possibility of being a superman.

In the end, there was no way to contact either one of them.

She was late to the meeting. The water activists were still exotic enough to be a little intimidating, a rough lot with histories of political action and arrests. There were three of them. Josh had recruited her—he was tall and thin and easy in his movement. He smiled her in and gestured for her to sit at the kitchen table, where they'd gathered. In a protest some years back, he had been beaten by the police. The resulting settlement had won him some money and fame. Even how he was dressed, with a dusty bandana around his neck ready to pull up over his nose, a ski cap and an unkempt beard, it was hard not to feel a pull of attraction.

The others at the table, Janey and Davis, were pissed at him for changing plans at "zero hour."

Renee watched them argue. Josh was the loudest thing in the room, and she wrestled with his simultaneous attractiveness and bullheadedness. He won his fights because he outlasted everyone else.

"Dude," Davis said. "What's a month of planning for if you change the plan on the day of?"

Josh shrugged and smiled broadly. "Because it's a better plan? What's a brain for if you can't adapt to a better outcome now and then?"

They were all nervous, and every time she became conscious of her own breath she had to work to slow it down again. She wished they could leave now. She wondered if this is what it felt like before battle, if her father had felt this way. There was a vibration in her guts that would not stop. To do something with her hands, she pulled a piece of scratch paper from the center of the table and folded it into a paper boat.

While Davis and Josh argued, Janey poured Renee a shot glass of water from her own unit gallon. "Ready?"

Renee sailed her boat across the table and left it in front of Janey. She had been asked this often but did not blame them. She was the newest and least experienced, the potential weak link. But Renee could feel her readiness, a coiled spring of it.

"She was born ready," Josh snapped. "I picked her, I know what I'm doing."

Renee frowned and shrugged. "Think so," she said. "Yes I am."

Janey squeezed her arm. "Good. You're pretty key, here."

Davis waved his hand in Josh's direction to end their argument. "We'll see who's right in the outcome, friend." He looked about at Janey and Renee. "KATU news knows to be there," he said. "Everybody have their flyers?"

Renee pulled a hand-printed flyer from the center of the table. It read:

WHO ARE THE THIEVES?

This truck carries unmarked
water to the West Hills!
The Portland Water Act is a sham!

She thought Josh must have written it; a wordsmith he was not. He pointed at her. "Speak through your part again."

She clutched the flyer, closed her eyes, and narrated her way through each action. As she did, she visualized it, every minute detail. She had practiced it constantly. It was automatic.

He nodded when she was done. "That was perfect," he said.

"No one will go thirsty," declared Mayor Brandon Bartlett into the nightly news camera. It made the mayor feel good to say this. He was handling things, he was taking charge. The agenda was on hold—that was OK. If just for once he didn't have to deliver bad news. He stared into the camera and smiled.

"We will all have to make sacrifices," he said, a political suicide of a line, but this was no campaign. He had just told them that water rations would be decreased to one gallon per day per person, and he expected the worst. He stood next to the weatherman, in front of the forecast, which showed an endless timeline of hot, rainless days. He wondered if he should put his arm around the guy, with his shiny hair and slick suit and handsome chin. As if to say: *See? I'm a friend of the weather myself. Rain could come at any time.*

A million gallons per day was distributed out to the city, one sixtieth of what had once traveled through the pipes. On Monday he'd lost forty thousand gallons in a fire in the Pearl district, and another eighteen thousand the following day. Bled out of their reserves reluctantly, letting buildings burn that could not be saved.

They played Patel & Grummus's new *prime the slime* water-saving jingle while an attractive woman demonstrated the amount. The whole thing made him squeamish and honestly, he couldn't imagine how anyone could portion off enough water from the ration to expel any waste from the bone-dry plumbing. But where else were they going to put it?

The city had enough water on hand to last for three more months with the new rationing. "Measures are being taken to secure water imports from Russia and New Zealand. Our city is in better shape than nearly any other remaining Western city." Except Seattle, he thought, envying their city-side desalinization plant. Still, everyone's first thought was the violence there, how the Emerald City was essentially in a state of civil war. Of San Francisco, with their power infrastructure destroyed, it was nearly impossible to get any reliable information. After the fires and subsequent takeover by a rogue branch of the National Guard they had gone dark. Or had the fires come after? Everything south of San Francisco was essentially abandoned.

"We ask that you stay calm," the mayor said. "We're Portlanders, right? We have thrived in prosperity, and we can endure hardship. To those who may feel the need to secure quantities of water, by whatever means, I ask you to have trust. Trust in your government, trust in me. We will provide. We will help each other get through. No one will go thirsty." He nodded to the weatherman, smiled, then exited the studio and got into the back of a Lincoln Town Car where Christopher awaited him. He'd stopped appearing anywhere where someone could ask him a question. Otherwise, the crowds lasted thirty seconds before the anger turned to jostling, or hecklers shot-gunned him with questions about hospitals and the police and reservoirs and desalinization plants and government water usage and imports and fuck all.

When the mayor returned home—or rather to his city hall office, which he and Christopher had taken to living in, for the view and the safety, but also because the work was never-ending—he paced around the conference room. He felt sick-hearted at the new restrictions he'd announced, and aggravated at the new reports of water robberies. He stared out into the view of the city. "Can't they all just stay the fuck calm?"

Christopher grimaced. Staying calm was not the people's job, he was fairly certain. It was the mayor's job. But he declined to mention this.

"Between the city council, the citizens, the news, and the fucking National Guard, it's like four piranhas in a fish tank."

"Eating you?"

"Yeah, eating me!" The mayor very much would have liked to put his fist through the sliding glass door to their balcony, but it was difficult to get replacement anything at the moment and so he reconsidered. It was city property, he was sure he'd be reminded.

"I'm not sure a fish tank is an apt metaphor," Christopher said.

The mayor turned angrily to glare at him, his finger pointing, ready to pound out a couple of points on Christopher's chest and then he stopped himself.

"Oh Jesus Chrissy, I'm sorry," he said and exhaled and turned back to the window. "OK, terrarium. Is that better? Piranhas in a terrarium. That's exactly it."

Renee rode her bicycle between taxicabs and clipped a mirror on a big yellow, jarring it out of whack. There was yelling and honking and she heard the distinctive sound of being chased by someone who had no business running, but she had no time to slow down. She gripped the metal rod she kept holstered to her handlebars just in case. The cars were trapped in traffic. There were far fewer cars, but the lack of traffic lights made driving a constant agony. If you wanted to get somewhere, you rode.

Tremendous precision was needed—the water truck would only be in the alley for forty seconds; everything needed to be exactly in place, as they'd practiced a hundred times. She found herself humming an old Genesis song and wished it were otherwise but it went over and over in her brain—fuck all, she thought, this wasn't the badass self she had in mind for herself. Still.

At an intersection she jumped onto the sidewalk and rounded a building cruising fast. There was a man in her way in an overcoat, completely immobile. She wondered if she had frozen him with her speed, deer on the tracks in the lights of the approaching train—there was no choice but to hit him or veer. She swerved to the left and her handlebar caught on a parking meter and jerked the front tire sideways. The bike came to an abrupt halt and she was launched, bouncing once on the roof of a parked Mercedes with a hollow thud and landing in the street, shoulder and face first.

For a moment she couldn't move, her breath gone and traffic rushing toward her, blood in her left eye and a feeling like her shoulder had come loose at the socket, like some toy, she thought, like a Mr. Potato Head, with its pullable arms.

"Fuck," she managed when she could breathe again and the man with the overcoat was pulling her to her feet. He said nothing, just gripped her bicep and steered her to the curb where her bike awaited. Its wheel was turned askew from the handlebars.

"What," she said and shrugged off the man's grip.

"Well, listen," the man said.

She jerked her chin at him and then noticed his expression. He wanted to help, she saw, and appeared now to have all the time in the world for her. One of those types who must have had a job downtown at some point, a manager of something, and now returned daily, donning his overcoat, pacing old routes, hoping for some something—anything—to happen. She righted her bike and yanked on the wheel to bring it back into true with the handlebars. The man hovered next to her. She held up one hand. "Listen, I'm cool. Just in a terrible hurry," she said, a little creeped out by his closeness and ready to deck him if he slowed her down.

"All right," the man said, "go on then."

"I will," she said. She mounted and rode off down the street, fleeing the stopped cars and the passersby who had begun to gather and wonder. Right now, to do this job, she needed to conjure up that deep inner hellion, that thing which is trained out, which civilization replaces, that thing that wishes to consume the world for its own damn self.

She felt a drop of blood trickle down her cheekbone and the dusty wind on the abrasion. She forced herself through the rickety, pulsing pain in her arm. She rode down a flight of stairs at Pioneer Square and just managed to squeak in front of a van.

The truck always took a shortcut through a back alley to avoid the busy intersection at Fourth. They'd studied it every day as it went to supply the big houses in the West Hills. A wind pushed at the traffic lights, swinging them on their wires, and for the briefest of moments she thought there was a smell of rain in the air but it was only a nostalgic trick, a nasal mirage.

The alleyway was one block away. She checked her watch and slowed, sighting down the street for Josh's sign. There he was, on his bicycle, a brown handkerchief stretched tight across his nose and mouth, the big baskets on the bike rack and the trailer behind. He held his hand up high in the air, five fingers, then folded them down one by one. When there were none left he shook the fist that remained. She swallowed the last of her fear and whooped with a warcry.

She cornered like she'd practiced, like she'd done a hundred times. She turned into the alley and smacked full on into the front of the water delivery truck, leaping before impact so that she hit the windshield on an incline, her body tucked into itself so that her side took the impact. She hit with terrific force—she hadn't practiced enough after all—and tumbled to the ground outside of the truck's trajectory as it squealed to a halt.

The driver knelt in front of her and though she could feel herself passing out, her vision dimming, the blackness coming from the edges, she felt sorry for him.

She didn't dare pass out. She pleaded with herself in the fraction of a second before her mind closed like a camera's shutter. Then time bloomed like a flower. The adrenalin that pumped through her body circulated uselessly. Her mind closed in to its own private viewing room and she saw Zach in a room full of water, glass jars of it, stacked in a wall about them. Each jar of liquid produced a hum. She could hear this now. The sunlight glistened and sparkled in each. They sat in this water library and listened to the sound of each of the water monologues like solo artists vibrating out a siren call, and they held hands. She was in her buried mind, and there the water sung to her its own song.

She groaned. It felt like her chest had been crushed. The driver was repeating an apology. She tried to find a hand to push against the ground with.

"Whoa, now. Stay there, an ambulance is coming—you got to stay there. If you've got something broken inside—"

She could hear the action at the back of the truck commence. The driver did not.

She didn't want to move; she wanted an ambulance to come, to be taken care of, to be lifted by her mother's arms and placed in bed. She wished Zach were there. But it would do no good to go to the hospital and be implicated. The plan was to flee, to leave the crime scene the way she'd come, to be a momentary decoy. She pushed the driver's hand away and stood up and swayed with dizziness and fell, but the driver caught her and she embraced him, tasted the sweat at his neck, the water that he gave off, the wastewater which could not be wasted. She rested her chin against his collarbone and felt herself slipping back into darkness. I'm sorry, she told him. She was aware of the crowd gathering, of her photograph being taken.

She stood by herself. Her bike was not damaged and while the driver yelled, *lady, wait!* she climbed on it and coasted toward the back of the truck where there were scavengers pulling bottles out of boxes. A few scattered flyers were on the ground, and others held them in their hands. It'd been a success, and now she was breaking plan. Her people had already come, filled up and gone, like the precise engines they were, their point made, and she knew she was supposed to get away, too. There were news cameras, alerted to this renegade truck, but they got something else entirely. They got her.

"Get back!" she yelled to the hoarders, feeling a sudden protectiveness for the driver, and perhaps because there was blood on her face the raiders eased back from the loot. She saw the bottles lying there on the ground and she thought the driver wouldn't mind if she had one sip. She was so terribly thirsty. Just one bottle to prove to herself that she'd done what she'd done. It was only fair. A crowd of people hovered in the alley now and she thought she could hear sirens. The driver yelled something, part surprise, part anger, and as a woman with a canvas shopping bag snagged a bottle he lunged for it. They pulled the gallon back and forth, her grip on the handle besting his. These were no unit gallons, ID'd and traceable, but anonymous and unmarked.

Renee pulled a gallon out of a box and turned to put it in her pannier and then she saw the crowd again. They searched her face, tried to make sense of the situation, greedily eyeing the boxes spilled from the truck like some dragon's mound of wealth upset. In front of them the stalemated wrestle between the driver and the woman. The crowd watched Renee, a woman with blood on her face and a cracked helmet and two long black braids, Hispanic maybe, her eyes vacant, or perhaps extra illuminated, more alive than they felt. They saw her drop her bike and take two bottles and approach them, giving one first to the woman wrestling with the driver so that his catch was suddenly freed and he lurched backward, another to a young boy half her height with dirt on his cheeks. She brought two more out, handing them into open hands, and two more. Then she handed another to the driver who stood on the side, his face grim, saying nothing. He was one of them, the crowd saw suddenly, a man with a part-time job, a driver, no more. She handed out more, and they were still, waited for her to place a gallon into their own arms. For a moment she thought she could do this forever, place water into the arms of those who needed it. This was what she wanted.

Then she stumbled, her bright eyes dimming. The crowd reached out, caught and righted her. She climbed on her bike. Their hands steadied her, but the sound had drained from the picture, as if someone had sucked the air out, averse to the low garble that the scene would make in slow motion. To the side, cameras caught everything.

The next thing she remembered she was riding her bike toward the river, that toxic mud slough, a gallon in each pannier, the world tinged red with the blood in her eyes.

At home she set her bike down on the front porch and a wave of dizziness overtook her. She went to her knees and felt how her shoulder and chest and head ached. She stumbled inside and found the couch and smiled to herself. She'd done it. They'd done it. She lay down. She needed to synch up with the others, but right now she needed to close her eyes for a moment.

When she woke it was dark, and her roommate Bea was there with a washcloth and hydrogen peroxide.

"Jesus Christ, Renee, I saw the news." Her roommate dabbed her face with swift, overly hard strokes.

"Ow—easy. What happened?"

"You happened, dude. We've got to go right now. Right now." Bea pulled her up by her armpits, as if she were a child, so that she wobbled unsteadily next to Bea, a head taller than she was.

"Bea."

"Right now." Bea pointed at the door. "They're calling you Maid motherfucking Marian."

"What?" Renee said, losing her balance.

Bea pushed her out the front door, across the dead dust-lawn, and down onto the bench seat of her '76 Dodge Dart. She slammed the door. "Stay down, for fuck sake, stay down, we've got to get out of here."

"Who is calling me?"

"The news, asshole, you and your people are already on the news. They're calling you Maid Marian."

"What's that supposed to mean?" The seat bench felt like a heap of granite. With each sway or bounce in the car a searing pain went through her ribs.

"You know. Robin Hood's girlfriend? You made a spectacle out of yourself. Just like you to go and make yourself a hero, dumbass."

Renee grinned and tried to hold on.

Nevel watched his slow, steady schedule with fascination, that of a working parent: the balance between trying to serve the mayor at work, a round with kids in the dust at the playground, the delicate chore of spousal relations, the upkeep of a home, the sustenance of life a dulling routine. The day divided into its major activities: Breakfast, Lunch, Nap Time, Dinner, Play Time, Bath, Bed—and then that sprawling chaos that enveloped his numbed mind after the kids went to bed when no one claimed his time but his own disorganized self, where, more often than not, after he'd kissed his wife good night, he found himself in the basement, chipping away at the wall there, digging deeper into the earth, building a tunnel for no particular reason that he could discern other than as a sort of military exercise against his anxiety.

Nevel poured a rare bath for the kids. They were down to bathing once every week or two. He abhorred the thought of bathing them in corpse water, as they'd taken to calling the non-drinkable family extra rations, and so he filtered it by running it through a hand-pump water filter. It was a slow, tedious process. A fetid, rotting smell wafted through the bathroom window and he had to put his face to the water to make sure the smell did not come from there. He wondered if the neighbor had killed his dog and buried it too shallowly in his backyard.

The kids scrabbled noisily up the stairs, one laughing and the other pseudo-crying for being left behind in the rush to get there. They crowded into the bathroom and he stripped them down, the dusty earthen child smell of a week's worth of play overwhelming the smell of rot, and plopped each of them into their proprietary sections of the shallow bath. A chorus of complaint was aired over the temperature of the bath which he pretended not to hear. The day was still warm enough. In the winter there would be only sponges.

The bath was pitifully shallow, but it was enough, and they happily played and splashed in it for nearly an hour. Water splattered out of the bath wastefully but he said nothing, wanting to give them, if only for a moment, a feeling of abundance in their lives. Their collective water ration didn't go far; bathing meant something else wouldn't get water. When their bath was finished, he would siphon the remaining water out to reuse for next week.

His lips were dry and he worried about the drought a little and, more immediately, dreaded the escalation of conflict that would come when he removed them from the bath and struggled them through the drying, the donning of their pajamas, the brushing of teeth. There would be crying and there would be laughing and wrestling and someone's feelings would get hurt and somebody would do something awful to someone else and then they'd read stories together followed by a half-dozen more rituals, teeth brushing and last-minute drinks of water—with each he would tamp down the conservation lecture they'd heard repeatedly.

His wife, Cora, was down in the kitchen cleaning up after dinner, and this is what their nights were like. The division of labor. Divide and conquer.

When the crying started Nevel thought seriously about getting up to go in.

"Nevel?" Cora shouted up the stairs.

"I'm on it," he said and rolled off the bed. "OK, guys," he said in the bathroom and the crying collectively increased a notch.

It appeared to be an argument about toy boat rights and bath water boundaries and for a moment he thought about making an instructive analogy about the state of the world. Instead he put toothpaste on their toothbrushes, dipped each into a unit of pure water and inserted them into their mouths, which quieted the last of the complaint.

Cora shouted up the stairs, "Make sure to help them brush their teeth" and he wondered how this could happen. How the trajectory that was his life, both of their lives, had leveled into this. "I'm on it," he hollered down the stairs, trying to keep the annoyance at bay. "Doing it now!" he sang.

Sure you are, Cora thought downstairs as she moistened a dish rag with the water she'd used to steam the imported broccoli which the children had refused to eat. She wiped down the plates but it was difficult to get the frying pan clean without letting it soak, and she stood there looking at it for a full minute trying to decide if she was going to use the water she had left to soak the pan or to water her last surviving house plant. She cried a little over the sink until she felt self-conscious and weak and poured half a unit of water into the pan and the other half into the plant. Later, she'd recycle the water from the pan.

"There," she said.

The power was still on. The mayor was on the radio and Cora had the same reaction she always did to hearing his voice. How could Nevel work with him? That slick eloquence that turned her stomach, the constant bad news laced with his strange reasoning on how they should be happy to hear it. She thought he said rations were being cut to one gallon per person. Her face burned hot, aghast at the news, and she waited for the news anchor to confirm it. She didn't know how they could survive this.

"Nevel!" she yelled, but he didn't answer. The radio had turned to a crime report of a woman on a bicycle who had robbed a private water truck and handed out water to people on the street. Fuck *yes*, she thought. She listened tensely as they talked about the manhunt. She had a moment of envy, wishing she was her. Or in her gang, a thief on a bicycle, and then she wondered if *Thief on a Bicycle* weren't the name of an old movie. She walked to the base of the stairs and listened to the squabbles over who got to pump the water back out of the bathtub. "Hey, Nevel?"

"What?" he yelled back, his tone that of a man who suspects he's being told to do something he's already doing.

She said never mind and went back to the kitchen and swept the floor in a hurry. She didn't know what she was going to say anyway. That rations were cut? That she'd had it, that she was going to go find a woman named Maid Marian and go outlaw? It was 7:25 p.m., and they had thirty-five minutes of power before the blackout.

After story time, Jason asked what would happen if they ran out of water.

"We won't, Jay—we'll be fine," Nevel said.

"But what will happen if we're not fine?"

"Oh, I don't know, maybe we'll go on a killing rampage until we find more water, and if we don't, we'll drink blood. Garrr!" Nevel bared his teeth and turned toward his daughter who screamed and giggled and flailed away.

"You kids with me or what?" He rose and thrust his fists into the air and it felt great.

"Yeah!" Jason said. "Yeah!" He scrambled out of the covers and stood on top of his bed.

"No. Stop. Dad's teasing. Back in bed, everybody." Cora said. "We'd probably pick up and move. The drought isn't as bad in Spokane, and we have family there."

"Is that where Calden moved?"

"Calden moved to Alaska. They still have a little snow in the mountains there."

Afterwards Nevel and Cora hugged in the hallway in the dark. The house was quiet with the whir of everything that whirred gone dead. The streetlights were all somber flagpoles now.

Cora held onto the news about the new rations, and a sickening hollow stuck in her chest. He'd been funny with the kids at story time, and adept, and she didn't want to leach any poison from the world outside the house into him just yet. He could spend the rest of the night wrapped in anxiety or he could spend it in his tunnel, so she decided to spare him what he'd learn at work tomorrow anyway.

They kissed, but each was already leaning toward the activities they'd set aside for themselves for the night. That which let the mind ease into solitude and quiet, the antithesis of child-rearing. She would read by candlelight, he would dig. Were it to happen, this would be the moment that passion took hold. He pressed into her subtly, experimentally. But when she patted his flank with a beat of closure his mind quickly moved on.

They went their separate ways, into the hermitage of their projects.

Nevel paced about the kitchen looking for any last chores so as not to make his descent seem overly eager, and then he opened the door and padded quietly down into the darkness and felt his way across the cement floor to his hole.

The hole was a reminder of his small cache of water and thus a reminder of his omnipresent thirst. The bottles glistened in the light of the flashlight down a branch of the tunnel. What water he could stand to spare from his daily routine was squirreled away down here. He had to trust the city—what choice did he have? He had a family. He had to trust and be steady until that time when he could no longer trust and then he must radically and decisively change direction to protect his family.

He was driven by hazy yearnings that bubbled up inside of him, unaware of their origins or meanings, and thus he dug, as if somewhere deep in the earth was concealed a clearer picture of himself. He patted the tunnel supports on his way to the end of the tunnel, listening for give or weakness. Then he moved to the back of the cave and tapped away at the clay and rock there, peeling back layers of time with each loosed rock.

He swung the pickaxe into the wall of earth, knowing that several floors up his children, were they awake, would hear only the faintest *tink tink tink*, as if a man were slowly hollowing out his prison passageway. A section of the wall gave way and buried him up to his knees and he yelled out. His hands shook, and he searched about for the bottles to make sure they were sound.

When the dust settled he tentatively freed himself from the rubble and sat atop with his head in his hands. What a stupid way to die. He wanted to believe he would sense this kind of danger. Especially now, as a parent, he felt a prescience of future disaster ought to be his right, a special power granted to all fathers. He stood and placed his forehead against the very back end of the cave. Felt the coolness of it and thought about how down here there was a safety and quietude. He'd begun to fantasize about burial here, about a sudden collapse of the cave that would leave him disappeared from the struggle to maintain, from the thirst. From his children and wife and the fumes of traffic congestion, the duties of work and the complicated ties of relationships. From wifi and cell towers and GPS signals and security cameras and radio and television and electromagnetic waves. Utility bills and wars, parents and climate change. The drought. It would be a stony, deathly peace. For a moment he imagined them all here, his family united in burial, laid happily together, wrapped cozily. Snug and still as mummies. He wondered if he was depressed and whether he ought to see a doctor about getting some medication. He pulled his headlamp down from the top of his head and shone it on the section he was working on. Veiny tendrils of dead tree roots, a layer at neck-height of century-compressed roadway backfill, below that black earth with stones the size of skulls. He picked at this earth with a spade, feeling around in it. He was looking for something, but he didn't know what. Chunks gave way—he'd hit a softened vein—and so he dug.

At night, thunder sounded in the distance but there was no rain. The city, the poor and the rich, sweated in their sheets. It was hot. A rare humidity laid a sticky grime over everything they touched.

As far as Renee was concerned, Bea shouldn't own a car. Now that she had the fear of the police, she drove even more erratically, as if subconsciously trying to flag the authorities by swerving, driving too slowly in fast lanes, too fast in slow lanes, turning in a giant arc in front of the few other cars on the road—the chorus of honking that followed her like a soundtrack that she couldn't drive without.

Renee felt sick in the back seat. Her head ached, and whether it was the nausea of concussion or the infernal swaying of the car, she needed to throw up. When the car stopped moving, she rolled down the window and did so.

"Renee . . ." Bea said, the word drawn out in sympathy and alarm and revulsion.

When Renee finished she wiped her mouth on the hem of her shirt and regarded her roommate, who gripped the steering wheel in concerned paralysis.

People had whispered "amazon" behind Bea's back her whole life, Renee knew. In the hallways at school, the boys on the bus, as she walked into restaurants. Her short, red hair and strong nose made her impossible to miss. Even Renee had, though she'd said it affectionately, appraising her six-plus feet and patting the muscles of the girl who was to be her welding partner. They liked each other immediately, and as Renee, a degreed perma-student, continued her tour of the course catalog—wood shop, chemistry, intro to German—French literature, gardening, auto-mechanics, algorithms, and on and on—settling on no theme she herself could decipher, they became great friends. Even now, as Bea recoiled at the puke-foam Renee had stained her shirt with, there was a wisdom in Bea's eyes that she admired. The wisdom of big people, Renee thought, the wisdom of perspective and contemplation, the wisdom of acclimating to one's abnormalities.

If it were up to Bea, Renee knew, and if Renee were inclined, they would have continued up that ladder of intimacy.

"I think you should drive now," she whispered. Several police officers on foot had taken notice of the stopped car with the woman puking out the back. "Where are we going?"

"I don't know," Bea said honestly.

Renee groaned. The implication of continued motion was enough to cause the nausea to return.

"Should we leave the city?" Bea said.

"How much water do we have? How much gas?" Outside of the city was an unknown. Like everything else, gasoline had gone up many times in price and wasn't reliably obtained. Farms had dried up. Beyond the city borders was a lawless wasteland.

"Just the two gallons you stole out of a *whole truck*. Just saying."

Renee leaned back into the seat and studied the drab ceiling in the car. Despite the pain, her body hummed with an excitement from what she'd done. She thought again of her father, and then the others. The plan had been to lay low and not associate with each other for a few days, but the plan had also been to not be caught on camera with their identities exposed, and she shrunk further into the seat and hoped she hadn't jeopardized them.

Inevitably, Bea found herself on the familiar route to her parents' house. It was obvious, she knew. The likely run-to spot, the refuge of all budding criminals destined to be caught. But Renee was tired and hurt and Bea's parents were the picture of stability and she wasn't sure where else to go. They would go quickly, to regroup.

Her own mother, Renee thought, would press Renee to turn herself in, pointing toward the door with mild disgust, cigarette smoke trailing in one hand, gin in the other: *you're just like your father.* Even so, despite the utter lack of romance her mother felt for it, she'd had her own heroics. Renee couldn't help wonder if the frustrated wrath her mother directed at her was instead a bent arrow, pointing back at herself. A frustrated marriage, a frustrating culture she'd adopted, sobriety a frustration. Even so, Renee felt like she'd performed some family rite now, some task that set her on equal footing with them, redeemed herself in their eyes: she'd begun her own fight.

For a moment she could see her father's face in her mind, the faintest touch of a smile breaking his beard's grimace. When she was young, she remembered sitting on his lap as he whispered alcohol-fumed fantasies of better times, a better life, a more just universe. Seeing her right now, she thought, on the run as she was, he would give her that same dreamy smile.

They parked outside and Bea gave Renee a shoulder to lean on as they climbed the concrete steps up to the house, a modern ranch on a rise. Bea's mother opened the door and came down the stairs to greet them.

"Oh Renee—you're hurt! You're on television!" Bea's mother helped Renee up the rest of the stairs while Bea went back to the car for their water.

The newscaster explained what was known of the crime. A still shot of her face encompassed the television screen, and she stared back uncomprehendingly, feeling woozy and not at all herself. Lining the bottom of the frame, block letters read "MAID MARIAN."

Footage played of Renee bleeding from a head wound and distributing jugs in a tender manner to a crowd of people who came forward one by one to accept them. The replay caught a magic that had not been there, or that she hadn't been aware of, and it contrasted radically with the water distribution they were all familiar with, with its display of National Guard weaponry. It was the kind of footage that made a cameraman's career—hypnotic and touching, and even Renee could see there was an emotional hook in there. You wished to cry and cheer a little. The station knew it. They replayed it again and again, between interviews with policemen and onlookers.

The police chief said there were three accomplices, water thieves on bicycles. "It means less for everyone else," he said. There was a menacing way in which he said it: *if you cross me again, citizens, no water for no one.* He asked anyone with information to please contact the police. One hundred and ninety four gallons were lost, he said. That's nearly two hundred people's daily rations.

"They weren't rations," Renee said into the room.

"Water crime's a felony," Bea's father said, absorbed in the newscast.

An image was shown of the truck, filled with unit gallons, and a large white question mark flashed over the top of it.

"Clearly, this was a robbery," the newscaster said, "but who was robbed? We were there on a tip, and we assume now the tip was given to us by Maid Marian's group. But where was the truck going with so many pre-filled water bottles? Flyers were found at the scene claiming that this is a private truck carrying water to the West Hills. Under the Portland Water Act this makes the truck itself illegal. The driver is missing and is considered a suspect, and in the meantime the city has seized it. Many questions remain. We'll stay on top of it for you."

"The city has seized it," Renee said and looked around the room at Bea's family. "Sure they have. Nice one."

Bea's dad got up and paced to the window and looked out. Renee thought she heard him say *fugitive.* She'd known him for several years as an amiable fellow who never said much of anything in conversation, but now he seemed a little frightening, and she wondered if he'd turn her in.

"Well, I think you look very heroic," Bea's mother said. Her voice trembled. "What are you going to do?"

"I have no idea." Renee leaned her head back on the couch and closed her eyes. She was exhausted and hurt, and yet there was something in the air. She could feel how her image was being broadcast over the city.

Zach watched the nightly news with amazement and horror as his girlfriend's image was played over and over.

After the blackout came he curled up on his couch and stared at the deadened TV and felt sick to his stomach. He wondered if she was already in custody by now. He went to the roof and listened to the night. There were sirens and the sound of people in the street. The night was hot and humid and the stars felt predatory, a billion interested eyes, recording. She was out there somewhere.

At three in the morning she climbed into his bed and spooned against him.

He scrambled up. "How did you get in?" and then after he'd wakened a little more: "I saw what happened." He clutched her forearm. "I hoped you'd show up."

She told him they'd gone to Bea's parents and had to run out the back. "We left the car. Look what I've got Bea into." She pushed him back onto his side on the bed and pressed her face against his back. After a while he could feel that she was crying. "I won't get you involved."

"I'm sorry," he said. "I'm really sorry. Are you hurt? Have you heard from any of the others?"

"No one. Bea's asleep on your couch. I fucked up with Bea's parents."

Zach turned them both so that he could get a grip on her.

"What am I going to do?" she said.

"You could stay here."

"And do what? Stay in your house and like be your house servant?"

Yes, he thought to himself, imagining the time they'd get to spend together, but dared not say it. Seattle or to the south were other possibilities, but there were rumors of regular carjackings in the rural stretches of the highway, and the occasional blockade. He didn't want her to leave. If the media played her image on an infinite loop it would get picked up on other stations across the country as the requisite "drought imagery of the day," and then nowhere was safe.

"Northeast Portland is spinning out of control," he said. "They'll either put it under martial law, or let it fall into a lawless slum. I'm betting the latter. There aren't enough police to patrol there and the rich areas too. You could hide in that mess. It's not safe, but it might be safe from the police."

She was quiet for a long time and he listened to her breathe. He wasn't sure he'd ever seen her scared before, but he could hear it now in her breath as a new and wholly different future opened before her. Or, he wondered, was he mistaking this quiet for fear, when instead it was a buzzing thrill, an adrenalin drunk for what she'd done.

"Are you hurt?" he asked again. He lit a candle. "Let's take a look at you."

This he could do something about, and he took pleasure in taking care of her. He carefully unwrapped her head bandage. She had a scrape on her forehead that needed cleaning and a deeper injury at her hair linethat probably needed stitches, though it was too late to do a lot with it. She had bruises on her ribs and legs, her yellow-brown skin turning the bruises a livid purple. In the candlelight her eyes flickered intensely as she watched him. He went rummaging through medicine cabinets and came up with a field cocktail of medical supplies, turmeric and super glue and began reworking the dressing.

"I want you to know, this hurts me more than it does you."

"Pfff," she said.

He took hold of her ear. "This, hmm, yes. I'm afraid we'll need to amputate."

"Come on," she said.

He cleaned her head wound, sprinkled in some turmeric and then, holding the wound closed, dabbed a thick seal of superglue over the top of it.

"Weird," she said. "If I find out the turmeric is a joke . . ."

"I swear, it's not."

"What other spices are you going to use? I'm like some kind of pizza now?"

"Curry." He noticed that she took a breath in the middle of sentences. "You having trouble breathing?"

"A little."

He felt along her ribs, conscious of her nakedness in the candlelight. "I don't know a lot about ribs, but it feels OK. I'm guessing you've got a crack, maybe a bruise."

"Just a bruise then."

"Correct."

"So you're saying I should stop my whining?"

"Pretty much."

Back in bed they lay on their backs and stared at the ceiling.

"I don't want you to be a fugitive," he said. "I want us to, you know, go out."

"I'm not sexier as a fugitive? With a head wound?"

"I don't think you're taking this seriously enough," Zach said.

"I need you to roll over and hug me because my ribs hurt too much to move. But softly, OK? I don't know what else to do. I'm just going to make jokes about it, because otherwise I'll think about it, and then I'll be terrified."

"OK," he said. "A little bit sexier."

After some time, she said, "I'll go to the Northeast—that's probably where the others went. If that doesn't work, I'll come back here. I'll be your housegirl."

"Mm," he said, and allowed himself to quietly ponder it for a moment. "You need some kind of a hobby to keep you from getting into trouble. Idle hands are the devil's et cetera. Promise to lay low?"

Renee didn't answer, and he could sense she was elsewhere, already on the journey across the city perhaps, or stuck in the infinite media loop of the truck robbery, or maybe seriously playing out a prospective stay at his house: how they might sit and have dinner-rations together in the evening, every evening, how she could be his for a while. He inhaled in her black hair and heard the deepening sighs of her sleep.

Zach pulled on a pair of shorts and felt his way downstairs to the dining room table. Outside a dusty wind blew and he could feel it nudge insistently against the old, leaky windows. He fetched a piece of paper and started to doodle so that his mind could relax into the project at hand. There was work to do—he wanted a day to think out a plan, to send them prepared and equipped. It was difficult to visualize anything that would lead back to normality—without jail time or violence or dying of thirst.

On a whim he ran to the roof of the three-story building he'd inherited from his mother to take a look where they were headed. The sky had begun to pale. He scanned the horizon to the north for tall objects. There were two water towers on 19th and Prescott to the Northeast that stuck above the line of brown trees. One was a great, bulbous thing, like a pustule from the ground, the other an awkward contraption on stilts. Neither held water now. He knew these towers—in high school he'd climbed the big one with friends and they'd gotten drunk on top, reveling in the view and the power of disobeying the law. They'd descended madly, laughing at the height and the danger, and then were sobered upon reaching the bottom and looking up at how high they'd been.

He taped a green laser pointer to the barrel of his telescope. When he pressed the button on the laser pointer, through the telescope he saw the small green bead appear on the fat underside of the water container. Ah ha, he thought. A communication link to the Northeast is made.

He lowered the scope until the green bead would be visible to those on the ground, and then cranked down on the tripod stand to freeze it there. Experimentally he tried out a message in Morse code: .. /—.. ... ... / -.———- ..- *I miss you.*

He fetched his video camera and set it up on its tripod, pointed it at the space on the water tower, zoomed in all the way. Then he attached a timer to that, set to start after sundown. An hour each evening should do. There was no reason not to leave the camera set up. Rain was not imminent.

When there was no other communication, they could still send these messages, at least. He felt like he was sending her across the frozen wastes or the desert, into space.

He scavenged for tools and supplies. He found two empty liter bottles and filled them out of his water savings—a pittance. They would need a map, bicycles, a list of friends or safe houses.

Back in his room he paused for a moment to watch her sleep. The bruises had darkened. Her right arm lay across the sheet, brown and muscular. Her hair snaked across the pillows and over her shoulder. He fought the craving to get back in bed with her for these last few moments but decided he'd rather prepare them for safety, a sort of insurance for her return voyage.

In the kitchen he looked for a better way to visualize the players. He needed to see the board in front of him and so he pulled down a few jars from his spice rack and positioned them on the table like opposing armies. The media, the city police force and the National Guard, the mayor, the rioting Northeast, Maid Marian, the drought, and the populace at large.

There he sat, the chess pieces laid out, attempting to figure out how to steer Renee above capture, while in his mind the video they had played of her sounded like a trumpet call of war. He positioned the spice jars in a circle at first and considered them, and then tried making groupings. Cayenne, curry, salt and dill on one side and parsley and rosemary on the other.

"Mmm, looks like breakfast," Renee said from behind him. "Right?" she asked hopefully. "You're fixing breakfast?"

"I have you here as salt." Unconsciously he gave the salt shaker a caress.

"I'm definitely cayenne, ask anyone."

"Well anyway—"

"Or pepper."

"I'm pepper."

"You're pepper? How'd you even get in this game? You're supposed to be my secret boyfriend."

"What? Why am I secret?" Zach said and gripped the pepper.

"Well, not secret, but, anyway, cayenne?—"

"—Is the media. I've been trying to figure out a way to lessen your crime so that—"

"It wasn't a crime," she said. "It was exposing a crime."

"Yes, but not really. Maybe in the people's mind, but robbing a truck is robbing a truck. And the police chief seems bent on calling a spade a spade. What are your possibilities here? At this point you're going to be seen by the police as the ringleader of an organized crime group. They're not going to forget that. Especially now that you're a media darling. They're going to use you as an example, and stealing water carries a heavy sentence."

"But stealing from whom? They were stealing, we were returning!"

Zach sighed. "Listen, *I* understand your point, but that water belonged to somebody. It was a lot of water, and worth a lot of money. You heard the police chief. They're going to find you. So what's your plan?"

She shrugged. "I'll go to Northeast Portland. I'll get in contact with the rest of the group and we'll bust more trucks and give the water to the people."

"What? What happened to staying out of trouble?"

"I slept on it."

"So, Robin Hood, you *do* want to be the ringleader of an organized crime group."

"I don't know about the leader bit, but otherwise yeah. Where's your outrage here?"

"At what—the weather?" Zach said it overly loud and slammed the edge of the table with the palm of his hand. His grandmother's salt shaker toppled over, spreading a thin veneer of white.

Renee pointed. "That was me, right?"

Zach took a deep breath. "I regret saying that." He stared down at his lap and noticed his shorts were seasoned with white grains. "I know you have some serious problems here. I think with a little planning—"

"Zach—you're always planning. And organizing and cataloging and recording and doing every preliminary step so as to avoid acting. I think what you do—writing ads, trying to make what the city needs palatable—is great. I mean it's a mixed bag, you know that, and you're doing what you can in there. But somebody has got to be out here on the front line."

"What front line? Why you? I'm here trying to plan so you don't get killed or put in jail, and you're doing the opposite."

"You know what I can do? I can make a killer foam leaf imprint on top of a latte. I can expound on the collapse of the Roman empire. I'm a lousy welder. I speak French and Spanish. I could probably fix your car."

"I don't have a car."

"Exactly. You know of any jobs out there for me with those skills?"

"Please—"

"But you know what is available, Zach? You know what I like? I like that chick they're showing on TV. That chick could make a difference. That's who I want to be. That's who *I am.*"

Zach sighed and swept his hand across the table, brushing the spilled salt to the floor. "That's not a job," he said softly.

"I've already done it, I can do it again," Renee said.

"That's a crime. If you want to expose issues with water distribution you should have gone to the press. That's their job."

"You think they're going to do something? They don't have people down there trying to"—Renee made quotes of her fingers—"'figure stuff out', not for real anyway. Rations got tightened to one unit gallon. Where do you think that truck was going? Does that not drive you crazy?"

Zach held his hands up, "All right, OK, we don't have to talk about the bigger picture. It does drive me crazy. But let's strategize for a moment—humor me—along your plan of action. Look at this." He held up his diagrams for communication methods and explained the laser pointer Morse code setup.

She patted his shoulder. "Neat, you dork. Of course you know Morse code."

"Wake Bea, we've got work to do." He handed her a hand-drawn card he'd made her with a Morse code translation. "You leave at dark."

———

Mayor Bartlett was late. He'd decided to walk, that they should all walk together, and enter the meeting hall in a triumphant micro-parade of optimism. But if he was not mistaken, when he claimed that they should do so, someone in his entourage clearly huffed. *Huffed!* A policeman maybe, or even, could it have been? His communications director. She had worked hard, as hard as he, on the proposal they were going to present to the city commissioners.

"What?" he said, turning to inspect each of them. "Is the car not hot and crowded?"

"Sir?" his police bodyguard said, gripping his thumbs through his police belt for adjustment, pausing for acknowledgement.

The mayor wilted, rolling his neck, knowing he was on the verge of receiving a security lecture he'd heard countless times. "Gary?" he said.

"Sir, it's not that—"

"It's fine, Gary, we'll take the car." He needed to save all his fight for the committee. The proposal, thick with hope and pleasantly weighty in his hand, felt like a sort of shield. Not just from whatever violence a random citizen might want to inflict, but from public opinion, too. They'd battled out the details for weeks and it was great, it was perfect.

"You don't mind that—"

"The car," he said, "to the car." He raised his fist to signal the charge, proposal and all.

Three advisors—the communications director, economic development director, youth strategies coordinator—and the policeman bodyguard shuffled toward the door, their queueing to exit awkward and apologetic. He followed behind, but dipped into his office at the last moment. There Christopher sat at the mayor's desk, helping to write a letter to community leaders.

"Ah ha," Christopher said, "so you're off. Come here a moment."

The mayor came around to the inside of the desk and sat on the edge. Behind Christopher hung a 1952 black and white aerial photo of the city, with its diminutive buildings and drab industriousness. Every time Mayor Bartlett stared at the photo he felt a sort of disappointment leak from it, for the future they clearly thought they had in front of them.

"You're going to do great," Christopher said.

"Yeah," the mayor said, wanting suddenly more than anything a moment of Christopher's pity, a comforting *humf* and back-pat.

Christopher reached up his hands and took hold of either side of the mayor's head and pulled him forward so their foreheads touched.

He whispered: "You'll give Councilwoman Sally one neat, ultimately meaningless concession. Councilman Edward will embrace it, but claim the ideas as his. Councilman Seth and Councilwoman Marybeth will rip it apart, but you've prepared for this. You'll take the high road, right, love? Answer their questions directly and easily. You'll smile and concede there are many other problems, but the city is tackling them one by one. You're going to do great."

"Yeah," the mayor said.

"Go on, they're waiting for you." Christopher patted his shoulder.

"Thanks, Chrissy."

The drive was short. They all piled into the car, and Mayor Bartlett wondered how he'd ended up in the middle, sandwiched hotly between his economics development guy, certainly no small man, and the communications director, who was fashioned entirely of hard right angles. She huffed again for reasons he was not entirely clear. He gripped the proposal to his chest and told himself: *I am the people's servant.*

Several blocks later, in front of citizens and other officials entering the building for the meeting, they spilled from the car like—the mayor tried to repress the thought of—a posse of clowns from a VW Bug. He smiled and shook hands while his team hovered close and his bodyguard loomed. The communications director huffed again, somewhere behind and to the left of him, her third huff, and this time it was clearly, he thought, directed at him.

He turned and studied her. "Are you alright?" he said.

"No, I'm not alright!"

Mayor Bartlett leaned in close and smiled to someone over her shoulder. "Yes?"

"I've tried to tell you half a dozen times," she whispered feverishly, "Councilwoman Jacobsen has a competing plan."

"You have?" He could not remember a single thing she'd said in the last several hours and he wished immediately to interview his team in order to verify they'd heard her speak. "She does?" A shudder spasmodically pulsed down his spine, as if he were just finishing at the urinal. "And you have read the plan? Is it any good?"

"No! It's a disaster."

"For whom? I thought—"

This was a moment which called for an executive decision. The wavering of his team, a sneak attack by an enemy at their flanks. Blindsided. Had the councilwoman already run to the press, touting her *whatever*?

His executive assistant, whom he realized now had been steadily trying to steer him into the imminent meeting, now simply pulled him from the conversation, leaving his communications advisor trailing mid-sentence. He heard only: "*Wastewater*," the word shouted as if it were the name of a pet ferret who had scurried into traffic.

At the doorway, Councilwoman Marybeth Jacobsen herself was there to pump his arm.

"Mayor Bartlett!" she said, and he immediately worried that in her sarcastic exuberance she was going to hug him or worse. Her smile slanted from her face in a vicious, made-up grin. A white T-shirt stretched tightly over her bust, emblazoned with the slogan *Young and Hung*.

"What?" he gestured at her shirt, startled by the grotesqueness, feeling suddenly woozy and unwell.

"I have a proposal!" she said, and signed off on her exclamation with a finger-jab to his solar plexus. "You'll find out!" Then she turned and strode to her council member seat at the broad platform.

"Marybeth," he called after her. "Can you please send these to my office so we can read . . . before?" but the last words of his comment were lost. The council president was speaking over the loudspeakers.

". . . even if the mayor himself has not managed to make it to his assigned seat, the rest of you should, and if you'd be so kind, Mr. Mayor?"

"Coming," he said. He waded through the citizen audience and noticed it was sizable, two hundred or more perhaps, with his bodyguard close in tow. He could feel the baleful stares he received from them as he went. There was a time, he remembered, when he was loved. "Sorry." He took his seat, "Yes yes, here now," and was temporarily blinded by the camera lights. Every one of them in the audience had some hurtful snip he wanted to direct at him, given an opportunity. He thought he heard someone say *Maid Marian*, but could not grasp the rest of the comment that bracketed it. In his hands, the proposal had grown slippery with sweat along its plastic cover.

"Thank you, Mr. Mayor," Council President Seth Langstron said. "We do like to start on time." The council president shuffled papers about in front of him and spent some time ordering them just so, into a few distinct stacks, as if each were a course—peas, ham, potatoes— he'd devour in time. When he finished he stroked at his thick beard and stared out into the room.

"And so," he said, "audience? There will be an opportunity to speak but you must *wait* for that opportunity if this meeting is to proceed within a human lifespan. Thank you." He paused again until the only sounds were a stifled cough and the *skirch* of a moved chair. "First on order is not one, but two proposals that intend to provide a solution to youth unemployment, with the mayor at-bat first. Youth is defined as, Mayor Bartlett?"

"To age twenty-five; we have ninety-three percent unemployment in our youth population between ages sixteen and twenty-five," the mayor said.

"That lucky seven percent," the council president said.

The mayor began his presentation, wetly pressing the remote control to turn the projector's slides, showing slick charts and the research they'd done. Reading from the paper in his hand an occasional choice sentence. They'd given it their all. "We call this the Opportunity Pipeline," he said, and smiled out into the audience's glare. Fifteen thousand eighteen to twenty-five-year-olds would be employed by the city over the course of a year to dig a hundred-mile pipeline ditch between the city and their coastal desalinization plant. While the plant supplied only a tiny fraction of the city's water, with time and budget it could supply much more. It was crazily ambitious, he knew, an idea for apocalyptic times, but exactly what his city needed. Putting youth to work meant fewer riots, less crime. And what would they be working on? Water issues. This was their Panama Canal, insurance against drought for the next hundred years. It was a perfect solution.

When it came to discussing the costs, he mumbled his way through. The money could be found, but the question of money was always painful. Some money would have to be diverted. In a year's time perhaps they could find funding to build a second desalinization plant. The existing plant distributed water to the city by diesel truck in tiny, expensive little increments. Opportunity Pipeline was long range thinking, he told them. "The idea is built upon the shoulders of grand successes, the Peace Corp and AmeriCorps, that have come before it. It gives an identity and provides meaning through useful works to the lives of our younger citizens. It is but the first of projects to come."

When he concluded a few people applauded and he grinned happily out into the audience but could not find the source. The mayor felt his heart beating in his throat and he put his hand there in case it visibly throbbed. To the side of the hall, his economics adviser raised his fist in the air.

There was a moment of silence, and then from the back of the room came a wavering, indignant voice: "I have one question, Mayor Bartlett. Do you despise our children so much that the only solution you can come up with is to exile them from the city?"

The mayor smiled again, a bland smile meant to serve as placid acknowledgement of the question, the smile a dike against his rage that he would not let them breach. "I don't see it as exile, but a chance to do something heroic for this city. Something epic," he said, and immediately regretted the wording, which sounded like he intended to send them on some odyssey. "This plan addresses two of our most pressing issues simultaneously." He wanted to use the term *visionary,* but fretted about how it might be attributed to him were it to come from his own mouth. "Imagine, if you will, how your own life might be transformed were you to spend a year or two on something this monumental, something that could help this many people." He was speaking in platitudes and superlatives; he could feel them swell in his chest and he looked for a way to ratchet down. "This is not an exile, this is a mission! This is a *purpose.* It's a chance to put faith in our youth, to charge them with a great task, to rally behind them. It's giving them a chance to live up to and exceed our expectations." He paused, partially for dramatic effect but also because he feared his voice would falter with emotion. "To create an artery that feeds the life to the city. Listen, there is no plan that is worthwhile that does not address our dwindling water supplies, am I right?"

"Well." Councilwoman Marybeth Jacobsen leaned deep into her microphone and breathed for a moment before speaking again. "We can debate the merits to such a plan after I present my own proposal. Council president, can I get a motion to present, since we have two proposals on the same issue, and then to discuss after?"

"Granted," the council president said.

The councilwoman winked at the mayor. "I call my plan *Young and Hung.*"

She pointed to her T-shirt, where the slogan was imprinted, and a number of the crowd laughed. The mayor scanned the audience to see if the laughers were simply her backers, or if the councilwoman was genuinely coming across as funny.

"Let's be honest with ourselves," she continued. "We're looking at employing mostly boys, are we not? To give a restless, and sometimes violent, part of the population something to do. I have four parts: jails, road repair, bridge maintenance, and wastewater treatment. Unlike the mayor's plan, mine is cheap, employs more youth, and will actually engage them into useful activities."

He tried to search out the eyes of the other council members for the tiniest hint they might support his proposal but got no response. The mayor sank in his seat and only half-listened to the grating sound of Councilwoman Marybeth's mic'd voice. He knew her plan, he could have drawn up her plan before she presented it, in his sleep, drunk or high he could have drawn up such a plan. It would have something for everyone, little crumbs for each citizen to devour so they could each claim, *I got mine!* No matter the useless pettiness of the component. In the oft-spoke words of the council president, it would "*be something we can all get behind!*" He could feel the work they'd done dying in his sweaty hands. He knew, politically-in-his-gut-knew, that the best thing he could do was to listen well and jump into her proposal with thoughtful changes, innovative ideas, that he should forsake the work they'd done in order to move any plan along. He could feel she'd already won. No matter that the work he held in his hand—and here he wiped its cover on his leg again—was the answer. He would stand when she finished and bear the torch of the great compromiser. Along the side of the chamber he could see his team deflating.

Bullshit bullshit bullshit.

His communication's director waved at him and he realized he'd been mouthing *bullshit* into the mic. It had gotten Councilwoman Jacobsen's attention but she continued heedless, bulldozer-like, her lipsticked mouth moving like a puppet's maw. There was far more applause when Councilwoman Marybeth Jacobsen finished her shrill speech, that was clear. Was he simply unpopular? Did they really think her plan so much better? He felt, and then managed to overcome, the impulse to throw something, an impulse that, admittedly, he'd not had the wherewithal to overcome in previous, they-would-not-let-him-forget-about-it council meetings.

He opened his plan again and read the summary to see how crazy it sounded. Opportunity Pipeline? It sounded insane.

But then he realized the essential question. The revelation vaulted him right out of his seat. *Keep cool, cowboy, keep cool.* Since he was standing, he plucked the microphone out of its holder and thanked Councilwoman Marybeth Jacobsen for her balanced plan, his arm pointing out into the air like Elvis Presley.

The council president was frozen, his mouth pressed to his microphone, on the verge of reprimand. "If you all will indulge me for one more moment," the mayor said, "I have an addendum to make." He tried to reel in his Elvis arm in a muted fashion, to keep his hips from shaking.

His advisers all seemed to be standing on the tips of their toes, leaning forward at thirty-degree angles.

"My friends, here is the essential question, the one each of us should be asking ourselves. Is this merely a long period of rotten weather. Or are we in a new era? Sure, your answer might pin you as an optimist or a pessimist. But it is vital that we ask this question of ourselves. It deeply informs the governing of this city, as well as our own lives. Do we make plans that make do, or do we stare hard into our future and create a city that thrives?

"You might call me a pessimist, then, when it comes to the weather. How many years more will we stumble weakly along, hoping for our deliverance? The drought is here to stay, folks. I'm a pessimist on the weather, but I'm a huge optimist when it comes to our city. I want us to thrive again! Fellow council members, as you consider these two plans I want you to look into your own hearts for your ambitions for this city. Are you planning to pass time, or are you planning for the future?"

If standing on the table now and Elvis-air-humping could in any small way add credibility to his speech, he would have done it in a heartbeat.

"My team and I have taken a stance. These are hard times getting harder. Our plan is skating ahead of the puck—" He realized he'd just used a sports metaphor and felt a moment of self-disgust.

"Thank you, Mr. Bartlett, Mayor," Councilwoman Jacobsen said. Her mouth had gone strangely askew, gnawed on, one horrid red lip dry-stuck on a tooth, leaving a vampiric smear there. A few strands of her long brown hair were sweat-glued to her forehead. "I don't think anyone here today is anything but hopeful and optimistic for our city. They're all here, right? We're all here putting in time to make the city better."

It did not feel natural to stand any longer, and so he sat. As he did so he saw at the back of the chamber, slouching deep into his chair, Commander Roger Aachen of the National Guard. Immediately he felt in trouble, chastised. The commander hovered over them all like some parent, the mayor thought, checking to see if the chore he'd tasked his children might need to be redone.

A man of seventy or eighty came to the citizen mic and spent some time adjusting the belt of his tan slacks, after which he told the mayor what he thought of his plan: He loved it. He then proceeded to tell a *well-when-I-was-a-kid*, with the hard work and etc. The mayor imagined and immediately dismissed the idea of embracing the man, foreseeing the heart attack it might give the elder heterosexual.

More citizens came to the mic and spoke, many he'd seen before, passionate activists who had caused him constant side-ache. His advisors had copies of his plans for anyone who wanted one. Questions were asked and answered. Councilwoman Marybeth Jacobsen droned on.

A woman of about sixty, dressed in a patchwork skirt and a turquoise blouse, approached the microphone. "Mayor Bartlett? Many of us would like to know if you have caught Maid Marian."

"Yes?" the mayor's voice came out gravely and he cleared his throat. He'd been slouching in his chair, only marginally paying attention, his body's gravity heavier in assumed defeat. Paying attention and not paying attention, a useful skill for weathering the umpteen million city council meetings he would attend in his lifetime. "I'm sorry, what?"

"This meeting stays on topic," the council president said. "We're discussing youth employment, not criminal activity, so I ask—"

"Have you caught Maid Marian?" she repeated.

The mayor had fixed the National Guard commander with a sort of internal tracking device, constantly aware of his movements, and at the repeated question felt rather than saw him lean in to absorb the answer.

"No," the mayor said, "though I prefer not to call her by that name. The police chief and I are working hard on it. While we do not know the age of the suspect, these proposals"—here he gestured vaguely in the direction of the other council members—"will certainly go a long way to address issues such as"—he held his fingers in air quotes—"Maid Marian, meaning crime. I don't think we're entirely off-topic here," he said, trying to win some small favor with the citizen at the mic.

"What about the illegal water routes that came out of her political action?" she asked.

"Ma'am?" the council president said.

"I—action? We consider her actions a crime, robbing a truck is a crime," the mayor said. "But of course the truck—we are looking into it, but having water itself is not a crime. There's no evidence that—"

"—If you do not stay on topic," the council president droned on, "we'll have to ask you to leave."

"We need water transparency! Unequal water distribution is a crime, not the other way around," the citizen said. Violent applause broke out across the room like a string of firecrackers.

"Ma'am?" the council president said in a voice laced thick with condescension and weariness, "OK, goodbye. Goodbye." He turned to a policeman standing against the wall, "Officer, please remove the lady from the microphone so that we may stay on topic for once."

"I hear that," Mayor Bartlett said. He looked up at the audience uncomfortably as the officer took the woman by the elbow and steered her toward the exit. "I completely, totally hear you, and my office and the police force are working to address those issues." He watched as she was maneuvered toward the doorway.

Commander Roger Aachen stood and followed the citizen out, and the mayor stared for a moment, transfixed by the closed doorway through which they'd exited, while the council meeting continued.

Riding in the dark, Renee was struck by the stench first. When they crossed into Northeast it was easily apparent that city services were breaking down. There were great piles of garbage at the curbs and it reeked of rot and dead animals. The houses were dark but she heard people on their porches, sitting on their dried-out lawns. There were sounds of argument and violence, of doors being slammed and glass being broken, and she felt conversations go quiet as they rode by. She was thankful they were on bikes and moving along at a good clip, even as they hurtled recklessly through the night. She tried to search the road in front of her for objects and gripped her handlebars tightly. Further in was a great bonfire at the center of an intersection. People carried items from their houses and dumped them and the fire blazed wildly, sending a plume of sparks upward. She could see the skeletal hulk of a car in the blaze.

The dust storm had covered everything in a fine grit, and Renee tasted this on her tongue now as she rode. She was scared, and immensely happy Bea rode with her, conscious of what it had cost Bea already.

They turned toward the Cully neighborhood and two streets up, cycling hard in the dark, they collided with something stretched across the street, made invisible by the darkness. It clanged metallically when they hit and Bea and Renee were thrown from their bicycles, landing hard on the ground.

Renee stayed down, her cheek pressed against the blacktop. She tried to breathe through the new pain, a complement to the old. She could hear the scrabbling of feet and someone calling out but she was disoriented and didn't move.

"It's a motherfucking fence," Bea said.

"Did what it's supposed to." A man's voice in the dark. "You head back the other way now, and quick."

Bea reached down for Renee's arms and pulled her to a sitting position. Renee couldn't get control of her breathing.

"We're just passing through," Bea yelled. "What the hell? Dumb droudies."

"This is a safe area."

"Safe from what?" Renee said.

"You," the man said.

"Asshole," Bea whispered. "We should go around. Can you get up?"

Renee stood and tried to see into whatever encampment was on the other side of the fence but it was too dark. They were a compound of some sort, she thought. "Maybe it's safe in there."

"You want to go in there?" Bea sighed disgustedly, and then yelled: "It's Maid Marian."

"No," Renee whispered.

"Who's that?" the man yelled back, but they could hear a hushed discussion on the other side of the fence and they picked up their bikes and waited, unsure of what to expect.

"You can pass when it's light," the gruff-voiced man said.

"But it's Maid Marian." This was a woman's voice, and more hushed argument followed.

Somewhere to the west of them they heard two gunshots in quick succession, followed by another some seconds later.

After a scuffling and whispers in the darkness, a woman's voice asked if they had a place to stay.

"We don't know if they still live up here," Renee said.

"Stupid to be out in the night," the man's voice said. "Come into the light."

He cranked up a hand-powered flashlight and they proceeded toward the glow.

Renee leaned into the light and pushed back her helmet, conscious of her wounds. She looked at their faces as the shadows flickered over them and saw a range of ages and races that seemed to have nothing to do with each other. They were neighbors, she realized, banded together.

"It's her," the woman said.

"You better stay here tonight." A woman emerged into the light, a pink headscarf wrapped around her hair, the tired marks of vigilance in her face.

Renee hovered close to Bea. It was only a dozen blocks or so to where they were going but her optimism had turned and running into the fence had jarred her. "Should we?" Renee whispered.

"It's safer," the woman with the headscarf said. "Sometimes at night there are raids."

"Zombies," the man said.

"—people on the lookout for water and food he means. They scavenge the empty houses, but they don't exactly turn back when they find someone still living in one."

They walked through a gate and passed men with guns and entered the block, fenced off at both ends. The woman with the headscarf walked in front and they followed in the dark. "I'm Lisa," she said. "Each night two families keep guard. We work together, like a wagon circle."

Lisa had two daughters, ten and fourteen, who scurried around preparing a guest bedroom by candlelight. She had an open intelligence in her eyes, the look of a woman who might have taught college or run a non-profit at one time, before the larger world turned violent and she'd turned inward to protect her family. She smiled at them, but couldn't hold their gaze, dipping her head in embarrassment or shame or because she was afraid, Renee didn't know which. Renee noticed her daughters stealing fleeting glances at her. She smiled back.

"What are you doing?" Lisa said. "I mean up here."

Renee shrugged and thought about the answer. "Looking for the rest of our group," she said finally. "We were separated." She hunted around for something else to say. "We're regrouping."

Bea cleared her throat. "We're going to find more trucks. We're going to redistribute the stolen water back."

Lisa looked up at Renee and she saw that there was awe there. It humbled Renee, someone older and wiser and more experienced looking at her as if she were someone who could really solve their problems. It made her feel like an impostor, like a sham, and she tried to rise to expectations. She swallowed and smiled. "My name is really Renee," she said, "and this is Bea."

In the morning, the Cully neighborhood in Northeast Portland felt like a strange desert outpost, with trash and dust blowing around in the street and people staring suspiciously from their porches. They heard another round of gunshots and accelerated toward their destination.

When they arrived they stood outside their friends' house and saw that it had burned. Dirt had been used to put out the fire, or to keep it from spreading to neighbors, but it had burned almost to the foundation. In the front yard there were scattered belongings and clothes, charred and filthy. The refuse left over after scavenging. Pieces of furniture and other unrecognizable items had been dragged from the scene and then discarded. Renee found among the detritus a trampled and heat-warped photo of her friends, the couple and their child posing in a pumpkin patch.

She couldn't bring herself to look any closer at the house for fear of finding remains. She sat at the side of the road and put her head in her hands. She wasn't sure where to go next.

"We need to find a house fast," Bea said. "Back to Lisa's?"

"We don't know what we're doing," Renee said. She pictured Zach, how sometimes the look on his face made her feel like she was telling him the greatest story ever told. She wondered about turning back and stabbed at the ground with the heel of her boot.

"Renee," Bea said, and took hold of her arm.

Four men came toward them from the end of the block, walking hurriedly. It wasn't easy to determine their ages for the grime and hollow eyes and untamed beards. They were armed with crude weapons, pipes and knives.

"Now, Renee." Bea put her hand out to help her friend up.

They mounted their bikes and the men broke into a run.

Renee turned and flipped them off and they pedaled hard to the end of the block. At the intersection she looked back. A shot rang out and the men scattered, ducking low and running toward the side of the road. One of them fell writhing on the ground.

They rode hard for a couple more blocks, putting space in between them and whatever conflict was behind. Every part of her ached, her injured ribs made the intake of breath a chore. She felt like crying. At Forty-seventh and Cully they stopped and Renee leaned over and breathed hard. "Fuck this." She wrapped her hand around the rebar she'd strapped to her handlebars as a weapon and listened.

A group of three kids in torn, dirty clothing approached them, speaking Spanish between themselves. Two twin girls of about six or seven, and a little brother. Renee and Bea waited.

"Hola, niños," Renee said. "Tengan cuidado en la calle, no? Donde están sus padres?"

"We speak English," one of the twins said indignantly. The children gripped hold of Renee's bicycle, the boy laced his fingers through the spokes. They stared up at her.

Renee looked back from where they'd come but they weren't being followed.

"Where are you going?" one of the twins asked. She wore a soiled baseball cap that said *Go Organic!* Both of the girls had their hair inexpertly cut short, as if they'd worked at each other's heads with a pair of child's scissors. The boy's hair was grown long. All three of them wore half a dozen pin-on buttons each, advertising some long-gone political campaign.

"We don't know," Renee said. "I like your buttons."

"Do you have any food?"

Renee pulled a nut bar out of her pack and broke it between them, and they devoured it instantly.

After the boy licked his fingers clean he studiously unpinned one of his buttons and handed it to Renee.

She pinned it to her own shirt. It said: *Ascend together!—¡Suben Juntos! Muskogee for Senate.* "How does it look?" she asked.

They stared at her blankly, too shy perhaps to tell her it was on wrong or didn't suit her. "Where are your parents?"

The girl with the hat pointed at a house down the block. "My dad is working."

"What does he do?"

"He runs for Gregor. Do you know Gregor?"

"He's the boss," the boy said.

"The boss of what?" Renee said.

They looked at each other in silent conference. "*Every*thing," the boy said.

"No," the girl with the hat said.

"Not at all," the other girl said.

"What's he like?" Renee asked.

"Nice. Fat," one of the girls said. Her thin shoulders rose in a shrug. "I don't know."

"And your mom? Who takes care of you during the day?"

"She's dead," the boy said.

"We don't need taken care of," the girl with the hat said. "We take care of our dad. We saw you on the TV."

"I wish I could show you my hiding place," the boy said mournfully.

"Are you going to get another water truck?" the other girl said.

"*Pow!*" the boy said.

Renee glanced at Bea and raised her eyebrows and said *phew*. Bea told her they should get going.

The children had her bike ensnared in a spider's web of small fingers, their eyes expectant and hopeful at the thought of being included on future adventures. Renee assured them next time they would definitely be enlisted.

"Do you have any water?" the boy asked.

Renee pulled out her water bottle and she heard Bea exhale in disgust. She poured a couple of teaspoonfuls into each of their open mouths. Little motherless birds, she thought, and tried to keep despair at bay. "Would you kids do me a favor? Tell your dad to pass on a message to Gregor. Tell him Maid Marian wants to meet with him."

"'Kay," the girl with the hat said. The kids all looked down the street toward their house, and the meeting seemed suddenly over.

"You got it?" Renee said. "What's the message?"

"You want to meet him!" the girl snapped. "Bye!" The children ran back in the direction of their house.

Renee watched them disappear between houses and felt anxious for them. "Was there some kind of dog whistle we missed, or did they just get bored?" she said.

After the kids, the block went quiet. A slight breeze shifted the big dead trees dryly over them. Renee stared up into the eerie branches and listened. There was no human sound.

Renee pointed with her chin toward a house down the street. It was obscured behind a wiry mass of leafless shrubbery.

The house was a Craftsman, but it had been built as if, Renee thought, the builder didn't understand the scale represented on the blueprints. Everything about the house was big, and it dwarfed the other houses on the block. It stood three stories tall and occupied a massive footprint. Like other houses in the neighborhood, it sat on a big lot, in this case a full acre. An eight-foot chain-link fence and the remains of a thickly treed perimeter encased it like an urban fortress.

Zach did the poster layout over lunch. He was cautious, but he knew he didn't need to be. No one would look at his machine except Berger, a project manager, who liked to glide around like some kind of inter-office eel and look at everyone's screens. But Berger had contracted E. coli and was in the hospital. Renee's group fled after warrants were put out for their arrests, their identities pieced together by video-tape and surveillance. They didn't dare use any traceable medium to try and contact each other. So he and Renee had schemed up the coded poster. Before becoming a copywriter he'd been a graphic artist and had enjoyed the work.

He hand-drew a robin with a leather aviator hood. Across the robin was strapped a quiver full of slender water vials. He scanned and color-ized the drawing and along the bottom he typed 147S@LHURST@9, which he hoped would translate to: The Robin Hoods (or, the robbing hoods, as it were) who lived at 147 Skidmore meet at the Laurelhurst Theater at 9 p.m. Then Zach would post vigil in front of the theater for a few minutes every night, waiting for one of them to materialize, unsure if this was what he really wanted in the first place. He could recognize them by sight, and some nights the theater still worked, showing a single short film, whatever they managed to get going while the power was on, imported from the East Coast or from their archives.

He was helping Renee, but were he honest with himself he could care less about the rest of her activist-crew. He felt certain they would only suck her more deeply into trouble—something she was fairly capable of doing already. He wasn't sure any of them were bright enough to turn his obscure poster into a private message anyway. And he felt it highly likely that he was endangering Renee rather than helping her. He leaned back from the design and appreciated his work. All things aside, it was, he saw, really fucking good.

Still, he had to help somehow. He thought of her constantly, up in some strange, dangerous neighborhood. He'd do whatever he could.

Zach stood up in his cube and eyed the printer down at the end of the hall. There were six office doorways—three sets, one on each side of the hall—to pass by in order to retrieve the side project from the large-format color printer. A layout of this size would occupy the printer for about three minutes. Zach stretched and then walked casually down to the printer. As he went he tried to eye which offices were occupied and which weren't, a thing he could never remember. A few had permanently closed doors, colleagues who'd migrated away, or in one case, died. The printer was off the break room, where Nevel appeared to be cleaning furiously, and so Zach turned around self-consciously and shuffled back to his desk. He hated this. He pulled out a legal pad of paper and quickly scratched out half a dozen word associations so there was evidence of work on his desk. They were trying to pitch a satellite telecommunications firm that sold equipment to the Middle East. One of the few companies with energy exemptions. Business must go on. One must work under the premise that the apocalypse was not nigh. And it seemed to him that money was sought after even more feverishly as people died, as if a wage, or the pursuit of, were some kind of shield against their own mortalities. They were all dying of thirst; money was one elixir.

We's in yo head!, he wrote, and then sketched a satellite with a lightning bolt coming out of it and straight into a stick-figure's head. He kept his ears out for Nevel.

Sputnik is thirsty for more.

The all-seeing eye.

He penciled out a quick sketch of Renee, giving her braids and a tin-foil hat. He remembered the first time he'd seen her in the cafe, joking with somebody at the counter, a warm wit to her. She gestured her arms wide as she made a customer laugh. When his turn in line came, he'd been struck with her spell. He'd lingered there, deciding long over the scones, as she spoke about the qualities of each, how this scone, with the chocolate, was for sadness, for mornings when you wake up and there's an unspeakable shadow right here—she tapped above her own heart—and this with the cranberries would be fire in the belly, like locomotive fuel, and this one with the apricot bits was for love, the finding and keeping of it.

He bought the one for love, red-faced and smiling and she put it in its paper sheath and drew on a heart with a Sharpie. Let me know how it goes, she'd said conspiratorially, sly with smile.

It had gone well, at least until now.

He admired his drawing and then became conscious of the fact that he'd just sketched the fugitive and written her name below it. He gave her a Frida mustache and unibrow and drew satellites and buildings and other bits around her, embedding and obscuring her in the image.

He didn't know what this satellite company was even selling nor to whom, though with the power issues most other sources of communication had gone dark, so he could probably figure it out. At any rate, they gave him the brand to steer, not a product to pitch. He decided to take the chance, Russian roulette style, and hit the print button. He would either get caught or he wouldn't. It was the designer's printer, he could always intimate that the poster belonged to her. And if the poster showed up in the news and on the police blotter the next day, well then fuck. Maybe he'd follow her up north. He made himself count to thirty, during which time he drew a giant eye on his scratch pad, spying down on civilian hordes, then he walked briskly down the hall toward the printer. Halfway there Nevel exited the kitchen and Zach started.

"Drought up," Nevel said on his way by. Nevel's office joke was that all anybody ever talked about anymore was the drought, so why not replace every word with that one?

"Drought up," Zach answered.

He could feel his face and neck grow hot as he watched as the printer head painstakingly snail-danced across the paper, the poster's tongue rooted in the cogs, so he could not make a run for it. From the back, his neck must surely look burned. But it printed, and it was lovely. He was, he thought as he admired it, a genius.

A few minutes later in the copy room he punched in 300 color copies. No one would ask what he was doing, he repeated to himself, everyone else had something to hide. He was working, there was no need for his skin to blaze fire-engine red.

"Hey, you're everywhere today," Nevel said.

Zach felt the copy room couldn't adequately hold two people. He knew his personal space requirements were on the high side, but still.

"How many are you going to print here, tree-killer? Should I go on vacation? You printing your novel or something?" Nevel leaned against the wall, blocking the door, in a manner that suggested he might be there until nightfall.

"No," Zach said. "I'm not even writing a novel."

"Oh? I thought everyone was," Nevel said. "What is it then, poster for your girlfriend?"

The container known as the skull which held Zach's brain expanded spontaneously a thousand feet in every direction, leaving his brain wet and small on the floor, amid a cavernous space, and it was there in that container that he wondered how in the hell Nevel knew what he was up to. He felt that in this new space where his brain sat in its own slippery goo, troops marched toward him, and his brain with all its power and inventiveness fought futilely to invent some utterly obvious reason why he would be copying a revolutionary poster for his fugitive girlfriend that would only prove to demonstrate his superior commitment to this very job. After a great long while, punctuated by the shuffling beat of the copier spitting out copy after copy, Zach said darkly: "It's for work." He couldn't think of one single damn time that he'd ever been called on in his history of working at Patel & Grummus to make a photocopy.

"Listen, man, I don't care. Seems like there might be a few tender spots there. You want me to turn around while you do your special thing here or what? Look, I'm printing stuff for the communist party." Nevel turned the piece of paper he'd brought into the copy room around to show Zach, and indeed it was a Soviet-era communist propaganda piece about mining.

"Oh," Zach said. "Is that for the TeleCelSys contract?"

"What? No, it's for my basement."

"Ah, should you be using the work copier for personal stuff?" he said, hating himself as he said it, wishing he were crushed under the boot of some great cockroach-crushing god.

"I guess that seems like sort of a silly question, Zach."

"I didn't really ask it. I didn't really mean it. I mean I don't even care. Will you make me a copy of your Russian thing too?" he said finally, to be companionable.

Bea and Renee stood on the sprawling wood porch and thought about knocking. The door was a giant oak defense, but the front window was broken and the house reeked of urine and and the cloying, putrid smell of death. They could see into the living room.

"Just a dog, probably," Renee said, the crook of her arm covering her nose. "Dead dog."

"It's abandoned," Bea said, "right?"

"Grab something." Renee picked up a long shard of glass and gripped it in her hand.

If there was someone there, they'd run, Renee thought. But she dreaded the thought of running more. She stared up at the height of the house and imagined it theirs. Fixed up and bustling with her people.

Bea found a damaged wood chair that had been thrown from the porch into the bushes and broke a leg off. "Glass is a bad idea, sweetheart," she said.

"You're the tough guy. I'm going to watch." Renee knocked at the door, and after a minute's silence yelled hello into the living room through the broken window.

"OK," Bea said, "here goes." She straddled the window and crawled in, and then padded quietly around a listing living room table toward a door at the far side. As she came to the end of the table a man leapt out of a closet and tackled her, gripping her in a full body hug that took her over the top of the table and to the ground.

Renee hurdled the window frame but by the time she was there Bea had the man in a cursing, spitting, snarling ball of a half nelson and wouldn't let go.

"Stop it," Renee yelled at him, "is this your house?"

"Yes!" He was bone-thin, wiry and brown-skinned and pungent. He flailed like a cat under Bea's grip.

"Is there anybody else here?" Renee said.

"It's not your house!"

"No, we were—the window was out."

"Get the fuck off me!"

"Not until you tell us if there's others," Bea said.

"Thom! Erik!" he shouted.

They listened quietly. Renee raised her glass shard and backed toward the window, staring at the ceiling.

"You're lying," Bea said.

"Get off me!"

Renee appraised the man ensnared in Bea's grip, their skin tones in stark contrast to one another. "Sorry," she said. "We're leaving now."

Bea released him from her grip and scrabbled quickly away. The man came to his feet, both hands filled with junk from the floor. A broken dish in one hand, a fistful of paper in the other. He was of an indeterminable age—a harshly wrinkled, hard-lived forty or an agile sixty-five.

"We're going now," Renee said. She backed toward the window and climbed out. Bea followed.

"Get out of here," the man snarled, his voice sounding more deflated than angry.

"We did knock," Bea said.

"What's your name?" Renee said from the front porch.

"Leroy. Leroy. I was here first."

"I'm Renee," she said. "We're leaving you in peace. You know of any empty houses, Leroy?"

"Nope."

Renee touched Bea's shoulder and nodded that they should head back to the street. As they left the yard, they heard a dish crash to the floor behind them. Leroy stood in the empty window.

"You coming after us," Bea said, raising her fists.

"Wait," Leroy said. He closed his eyes tight. "It's a big house," he said. He stepped backwards a few steps and brushed himself off with an agitated ferocity. "Never mind! Never mind!" he yelled.

"We're looking to find a house. We need a place to stay."

For a moment nothing was said. It was obvious that the unasked question was being weighed, and the moment to say *you can't stay here!* came and went. She could feel the complications of the question, how against what neighborhoods they'd come through being alone might be more frightening than not. Renee came forward and leaned against the porch railing but it complained loudly and threatened to give so she stood again.

"Careful!" Leroy said.

"This is Maid Marian," Bea said. "We need a headquarters."

"A what?" He inspected Renee from head to toe. "What do you do?" He eyed them suspiciously and then began shaking his head. "That kind of shit brings trouble."

"That's not—" Bea said, and then, offended, began to reach for him again and he threw up his hands.

"All right, I don't care what you do! Let me show you the empty rooms. But I have the third floor. Everything's exactly as I like it. Don't touch anything up there. Don't even go up there."

Renee smiled and started to ask if he was sure, but changed her mind. It was far better to be bound to those you disliked than to the unknown, she thought. And it was scariest of all to be alone. After Bea and Leroy had ascended Renee closed her eyes where she stood. She could hear them squabbling in the rooms above, and heard how the squabbling came easily to Bea—a good sign. The thrusts and parries of light argument, of testing one another. She could sense who Leroy was, a scavenger, a survivor. They were like him now, too. Most of all, she wanted to sleep. To have a room and to sleep in it. She felt like she was home.

Later, Renee strolled through the house, taking stock and picking off the easy targets in damage control. While still a splendor to behold, the house had been been ransacked often enough that the halls were filled with trash. Someone had written *I am the motherfucking king of Egypt!* on every available surface on the first floor with a black Sharpie.

"Is this . . . did you write this?" Renee asked Leroy as he hurried through on his way somewhere.

"I'm not the king of Egypt," Leroy said matter-of-factly, putting emphasis on the word "king," as if to leave open the possibility of another position of note for himself.

She chose a room on the second floor at the back of the house. The room had been a child's room at one time. The walls were a light turquoise and trimmed with flowers. A bookshelf contained a wide range of titles, from Richard Scarry to the *Chronicles of Narnia* and the Earthsea Trilogy, and in those books she could see the passage of time in the room, could feel how the girl had grown older there. The abandoned conclusion of that progression, whatever the girl's fate, saddened her. One dejected stuffed rabbit lay on the floor in a corner. Out the window was a large backyard that at one time had been beautiful. Now brown earth stirred up into small plumes of dust in the breeze. A wood swing set sat forlornly to one side. She wanted to know where the family had gone and whispered a well-wishing for them, thinking of the girl.

Bea pulled in a twin mattress from down the hall. "I don't want to sleep alone," Bea said.

"It's a lonely feeling," Renee said, "moving in like this, to be on the run."

"We should plan escape routes first thing," Bea said, and then sat down on the bed and put her face in her hands and cried.

Renee was taken by surprise. She sat next to her and stroked her hair, trying to think of something to say. "I am so sorry. Let's get a message to your parents." She embraced her back.

Renee heard Bea take a deep breath from behind her hands.

"No no, I'm fine, I'm going to be fine. I wouldn't change it," she said. "I mean beside the drought, there's nothing that I would change about this." She wiped her eyes, took another deep breath and said, "Whew!"

"Why don't you take it easy for a bit? Sleep if you need to."

Bea shook her head, stood up and walked out of the room.

"Bea?"

"Escape routes!" she yelled from down the hall. "And I'm going to check on Leroy."

As if in answer, from upstairs, came the sound of energetic furniture moving.

He found the letter tucked in his pillowcase a couple nights after she'd gone. His pillow had crinkled and rustled annoyingly, and he'd wrestled with it, punching it into shape as he slept fitfully, waking each time to rediscover sadly that he slept alone. By then, the paper was a bit worse for wear. In the center was drawn a nude woman, her hips thrust cockily to one side, her breasts nicely full. Around the drawing Renee's sloppy handwriting traced the woman's shape.

Hey Boyfriend!
Look here, right? Introducing ENREE 2.0. My papery clone, to keep you company. She'll tell you the same bad jokes and perform—OK, nearly, but not exactly—the same sexual services, provided your

imagination chips in substantially (—I'm sure you'll have no problem there.)

CARE AND FEEDING:
At night: sleep with her pressed against your chest. Stroke her gently. Brush her hair with the tips of your fingers.

During the day: fold and place in the shirt pocket over that hungry organ that pumps with hope. Alternately: in your front jeans pocket, next to that other organ that has its own sort of pump (vroom!).

Requires: very little feeding or watering. Ironing: on occasion, with cool iron.

See, she's almost better than I am. I'm already a little jealous!

Please don't worry. I'll be back soon enough. (She says for herself, as much as him.)

yrs,

-r

The first definitive copycat was spotted on I-84. A truck identical to the one Maid Marian robbed was pulled over to the shoulder at a severe angle, its back doors spread open. By the time the news crew arrived, only a few bottles remained, which a crowd of scavengers quickly whittled down and distributed equally among them. The driver was nowhere to be found. Among the news anchors' Maid Marian speculation, some wondered whether the driver himself wasn't responsible for the act, blending anonymously into the onlookers.

Most notably, crudely spray-painted in red along one side of the truck was written:

MM

The underline below the letters was shaped like an arrow, as might be seen in a quiver.

After the news showed the latest episode with the still-frame of the truck's side, the symbol bloomed across the city.

Nevel found an M.M. traced in crayon on the sidewalk outside his house. He turned to look at his son Jason with one eyebrow raised. He called to his family and they stood around and wondered where it'd come from. He looked up and saw the same symbol drawn at intervals down the length of the block.

"It's Maid Marian," Jason said. "She's been here!" And then he turned and ran into the house for his own crayons.

Zack saw it first drawn on the backs of hands of women in line at water distribution, a few days after the copycat crimes began in earnest. Drawn on like tattoos, sometimes with a heart encircling the symbol. Their expressions bold and steely, and they appeared to be organized, together perhaps. Were they watching distribution for fairness, he wondered, or at ready to rob from it, or admirers in solidarity?

Sometime in her first week at the new house, Renee found one outside, painted in arching letters in the middle of the street, the arrow pointed directly at their house. She sat down among the large letters, feeling startled and amazed. It was another gift. The longer she stared at it, the more she felt like it was a visitation from an oracle, a sign in the oldest of senses. It wasn't just about her, she knew that: It was a *thing*. She took a pen from her pocket and inscribed the symbol on her forearm, branding herself with the symbol they'd given her. Yes, she thought, admiring it on her arm. I accept. She would be theirs. She would do her best for them.

Nevel sat at his office desk—his own, now, a private place in which he could utter obscenities without aggravating those around him. The view was of the rust-dusted light rail line on the street below, which had long closed down. He reread the document he'd received, entitled: New Westside Water Distribution Creative Brief. He kept losing focus. He was tired of all this. Before this job he'd been in a string of failing companies. Places where you sat at your cubicle and rotted and waited for someone at the top to give up. To realize the company was irreversibly dying.

But now it wasn't the company, it was everything: The city was dying, the west was dying and turning to desert. A long, boring, despair-inducing decline.

Nevel stood at his office window and watched people pass below. A shiny black car pulled up in front of the building and he recognized it as the mayor's.

He watched the mayor's bodyguards shoo away the homeless who gathered to see what the commotion was. And then the mayor emerged. Their chief. His hair shone.

You cannot close a city down and give the money back to the shareholders. There was no larger, wealthier city hovering about to buy up Portland's assets. You must soldier on, keep your shovel to the bottom of the hole until something turned up. Everyone waited for a change of fortunes.

Nevel turned to his desk to tidy up. The mayor would be in his office in approximately three minutes, six if he stopped to talk to anyone else.

The East Coast was luckier, better off, at least in terms of weather. But for all intents and purposes, they too had devolved into interconnected city-states. In each of these little hives of civilization there must be a mayor, he thought, very much like theirs, or perhaps a governor or some military figure, and there must be one of himself, too, the bee whose job it was to cobble together optimistic, educational campaigns for the chiefs of these failing cities. In charge of publicizing the good works, as they were.

After he'd straightened the place up, he sat in his chair and waited, staring at the door, preparing himself mentally. He was in advertising. A flexibility was required. He scratched out a few obscure notes on a blank sheet of paper so that he could place something between them, an artifact of work in progress to defer to.

When you pitched a product, there was the side of the story you wanted the consumer of the product to know, and then there was the whole story. In many ways, the city's campaigns were a welcome respite, in that instead of being intent on selling, their job was to help and to educate. At least in theory. Though still, as with any good ad campaign, they buried a story here too.

After a few minutes the door opened. The mayor did not knock, a man who must barge wherever he went.

"Mayor Bartlett," Nevel said. He stood and held his hand out. The mayor took it.

"Nevel! How are you?" the mayor said.

The mayor liked him, he remembered with mild surprise. He seemed to like both Zach and him, and while he could understand why he might like the brainiac, Nevel could never quite fathom what the mayor saw in him.

The mayor paced back and forth in front of his desk and then scratched at his collar line. "Have you been itchy lately?"

"Itchy?" Nevel said.

"Probably just me." The mayor stopped mid-stride and turned back to Nevel. "Listen, have you got one of those blood pressure gauges? Tester things?"

"Sphygmomanometer?" Nevel said, feeling immensely pleased with himself for knowing the object's name.

The mayor paused, perhaps startled at the word, and then said: "Yes, that thing."

"A partner might keep one—shall I ask?"

"Yes, yes, good—can you? You know how?" the mayor said.

Nevel left his office, glad for the chance to have a task. He made a query of the firm's partners, resisting the urge to tell them it was for the mayor, though they would infer anyway. He rummaged through their meager first aid supplies and came up with nothing. As a last-ditch effort he queried the creatives in their burrow.

"I do," Zach said.

"Not really," Nevel said.

Zach rummaged in his desk drawer and pulled out a blood pressure monitor, stretching the tube long as the gauge snagged on some other bit of electronic shrapnel in his drawer.

"You're worried about your heart?" Nevel said.

Zach shrugged. "Who isn't? How's the mayor's?"

"I'm about to find out."

Zach nodded. "Let me know how it goes."

Back in his office, the mayor had rolled up one shirt sleeve of his sky-blue button-down shirt. His elbow rested on the desk.

Nevel pulled his chair around, conscious of the closeness in which they now sat in his small office.

"Shall I?" He gestured with the sphygmomanometer.

The mayor looked away thoughtfully and Nevel took it as a sign he should proceed. The mayor was better built than he was, he noticed, his bicep boasting a potato shape. He Velcroed the strap to the mayor's upper arm.

"Are you flexing?" Nevel asked. "You should relax."

"Oh," the mayor said. Nevel tightened the strap on his arm and began to squeeze the rubber pumper. He had not done this since he'd cared for his mother, but for nine months he'd done it nearly every day, until her death. Each time, he'd joked with her: *I'm going to pump you up!* Or: *you'll be the size of a life raft when I'm done with you!*, or some other pneumatic joke inserted to add levity to their role reversal. The mayor cleared his throat, smiled, and then looked away again. Nevel began to release the pressure, counting the ticks as the contraption hissed. He imagined telling his wife about this later, but decided he would not. Some stories were better left untold.

"This is kind of high," Nevel said. "One fifty-seven over ninety-six."

The mayor exhaled violently, "I knew it!"

"Were you—were you holding your breath?" Nevel chuckled with surprise.

"Was I?"

"OK, I think you should—do you ever do deep breathing?" Nevel was going out on a limb here, he knew it, but the care he'd given his mother was taking over, and so he proceeded. "With me, inhale."

The mayor sat up very straight and inhaled dramatically.

"It looks like you exercise regularly?" Nevel said.

The mayor shrugged again, but could not repress a self-conscious smile.

"Relax your shoulders, exhale. All the way out, pause."

"Mm," the mayor said when he'd finished, "that *is* nice."

"Now inhale, good. Keep going, close your eyes if you need to."

Nevel inspected the mayor as his eyes were closed. He had perfect skin and impeccable hair, but his eyes were drawn to a spasm below the mayor's left eye, the dark topography there. The tic throbbed.

His nose was an arrow, a geometric perfection. The man could probably grow a full beard—beards were near-ubiquitous now in the absence of shaving water—but the chin was swept clean, meaty and handsome. Despite the obvious care the face underwent, there was a sadness there. Or maybe, Nevel thought, looking at anyone with their eyes closed made them appear sad, the spark gone from their face. When his daughter was younger, a year old, she'd wanted to pluck the eyes out of faces, as if they were but jewels you could hold in your hand, or the very flame that powered a person, that you might wish to extinguish or have for your very own. Nevel wondered if, given the head start the mayor's closed eyes gave him, he'd have time to snatch one of his.

"Good, let's try again." Nevel pumped the rubber stopper again to inflate the blood pressure monitor.

"You heard of this Maid Marian character?" the mayor said. His eyes were open wide, now, beaming with a mad and intelligent brightness.

"I have, but right now let's just relax."

The mayor let out a grumbling sigh. "What should I do, Nevel?"

"You're asking me? No, now this is higher," Nevel said. "You're not relaxing."

The mayor ripped angrily at the Velcro. "Goddamnit!"

"Now hold on—"

"Meanwhile, I've got these a-holes who've got me by my balls, buying up portions of water, or sending little hinting threats, and fuckward National Guard, they've got to have their share too. Commander Aachen, you've met him?" The mayor balled his right fist and released it. "No, of course you haven't. Who even knows how much they're skimming off the top, see? If they are, if they are, I mean."

"I see," Nevel said.

"So we ratchet down rations, but something's going to give, right? I'm stuck in between them."

Nevel realized what the mayor was telling him. His face felt hot. This was the reason they had a job, he reminded himself, sitting right in front of him. Nevel wrapped the tube around the meter portion of the blood pressure monitor and set it carefully on the edge of his desk. He had no idea what to say.

The mayor paced in the tiny runway of the office, between the desk and the door. He stopped and leaned against the door, resting his forehead there. "Sometimes I feel like I run this city as much as a figurehead steers the vessel she's affixed to." His voice was muffled against the wood.

"Who does run it, then?" Nevel's voice came out flat and disinterested.

The mayor turned, suddenly angry. "I do!" His arm jerked out, as if he were skipping a rock down the pavement. "Ah, fuck it. I'm trying to."

"Do you want to talk about this campaign?"

"No. What's it about? No, you do it. You get your people to do it. Get Zach. Do a good job." He rolled his sleeve down and buttoned the cuff. "OK? Thanks for that." He pointed at the sphygmomanometer. "Anytime."

"Keep it around. I'll be back in a few days. Deep breaths. You've got to help me make this work, Nevel." The mayor turned and closed the door softly after him.

Nevel rolled his chair back around behind his desk. He picked up his unit gallon and unscrewed the top, and then rolled to the window and waited, watching the black car below until the mayor had entered it and driven off. He took a long draught of water. Why me? he thought.

Then he unrolled the blood pressure monitor and wrapped it around his own arm, filled as he was with self-loathing, and began to pump.

They locked down as much as they could, but there was not much to be done about the broken front window. In the back bedroom Bea and Renee sat close in the dark on the bed and listened to the night. Far away—far enough away—there were shots. Closer in, some yelling. It felt like a transformation took place upon nightfall. The citizens of Northeast Portland began to hunger for each other's flesh; they were eating each other alive out there. Renee thought about the kids they'd met in the street and hoped they had a real place to tuck into, and someone to tuck them in.

She and Bea slept in their clothes, side by side on the same mattress, holding hands, each of their other hands around a makeshift weapon. Bea held a large standard screwdriver and Renee had laughed when Bea made a joke about "really screwing someone up." Renee gripped the stout handle of a broken pair of pruning shears. Upstairs, Leroy had gone quiet. They feared him, too, even as they took comfort in their united location.

Some time deep in the night Leroy appeared silhouetted by moonlight in their doorway. "Girls," he called quietly. "Girls," he said again, and when no one stirred he said it again until they'd woken.

Bea scrambled to her knees and held the screwdriver in front of her.

"Shhhhh," he whispered. Leroy eased his way into the room, stepping with exaggerated slowness so as to keep the wood floor from creaking. He squatted next to them.

"Don't you come any closer," Bea said.

Renee tried to clear her head of sleep. The pruning shears handle had gotten away from her somehow and she groped around for it even with him right beside her.

"There's someone downstairs," Leroy whispered.

The hair on the back of Renee's neck stood up. They listened.

At first she heard nothing, only the sound of Leroy's breathing next to her, a call somewhere far off in the night.

Then they heard plodding footsteps. An item dropped, perhaps bumped from a table.

"How many?" Bea said.

"Maybe one, maybe two," Leroy said.

What do we do?" Bea said.

They listened—there was the sound of scraping, or something being dragged. For a moment, Renee pondered what it would be like to go and fight for these two breathing bodies beside her. The mass of her charging blindly downstairs toward their intruder, readying her body for collision. There was a rightness to it.

There was a crash from below.

"Let's dance," she said suddenly, "come on!" She let out a terrific whoop and then began to jig about the floor, knocking into objects in the dark as she went, off-balance but reeling onward. On the first go around she grabbed at Bea and Leroy, who remained squatted and bewildered. "Come on!"

They took to it, finally. The three of them whooping and calling and stomping about in a circle, beating on the floor with their feet. They sounded like a buffalo stampede, and it was a fantastic feeling to make this much noise, to fight back the night this way. Below them, she hoped the scavengers hurried away, terrified by the clamorous haunting from above.

They kept at it as long as they could, dancing together out of the room and down the hallway into the other rooms and back again, avoiding the stairway still. She didn't know how long they lasted.

"Now we go check?" Renee said when they finally petered out. She wiped the sweat from her eyes and tried not to think about the dwindling amount of water left in her bottle.

"I'm not going," Leroy said. He was panting hard. In a glance of light Renee had seen him smiling while he danced.

"Phew," Bea said. "How long until light?"

"Three, four hours?" Renee said.

"Let's sleep in the same room and wait for light," Renee said.

"With him?" Bea said, pointing her screwdriver at Leroy.

"Of course."

Renee patted Bea and Leroy on the back as she steered them back to where they slept, closing the door behind them and putting a chair against it. She directed Leroy toward the other twin mattress and they lay down on the first. Their breaths still came fast, but there was no sound from below.

"Well, OK then," Leroy said after a while into the dark, in answer to nothing in particular, and Bea and Renee laughed.

Renee did not sleep until dawn. Her bunkmates drifted into heavy breathing and she remained awake, thinking of the neighborhood outside. She wondered where her fellow water activists were and decided soon she'd go use her Morse-code system to talk to Zach. A hazy plan had started to take shape in her mind. She wanted to see the boss of everything.

In the morning, they crept slowly down the stairs together, armed with what they had, but the house was empty.

"Maybe we should board up the whole first floor," Bea said.

"Or dance every night," Renee said.

Bea and Renee sat at the dining room table and looked at each other. They were hungry and thirsty, and had no rations left from those Lisa had given them. They watched Leroy pass toward the kitchen and wondered about asking. They knew he could go to the distribution up the street at the elementary school field each day, where they would be arrested.

The wallpaper had begun to curl away from the wall in the dining room, and the light fixture that hung over the table only had a single light of the five that had been in it. Bea drummed her fingers on the table.

Renee whispered that she'd ask him and Bea shrugged and hung her head. Ahead of them, Renee knew, there were days filled with nothing but trying to secure rations for themselves.

"I'll get you a drink." Renee walked to the kitchen and leaned against the counter. The power was on and Leroy hurriedly cooked rice with some kind of ration-issued vitamin-enriched protein powder over the top of it.

He looked up at her and knew what she wanted and turned back to his task.

"The police are looking for us. We can't go to distribution," Renee said. The pot of rice was small, only enough for a single portion. "You probably knew that already." Even the bland smell of cooking rice made her stomach ache. When his back was turned she leaned over and inhaled steam. "Do you have savings?"

"No, I don't have savings. Every time I get something together I get robbed or a couple of white girls drop in."

Renee handed him a spoon. "You better stir that."

"I know what I'm doing." He stood back and stared at her. "I know how to cook rice."

"This is short-term. Two, three days max. We could trade work on the house. We need to get on our feet. It was good last night, right, with the intruder?"

Leroy shrugged and then grinned despite himself.

"Do you know Gregor?"

He scowled. "Of course I know Gregor. Listen, lady, I ran the Bottle Route."

This seemed to be something she should know, and she shut up as he finished cooking. In the cupboard she found three cups and three bowls and laid them out next to him on the counter and he sighed.

"I don't remember what the Bottle Route is."

"Bottle route, cans and bottles, ka-ching? A shopping cart? For fuck sake. Ten years. I know everybody. I don't forget anything. *Anything.*"

She put her hands up defensively. "I just need to meet Gregor."

He shook his head at her and turned to finish the rice. "It's a thing, OK? Like a disease."

"What?"

"A disease."

"What is?"

He pointed to his head, his finger tapping his temple. "Forgetting. Not forgetting."

"OK," she said and busied herself with kitchen tasks, trying to stay out of his way. After he served the bowls—he took great care to split them equally—she scraped the pot clean, dividing the last teaspoon of rice cruft between them.

"Thank you," she said, and he stared at her, one eye open wider than it ought to be, a tuft of his sparse beard standing out oddly on his chin.

Finally he said, "Yeah, it's all right." He turned away with his bowl toward the back door.

"Leroy?"

He stopped.

"Come eat with us. We're not so bad."

Leroy scowled and stood by the door.

"Can you take me to Gregor?"

"You don't just go knock on his door."

"What else have I got?"

Leroy made up his mind and she followed him to the living room, handing a bowl of rice and a short glass of water to Bea. "What else? Everything else, everything but that."

"He's no king of Egypt, right? Can't you help me set up a meeting?"

Leroy shrugged. "He's close enough to it."

Zach stood in his underwear, pants in one hand, shirt in the other, and watched the morning news dominated by Maid Marian. The manhunt continued, risen now to a fever pitch by the copycat crimes. The city was going to make a lesson out of her. People were putting signs up in their windows that said "MAID MARIAN SAFE HOUSE," the news reported.

A bearded man on a bicycle with a tattoo of a pigeon on his neck was interviewed. Three other bicyclists, two men and a woman, were in the background behind him. They were going to find her before the police, he said.

The interviewer said: "But—I'm trying to understand, what will you do when you find her?"

"We'll hide her. She's a truth-exposer." The bearded man turned to the camera and pointed. "You can't trust the city!"

Behind him, the woman cyclist called out, "We'll join up with her!"

"Well," the newswoman said into the camera, "as you can see, Maid Marian has stirred up a tremendous amount of emotion among Portlanders."

Next they interviewed the sheriff, and Zach watched with amazement as his girlfriend transformed into a brand. First, there was the iconic image, a woman distributing water to the thirsty. Next they affixed legendary connotations to the image—Maid Marian of Robin Hood—giving the "thief" an irreproachable sense of morality and ethics. The news qualified this tongue-in-cheek, saying the word *thief* as if they should all be lucky to know such thieves. Then a fan base sprung up—good god, not more than a day or two later—deepening the brand and making it socially acceptable—nay, *desired*. They wanted her to win, they began to need her as a conduit for their hope. People were actually putting signs on their houses to indicate their fealty to brand. It was an advertiser's dream. He watched as the police obliviously made her image stronger. At this point, if she were caught the city would riot. They'd already rioted once this week, he remembered, after a horribly orchestrated water distribution fell into chaos and a nine-year-old boy was trampled.

A symbol had been created for her, and it was stenciled on the street. Her name and likeness surely would already be scribbled on bathroom stalls, bus stop shelters, cop cars. If teenagers bent their energy to her, if she became part of the culture's consciousness— then she would have ascended beyond what was possible as a commercial brand. Then she would belong to the realm of Che Guevara or Joan of Arc or, he realized, Robin Hood. It was too early to tell, but no matter the situation, he knew it couldn't be helping his relationship.

Before dusk, Renee and Bea rode for the unused water towers. Now that they'd been in the neighborhood, the mile and a half ride felt like a long, hazardous journey, and they embarked with trepidation. They rode hard, pausing for no one and memorizing their route and the obstacles in it, complete with its burnt-out cars and trash heaps, the charred remains of houses, roving bands of wary youth. Renee sensed that each block had its own impromptu system of arrangements and connections, of safeguarding each other, or in some cases a single group that antagonized all others.

At Nineteenth and Prescott they pulled over to the edge of the street to inspect the park. Two water towers rose in front of them. At their feet there was a playground. One water tower was shaped like a massive thimble, the other like some old Russian moon rocket, suspended on eight legs. They were empty now, monuments from a different time.

The park was tiny and crowded with objects. In its half-dozen city lots were stuffed the two towers, a playground, and a couple of maintenance buildings, but there were still plenty of places to hide, and so they wheeled their cycles in carefully. Bea gripped the kitchen knife she'd strapped to her handlebars. But the park was quiet. They sat underneath the big thimble tower and chatted in a whisper while they waited for sufficient darkness.

Renee unwrapped the green laser pointer from its Morse code instructions, and it made her smile. Renee had studied the Morse code off and on all day in anticipation of this moment, reading his handwriting and trying to commit what she could to memory. Bea would help her write down and translate the bits, but she had much to say and much she wanted to hear.

She tried to imagine him out there, climbing the stairs of his funny old building, opening the metal door that led to the roof where he worked on projects or watched the street below. Sitting cross-legged on the black tar and rubbing his hand across his clipped head.

The light was dim enough to begin, and she hoped he was there. If only it were possible to compress the space between, so that she could whisper into his ear with her eyes closed, her nose brushing against his cheek.

This would have to do. They stationed themselves on top of the plastic playground slide and faced toward the big thimble tower. She opened up the beam of the laser pointer and traced a circle up high on the tower in intervals, a hard, bright green dot the size of her thumb tip. She felt spooked by the alert they were broadcasting, but to hear from him was worth the risk.

She traced circles a few more times. If there was no answer, she would tap out the message she'd memorized for his video camera.

She patted Bea's leg in the anxious anticipation of anything happening, grateful she'd come.

A new dot appeared on the tower, this one the size of a fist, the beam gone wide from the distance. It was him. It flashed a series of rapid blips—it was easy to read excitement in the reply.

The messages came fast. Bea read them off the tower to Renee, who scratched them out on paper and tried to decode them as they came in.

"Dash dot dot dot space dot space dot dash new word," Bea said.

"Hey, that's your name. He wants to know if you're here, Bea." Renee answered back a yes: -.—. ...

His light shone on the tower to reply and she left hers there, circled around his. Their lights flirted around the edges of each other. This was silliness, she knew it, and dangerous too. Morse code was a kludgy, awkward way to tell someone how you felt. But for a moment, she couldn't bring herself to remove her beam from this approximation of him.

"What's going on?" Bea said, and then after a moment she sighed with disgust. "Never mind."

Zach's light began to relay messages again. He had found Josh, whom he was sending up, but no others. She told him what she could of their house, but tapping out the messages was painstakingly slow, and she began to grow more nervous as the night went black.

"We better go," Bea said.

Renee nodded. At the other end of that green dot was Zach. She sat for a while longer. They didn't have anything else to say, not really. After a while Renee tapped out: "love bye."

As they were leaving they watched one last quick reply, the bright green dot pulsing out its last message on the tower. "2MROW?"

-.—. ...

In the morning they were in the living room removing glass debris when an older woman stopped in the street outside the house.

After a while she leaned against the front gate heavily, as if preparing for a long wait. She stared in blankly, something about her movements at the end of things. She reached her dark brown hands through the gate's slats and was still.

They watched her from the living room window, wary.

"She doesn't look armed," Bea said. "I wish she'd move along."

"She's waiting for someone," Renee said.

"Leroy!" Bea called. "You got a visitor!"

"Not for me!" Leroy yelled from the third floor.

Renee picked another handful of tiny shards of glass from the carpet, painstaking work. After about ten minutes she looked up to find the woman still there.

"You want me to go talk to her?" Bea said to Renee.

"No, let her be."

Forty minutes later Renee found her sitting on the front porch, her hands folded across a gold and pink polyester dress, trembling slightly. She was in her early seventies and her black hair was smoothed to a plasticky perfection. A wig, Renee surmised.

"Oh," the woman said, when she saw she'd been spotted.

"Can I help you?" Renee said

"Are you Maid Marian?" the woman said, and then waved her hand dismissively and clumsily stood. "Never mind," she said.

Renee swallowed an instant of confusion. "That's what they call me."

"I heard you were up here." The woman stopped and stared toward the gate. "I don't even know what I'm doing here."

"Heard it from who?"

"Everybody."

"Everybody?"

"Well not *everybody*," the woman said, as if Renee had made some outrageous claim. "Just people talking."

"What'd they say," Renee said.

"Nothing," the woman said crossly. "We all saw you on TV, what's there to say?"

"I see," Renee said, but wasn't sure she did. "And you're looking for—do you have a place to stay, sleep?"

"Well, yeah," the woman said angrily and took one step toward the gate.

Renee felt like she'd crossed some line of propriety and looked for a way to apologize.

After a while the woman said: "No, I don't."

"OK," Renee said. They sat there for a while in silence. There was a touch of sea air in the morning breeze, and yet despite the tease, no rain came. The weather had snaked its way up the channel the Columbia river had made and sat there in the city with its arms crossed, as if to say, What are you going to do about it?

"You can stay here," Renee said. It came naturally. She made the decision without consulting Leroy or Bea. "It's a huge house. There's work to do. What's your name?"

"Julia," the woman said, and fought a smile.

Renee instinctively sensed an exchange was in order, that for Julia to stay here without a contribution would lead to an unfortunate debt in Julia's mind. She hunted around for a trade, no matter how small.

"Are you a good judge of people?"

The woman reared back and inspected her. She gave Renee a bird-eyed stare. "Kind of question is that? Everybody thinks they're a good judge of people."

Good answer to a dumb question, thought Renee.

As they walked into the house they heard Leroy yell, "Third floor is off limits!"

Julia paused and leaned heavily on the banister. She was a little out of breath and Renee thought she might not be well. "That Leroy?" she yelled up the stairs, but no answer came.

"You know him?" Renee said.

Julia shrugged. "Everybody knows Leroy."

Renee gave her a choice of rooms on the second floor, and let her know she might have to share eventually. "You get settled, then come back and we'll talk about what needs doing." Renee watched her pause in a room and inspect the things that had been left there—a torn mattress and dresser, a cracked mirror on the wall, a door that led to a shared bathroom with no running water. She appeared tired and Renee struggled against the urge to tell her to lie down.

"I'll bring you a drink," Renee said, realizing she'd have to borrow it from Leroy. "We'll all be safe here."

"OK," Julia said, her voice turning suddenly meek and conciliatory.

When Julia came back down they sat on the front porch and talked.

Renee wanted to hear more about "people talking" but she couldn't figure out how to get the subject up again. "Do you think others will come?" she asked finally. They stared at each other; a plastic bag blew by and somewhere a door slammed.

"They'll come."

"Because of . . . ?"

"For Maid Marian." Julia shrugged and appeared to be done talking. They sat in silence for a while. "These are pretty low times," she said.

Renee agreed.

"People—they haven't had something to come to. They need something to come to."

THE RIOT

Next came a man named Chris, in his mid-forties, thin and busy. He wore a baseball cap and worked incessantly at some invisible thing in his mouth, a stone or chipped tooth or perhaps his cheek. He was quiet and Renee could see it was painful for him to look her in the eyes, his own blue eyes big and hurt and uncomfortable. Julia said she knew of him from her old neighborhood.

"I've passed his block, seen him working in his yard," Julia told Renee. "Always working, out there mowing. His yard was nice."

"What do you want?" Renee asked him.

He shrugged. He'd seen her on the news, he said. He didn't need a place to stay, he needed something to do. He'd been unemployed for three years and the restlessness was killing him. After that first day, he showed up at 8 a.m. every morning to work.

"Here," he said. He pushed a full unit gallon into her arms and two days of rations and then stared at the floor. "I don't need it."

"Thank you," Renee said. "But no, we can't take that."

He raised his hands, refusing to take it back. "Please. I know you can't get any. You keep giving yours away, ha ha," he said, and then blushed. "I want you to have it."

She set him to work on the house, and he turned his nervous energy on it with fervor. He built an outhouse. He made bunk beds in preparation for more that might come, the wood pulled from the walls of abandoned houses. He cleaned out junk piles, fixed latches, sealed windows, whatever it was that needed doing. His projects spawned new projects, which spawned new projects, so that Renee would come in to find a lightbulb replacement task had resulted in part of the ceiling torn apart.

"Don't fix any leaks," Renee said. It was her running joke. If the roof leaked, they could all go home.

Then others came, drifting in off the street like leaves blown in. Some arrived fired up, kids in their twenties having found her, ranting

71

about the Portland Water Act and distribution inequality and looking for ways to fight. Many truck robberies were proposed, and each time Renee pushed back. No, they were gathering. They were building. No need to flag themselves. They chipped their ration allotments into the communal meals and hung on. Some needed a place to stay—refugees in their own city—while others just came to take a look at her, she supposed. With each arrival she felt a greater need to live up to what they expected, but also a greater sense of who she was. Authority began to come more easily. Her visitors assumed she was in charge—and they seemed to need someone to be in charge. She placed each of them in some small routine, giving them a moment of purpose, allowing herself to believe they were all working toward something larger. As of yet she had only a vague idea of what that larger thing was.

Renee set Chris to work on creating an office for the house. She chose a medium-sized second story room across from where she slept, leaving for now the big room on the second floor empty. The office was not large—but perfect for private audiences. She'd churned the idea for the room about in her mind for a few days. First realizing she wanted it, then trying to get a feel for it, how it would look, the meaning it would impart to visitors. The office needed a big chair, an enormous chair to sit in, and a desk that spread nearly the width of the room. As if to say: Here everything is decided with the utmost solemnity. The office was spare and unadorned—though she amused herself with the thought of having Leroy scrawl *I am the motherfucking queen of Egypt* on the wall. On the desk she put a neat stack of blank paper on one side, and reserved a space for outgoing documents on the other side.

When it was done she shooed curious volunteers out and closed the door behind them. The walls were scuffed white, the floor was scarred fir. For a moment, she laughed at the whole project, the preposterousness of an office with a slot for outgoing papers. She stared out of a window that looked down on the big backyard. Then she sat at the desk in the big chair and stared at the door and rehearsed, quietly, a voice that was beginning to surface, someone else that she'd had hiding inside of her all along.

She thought about what Chris had said, the rumor that she was starting some kind of an organization. She pulled out a pencil and paper and wrote the word "OK" at the top of the page, and then double and triple-traced it. They needed water.

She thought of Josh on his way up from Zach's house. She put off the fear of what they must do. Wait until Josh came, and then they could case the trucks that smuggled water. Josh and she could get a crew together. She'd be the new Robin Hood. She'd be Maid Marian.

Renee and Bea armed themselves and went scavenging for clothes. It was a mysterious process—standing in an abandoned house and sifting through clothes that had been strewn around like a great wind had whipped through the place. Sometimes there were feces on the floor or the remains of campfires. And the clothes: Bea picked up a few pieces until she found clothes that fit her and she was done. Renee picked up each piece and marveled at it, trying to parse out who it was she was becoming and to match up those branching possibilities with the shirt that dangled from her fingers. A cowboy shirt with plastic-pearl buttons? A green canvas shirt from some past war? A pink tank top, a black tank top, a dress? Was she dressing for herself or Maid Marian?

She picked up something blue and satiny and shied away from a stain on it that could only be blood. Bea stood by and scarred a dresser top with the point of her knife. She sighed impatiently.

"Stop it," Renee snapped. "Go home if you want."

"No, I'm staying."

But Renee didn't find anything in that house either.

As they walked down the block they looked for signs a house was abandoned. A front door off its hinges, windows smashed out, but these signs were not always telling.

At one such place, a small green house a block from their own, they stood on either side of the entrance and tried to peer in. The branches of a great dead tree did a poor job of shading the place. There was a screen door between them and the inside that had been spray painted black, the drips hardened into little black pearls. Through its few tiny holes it was too dim to see inside.

"Hello?" Renee called in. "Is this house empty?" The words came out muddy, her syllables dulled by a dry tongue.

There was no answer and they waited, listening.

Renee nodded and Bea opened the door. They stepped into the gloom and waited for their eyes to adjust. Sitting in a rocking chair was an obese white man in his forties or fifties. He held a shotgun pointed at them and did not move.

Renee screamed and dropped the few clothes she'd gathered—socks and underwear and a military beret. She turned and fled, banging back through the screen door and Bea followed.

As she ran she waited for the gunshot but it did not come.

They sprinted, panting with fear, back to the front of their own house and stood there in the street.

"Dude," Bea said, "don't fucking scream."

Renee threw her hands up. "I didn't! I mean don't normally." She paced back and forth. "Was he alive?"

"Yes," Bea bent to catch her breath. "I don't know."

"We'll have to send someone to check on him."

"No way I'm going back there," Bea said.

"Goddamnit," Renee said. She sat on the porch and held her head in her hands. "If he isn't, we can't leave him there." She went over the details in her mind. His eyes had been open, his head tilted just so. "What do we do?"

"Nothing," Bea said.

"I have to know if he's alive."

"You've got no survival instinct."

"Let's go back." Renee stood up.

"Seriously," Bea said. "Come on."

"Walk me back there, I've got to know."

Bea swore and stood up. They walked cautiously back to the house, spooked now, as if every house held a man in a rocking chair with a shotgun.

Outside Renee snuck up to the side of the doorway while Bea stood out at the street.

"Please," Bea said one last time. "Don't."

"Sir?" Renee said breathlessly through the screen door, keeping out of view. She worked at a piece of peeling paint in the doorframe with her thumbnail and felt an immobilizing wave of fear pass through her. She wanted to look into the dark room beyond but she couldn't bring herself to do so. It was utterly silent inside. "Sir? I'm just checking on you. Making sure you're OK. Just say something and I'll go away." There was no sound.

She snuck a look inside then. He was in the same chair, still. A violent chill shook her and her teeth began to chatter. She opened the screen door and approached. She was shaking now and she clenched her teeth to keep them still. He was massive, with an enormous, mostly bald head and a fleshy face. His eyes were open. She thought maybe she saw him breathe and she stumbled sideways and crashed objects off of a coffee table. He wore a blue T-shirt and blue jeans, dust-covered and sweat-stained. His eyes did not track. "Sir?" she whispered. She wanted to touch him for a heart rate but each time she got close to his neck she pulled back. His eyes were sunken and rimmed with dark, and his skin slack, his lips parted. She settled on the shotgun, grabbing the barrel and pulling it from him slowly. It slipped from his hands. She didn't judge its weight properly and the butt clattered on the ground. She leaned it against the door, and then checked the pulse at his neck. The skin felt odd to the touch, as if he were wrapped in wax paper, and it depressed as if the insides were hollowed out. There was no pulse. Renee backed away a few paces and leaned over. For a moment she thought she would vomit. "Bea!" she yelled.

Renee grabbed the shotgun and stumbled outside. "Never mind," she said. "Let's go find a crew. We have to bury him."

"Ah," Bea said.

"Damnit," Renee said. "Damnit."

They stood there at the end of the walkway for a moment. The neighborhood was quiet. And then about five houses down they heard what sounded like hammering. "I wonder if—his neighbors?" Renee said.

"We're not really on our feet here ourselves." Bea eyed the house again.

The hollow her fingers made in the man's neck was stuck in her mind. She wiped her hand on her jeans again, and then again. "I know." She shrugged. "I can't leave him there."

His name was Harold, or at least the ID at his house claimed so. They buried Harry the Giant, as they'd taken to calling him, dubbing him with a friendly title to insulate them from the gruesome task. They dug four feet down into the dry earth, the best they could do before dark for the size of the hole. Someone turned up a cart for hauling lumber, and the lot of them, every resident of the house on Going Street, transported him out of his house and onto the cart and through the streets to the Rose City Cemetery. The task took most of a day, and they walked through the streets with him atop their cart like a tiny parade with one float. Renee felt people watch as they passed.

For a moment, as they put Harry in the ground, she hovered between satisfaction and sadness. She wanted to spring up and search other houses for the dead. As if inside her were a bell, and having done one ennobling thing, that bell rang clear and loud and her body hummed with it.

Later that night, with the job finished, she stood in her room and inspected each item of clothing she'd scavenged. Each had a memory to it, the ghost of its previous owner still inhabiting it. There was something wrong with all of them. They came from the past, from the dead and a dead era. As soon as possible, she resolved to have someone make her clothes. She needed to look it. Were she to be what they asked of her, chieftain of this new tribe, she needed to part ways with the past.

In the end, she chose a black T-shirt that had a hole in its sleeve and blue jeans that had the worn mark of a wallet in the front pocket. Men's jeans. For shoes, she'd had a lucky find in a pair of worn boots that thudded reassuringly against the wooden floor when she walked. They would know she was coming. The outfit would have to do for now.

In the mirror behind her door she looked at herself. There was a long thin scratch down her right cheek that she had no memory of getting. The blood had smeared, starting bold and red and fanning out on the end like a comet.

Downstairs, atop their listing table, someone had pencil-drawn a likeness of her. No body, just her face, the extra dark eyebrows, the twin braids she wore all the time now—the face looked sad, she thought, or angry, and yet there was an expression she didn't understand. She stared at it self-consciously, as if come face-to-face with a living, breathing doppelgänger of herself, someone who might know her thoughts before she spoke them. There was a hardness about her.

And then she realized it was not of her. It was a drawing of Maid Marian.

Zach sat perched on the stone edge of his building's top, a three-story drop to the sidewalk below him. A capricious, unsteady wind blew from all directions. Gusts of it pushed him this way and that. It was most apparent in the street below, where heaps of detritus that had rotted in place for weeks suddenly moved, rose Frankenstein-like from their resting places into cyclone characters that stumbled down the street, reanimated and careening, an instant army of the undead, until their life-sparks moved on and they settled back into newly rearranged piles.

Dust particles bit at Zach's face and stuck to him. He sighed and gripped the letter and sighted down the street toward the city where, later, he would be expected to show up at work. He thought about not going. He thought maybe he'd curl up and reread the letter all day.

In the distance, to the east, the big mountains rose from the ground brown and lifeless—Mount Saint Helens and Mount Hood, and beyond, Mount Adams and Mount Rainier and Mount Jefferson, lost in a dust horizon. With the snow gone, they'd lost their beauty. Just looming piles of dirt now.

Hey Boyfriend!

So it's been by my count ~8 days, aka 11,520 minutes (since I know these sorts of exacting numbers make you hot: 691,200 seconds, plus or minus, and every last one of them more dull/less good/ more boring/less happy/more horny/less sexy) since I left your front porch and bicycled my way up here into the wasteland of the NE. Each of these days, for lack of Zach, I've had to share a bed with Bea, who snores not a little, I do not hesitate to inform you. And I'm not talking about the soft, thoughtful—even somnulent(sp?)- inducing—hum-buzz of my boyfriend's snore, but a rip-roaring, jake-brakes outside your trailer home type snore, that rattles the window panes and makes your teeth chatter into rearrangement, bless the girl.

In the morning, in front of the mirror, it is not unusual that this narrator needs to re-position her molars back to their starting gates. Just saying.

How are you? I wish you could stop by to [redacted] me so [redacted] that I [redacted] all night making [redacted redacted redacted]. Right? I mean come on, how long must this separation last? With the dry tongue and the anxious looks over one's shoulder and occasional—cannot deny, it must be told—masturbatory episodes in the rare moments of free time to oneself? How long?

I think of you often down there conversing with my supposed-arch-enemy Monster Bartlett, explaining to him patiently how to save the people of our fair city while he ignores, nose pointed askew, hair glistening-hard and ready for take-off, the pointed dome of a space rocket that surely it is fashioned after. I know you're fighting the good fight, and it makes me happy to think of you there.

Things are going well here. For instance, today I went the whole day without withering into a broken pile of bone-flesh and tears, wasteful tears, need us not remind us. A good day really, with a sense of accomplishment. There's much to tell. The "King of Egypt" (long story) is still providing some of his own rations, and others have chipped in too, whatnot and so on, so that we're keeping sustained, if not rail-thin-thinking-of-one's-hungers-non-stop. The curves you admired? Hope you like angles instead.

Lots of nice folks up here, not saying there's not. And lots to be sad about. I know you suggested I take up a hobby (idle hands do the devil's etc) and hey! Does the finding and burying of dead people qualify? Is there accreditation? Small scholarly circles devoted to the study of? Society ladies gathering with the white wine and the foie gras and the shovels? Well anyway, I hope so, because I will have lots to share with and laugh about to said people when such hobby groups form, with hugs and the shedding of we've-all-been-there! type tears.

No but seriously I'm kind of sick of all this and losing a sense of whatthehell I'm even ontheplanet to do. You have a handle on that for yourself or are these the type of questions a person doesn't necessarily go down the road of asking oneself, for the possibility a person might discover that these are questions with no answers, like light bulbs with no sockets? Just tell me, I'll take any old sort of answer.

And so lastly, here I am here waiting for the, shall we say, subsequent parts of our relationship, as in the what-happens-next parts, where most likely I fly this coop, deciding that the burying of dead people is not the exciting up-and-coming hobby I thought it was, and head back down through the rough and tumble to your place, or you decide to give up on your career of mayoral counsel (but why, right? you have a job. I'm an outlaw, turns out) and come join me up in my Pharaoh's lair. Odds are high on the former, things considered. Going to pretty much give it one last shot here, over the next

few days, and then please be expecting me, wafer-thin, all angles
and smiles, on your doorstop.
W/love/and/so/much/more
-r

She pulled together a small group of six. Armed with the newly
acquired shotgun and other implements, they traveled her neighborhood, introducing themselves to neighbors as the Sherwood Club. At
each house she knocked tentatively, fearing only deadened ears listened on the other side, his or her heart long ago having given up
whatever losing fight it fought. It was hard to sleep at night thinking
of them, their eyes seeing nothing.

When the wary "*who is it?*" called back, she became used to saying her assumed name in reply: "Maid Marian." It grew easier on her
tongue with each repetition.

"We're establishing neighborhood security." A curtain would
flicker, or the door's peephole. She imagined the Sherwood Club as
a citizen force, taking up slack for absent city services. A safety net
for people who could not fend for themselves. Usually they let her in,
knowing her from the news. Sitting on the edge of a chair in a family's living room, she felt how they simultaneously leaned toward and
away from her, hopeful and anxious, this idealist warrior—or criminal, was it?—terribly real and in the flesh, in their homes. From them
she learned of the bully down the street, who lurked at the perimeter
of distribution, looking for water rations to steal like lunch money.
She learned of the couple across the street who screamed at each
other deep into the night, until the darkness filled with the sounds of
glass breaking and things thrown and hurt. She made sure to speak at
length to each house about their neighbors, for to know those around
you, she thought, was to lose your fear of them. To bind your story
to theirs. They were islands no longer, each of these houses, she was
sewing them together.

She tried to fix what problems she could. She held an impromptu
court at the water bully's house, inviting all of the neighbors from the
block to show up and listen to him speak his crimes. The domestic-
violence couple she invited to live under her roof, that they might be
tempered by community, or separated if need be. Many problems,
she found, only needed a slight bump to jar them from the hard track

they followed, and many more were not in her power to affect. Like a halo it spread out from her house, she imagined, a ring of safety.

But the deaths were hard. Three blocks from HQ they found a locked house with boarded-up windows. Bea used a crowbar to remove the wood from a window. Amid the squalor inside they found the bloated corpse of an old woman lying in bed. They wrapped her in her blankets and buried her in the cemetery. Among the items on her dresser Renee found a water identification card.

Two days later they found another body, eleven blocks away, this one covered in a storm of insects. An elderly man, they thought, but it was difficult to tell much else. They buried him, too.

After the burial Renee sat next to the grave and stared at her shoes. One week and three dead buried. The bell no longer tolled inside her like it had. She'd become afraid of what they might find in each house, and while they'd had successes, her Sherwood Club became dispirited.

That night a man walked into the house late at night and Leroy, hearing him from the third floor, began calling "intruder!" in what to Renee's ears sounded like the electronic tone of a warehouse alarm system.

As people gathered weapons and filtered cautiously downstairs, the man claimed he was a friend of Renee's.

There was barely light to see by, enough to catch a glint off the pistol the man had raised in the air, surrender and not surrender.

"Listen y'all," he drawled in an accent that was in no way convincing. "I know Renee is here."

"No one here by that name," Julia said.

"Maid Marian then?" He smirked. "She and I did the heist downtown. We did that together, OK? I'm one of the good guys."

From the top of the stairs Renee said, "This is Josh, everybody."

"Everybody," Josh said.

"Come on up," Renee said, "but put the gun away." She brought him into the big room at the front of the house on the second floor that she'd kept empty. There was an old couch there and a couple of chairs. She lit a candle and it flickered dimly against the walls. Members of her Sherwood Club gathered round.

Without sitting he began to dig in his pockets. "Look what I've got, kids." The accent gone.

He'd cut his beard close, Renee noticed. He moved with a nervous and excited energy, checking the pockets in his backpack. His hair an uncertain color, blond and brown with premature gray in it. Were it not the for the drought, she would have suspected him of adding the gray himself.

"Now wait a minute, it's here somewhere. What an operation, right? You've got bodyguards, you fruitcake. Ah." He pulled a dozen laminated cards from his pocket and spread them in front of them on the floor like a winning card hand.

"Water IDs," Renee said.

"Water. IDs." Josh pointed at them with each word and bounced on his feet.

"But where is everybody?" Renee said.

"Janey's in jail, Davis's MIA. And look at you, all the reputation."

"You saw Zach?" Renee said.

"Your boyfriend. That was a surprise. So my idea is we start harvesting these IDs. We set up a mini distribution and make a profit besides. It's good to see you, Renee." He leaned in and gave her a brief hug.

She studied him in the candlelight. He was a white-collar radical. Well-schooled and tall and athletic. She didn't know his background well, but had always assumed he was one of those kids from a wealthy conservative family who had eschewed his parents' ideals and gone to some hippie college to snowboard and smoke pot. But his parents could not be stamped out of him, and before long he was morphing into an amalgam of the two creatures. Underneath you sensed someone whose ambition was unceasing. Even if the tenets of the ambition aligned closely with hers, he intimidated her with his relentless pursuit of them. There would have been no water heist without him.

He could be running this, she thought. She felt a sense of relief then. She wouldn't have to do all the heavy lifting, to be in charge. She could just participate in the movement, whatever it was, this citizen-gang or Robin Hood–whatever, a hollow figurehead perhaps or simply a worker bee. She wouldn't have to be responsible for everyone else.

"What have you heard about us?" she said and remembered Zach's advice: to listen and assess, and then refine and replant the rumor you want perpetuated. And as she said it she knew there was something else here too, something that she could not let go of.

"Zach said you came up to hide from the police. Everybody is all Maid Marian this and that. A dude three blocks down said you were watching out for him." He chuckled.

Renee shrugged. "Anyway."

"You're not doing that great at the hiding, if that's what you're doing."

"The chaos up here hides well enough. The people hate the city government, and the police never come north of Fremont, as far as we can tell." She reached over and grabbed the mug she drank water from, but it was empty. She felt exposed in front of him. "We're making something," she said quietly.

"Still. You're going to make yourself in police custody, is what."

Renee didn't feel like answering. Josh took a unit gallon out of his pack and filled her cup. Bea appeared in the doorway and Josh filled her a cup, too.

"Yeah, well anyway," he said, "what do you think of my idea? This could be twelve gallons a day, right? First we steal a scanner to verify them. Then we make a little salon here gussying up people like the pics in the cards. You got people. We run these through the system—that's a lot of extra water, right?"

"And the water?"

"Same as before, to the people. Or you know, what happened, like at the heist."

"But that's taking from distribution—I'm not sure that's the rich I intended to rob."

"Distribution is the system, the system is a tool of the rich."

It sounded like it belonged on a bumper sticker, and for a moment she felt like kicking the legs off the closest chair. Josh just wanted to fuck the man, she could see now. He was a disruptor. She could smell the water he'd given her in the cup in her hand. She took a deep breath and stood.

"It's a clever idea, Josh," Renee said. "Let's do it. We're desperate for water, it's true. Bea and I have been skimming food and water rations from the others. It gets old." Bea made an exclamatory noise in the background. "So I'm game. But you understand," she said, "this is a survival play. It's the means to a goal, but not a goal itself."

Groundbreaking ceremonies were once the type of dull, idiotic event the mayor would have attempted to avoid at all costs. But all that had changed in this landscape of bad news. An event where he could appear without people specifically seeking him out as the target of their raging invectives was an event worthy of consideration. These types of ceremonies were poor venues for protest. And so, after his brief speaking role and television shot, he left with a whistle on his lips and a buoyant bump in his stride.

Now he splayed his feet out across the backseat of the car and relaxed. There was a police car following, and it was a short ride back to his office-home. This gathering had been about the construction of a new shelter to accommodate refugees. In the end, it was an emptyish gesture, the result of a long, drawn-out fight between various council members, several of whom he'd shared the stage with. Each had diluted the others' ideas until what was left was but a token. But officially it was a *good thing*. No one could say that refugees did not need a place. No one could chant out *Heartless Bartlett! Heartless Bartlett!* with tuneless volume at the construction of a shelter. And any victory, no matter how small, was worth notching up in one's mind, a reminder that *yes*: He was there to do good, and good could be done. Right?

The phone rang. It was the chief of police. There had been a tip: They had found Maid Marian's hiding place. The mayor sat upright in his car and pounded on the driver's seat-back.

"Stop! For god's sake, stop for a minute." He plugged one ear and pressed his other to the receiver. "You're sure?"

Yes he was sure, the police chief replied in his easy, lethargic style, as if, the mayor thought, he'd eaten a side of beef and was swilling the last of the cognac in his leather smoking chair. He informed the mayor that she was deep in Northeast Portland in a red zone, an area of the city no longer actively patrolled by police.

Somehow he'd pictured her close in, waiting to pounce again, and to learn that she was up in the city's wastelands diminished his opinion of her. "What the hell is she doing up there?"

The police chief didn't have a good answer for this.

"And the National Guard, they already know?"

"No, not at all, sir, you're the first to hear," the police chief said.

"Well, that's fine, fine, not sure they need to bother with this business. Shall we keep it to ourselves? What do you propose, Freddy?"

The police chief hummed into the phone and the mayor drove one thumb into his forehead as he waited for the man to speak.

"Perhaps? In the morning, they could. Strike first thing," the police chief ambled. "At dawn? Catch them sleeping when the neighborhood was at its coolest."

"Yes, put that together, Freddy. Tomorrow morning, right? We're not talking about sometime next August. And Freddy? No killing. She's got to come in safe."

The mayor hung up the phone and smiled. This was something to look forward to. He relished the idea of sitting down to chat with her in a jail cell.

He spent some time pondering this and knew exactly how he would behave with the city's new hero and news-hog, their water thief and prospective false savior. Cordially, of course. Gracefully. But she would spend the rest of the drought—if it ever ended—in jail, that was for certain.

Let's see what the National Guard and the citizens have to say about that, he thought.

Josh held the scanner up like an Olympic torch when he returned. Renee sat at the main table on the first floor and he deposited it in front of her. It was a simple machine—a black plastic handle with a three-by-three-inch screen at the end, the barcode-reading red of a laser emitted from the back.

"Where in the hell did you find that?" Renee said.

"You ever heard of Gregor? I went asking, you know? One of his dudes. Cost a freaking lot, right? Check it." Josh held up a card and turned on the scanner.

"Wait," Renee said. "For fuck sake, you idiot. Wait."

Josh gave her an irritated look and scanned the card anyway. "You realize the power we have here? This is the root of our whole operation." The scanner read the back of the card, and a second later a picture of an older, paunchy, Hispanic man appeared on the screen, and below him a few details.

- Jose Ramirez
- DOB: 04/07/1952
- Distribution: Alameda
- Last pickup: 9 days ago

A green light pulsed next to his name.

"Whoa," Renee said. "That one's good."

"Fucking right it is."

"Where do you suppose he is?"

Josh shrugged. "Dead or gone, amigo." He pulled out another card and scanned again. This time it was a light-skinned girl in her twenties. Renee shuddered. "Ugh. How did you get these cards again?"

"Could be in jail," Josh said, "or maybe she left somehow, I don't know. If you distribute water, you hit this button here and it registers the location and water given out. They do that when we pick up."

"How do you know this gizmo isn't sending your coordinates up with the request? We're not exactly a water distribution here."

Josh looked at her quizzically and then blanched.

"I mean it's got the—fucking hell, the location is right there, right? You don't think they keep track of these scanners?" Renee rose in alarm. "Bea! Get your shit!" She turned to Josh. "Nice one, dipshit."

"No—there's no way," Josh said.

"Of course there is, if they're missing one they'll want it back. It's sending your location. We're out of here."

Bea charged down the stairs and Renee instructed her to rouse the house for leaving.

"Josh, turn that fucking thing off."

"You're being alarmist."

"You stay if you want. They don't even know who you are."

They gathered solemnly, called from their various jobs at HQ. "We think there's a chance someone is going to come looking for us, and because of this,"—she pointed to the scanner—"a water card scanner, every one of us has got to jump ship. This house has to look abandoned and we've got to find a place. Ideas?"

"Jeffersons would take us in," Bea said. They had met the Jeffersons during the burial runs, a small house up the street.

"Good—but not all of us. Julia? You stay there and keep an eye out on HQ. Leroy, you and Chris go with her. Anyone else? I propose the rest of us camp at the water tower park."

"Ma'am," Chris said, ducking his head. He pointed to the slatted barrier he'd built over the big broken window that led to the front porch. "If you don't mind my saying it, this could be caved in for effect and"—he turned red and studied the floor for a moment—"if I were you, well, it'd be effective if someone defecated on the porch. In front of the door. Make it seem like no one lived here, you know."

Renee nodded. "Brilliant. Thank you, Chris. Everybody else, clear out!"

———

That night at the water tower Renee wrapped in a sheet and huddled next to Bea on top of the playground structure. Below them the others crowded together to keep warm. The night had turned chilly. Under the sheet, Renee could smell the body sweat and rankness on their clothes, grime and dust and sourness. In this moment hiding atop a playground structure, ejected by fear from their new home, the task of cleaning one's own body felt monumental.

Josh had apologized, and then he had ridden off with the scanner to test the rest of the cards in transit, to leave a wandering trail for the thing. When he met up with them at the park he announced he had seven working cards.

Despite the news, Renee felt sick-hearted. She wondered if they'd lost their house. She suddenly wearied of fighting back, of feeling like she was in charge, of being on the run; daunted by the work ahead of them. The dust dried the saliva in her mouth and she did not feel like speaking. She wished she could see Zach. She tried to call to him with the green laser but he did not answer, and so she tucked her head into the sheet and wept, but no water came to her eyes.

Late the next afternoon they tentatively returned, collecting Julia from the neighbors on the way. Julia told them she'd wakened to see the police at their house. There were signs of them throughout—the feces on the front porch had been tracked into the house, then back-tracked and scraped off on the edge of the porch, likely with much cursing. Their ruse had worked; it was highly unlikely they'd come back to the same house, and there was hope in that.

Her first official visitor was called Martin Ostrovsky. According to Leroy he traded in drugs and water and gasoline and had half a dozen men working for him. In other words, medium-small fry in the neighborhood bigwig business. He ran his operation about twelve blocks to the east, and theirs, the Sherwood Club, had extended into his area. There were others of these kind that would come to confront her, she thought with anxiety, and ones with a lot more clout.

She stationed Bea at the door of her office, so that she would loom behind whomever was having an audience with her, a big sentry there to intimidate, and she asked the volunteers to make regular foot traffic up and down the hall outside.

Renee stood and offered her hand, making Martin lean deep into the desk to shake. He scowled. He was big and thick with a shiny bald head—a subtle mark of wealth, for to shave a head required wasted water. From his just-visible whisker growth she could see his hair had gone gray. The two henchmen he'd brought in tow she made stay outside the house, and he was not used to being treated this way.

He asked her what she was.

"What have you heard?" Her chair was about eighteen inches higher than his, making it seem as though he was sitting in a child's chair. It also meant that his head was about the height of her bust, which he kept glancing at, and she wondered if she might need to have her desk adjusted.

"I've seen the news and I know Ronny left to come work here, that backstabbing son of a bitch. How much do you pay him?"

"We're all volunteers."

He looked surprised and she could see him trying to figure out a business model that kept its employees without pay. "What are you shelling out then? What's the scoop here?"

She gave him the pitch she'd given others, about neighborhood security and the inequality of the water system. About rebuilding and providing where the city had abandoned them. A network of citizens that looked out for each other. For a moment she heard her father's voice in her, felt his power and persuasiveness rise up out of her and fill the room. How as she painted the vision she herself became lost in it, said it as if she might suddenly stand on her desk, or put her head down and cry out a spell, feeling her own words and her purpose dig deep into her gut. That by merely saying it made it happen. There was a rightness of it.

His facial muscles were taut, bunched into a grimace of puzzlement. For a moment, she thought, he had bought the vision she wove.

"We're the neighborhood's net. We're its keeper."

He said nothing, his eyes blank and startled. He tried a smile, and then one corner of Martin's lip slowly raised into a sneer and he swore. "Keeper? What's that supposed to mean?"

She saw that it was over, then. No alliances would be built here, their intentions were at odds. If the Sherwood Club continued to grow like they were, they would overrun his territory and their aims would clash. "You can go talk to Ronny if you want to." Her voice hardened. "But it's his choice. If he wants to stay, he stays. You know, as a leader yourself, you could make a difference. We would be happy to have your service."

Martin scoffed, "Oh, I'll talk to him." He pointed at her. "And I'll be back."

Renee pulled a sheet of paper from her stack. On it was written the name of every "boss" in the Northeast that her volunteers had come up with. She found Martin's name and crossed it off. "Good luck," she said.

After he left in a huff of disgust and confusion she went over her list. By each name she had written the estimated number of employees, what their business was, and any notes she had about their reputation. She would invite each of them to meet with her.

"You're going to make a lot of enemies," Bea said.

Renee startled, having forgotten that Bea was in the room, as still as a statue and holding the shotgun. She leaned back in her chair. "Yeah. His employees would rather work here."

"I think you need more guards."

Renee nodded. She stared at her friend, leaning against the door of her office and could hear in her voice all the ways Bea thought she was being foolish, and Renee wasn't sure she disagreed with her. "Would you take care of that for me, Bea? Also, maybe you ought to have someone tail Ronny for a few days."

The plan with the tunnel was not entirely clear, but that did not bother Nevel in the least. He was driven, mainly, by the fervor to dig. One must trust that one's subconscious has an intent, he thought. But then, as he remembered some of the dreams he'd had lately, he worried that perhaps his subconscious was not to be trusted after all. Perhaps his subconscious was working against him, rebelling against his conscious mind, assuming control, propelling him to do things that he should not be doing.

But what harm is a tunnel, he thought. Other than, say, the threat of collapse. He wiped the sweat from his brow and left a long dirt streak there along his receding hairline. "But you won't, eh?" He patted one of its supports, which felt firm enough under his hand. Maybe the harm was that he was obsessed with it when he should be doing something else. Averting some catastrophe he was not yet aware of or making a solid plan for survival for his family's future.

He suddenly craved to ask the question of his sleeping daughter, who'd only started speaking, and subsequently began spouting out pidgin prophecy like an oracle. This was silliness, he could see that, but he couldn't shake the feeling that she might still carry with her some omniscience from the other side, before birth, before she was anything.

He removed his shoes at the basement door and did his best to scrub himself off with the towel his wife had thoughtfully installed for him there. As he ascended the stairs he remembered that in one of his dreams the mayor had appeared with giant wings. From his bed he had watched the winged mayor flutter against his bedroom window as if he were a moth drawn by the light inside, his efforts frustrated by the glass between them.

At his daughter's bedside he saw that she was sleeping hard, deep below dreams, and his desire to wake her for divination evaporated. Instead, he pulled the sheet up to her shoulder and admired her. These were questions he needed to answer himself.

In one quick motion she raised up on one elbow and stared intensely at him in the dim light, her eyes sparkling black beads, and he put his hands to his chest, waiting for the oracular blow that was to come. But after a moment, she only asked for her bear.

He located the dirty little stuffed animal wedged between the wall and the mattress. She wrapped it tightly in her arms again and fell back into sleep.

It was time to fly right, he told himself as he trudged back downstairs toward the basement. To stick up for his family, fists a-blazing. Once back in the tunnel, though, he picked up his shovel and began to dig anew.

Water distribution in Cully happened at a dysfunctional elementary school. Parents with younger children had been the first to migrate away.

A water truck pulled into the large open-air structure built over the basketball court, to the side of the dry field. Behind it, eight National Guardsmen pulled in in two jeeps. With their rifles out, they guided people back to the perimeter while distribution was organized.

Renee and the others stood on the edge of the crowd and watched. She had a sweatshirt hood pulled deep over her face. Of the nine days she'd been to this station, three days had been violent and there'd been one death; a heavyset man attempted to steal the truck while it was in operation. He was killed brutally by a guardsman who wasted no bullets, but beat him to death with his rifle butt.

The crowd surrounding the truck was irritable with dehydration and hunger, and the system was slow and hostile.

She imagined the feel of carrying her own unit gallon home. The heaviness of that wealth.

The criminal database and the water distribution lists cross-referenced, so known criminals regularly emerged a few days after a crime, delirious with dehydration, or showed up in the hospital sick after having tried to drink from the river sludge, or fled the city to join the shadowy gangs that roved outside the governed area.

Renee crouched and watched. It was a lot of fucking work, she thought, just to survive. Today they were trying a couple of cards and Josh would be their guinea pig. Tomorrow they would try more, letting those with cards run through and then dressing them up for another go-through.

Someone patted the top of her head insistently, and she looked up to see Leroy.

"What?"

"Look."

She stood and tried to follow where he pointed. "I don't know what you're trying to show me."

Leroy pointed again, and then turned his back to where he'd pointed, as if bracing for a blow. She looked around his shoulder.

"Brown shirt, brown shirt," Leroy whispered.

She saw him, a black man in his late twenties or early thirties. Twenty yards away, mingled into the crowd. He had woolly hair and a well-used light brown T-shirt, a hole below the collar. His face was angular and lean, his beard sparse, and then he looked directly at her and smiled. Renee shifted so that she was hidden behind Leroy. "Who is he?"

"Jamal Perkins. Ring any bells?"

Renee shook her head. She couldn't be recognized, not here.

"*Perkins.* Gregor's son. This wouldn't be his distribution, if he even goes to one."

Renee shifted so that she could take another look at him. He smiled again, as if they were old friends, and began to walk toward her. She couldn't be sure, but it looked as though several others peeled off of the crowd and began to mingle slowly their way as well.

"He's coming," Renee said.

"Shit. Shit," Leroy said.

"Should I be scared?" Renee stepped around Leroy and began walking toward Jamal and they met halfway. Behind her she could feel her group fall in around her, protectively.

Jamal held out his hand, "I'm a big fan." He smiled again, as if the punchline to a joke about himself had been told. He leaned in close and whispered, "Maid Marian. Right?"

She took his hand and he pumped it with warm exaggeration. It was hard not to like him immediately. "I've just been told who you are," she said. "Someone suggested that I run."

"Oh?" he laughed. He inspected her group and nodded to a few he seemed to know. "You've got me mixed up with my father. I'm only a fan—" he lowered his voice so only she could hear "—I'd be interested to hear your plans."

Renee shuddered momentarily, as if he'd somehow spied her out, her pencil and paper that morning. She nodded and looked away and wondered if he was mocking her.

When he spoke again all of his charming veneer was gone, replaced with earnest haste. "Can we talk?" he said in a voice that was barely audible. He still held her hand embraced in a handshake and Bea came beside them and stood with her arms crossed.

Renee said she'd love to and straightened. "What about? Come back to our headquarters," she said. "We'll talk. I'd love to meet your father, too."

Jamal's face clouded briefly, "Sure. I have a few others."

"You're with people?"

Jamal smiled and then merged back into the crowd.

Renee scanned the distribution and felt a tingle of fear and excitement.

"Who was that?" Josh asked. He had done something to his hair for the card scam that made him look surprised.

"You should be in queue," she said.

That night they sat in a circle around a campfire in their big backyard, all of them, plus Jamal and the three that he'd brought along—young men who seemed ill at ease among them. It was a rough-looking bunch, every one of them, Renee thought. Herself, surely, included. After Josh's success they'd made up others and some still wore their disguises to fool the ID checkers. They passed around a couple of contraband unit gallons like jugs of moonshine, excited at their sudden wealth. For the first time in weeks Renee quenched her thirst, and in so doing she felt a residual exhaustion fall away.

Josh was cocky and relived each gallon they'd acquired, already excited for the extra units that would be theirs tomorrow.

It did feel good, but as they drained another gallon dry, the small victory began to feel like an embarrassingly small win. In her belly she felt the water slosh, turned fishbowl. She began to work at a plan in her mind, an ambition. Like a seed stuck in her teeth she pressed against it from all angles, trying to pry it loose.

Jamal pulled a small flask of some kind of alcohol out of a ratty canvas bag he carried with him and passed that around. Alcohol was hard to come by, especially that which wasn't the awful swill distilled from rations. She raised the flask to him in cheers and studied him to get a sense of his purpose here.

"What's your story?" she said.

Jamal paused. The expression on his face was that of someone who wishes to choose his words wisely. In the space of his careful pause, all other talking dried up and attention focused on him.

After a moment he noticed everyone staring at him and he smiled and poked at the dirt in front of him with his feet. "Hey all, it's not very complicated," he said. "I was impressed." He gestured to Renee with his chin. "I saw you on the news and I thought, good stuff. I want to do that. Just like you did, but up here, in the 'hood." He considered Renee. "I've been trying to find you. We've been hearing about Sherwood Club. I wanted to see what you were working on—and here you are."

"And here I am." She wondered if she was living up to the expectation Jamal had of her, and knew she wasn't living up to her own. "It's a beginning," she said.

"Sure." He turned to Josh and hefted the dead unit gallon. "This is a good plan. You could do more. But this is a smart plan." Jamal picked a stick up and rearranged the logs on the fire, which burned hot on their faces.

"Thanks," Josh said.

"But I wonder if it could—you know, scale," Jamal said. "It all depends on one's objectives."

"I've been thinking about another truck," Renee said.

"There you go," Jamal said.

Next to Renee, Leroy twitched in place, stretching his neck and adjusting his feet and mumbling to himself so that Renee finally turned to him. "Yes?"

He sat up quickly on his knees and his eyes glistened blackly with the reflected firelight. "Gregor," he said into the fire, and then finding no words that fit into the well of silence he'd created, said it again.

"I hear it," Jamal said. "I know. This is only me, though. These smart-asses, too." Jamal jostled one of the men he'd brought with him. "A real talky bunch." The flask was passed to him and he held it for a moment. "Pop does one thing, I do something else. We share a name. He's old, you all know that. Mostly he just widens his middle and lives off reputation these days. I'm not him." Jamal took a small pull on the flask. "I am not him. I understand that you might not see that all at once, that it's going to have to be shown."

"Tell me more about Gregor," Renee said.

"I live at his place, I'm not going to deny that. These guys have all worked for him. But Pop's operation is—well, *diminishing*," he said and drew the word out. "He wants it to. He does a lucrative trade and he's, you know, respected, in his way, but he's tired. Everybody knows this. Am I right?"

"The Governor," Leroy said.

"Yeah," Jamal said, "a nickname."

"The Hammer," Leroy said.

There was a smattering of uncertain laughter and Jamal stayed silent.

"The Arm," Leroy said.

Renee put her hand on Leroy's arm to silence him. The fire crackled. She leaned back and rested on the ground. Outside the circle of firelight the stars shone brilliantly. She liked how the man sounded, portly and riding a slow empire into nothingness. He had won the drug war of some years past, she knew. She'd invited him to meet with her but had not heard back.

"Scary motherfucker," someone said.

"Not like he used to be," Jamal said. "I can tell you."

"Here's what I'm thinking," she said, her voice pointed skyward. "What if we steal the truck *before* it has water in it." She let that sink in for a minute and could hear Josh gearing up to protest. "We drive it right off the lot where they park them at night."

Jamal laughed and it was a pleasant sound. She felt stronger with him around. This was not someone from their activist group with a history of sparring with her, and it was not someone come looking for help. He had sought her out, a person of note.

"We're not even stealing the water," she said. "We're filling up. And we don't steal it publicly. We don't do it in protest. No news. We steal it to have it. Then we start a new game entirely."

"New game?" Josh said.

"An entirely new game."

"We'd have to research the piss out of it," Josh said. "You're talking about driving through water pickup? The piss out of it." He swore. "Say we acquire a couple of uniforms? Yeah."

Renee closed her eyes and listened to Josh continue on. Once an idea was set in his mind it festered there like an infection, each facet of it ferreted out until all unknowns were revealed. She smiled, listening to him prattle on, clever boy. In this way, she would utilize him, let him do what he did best. Maybe this was the secret. To design a system that made it easy for others to choose her steerage. To govern by suggestion and the planting of seeds.

Some days the house felt like a non-stop party her roommates were having, or a busy political campaign office. A constant trickle of people she did not recognize showed up and Julia, whose initial meekness had transformed into a hard-staring, voice-of-power when tasked with command, put them to work or sent them away or catalogued their needs so that they could be assisted. Renee made herself available to the newcomers that came to meet Maid Marian. As if they were on some pilgrimage to see a statue, she thought. The first truck, the copycats, the burials, the neighborhood security that spread out from them, all of it had continued to accelerate visitors. She pressed their hands warmly and welcomed them. She had a knack for names and she burned their faces into her mind. She felt grateful toward them, each a sand-grain of confidence.

On any given day there was a cadre of people gussied up in disguise for water ID card duty, or outfitted with tools for a backyard construction project, or huddled over the living room table sketching out a plan. Renee ran a distribution project once a week. Her neighborhood burial crew, the Sherwood Club, brought her names of those who needed it as they went door to door. She sent water with them for delivery.

Demand was high and need was hard to verify and what she offered was a drop in the bucket, she knew. At the end of the week, they averaged an extra sixty rations now, and these she delivered to those who were the most needy, carting the unit gallons and food in child bike trailers with Bea and the Sherwood Club. Families with young children, a few infirm, and so on. A tiny stipend she reserved for a master gardener who had come on staff, and who was slowly etching out a garden space in the backyard.

On one such delivery run, as she handed a unit gallon across the threshold to an elderly man, a woman dressed in a red skirt appeared out of nowhere and asked for a moment of her time. On the sidewalk the interviewer smiled over-broadly, her nervousness infectious, tilting slightly from her inappropriate shoes.

Renee faltered. Her hands, emptied now of anything to hold on to, fidgeted with her sleeves. Behind the woman stood a cameraman and the news team's security guards and van.

She stared at the woman in red and tried to read her expression, with her painted, overly large eyes. Was she being mocked, or were they genuinely interested? Would this give her away to the city?

She was already being filmed, she saw. The cameraman fine-tuned the controls of his camera.

"Please," the cameraman said in a Mexican accent. "Stand in front of truck, that way they don't find where you are. You are safe with us."

Bea grabbed the back of her shirt and leaned in to whisper. "Goddamnit *no*, Renee, *no*," and then Renee found herself nodding yes. She stood in position and smiled into the lens and winked.

The newswoman, who introduced herself but whose name Renee forgot instantly in the giant glassy stare of the camera, asked: what was she doing? Why was she doing it? How did the people respond to receiving water? Did she have a message for Portland?

"Hi, Portland," Renee said. She glanced at Bea off camera who fumed at her. "How are you?" She brushed a braid back from her shoulder and realized she had not seen her face in a mirror for days. The last time there'd been a bloody comet streak down one cheek. "I wish you were here with me, going door to door. If you could all make a few stops with me and our Sherwood Club. We're weaving together neighborhoods."

"By weaving, you mean?"

Renee held up her hands for the camera, her fingers woven together. "Connecting them, providing safety and sharing rations, caring for each other. We're creating a fabric upon which we can all depend. It's hard work, I've buried a few people in the last week. And we like to think we kept a few from needing burials. I believe—I believe we're now one of the safest parts of the city. Mayor Bartlett, the city council, everyone is invited. I'd love to have you on our side. Step into one of these rooms in Northeast Portland and it alters you. Mayor Bartlett, I'm afraid you would feel inclined to resign on the spot, for it's difficult to imagine the gall one would need to carry out thieving water from public rations in the face of the kind of misery that exists here. You are free to do so, upon my suggestion. Resign or tag along, either way." She winked again. "I'm sorry, tell me the question again?"

"Rumor has it that your Sherwood Club provides extra rations to families in need. Where do you obtain the extra rations?"

It is moments like these, Renee thought, where an opinion is transformed. In her mind she saw Josh's water scanner and she made her eyes hold steady. "An excellent question. What we have is a pittance, a few gallons here. Where does the mayor get his trucks? You are familiar with Robin Hood? Well, the difference between that king and our Mayor Bartlett is that one over-taxed and the other steals." She smiled. "A system that criminalizes a whistleblower is wanting in introspection."

The woman asked her another question, but Renee spooked, realizing the danger she was putting them all in.

She nodded to the camera to end the interview and said thank you. Then they mounted their bicycles and rode as hard as they could, weaving through the streets recklessly with no thought to the safety of each neighborhood they passed through, in order to lose any trace of the van. After an hour they found themselves at the empty water tower.

She felt sick to her stomach with her own stupidity, and buried under that a rising excitement as she thought of herself and their mission on everyone's screen that night. She wondered how they'd make her out, how the newscasters might idly chat about the Sherwood

Club. She imagined their jovial laughter ringing out over hundreds of thousands of televisions as they bandied about the fruitlessness of her task. Petty thief, petty charity. She lay down on top of the wooden playground equipment and buried her face in her hands. She'd screwed up, she could see that now. With a few idiotic moments of bravado and self-importance she'd fucked up everything they'd built so far and put all of her people at risk of arrest.

As the sun went down and the sky began to darken, she fumbled about in her pockets. She found the green laser, and she gripped it tightly, a lifeline.

.... . .-.. .-..—- ..—.. *Hello?* She Morse-coded on the side of the water tower, her thumb tiring with the first word. She lay on her side and stared up at the structure's great belly, iron and empty, and waited. Every few minutes she traced out a circle on it, in case he plugged in.

The reply came at last: *You were awesome.*

Renee sat up and her heart raced. She traced a question mark directly on the tower.

On news. Be careful. But yes.

Josh led up the truck operation, and Jamal formally joined Sherwood Club as Josh's partner on the heist. Extra water was set aside for them to clean themselves and the uniforms they'd quietly purchased.

On the day of, they clipped through the cyclone fencing that housed the city's twenty-two official water distribution trucks, in the big parking lot under the freeway where city buses, snow plows— from more optimistic times—and other city vehicles were stored.

There were usually three or four trucks left behind in the parking lot, alone and dormant, waiting to be called into duty. Fewer trucks were needed as the population continued to dwindle.

On the night before the heist they piled cardboard boxes and other debris against the back fence of the parking lot. They slept underneath this and watched as the city drivers each came to claim their truck early in the morning.

After the trucks had pulled out, Josh and Jamal squeezed through the hole in the fence, dusted themselves off, and walked toward one of the remaining trucks in the lot.

Josh concealed a framing hammer up his sleeve, to puncture the window if need be, but, mercifully, the passenger door was unlocked.

They climbed into the barren truck and grinned tensely at each other, keeping their heads ducked while Jamal hot-wired the vehicle. When he'd finished and the engine started, he pulled two guns from a plastic bag and handed one to Josh.

"Just in case," he said. "The intent is not to use them."

Josh studied the gun and then put it under the seat. "I've never actually used one."

"Then let's not make this the first time."

Jamal accelerated out of the lot and caught sight of the last of the vehicles turning onto Highway 30. As the trucks ahead passed a National Guard base, they slowed and spaced themselves out, so that a military jeep could pull in behind each.

"Shit. Here we go," he said. They waited tensely to see if a jeep would pull in behind their truck, the last in the long motorcade.

Josh stared into the rearview mirror. "Nothing."

At the airport checkpoint they pulled to a stop at the entrance. A security guard with a thick mustache and plump cheeks waited in a telephone booth–sized compartment. He looked as if he needed to be pumped in at the start of each day and pried out at the end. He inspected his laptop and eyed them. "I don't have this truck in the queue today."

"We're taking it up to the workers at the wind fields," Josh said and swallowed. "New workers. I guess they're bumping up power supplies." He nervously fiddled with the door handle.

"Well, that's good, I suppose," the security guard said. He pointed up to the small solar panel on his roof. "These damn things are impossible to keep clean with the dust storms. Always fritzing out on me. Where's your escort?"

"One never pulled out." Josh shrugged.

"Hmm," he said, and there was a long pause as he worked at his keyboard. "Must be a bug in the software. The wind farms are delivered by helicopter. When did the truck get initiated?"

"Just this morning," Josh said.

The security guard studied them both for a long awkward moment and then leaned out the window to sight along the truck. "Well, I'll call you in an escort. Don't leave the grounds until they come in."

"Perhaps they're meeting us on the freeway toward the dam?"

"Nope, doubt it. Worst case scenario, you get two escorts. I wouldn't want to do that route. You'll be glad for the extra help."

"True, true." Josh smiled and thanked him.

The guard waved them forward and Jamal drove into line behind the other trucks and they waited. The trucks were filling from a nozzle that hung from the underbelly of a behemoth plane. When a plane emptied, another rolled forward.

"Shit," Josh said.

"It'll work," Jamal said.

"Shit."

"Stay calm."

They waited their turn and watched the exit gate, looking for the jeep that would be their escort.

Josh began to have that hopeless feeling he imagined spies and double-agents had, the sense of doing the enemy's job for them until that's all you knew. The fear of discovery keeping you on task in their service until you were found out. He wished they'd told the security guard they were running a job in town, but they didn't know where the other trucks were bound. Between the city and the wind farms, rumors of violence and robbery were prevalent.

Their turn came and Jamal pulled the truck up under the nozzle, missing the mark so that the ground crewman swore and he had to back up. He felt the crewman stare at them, whether to register his scowl or to root out their fraud, he didn't know.

When the truck was properly under the nozzle they began to fill it. It was the most enchanting, bewitching sound Jamal felt he'd ever heard. Gallon after gallon splashing into the deep metal tank. The sound of such wealth. It made him intensely thirsty.

When the truck was full, the crewman capped the top of their tank—the drivers were forbidden from exiting the trucks at the National Guard–run airport—and Jamal started for the gate.

There was an identical phone booth–sized checkpoint on the way out, stocked with what appeared to be the identical twin, minus thirty pounds, of the incoming guard.

"Destination?"

"Wind farms."

The guard looked up from his computer. "Oh yes." He folded his hands thoughtfully and set them on the window sill dividing them. "This shit never works. Data sync issue maybe? Wish I could say it was the first time."

"Huh," Josh said across Jamal, "should we drive it back to the garage then?" Suddenly he felt more than willing to give up the whole thing, to put the truck, full though it was, in the lot and bicycle home. They could come back and lift it at night.

"No," the guard said, drawing the word out. "Can't get off that easy. You know what I think? Piece of paper and a phone call. Boom. Job's done." The guard picked up an old style phone with a cord and held it out toward the truck. "Doesn't work either." He raised his eyebrows for effect and then looked at his screen again. "Instead we rely on some half-assed software. I can't think of one thing I ever done where these things"—he tapped the side of his screen—"have made it better."

Josh and Jamal waited. The man seemed to be chewing on some kind of decision.

"Route's not used much anymore," he said.

"Oh?"

"So you know what I think that means?"

Jamal inched down into his seat and felt their moment was up. The guard had worked through the situation and deduced their crime.

"I think it means the copter's broke." He stared at them. "You know about this route? I don't recognize you guys."

"We work distribution usually, sir," Jamal said.

The guard slapped the sill of the booth with his big, meaty hand. "What can you do?" He pointed out the window beyond his booth. "Your gunners are waiting out the gate, better stick close to them."

Josh nodded.

"Well, pull on out then," he said, "off you go! There's thirsty folk out there!"

Waiting for them on the other side was a military jeep with four National Guardsmen, looking sleepy and not at all alert.

Jamal gave them a quick wave and waited to see if they wished to talk to him. The driver signaled emphatically for him to carry on and he pulled forward into the street, pointed toward their rendezvous with Maid Marian's people, where the plan was to drive the truck into a warehouse and fake a riot while they hid it away.

After Jamal's first turn toward their destination, though, the jeep began flashing its headlights and honking furiously and then tore out around, veering to a skid in front of them. The driver strode furiously toward them.

"Where are you going?"

"Marine Drive?" Jamal said.

"You'll get hijacked on Marine Drive! We take the freeway, that's the secure route. How long you been on this job?"

"But I thought . . . We—we can take that way if you want, yes sir."

"If I want?" The driver scowled at him and told them to turn around, and then strode back to his jeep.

"Well?" Jamal exhaled, and put his hands over his face. Their plan had spun off into the unknown. "How many of them can you take?"

Josh closed his eyes and sank down in the seat.

"I guess we're driving to the wind farms," Jamal said.

Along I-84 the hills to the right of the freeway were ominous with a great yellow-brown forest, the needles gone brittle and brown for thirst, the trees long-dead. It was to the hills that they watched for ambush, in front of them for road block.

They passed two burnt-out cars discarded on the side of the road and Josh remembered how the news had covered the first ambushes outside of the city a couple of years ago.

"What are we going to do?" Jamal said.

Josh shook his head, grim.

"I could get up top, shoot their driver and see if the jeep rolled," Jamal said.

Josh smirked. "You can do that?"

Jamal shrugged. He wouldn't know if he could until the moment came.

"We may need their protection," Josh said.

There were no other cars on the road.

They drove the truck in silence for half an hour. They were going at a careful pace, slowing down to dodge debris in the road—fallen trees, a tire, the remains of a campfire. They watched in front and to the side for movement, and behind them to keep an eye on the jeep that followed.

"We might as well be wearing a suit of money," Jamal said.

"We're driving a suit of money."

At Multnomah Falls, the now-defunct tourist stop, the jeep pulled ahead of them and began to slow down, bringing them to a stop. They came to a rest fifty yards from the stone gift shop. Its windows were blown out, the interior was dark, and there was a burn mark along the eaves. It appeared as though someone had been having campfires in the place.

They waited in the truck, letting it idle. Jamal watched the guardsmen get out of the truck and feared suddenly that they might be
robbed by their own soldiers. That perhaps they'd been eager to go
along with the ruse in order to hoard the water for themselves.

In the rearview mirror he watched one walk toward them while
the others stayed with the jeep.

"Get your gun ready," Jamal said. "Keep it low."

The guardsman was older than the others, in his late forties, with
a scar along his chin. He came to the passenger side window. After
looking around the truck compartment he exhaled with impatience.
"I talked to command a few minutes back. There's no delivery out this
way today." He raised his eyebrows at them.

"Oh?" Josh said, "You're sure?"

"Of course I'm sure. This makes this a lost truck. Who'd you get
your orders from?"

"The usual place," Josh said weakly.

"The usual place?" The guardsman pulled out a military-issue
phone and dialed a number, and then swore when he realized they
were in a dead zone, off even the guard's own network. "What's your
name?"

"I—I wonder if it's safe here," Josh said.

"Get out of the truck. Right now." The guardsman looked toward
his jeep and his men to signal for help. The driver of the jeep took one
step toward them and then a red gash appeared across his neck. He
made a gurgling sound and fell.

"Jesus!" said the guardsman at the window. Jamal jammed the
truck into reverse and stepped on the gas, backing down the freeway
as fast as he could go, leaving the fourth guardsman exposed and hol-
lering at him.

"Switch places!" Josh yelled. "You're better with a gun."

"No!"

"Switch me, damn it, I can't shoot."

Jamal skidded to a stop. As they fumbled across each other to
switch places he caught sight of people in the old lodge.

"That building!" Jamal yelled, and Josh looked to see a face and
rifle appear briefly in the window of the gift shop to their right, and
then another guardsman was on the ground.

"Oh my god," Josh said. He accelerated backward again and yanked
the steering wheel to the left. The truck skidded partway around, stuck

in the middle of the freeway at a perpendicular angle, facing the forest. Their windshield exploded, splintering glass over them.

Jamal waved his gun about looking for a sign of the attackers. Ahead of them was a dark brown, dead forest. "Drive! Fuck, drive!" Jamal shouted.

Josh stepped on the gas and yanked the wheel to the right. The turning radius was wide and he accelerated into the turn, driving them into the ditch at the side of the road. The truck's grille hit the bank and the truck would turn no more. "Shit!" Josh yelled. In the side mirror he saw the two remaining guardsmen under cover behind the jeep. He felt the truck shudder as it took bullets. He ground into reverse and freed them from the ditch. Up the hillside to his left a small band advanced toward them. Two had rifles pointed. He ducked below the steering wheel as his side window blew out, the bullet cutting a path across them and embedding in the passenger side door, above Jamal's thigh.

Josh put the truck in gear and floored it. The lumbering beast pulled away. He felt the truck take another bullet, and then they were out of range.

In the mirror Josh watched one of their attackers fall under Guardsman fire and then they rounded a bend and were free.

"We're losing water," Jamal said, he watched the wet trail they left in the road in the rearview mirror. The wind blew hard in their faces and it was difficult to hear each other.

"Can't help it," Josh said.

"We have to stop," Jamal said, "we have to stop now."

Josh realized he was right, that the waste would haunt him, lives were pouring out the back of the truck. The emptier the truck became, the more meaningless the entire effort was.

"One more minute," Josh said. He drove hard, dodging the same obstacles they'd already passed, and then skidded to a stop.

Jamal jumped out to look at the damage. Four holes sputtered out water in bullet-sized jets through neat, circular incisions. Jamal stripped off his shirt, tore it into pieces and screwed tight wads into each of the holes.

"Better than before," he said. There was a dribble down each.

The road behind them was empty and quiet.

They drove again. But in a long straight stretch they could see they were being followed, the jeep's outline distant but clear.

"See them?" Josh said.

"Fuck," Jamal growled, "Guardsmen?"

"It would be a miracle," Josh said.

Josh took the truck as fast as it would go, a vibrating, frightening pace, but he knew its speed would be no match for the jeep. He plowed over the top of obstacles he'd dodged before.

"We have to get off this road," Jamal said.

"There's no way we could hide this thing." Josh thought about the thirty minutes it'd taken them to drive here—the jeep would pull even with them long before they hit town again. In the distance they spotted a green highway sign advertising an exit.

"Speed for that, man," Jamal said.

"No way, it'll slow us way down."

"Do it. We'll fake it from there." Jamal placed his feet against the dashboard to brace himself against the vibration and made sure all was right with his gun. "Any idea how many of them died?"

"No."

"And now they've got a jeep and serious weapons."

"I know, Jamal. For fuck sake."

"You coming apart, man?"

"No!" Josh said. *The plan* had come apart, he thought, not him, and now it was only a matter of time before it would be them. He kept trying to make a new plan, and then panic overwhelmed him and he'd have to start from scratch. "Our plan was shit. This is shit."

"No," Jamal said, "we have the truck. We're in this game."

"It was a shit plan!" Josh checked and rechecked the side mirror for the position of the jeep.

"The plan was good, Josh, but that was then. Take this exit, man. Take it!"

Josh jerked the wheel to the right and descended down an off ramp into what appeared to be a recreation area turn-off. The road went a short ways toward the river and ended in a parking lot.

"Fuck! What do I do? There's no out."

"You're losing it," Jamal said. "You want me to drive?"

"No!"

"The on ramp is hidden from the freeway. Go hide on that."

Josh pulled onto the on ramp, which was in a natural depression. They idled the truck and waited. After another minute they heard the jeep pull off onto the exit.

"Go!"

Josh pulled onto the freeway, trying to keep the truck from roaring in its lower gears. They could not see the jeep and he gunned it to full speed.

After several minutes they could see the jeep trailing them again. It was markedly closer.

"I'll watch the jeep," Jamal said. "You keep your eyes on the road. There, look—" There was another exit ahead.

"It's the old highway," Josh said.

"Jump the lanes and go down the hill."

"No. No way, we'll roll." Josh shook his head.

"Do it now," Jamal yelled. When Josh hesitated Jamal yanked the wheel hard and steered them across their lanes and through a metal guardrail. They plunged down an embankment onto the old road, the truck rattling and bouncing violently.

Josh floored it. The road climbed into the hills, quickly entering into treed, semi-rural plots on the outskirts of the city. He drove hard, looking for a suitable driveway to pull into.

"You got to decide quick, man!"

Big ranch houses nestled deep among stands of tall dead trees. Josh picked a lane and pulled in. A brick house stood in a clearing in the center of a skeletal forest and he gunned toward that, aiming to hide the truck behind it. It was a long driveway. As they got closer they saw barbed wire tangled into a low barrier around the house.

"There's someone here," Jamal yelled. He saw a brief flicker in the curtain and then he heard a thump.

"Oh," Josh sighed. It was an exhale of disappointment and disgust.

Jamal looked over and saw red blossoming across Josh's shirt. Josh's grip went weak on the steering wheel.

Jamal ducked below the windshield and felt the sudden impact of a bullet embed into the seat where his body had been. He yanked the steering wheel to the right toward a standing garage and killed the engine, coasting into a bumper-kiss with the garage wall.

"God*damnit*. Goddamnit, Josh," he said. Jamal grabbed his arm and yanked him down and out of view.

Josh emitted what sounded like a sigh of acknowledgement, and then slowly slouched onto the seat. The truck went into a backwards roll and Jamal struggled to engage the emergency brake on the floor.

His shoulder smeared with Josh's blood and he wanted to fire his gun into that house until it collapsed. With the brake finally on he opened the passenger door, shielded by the garage, and carefully stepped down from the truck.

He swore and stood there a moment. Another shot hit the dirt close to him. "Wait!" he yelled toward the house. This is so not my territory, he thought, a shirtless black man in a white neighborhood, pursued by white ambushers. Behind him were trees, the remains of trees. He could make a run for it and live, but the distance home through hostile neighborhoods was great, and he'd lose everything they'd come for.

"Wait!" he yelled again. "You killed the driver. We're being chased!"

"You got no reason here," came a man's voice from the house.

"We're being chased," Jamal repeated.

Jamal eyed the distance between the truck and the garage. About fifteen feet.

"Get in your truck and get out."

He didn't trust them not to shoot him, and did not want to be back on the road. "There's no time." He yelled back. He realized they hadn't realized it was a water truck. He weighed his options. "This truck is full of water. Water thieves are coming."

There was silence from the house.

Jamal sprinted for the cover of the garage. It was a large, two-car structure and in the window he saw a variety of standard garage trappings: dusty lawn mowers and bicycles and a car. He tried the door but it was locked.

"You steal the truck?" the voice said from the house.

"It's for the Northeast neighborhood," Jamal said. And then he yelled, "Maid Marian."

A second later the jeep roared up the driveway. As with Josh, the first bullet from the house killed the driver instantly. The other two men jumped from the jeep while it was still moving and scrambled for cover behind the water truck.

"Motherfucker!" one of the men yelled.

"You got no reason here," came the voice from the house.

Jamal hid on the far side of the garage, out of view of the house, and watched the men conference. They went to either end of the water truck and fired on the house with their stolen assault rifles, blowing the windows out and doing a tremendous amount of damage. They had not seen him.

One of the attackers opened the passenger door and Jamal aimed, holding his gun hand steady with his other hand. He fired a round into the man's back, not twenty feet away. The man fell against the truck and onto the ground. He rolled facing the garage and Jamal hit him again in the chest and he went still. There was a code of honor about shooting a man in the back. He could feel that burn in him briefly, as if the ghosts of old Westerns shook their heads sadly at him, but in the end all he could feel was an exultant joy that it was not him, and that there was only one left. There was nothing honorable about any of this.

The other man paused firing and looked down the truck to see his partner fallen. He panicked and ran down the driveway. A shot from the house leveled him. He went from a dead run to dead and skidding face down in the dirt road.

Fucking marksman, Jamal thought. He didn't know what to do now, but he felt sure he didn't want to surprise them. After a few moments Jamal said, "I'm still here! They're both dead." And then, "I'm not your enemy!"

The house was silent.

"Don't shoot," Jamal said. He sprinted the short distance back to the truck and waited, unsure of what would happen next. He studied the dead man at his feet. A fine dust covered the man's face and clothes. The dried-out topsoil that lifted into the air, weightless, as if they were on the moon, the gravity gone weak. His cheeks were hollow and there was a translucence to him. His lips were cracked and dark circles rimmed his eyes—dehydration. He wore a torn black concert shirt with "Giant Tim and the Tiny Turds" emblazoned on it above a futuristic-looking spaceship. Jamal soft-prodded him with his foot. His clothes were ragged and excessive for this time of year. He probably wore everything he owned.

"This is too much for you to keep," Jamal yelled. "I'm bringing it to a whole neighborhood. Thousands."

There was no word from the house. Jamal checked his gun again and wondered if he should pick up one of the assault rifles, and then remembered the marksman's aim. He crouched down beside the truck and peeked around a tire toward the house, where he could see no movement.

"Well?" he yelled.

"Throw your guns into the roundabout in front of the house. All of them."

Jamal tried to figure out which window the voice was coming from. "We are peaceful, we mean to help our neighborhood," he said, thinking of Maid Marian, an edge of righteousness entering into his voice. He would bring the water back.

"The guns!"

Jamal thought he saw a curtain move in the house, now ragged with bullet holes. Unlike his father, Gregor, he'd always been mediocre with a gun and thought his chances of taking out even one person in the house minimal. He had no idea how many were holed up there.

"I can drain this tank right here," Jamal said. "Ten gallons a second. By the time you've killed me it'd be gone in a wash over your driveway."

There was quiet from the house and he realized there were several there, discussing the plan of action.

Finally they said, "Give us some."

"A hundred gallons," Jamal said, "in exchange for safe passage out of here, and the good will of the people of Northeast Portland."

"Two hundred, and we keep the jeep and the guns."

"For two hundred I keep the guns, you get the jeep."

"Give us one of the assault rifles."

He wondered if this were a means to lure him into the open.

"Throw your guns into the roundabout and show yourself."

"It's a deal. Is it a deal?" Jamal didn't know if they had seen him, and he worried at the reception and instantaneous discarding of plans that the appearance of his skin might bring, a savage here among the righteous. Shirtless and brown. He sat back against the tire and breathed deeply, trying to calm his heart.

Then he had an idea. He stood up and took a deep breath. "I will bring you water," Jamal said. "I will bring you water." His voice came out like a river of black tar, smooth and confident and unstoppable, and the rest of him tried to catch up.

He tucked his gun visibly into the front of his pants. He opened the passenger door to the truck and retrieved a couple of unregistered unit gallon containers. The trucks kept several dozen spare to replace those that had broken. His hands were shaking.

He went to the back of the truck and filled them from the spigot—still out of view of the house. And then, taking a deep breath, he turned slowly, holding the full jugs of water before him, his body exposed. "I will bring you water to seal the deal," he said.

"Drop your gun!" the voice shouted, but he felt he heard an uncertainty in it now.

"No one will drop their guns," Jamal said, "I am bringing you water. I will leave two hundred gallons. We will trust each other."

When he'd made it to within twenty feet of the house he heard another voice say, "You're black." Had they only now figured it out, he wondered, or was it impossible not to make such an obvious statement in the face of things?

"I am bringing water to share," he said. "I will leave two hundred gallons. We will trust each other." He wasn't sure what he was doing any more, but he could feel his father's tea ceremony rising in him like some mantra, felt he could understand how the ceremony took control, how the routine of it, of sharing water, could dominate an exchange.

"Don't come any closer!"

"I am bringing water to share. Bring glasses out and we will drink to sharing water. We will trust each other."

From the house he heard someone's voice say "don't you dare" and understood that they were talking among themselves, arguing over the outcome. He got to within twenty feet of the front door, to the edge of the barbed wire, and sat down cross-legged on the walkway which had once been surrounded by a well-kept lawn but was now a scarred dust scrub. He put the gallons in front of him and waited.

"I have brought you water to share," he said. "We will trust each other. We will drink to trust."

They buried Josh in the backyard in a quick, quiet ceremony. Chris and Renee and Jamal dug the hole together and Renee wielded the shovel like a weapon, punishing the ground with it. After they filled the hole back up, over the top of his long, handsome body, she swayed in the heat as Julia said a few words. After she was done no one said anything, and no one moved.

Renee was the first to break the circle they made around the grave. She gave Jamal a hug and told him she was glad he was safe, and then she walked in a straight line away from headquarters, away from the house on Going Street, down the block and into the next. At some point she became vaguely aware of Bea yelling at her, pleading with her to return, but she could not stop.

She did not care. Were it to come by gunfire or knife or some other means, it was all the same to her. She willed it on herself, even, wanted the taste of her own blood in her mouth, wanted as much of hers spilled as Josh had lost, some retribution for her own ambition. She walked numbly down the middle of the road, past barrel fires and local conflicts, past kids playing, past people who taunted her. She walked as long as she could, blocks upon blocks, looking straight ahead, wishing to walk off the end of the earth. She walked until she reached the bluff's edge of the defunct river and she sat down there, her legs dangling over the edge as the sun dropped below the far hill.

She felt lonely for Josh, alone in his grave, and for the struggle she had in front of her with him gone. She was tired of being hunted. She stared up the river toward the city center.

She didn't know where to go next, but every time she turned back toward the house she felt deflected, the guilt a barrier that warded her away.

In the end she found herself at the water tower. She stood at the edge of its grounds and thought about walking to his building, three or so miles away. She paced there in front of the tower considering it, knowing that to walk to his place meant a defeat, that she would not leave again once she got there. She was between things now, in a hellish limbo, the stakes of the game she played unbelievably higher. She dug in her pockets and was relieved to find the green laser.

From atop the playground equipment she traced out his name, but realized it was far too late in the evening for him to expect her. Then she began to write, a sloppy cursive she wasn't sure he'd be able to comprehend anyway, and in that she poured everything: Josh's death, the incredible wealth that'd come under her power, the feeling that she was at the end of it all, on the verge of Josh's fate herself.

She wrote until she exhausted herself with the piteous outpouring. She hoped he hadn't recorded it. Idly, and she supposed to punish herself, she wondered if Zach had found somebody else. She lay down on the top of the playground equipment and gave in to her exhaustion.

Sometime in the night she woke to the green of Zach's laser pointer criss-crossing across the water tower. When she crossed his green with hers he excitedly began to send Morse code and she had trouble keeping up.

Watched vid. So sorry about Josh, he signed. After a long pause in which she could think of no response he said: *What will you do now?*

She said she didn't know.

Wish I were there.

Come, she said.

40k gals. Secede.

What? She signed back, sitting up and trying to blink the sleep out of her eyes.

City not distribution. Bargain with feds. Make your own country.

Don't understand. She said.

Human rights.

Zach. I don't understand.

Your own country. Take NE. Be up soon as I can.

How? She said.

Riot.

Renee sat with the laser pointer in her lap and let Zach's last word echo through her. For a brief moment she imagined herself as a sort of prime minister, her people stretched out before her in old Portland bungalow houses as far as the eye could see, all of them her charge to protect and care for, and then the weight of such an enterprise leveled her again, so that she flattened out on the playground equipment and shivered in the virtual company of Zach. He was joking, surely.

Ha ha, she blipped back.

Riot. Borders. Negot. H2o dist. Security force. Only way to stay out of jail.

Right, she said. She could tell he was on fire there on his roof across town, humming with ideas. *Not me. No way it would work,* she signed.

You have the reputation to do it. So bold it would throw them.

Crazy.

Yes. Big crazy. Stay out of jail.

She rested her eyes for a moment, exhausted, and continued to see the stark, ultra-bright light of the laser through her eyelids. In her dreams, the racing green line traced out an outline of neighborhoods, seven miles square. A map. When she woke it was still dark and she had no concept of what time it was. Her body was sore from lying across the wood playground equipment, and the water tower had gone dark. She eased herself up, traced out a quick *bye love,* and walked home.

———

At HQ she stood outside the big garage and tried to make up her mind. Inside was her new truck. She nodded to the guard posted outside and went in. Standing with her hand on the truck's great swollen belly, she felt like a dragon must, counting her pile of gold, the war spoils. The space felt cooler, the great mass of the tank changing the climate of the room.

They had filled a number of unit gallons from it, and she drank deeply from one of these now. She drank recklessly, not counting gulps, not heeding the digital readout.

She thought about the number of people who had died to bring it here. In her mind the water mass of them, the blood weight, was roughly equal to the contents of the tank. When Jamal had first pulled it into the garage, before she knew Josh had died, it was the most glorious of moments. Like life had just begun for them. There were many in her care now. They were at war: against the city's neglect and scorn, against the drought, against their own nature.

With the water they had an immense wealth. She could sustain innumerable lives. She could use it as an agent of change.

"Sometimes people have to die," she said to the empty room to try it out. A wave of nausea hit her so that she braced herself with the truck, let her head rest against its belly.

It was a lie and it was not a lie.

Tomorrow they would empty the contents of the truck into tanks they'd built in preparation in the backyard. Then they would disappear this unlucky truck, with its bullet holes and blasted-out windshield and the role it had played in their cause.

She patted the side and felt the dampness below its plugged holes.

She would recruit more, she thought. They would expand. They would go out on bikes, weighted down with a cargo of unit gallons, repaying with life the debt she owed.

That night they hunkered close about the campfire in the backyard, quieter than usual. Jamal sat across from Renee, and she avoided his eyes, knowing now what she'd put him through. She had apologized until he'd asked her to stop.

"You can't do that again, dude," Bea said, referring to how Renee had disappeared.

Renee scanned the faces at the fire—beside Bea and Jamal, Leroy and a few others were there, their heads bowed toward the heat. "I went to the towers and talked to Zach."

Bea grunted.

"He says we should secede. Went on and on about it. He used to be all cautious before. He's worried I'll go to jail."

Across from her, Jamal fixed her with a peculiar stare and she smiled nervously and stared at the fire again. She didn't feel herself. She should go to bed, she knew, start again in the morning.

"That's what I'm talking about," Jamal said.

"Hm," Bea said.

"Can you imagine?" Renee said. "Might as well stand at the bottom of the mountain and holler the avalanche down."

"Renee," Jamal said, "that's exactly what we need. New rules. New police. City out of here. It's fucking genius. You got to do that."

"I have to do that? I'm building a neighborhood support network. I don't want to be mayor."

"Mayors don't run countries, you'd be like queen or something."

"Fetch Queen Marian some pie," Renee sing-songed. She pulled a handful of sticks from the wood pile behind her and methodically snapped them and fed them to the fire.

"I'd vote for you," Bea said

"Bea," Renee said. "You're supposed to be the rational mind."

"Never thought I'd say this, but I agree with Jamal and Zach."

"Yep," Leroy said. There was a moment of silence, and then he added: "Their rule is an agreed-upon system for the maintenance of order and the continuation of services. The services have all gone, but the government wants to go on anyway. And yet the representative nature of democracy means it's too hard to course correct when the situation calls for it."

"Hear, hear," the woman sitting next to Leroy said, whom Renee noticed was holding hands with Leroy.

Renee smiled at Leroy and he shrugged and looked away shyly.

"City isn't even here, but their shadow is," Jamal said, appraising Leroy in a new light. "Chase it out."

"Listen. Someone else can. I don't want to do that. We already lost one person, are you guys not seeing what would happen? We have a good plan."

Jamal put his legs behind him and lay prone on the grass, his chin resting in his hands. "You're not seeing it. Think about it. You've already got a robust neighborhood network. Work with rations distribution, make it safe, do all the stuff you're doing already—just with scale, and with everyone in, and no outside government to fuck with us. Like I was saying at the start. It'd be powerful. You're already part-way there—it's got to be you."

Renee leaned back and looked up at the stars and began to shiver. As the night wore on she heard them get up to go, one by one.

"Come on, let's go to bed, your highness." Bea stood over her and offered her hand.

Renee snorted and stayed where she was.

"Come on, I'm teasing."

"I'll be up shortly, love," Renee said.

After a while she was alone. The fire died next to her. A breeze came and she wrapped her arms around herself and stared into the sky. The stars tilted and turned, until they'd traced their way across the black expanse and went to rest at its brim, replaced by new ones along the other edge. A few shooting stars blazed white and were gone. What journeys they'd had, she thought, born in some distant part of the galaxy. Perhaps birthed in the time of Tiberius Gracchus or Hypatia, or earlier, when the Earth was wild, hundreds of thousands of years ago. All of them, the meteors and the Gracchi and Hypatia, they burned bright and came to unpleasant ends. Still, she could see how it was a time for which ambition was called. A chaos through which order could be made. Finally the dawn came and the stars faded away and the sky filled with blue.

Among the meetings Gregor had lined up for the day was one with a woman who called herself Maid Marian. He'd seen her on the news, but for the most part he assumed it was white people trouble.

Some days back she had "requested" an interview with him *at her place* up in the Cully neighborhood, and he'd stared at the written card with puzzlement. At the bottom of the note was a different hand-writing: *Please come, Pop—Jamal.* He wondered if Jamal had found the card and used it for scratch paper. And then he forgot about the whole affair. *Come to her place*—If you did not understand that there was a certain order to the universe, you did not warrant a reply.

And now he'd been informed she was coming for a visit. He sighed heavily and shifted in his chair. It was trouble, he could feel it.

Gregor had a crew of twenty and ran the Woodlawn and King neighborhoods. His operation was diminished significantly from the old days, the drug war, but it was what he needed. When he had it, he dealt what there was to his dealers and a few freelancers—dope, crack, coke, heroin, ecstasy and if the white kids came looking for it he could turn up LSD. It was harder to obtain nearly all those, but the demand was high. It was a tightly run operation. He'd been running the ship for a little over two decades and he felt like he'd mellowed into a relationship with the neighborhoods, his business clean and efficient, a regality of sorts. The reputation he'd earned over the years far outsized the operation he ran now, and far surpassed the borders of his domain, and that was fine with him. He thought of himself as the standards body, and his structure provided the DNA for every other operation within miles. When the others needed advice, they came to him.

He was lenient when leniency was called for, hard when hardness was called for. In a word: Just. Nobody had been killed on his account in the last five years, and there'd been no police trouble for three, and so he'd begun to think of it as "just a business, like everybody else." The peaceful success had a few side effects: a Buddha-sized paunch—though shrunken somewhat from the drought—diminishing ambition, and a tendency to lapse into nostalgia. The Woodlawn–King War had taken his wife and the youngest of two sons. Jamal was all he had left. Perhaps that had mellowed him, too.

Over time Gregor had earned a host of nicknames, a few of which were tolerable, and a number that he loathed.

"The Pirate" had a nice ring to it. It suggested, perhaps, that he was able with a sword or might possess a prosthetic limb, likely hollowed out, with some devilish map encased inside. It suggested he might have exclusive knowledge of a buried chest of treasure somewhere.

"The Hammer" he didn't care for. It was given to him because of a rumor that he'd beaten a man to death with a hammer. Occasionally a hammer would be left on his doorstep, which he supposed was some weak-minded threat against him by the family or friends of the victim. 'The Hammer' sounded brute and haphazard, the weapon of dullards.

"The Arm" was marginally better. There was a hint of reach and length about it that he liked. Though when he thought of the name, it was difficult for him not to evoke a teeming mass of arms, thin ones and strong ones and tattooed ones and fat ones and all those arms together, jumbled and sweaty in their fleshiness—appropriate for some kind of commercial about human diversity, sure, but it seemed entirely the wrong kind of message he hoped to project for himself.

He hated "Spider." Something about webs and conspiracies. He had a deep arachnophobia and checked his shoes each morning and needed to look in any darkened space—a glove box, a sock drawer—before pulling an item out. No matter that he was told one had to face one's fears. It was Batman's fear of bats, after all, that made him what he was. Well. Not for him.

There were a number of names that suggested generosity in some vague way, or that he was the source of something. The father, dealer, the giver, the bank. All true, in some way. Simple words to describe a simple function. Honorable enough, but boring.

His favored nickname was simply "Pop," and it was what his men called him. There was a fatherly tone to it. In his mind it was written comic style, the *pop!* of a gun or simply the sound of something becoming suddenly unstuck and free.

When Maid Marian arrived with an amazon of a woman and Leroy, he did what he always did when he had a visit. He made tea. The making of tea in these times was an exorbitant and troublesome affair, but Gregor appreciated ritual and protocol and what it said about a person. No matter the circumstances or purpose of the visit, when you came calling at his house you were going to drink tea. He kept a number of gallons stashed away expressly for the purpose. In the past it had been bourbon or rum, but a man could not quietly sustain his affairs for two decades on that kind of a ritual, especially if he preferred not to have the complications of bloodshed in his house. This he had learned.

"We've come to negotiate," Maid Marian said, after she told him her plan to take control of the entire Northeast of Portland and to secede from the city government. He'd had to ask her to speak up. His ears weren't what they used to be, and he'd noticed that the nervous dribbled their sentences into wispy puffs of air at the ends.

When she repeated herself her voice rang out with a bold certainty. Gregor stopped pouring tea. He wondered if he was being had. He turned to Leroy for clarification and noticed that the man had picked up an empty ashtray and now spun it end over end in his hands at a speed that could only suggest he'd spent the better portion of his life practicing just such a move. Leroy looked up at him and shrugged and continued with his spinning.

"You're inside the city," Gregor said and handed out the cups. "You can't secede with a few piddly neighborhoods. You've got no services, no power source, no water."

"Water is supplied by the federal government and run by the National Guard. We will negotiate as a separate entity. The Northeast sits over the aquifer, what's left of it, and a couple of wells will be within our domain. They say there's a little that can be had there if we can dig deep enough."

"So." Gregor scratched his head and took a sip of his tea and then made eye contact with his men to make sure they were alert—they were *bodyguards*, really, but he felt there was a physical intimacy to the word which made him uneasy about using it. "So, you are here to—what are you here for?" He suddenly felt like ten years of success had made him go soft, that there were large new ideas at play that hadn't yet scuttled their way into his dusty spiderweb.

"We want you to be part of the organizational structure."

Gregor made eye contact with one of his men again, this time to register disbelief.

She nodded to affirm what she'd said. "Your son is already with us."

'Well, the boy does what he wants to do. Listen, I've peaceably cohabited with many other organizations, of all makes, for over a decade. I don't run in turf wars, not if I don't have to."

"That's what I've been told. I'm not bringing a war here, I'm asking that you bring your operation into the folds of ours, and then to expand your duties. Your"—and he saw her struggle for a word here—"concern, at the very least, will remain yours."

Gregor made the kind of sound those in charge learn to make, meaning: I will need to hear more before I say no, but no it will likely be.

"I need leaders in the government."

Gregor studied his tea. There were leaves swirling about the top of it, suggestively, and for the hundredth time he wished he could draw some meaning from them. "You know what business I'm in?"

Maid Marian nodded. "I do, and one of the things I would ask is that we put some safety controls on the more addictive drugs. But right off the bat, legalization would take out a good deal of future conflict."

"Huh." Gregor smiled and leaned back into his chair. He held his tea with both hands, enjoying the feel of the rough cup and the quiet affluence of it. "Lady, I think," he said and paused. "I think you are operating in a fantasy. I need this business to be here at the end of all this. What do you hope to accomplish with a secession? You're suggesting a sort of suicide. These are not end-times, this is not the apocalypse."

"Not yet!" She stood.

Gregor was impressed with her brazenness, even as his men leaned in.

"That's what I'm trying to avoid," she said. "You've had riots in your neighborhood. How many houses burned down? You know how hard it is to put out a fire. There's not a single occupied government building in the entire Northeast. When's the last time you saw a police vehicle? The city has abandoned this quadrant. I know you've stepped up security in your neighborhoods. When will they cut rations entirely? We're fighting for survival here—maybe not you, but most are. This entire section of the city is going to fall into complete chaos. How can that help your business? The proposal I'm making to the city is simply that we handle security and water distribution, and perhaps we'll pick up a few other services along the way if they fit."

"Sit. Sit down. Let's talk at least. You're talking about security again—what about the others?"

"Other what?"

"You know what I'm talking about."

"I've talked to most of them. Look, Leroy vouched for you, I know your reputation. Some cannot stay. I need a patrol, and I need someone who can lead."

Gregor studied Leroy. He knew Leroy only vaguely as a homeless man who pushed cans around his neighborhood in a squealing grocery cart, and he wondered what weird role the man had ascended to in her play organization.

"He said you ran an ethical operation here."

"You're talking about war," he said quietly. "You're asking me to go to war against the others."

"I'm asking you on behalf of the people in all the neighborhoods in the Northeast to stand up for them. I'm asking you to be the police chief of a new country."

"You have no country. The answer is no."

There was silence in the room then. The conversation was over for him. He waited for them to understand and leave.

"You understand I will go to someone else."

"Lady? Jesus Christ. Lady. I understand you have some popular support—"

"As do you."

"Not the same thing. You're going to squander yours anyhow. How are you possibly going to manage this?"

"I don't know," she said, and then she pointed at him. "I'm going to do it with you."

Gregor sat back in his chair and appraised each in turn. Leroy he realized he might have underestimated. Leroy always appeared to be on speed, and Gregor had just assumed he was getting it elsewhere. The few times Gregor had spoken to him, he'd frenetically rambled, aggressive and near-incoherent. He looked more settled now than Gregor had imagined the man capable of, the mania concentrated in the actions of an ashtray. The amazon woman was alert, but in the way his men were alert. Her tea sat on the table untouched. There was something coiled about her, a well of potential energy. She was listening to the conversation, but also to the room and outside the room. She was a soldier.

The Maid Marian woman he couldn't make out at all, other than she obviously had no sense of self-preservation. With her impassioned argument she had raised some buried instinct in him, to his surprise, and he contemplated this. For an instant, he'd felt a desire to join in, to bind and save the neighborhoods.

After a while he said, "I am sorry. But there's no way in hell your plan is going to work. I wish you luck."

After they'd left, he stood at the window for a long time watching the dust and debris blow around in the street outside. He realized the city, like his tea, was in the act of divining. When the wind stopped, the future would be declared across its geography.

He needed to speak to Jamal.

The mayor and Christopher were out for a drive. Except you couldn't ever go alone anymore, Christopher thought. They were *driven*. The idyllic romantic wanderings of a couple in the car became more of a traveling circus of mismatched personalities.

The driver, who wore a hat in such a foul, bedraggled state that Christopher could only imagine the man had fished it from the bottom of some cabbie's grave, ran a barely audible Mexican-accented commentary about everything on the road. The only coherent parts were when the dialogue crescendoed hotly into profanity. In the passenger seat beside him sat an *officer of the law*, a quiet, brooding man in his forties who had told Christopher his name enough times that he could not bring himself to ask it of him again. He was, Christopher thought, the type of man whose personality is like fog. You grasp at it, and when you open your hand, there is nothing there.

He and the mayor sat in the back like two kids strapped into car seats on the way to a soccer game. It had been Christopher's idea to take the drive. He couldn't stand being inside any more. He'd complained that they were holed up like they were under siege. He argued that they needed to see what the mayor governed in order to govern properly. Begrudgingly, the mayor set down his video game controller and agreed to go.

Christopher reached out and looped his index finger through the mayor's, and the mayor took it absently. He remembered when the two of them would go on drives. They'd make a day of it, lazily wandering east through the Gorge, eating a nice dinner in Hood River, sleeping at a bed-and-breakfast if the mood hit them. Happier times, he thought to himself.

The mayor sat forward in his seat, anxiously looking out the window as they moved from one neighborhood to the next. A squad car tailed them, as ordered. As they drove from Southeast Portland to Northeast Portland, the vista became progressively worse. The windows became coated in drought-dust, whipped up by a wind that came in overnight, blowing wispy, insignificant clouds across the sky and reducing visibility.

As if to taunt them, mid-drive a dozen fat raindrops hit the car in an agitated pattering, their dirt consistency and weight more akin to a squall of bird droppings.

"What was that?" the mayor said, his hand pressed against Christopher's chest protectively. He cursed when he realized it was a weird rain, ejaculated from a sky empty of rain clouds. Minutes later the windshield was dry again.

In the Southeast many neighborhoods still had the feel of being generally intact. But as they progressed toward the Northeast they saw burned-out or abandoned houses with children garbed in only underwear standing on desiccated lawns, watching them go by.

It was depressing. Christopher would not bring it up to the mayor though. There was a history of poverty and crime here, and he knew they were repeating a cartographic racism that had been institutionalized. Parts of the Northeast had perennially diminished city services and in the past violence tended to be the police force's first course of action. It was no wonder they were worse off during the drought.

Each neighborhood tended to resemble its former self: the harder neighborhoods were that much harder, and often run by the strongest individual on the block. The better neighborhoods were hardly better. He knew the mayor perceived the same things, but bringing up any observation would cause his partner's blood pressure to rise, cause him to spout out invective that ran on parallel tracks of guilt and defensiveness.

But he couldn't help it. Christopher squeezed his shoulder. "It's not your fault, Brandon, you know."

"Of course it is," the mayor said. The mayor was turned away, but Christopher observed him shift subtly, so that they no longer touched.

Christopher stared out his window, wishing he'd said nothing.

"We need a campaign for here," the mayor said. "We need people in these streets."

"Doing what?"

"I don't know. Something—*goddamnit*—something fucking cheerful or something."

Christopher nodded. "A job might be kind of cheerful."

"Security has to be first. We'll put together a task force when we get back. Have Sue head it up." The mayor linked his fingers back through Christopher's as he spoke. "Six, eight people—who do we have that's from the neighborhood? If only there wasn't a mud sinkhole of a city council to wade through."

The driver swerved and squealed to a stop as, this time, a patter of small stones hit their car. Half a dozen children were in the street blocking the way. The driver accelerated to the right and the tire bumped joltingly over the curb. Behind them the squad car turned on its siren and the children scattered. Another series of stones hit their car.

The mayor sank down in his seat as they accelerated. "Oh Chrissy, I feel sick."

Christopher nodded grimly but said nothing to the driver. He wondered if the mayor could stand to feel this sick a little more often. He noticed another squad car had joined behind them now. The police didn't like them driving in a red zone—lone cop cars for miles around. "I doubt they knew it was you, love. They're pelting cars. Let's drive straight across to the river."

The mayor nodded and looked out the window.

At an intersection they paused and a group of six bicyclists rode by in formation in front of them, all of them dressed head-to-toe in green. The mayor and Christopher watched as they glanced over at the car, some smiling, and continued on.

"What was that?" The mayor said.

"They had outfits. They matched."

"That looked like that girl . . ." The policeman in the front seat said and then his voice faded away unintelligibly.

The mayor sat bolt upright. "Maid Marian? In the middle? Follow them!"

The driver stomped on the accelerator and they turned the corner in pursuit. The bicyclists were easily a block ahead of them now, and the street was littered with debris. Couches and burn barrels and discarded trash were everywhere.

"Go, man!" the mayor said, but within a few minutes of steering their way through the obstacles, the bicyclists had turned and were out of sight. "*Goddamnit.* What's with the fucking uniforms?" There was something about seeing them that gave the mayor an immense chill.

The driver cursed his way into the street until there was no more going forward. "Look at this," he said, "just look at this." There was a makeshift barricade in front of them that had been disguised by debris until they'd gotten closer. Burnt-out cars had been pushed together in such a way that nothing beyond the size of a bicycle could pass.

"Sons of a bitch," the driver said, "we will have to back out now." He leaned out the window and waved frantically at the two police cars behind that blocked their return. There was chatter over their police radio, mixed with static and too many voices trying to talk at once. "Go back, *pendejos!*" the driver yelled, swallowing the last word, and then he took one sweeping look at their situation and ducked his head down. "It's trap!" He punched at the window controls frantically, causing the windows to pulse erratically upward.

"Trap?" the mayor said, lowering himself further into the seat. "No?"

The cop leveled his gun across the dashboard.

"I don't see anyone," the mayor whispered. Behind them the two squad cars were slowly orchestrating the logistics of backing up through the maze of the street.

"It does look like a trap," Christopher said, "but no one is here to claim the prey. Maybe we're too big a fish for this trap."

They watched the streets for sign of attack while the driver jerked his way backward.

"Let's go, man," the mayor said. He had seen someone watching them from a window. "Get us out of here."

On the way home they held hands, the ability to be intimate eased by adrenalin and its subsequent letdown.

"That was her, wasn't it?" Christopher said after a while. "In uniform, too."

The mayor sighed with disgust. Among these other problems, why her? Why does it have to be a coffee barista. A Latina college student. In his mind her citizen-ordinariness loomed as a super power against him in the fight for the public's heart. He stared out the window as they cruised back toward their mayoral encampment downtown. He wanted a bath and a cocktail. "What should I do, Chrissy?" the mayor said.

Christopher shrugged. "I think the Northeast needs to think you're still on their side." The mayor extracted his hand immediately and Christopher looked wryly at where his hand lay dejected on the seat of the car.

"I *am* on their side!" The mayor gripped the seat back and glared off toward the front windshield, not quite meeting Christopher's eyes. And then he dropped his shoulders. "I am on their side," he said again weakly, "but I see your point."

"You asked, love," Christopher said. "How about spearheading some kind of neighborhood association that works in conjunction with the police. How about a neighborhood patrol."

"Yeah. We need security back there. Nothing is going to happen until the people feel safe. But where will the money come from? Where will the police come from?" the mayor said with increasing despondence. In his mind he saw only her, surrounded by a small troop of bikers. "It needs to be secure and cleaned up." *Why was she in uniform?*

Hey Boyfriend!
Yeah so like all things being what they are this is like, boom. Right? Happening. This is time for one of those will-like letters where I'd bequeath to you the pearl necklace my mother gave me and my collection of first edition novels, were such things to actually exist. Things are so tense here I run around quaking in my cowboy boots, no joke, and at any moment—not to cause any concern to himself, please, things are what they are and what they are is what they are—I might end up in a hole too deep for the shovels this life has equipped me with.
    But.
    But I feel like what I've begun to build here is like a dust devil that's begun to suck up its surroundings, and for each thing it devours it grows in size. At the edges of the periphery it hovers close to a house, equal-sized to itself. What will happen? They want to know. Is the house too stable a force? Or, instead, does the dust devil grow and devour, disassemble the house shingle by shingle, sucking it in, loosing nails from the sheathing, glass panes exploding outward, furniture pulling from the gaping maw and into the dervish. And again, the dust devil becomes more powerful. . . .
    No please, don't put the letter down, I can desist with the long drawn metaphors, serious, scout's honor! But what I'm saying is, things are starting to be the shit, here. And I've a captain-ish feller whom if he joins in, well then a tornado are we, with bells on.
    If he, the letter recipient, will remember how 100 thousand years ago she was losing a sense of what the hell she was even on the planet to do? So the narrator figured that shit out, ok? At least for the time being. It's in the sack. Packaged up, receipt dangling out, bought and sold.
    I hope this finds you well, good sir, who were he here his ____ she'd put in her mouth, until roofing nails & dust devils, etc. She

would, if he knows what she's saying, make it worth his while. & she does love to make his cheeks flush so by the saying of said things. But also listen here's the thing.

There's an aspect of this I don't know how to properly say without the way it's said sounding . . . off. I'll go ahead and say it, then you tell me how it sounds.

Actually no, let's take the weakling's offense and fall back on metaphors again: Imagine you're juggling a whole lot of balls. Cupcakes. Whatever is his fancy. A lot of them, more really than you've ever done before, by such a wide margin. At any one time there are what, four or fourteen or forty of them in the air, and only one, really only goddamnit ONE in your hand. There's only a single ball at rest in your hands at any given microsecond. That's the one you know. That's the one you can depend on. That's the one you can trust. All the rest of them are in their arcs, bent under the pressures of gravity or acceleration, liable to run into each other and go spinning off, their collisions a sort of betrayal to the juggler who has set them in motion.

Crystal clear now right? Dustdevils and balls, cocks and cupcakes. She's gone batty, he says, shakes his head, crumples the letter and tosses it in the trash.

A few minutes of pacing later he retrieves it, oh he does! And continues onward.

Hello Boyfriend!

But see what I'm saying here is: You're that ball in hand. Why are you not here, on-hand?

Balls!

—W/so/much/love: -r (MM)

Gregor sat on his raised wooden front porch in an old rocker and stared out into the neighborhood. There were many smells in the air—rot; the dry, stifling smell of dust, smoke from something that should not burn, a car perhaps. He did not flatter himself that he could, as the saying went, smell change, but there it was, clear on the air, an edge that insinuated a new front. It was an indefinable wisp, a whisper of something else in the decay of the drought. With the stem of the pipe he carried with him but did not smoke he tapped out a rhythm on the arm of the chair. Or perhaps, he thought, it was simply the perspective with which one inhaled. Not an external scent, but an internal revision.

He called to his man on the porch for a cup of tea, and the message was passed into the house. There was always someone with him. He was not without enemies, and he was not incautious.

It was probably too hot for tea, but the tiny cups—served in sake-like earthen mugs—hardly warmed one, and they helped him think.

Jamal had been with Maid Marian for a few weeks now, he'd learned. The converted. That was fine, the presence of Jamal would keep Gregor in her thoughts. Her organization grew every day, Jamal told him. A small army of fresh workers showed up at her house. Word of her spread across the neighborhoods. A day did not go by when he didn't hear at least one weirdly enthusiastic account of her. He still could not understand how she held sway over others—other than they so desperately needed someone to believe in. By all accounts she was doing what she had claimed she'd do, that day in his house, with a touch of insolence. Perhaps, he thought, tapping his pipe on the arm of his chair, he'd been hasty to dismiss her. But no.

How was she not yet in city hands? Did they think her too hot to handle? They must be willfully ignoring her, he thought, hoping her plan might fizzle into complicated community politics, or be overly burdened by the dull routine of survival. Perhaps they did not yet realize it was survival that birthed such plans. Perhaps they did not know about the truck.

It was a silly pot to throw in with. After all these years of running a successful business, he was comfortable and could obtain what he wanted, could provide for those he cared for. But if change were upon them, if she were going to challenge the city for the whole of the Northeast, then he would inevitably be involved, on one side or the other. It was a trap she'd laid for him. She was choosing a general, and it could either be him, or not him. A binary choice, and the implications of each spun out in terrifying fractals.

He sipped the tea and scratched at his beard with his pipe. There was no possible way he would be allowed to coexist with a power that bound all the neighborhoods together. Already her organization was many times the size of his, sprawling and absorbing.

Gregor watched as a bicyclist rounded the block at the corner and shot toward him. It was Jamal, riding at breakneck speed, as always. Jamal picked up the bike and leapt up the steps.

"Pop," he said and grinned. Jamal grabbed a rocker beside his father after he'd leaned his bike against the wall. He panted from the ride.

"Hey boy," Gregor said fondly. He'd enjoyed watching Jamal change over the course of the drought. He'd transformed from a softer, bookish early twenties to a ropey confidence over the last few years, so that Gregor, though he was loath to admit it to Jamal, would trust him with most anything. "News?"

Jamal shrugged and took a pull off his canteen. Gregor motioned for his man on the porch to bring another tea but Jamal stood and said he'd fix his own.

When he returned he'd regained his breathing and sat on a wooden chair with his small cup. "They're making an army."

Gregor eyed him. "You mean, you're making an army." That Jamal had fallen in with her organization so deeply was a troublesome bit. The trap she'd built for him was complex indeed.

"Yeah." Jamal gave him an elusive smile.

"Anybody we know?"

"A few familiar faces, but nobody that big yet."

"You. They've got you."

"Yes," Jamal said. "They have me."

Jamal turned and Gregor felt the boy search his face, his two steely drill-bit eyes aimed deep into his cerebrum. He could see what the look meant. Jamal had chosen a new leader and didn't know how dangerous it was for their relationship. He could see how the boy was hooked, how he'd always been a dreamer and an ideal-ist, that he'd done the family business only because he'd been born into it. Because there was the shared loss of the other half of their family, mother and brother, that kept the remaining father and son inseparable.

"Come on, Pop." Jamal turned away and watched the street. "Everything's changing, man."

Jamal sipped his tea and watched a couple of guys push a bur-dened shopping cart with a stuck wheel down the street. Their bodies bent at severe angles behind in order to push. They knew better than to come calling at Gregor's house. "They're talking about things like farms and schools."

"Farms," Gregor said and smiled, the word felt like some relic from the past and flooded him with nostalgia. They hadn't dared leave the city for more than a year, but there were no more farms out there. No fields of apple trees, no vineyards, no peaches. He'd taken Jamal and his brother to the U-Pick strawberry farms when they were children. The whole memory floated intact and unreal in him as if a dream. He'd been high, of course, but still it was one of the few times in his memory he was proud of his parenting. They'd settled into a sort of comfortable rhythm for an afternoon, the three of them on their knees eating strawberries straight off the bushes, not bothering to save any to their baskets, their hands covered in juice, the berries giving them a prolonged closeness. Last he remembered, there'd been a series of water rights uprisings as farms died. A lot of blood was spilled. "And the city?"

"They tried one raid before I got there. Nothing else. They either don't know or feel like it's too risky with the status she's built. Her people disappear her when they need to."

"Hm," Gregor said.

"It means a lot to me, Pop."

A Hispanic boy of eleven or twelve approached and Gregor's guard intercepted him.

"I'm here for Pedro," he squealed, as the guard blocked his way.

"Where's Pedro?" Gregor said.

"Pedro's dead," the boy said.

"Let him by," Gregor said. "Explain your story quickly, boy."

Jamal closed his eyes and sank into his chair and felt sick of the whole thing. Every last needy fucking user, the rampant stupidity of the entire network. It was a different kind of power that Maid Marian wielded, and he found himself pulled toward it, his thoughts like iron filings toward a magnet.

After the boy had left they were quiet. Jamal hadn't heard every word but could sense his father's anger. Something about an altercation between Pedro, a runner, and a user, and then Pedro's son showing up to support the family in his stead. Depressing, but a gratingly boring story for its redundancy. Each of these incidents riled Gregor—he liked smoothly functioning machinery, a system at peace with itself—but to Jamal, it was the same inevitable incident occurring over and over.

"Pop?"

"Don't. I know what you're going to say," Gregor said. The problem with Jamal, Gregor thought, is that he believes things really change.

He believes that it really is an end-time, an end-time that allows for the reinvention of everything. A whirl of dust and debris blew down the street in front of them. And so: Was it? Would his inability to see that change break him in the end?

He pondered bringing up the water truck heist, about which they'd fought virulently. The boy was going to get himself killed, and that was one reason to ponder things. Somehow they'd pulled it off, despite a half-baked plan. She was wealthy now.

"It's time to decide," Jamal said.

"No, not yet."

"Shit or get off the pot."

"There's time still."

Jamal finished his tea and leaned his head back against the house. "No," he said firmly. "There's no more time."

Renee sat on the floor of her room with Bea across from her. They'd found a cribbage board and cards and had been dealing games since. It felt good to have the distraction, and they played in a giddy, amped manner, calling out their wins and smack-talking each other.

Bea looked good to her, sitting cross-legged with a fan of cards on her knee. She was backlit and her hair shown a golden-red on her head, the freckles across her face like a paint-spraying of summer.

In here, they were safe, and the world she'd spun into motion moved outside the door without her.

"Fifteen for two, fifteen for six, and a pair makes eight, *sucker*," Bea said.

Renee dealt out the cards and thought about going to the tower to talk to Zach. She needed someone with whom she could strategize. There were those who trusted what you did, and those who followed blindly, and those who made suggestions, but with Josh gone she didn't feel like she had anyone scheming on the same level, arguing and contradicting her. Could Gregor? she wondered. She had made a fool of herself in front of him, she thought, she had over-extended and squandered the opportunity for a genuine ally. She reached into her pocket and fingered the green laser there.

"You put down the crib?"

"Sorry?" Renee said.

"Dude."

There was a knock at the door and they stared at each other for a brief moment before Renee yelled come in. It was Jamal. Renee invited him to come sit with them.

"Cribbage," he said.

"You should take my spot," Renee said.

"She's thinking about your dad," Bea said.

Jamal nodded. He opened and closed the palm that held his list of things-to-do, permanent-markered there in black. At the top was: *Pop.*

"Chances?" Renee said.

Jamal shrugged. "I worked on him, and . . . I'll keep working on him."

"We don't have much time," Renee said and stared at her cards, confused as to where she'd left off with the game. "We're getting noticed. We've got a tank of water burning holes in our backyard. I need to make a decision. If Gregor isn't going to do it, it's got to be someone else. Link, Martin, Salzar, Charles." She shrugged. "I haven't decided who's next." They were not, the rest of them, a basket of Easter eggs from which any choice might be pretty, more like deer droppings, or worse. She needed someone with a deep history here, a wisdom and influence. There was just the one that might work, and the rest she wasn't sure she should bother with.

Jamal nodded. Hearing those names brought a flush of heat to his face. If any of them did come in, there would be some talking to do. He wondered if he could fight against his own father. But he'd made his choice. You could not make an allegiance to a family-run drug trade. There was no idea there, there was nothing to swear to. He balled his fist, closing the to-do list from view. "How much time?"

"Twenty-four hours," Renee said.

"Is anyone even playing?" Bea said.

"I'll play. I'll totally play," Jamal said.

Renee handed him her cards. "I'm lost here, you take mine."

"I warn you, no one's more lucky," Jamal said.

Renee swallowed hard at this as she made way for him. She had firsthand proof of Jamal's luckiness.

"And also, I cheat." He shrugged as if that were just the way things were.

Renee lay back on the cot and listened to the two play and decided to give herself two minutes there. After the recruitment of a strong arm, the number and scope of items that had to be done was dizzy-ing. *Lieutenants,* she said to herself, the word arising up from some Napoleonic history lesson, conjuring up someone who might wear tassels on his suit coat and carry a saber and wear a handlebar mus-tache, which Bea would look nice with. She chuckled at the thought and could hear the two of them pause to look over at her. The smell of their unwashed bodies was rank in the room. *Lieutenants* playing cribbage. She loved them, and loved listening to their game banter, manifesting in counting and cursing at each other: *fifteen two fifteen four a run for three makes seven. And the crib—fuck. really? fuck—that's right, for fourteen.* Lieutenants she had put in terrible danger and was on the verge of doing again, digging their hole deeper, and this sobered her so that her muscles locked in place, frozen, with her breath held. *She* was the one playing the game, the one pushing the all-in bet into the middle of the table, gambling them like chips.

Gregor decided to go there himself. If you were going to do this sort of thing, you didn't call her to you. He knew that. For the first time in a long time, the roles were reversed.

He didn't leave the house much anymore and felt odd preparing himself for the out-of-doors. He sent people scurrying about in front of him: prepare his bike, find his clothes, tell her he's coming.

When he was finally on his bike in the front yard he looked up at the neighboring houses, trying to remember which unfortunate interactions he'd had with each. Which were his allies, which not. He felt a sort of mortification. Like a man raised from his tomb into a different time, blinking into the sun. Gone soft and dead in the inter-minable years.

He wore the eight men who accompanied him him like a suit of armor as he rode, a Roman phalanx of pedalers. He could have fired up the Cadillac, but it was so out of repair at this point, and carried so few. Nor did it seem appropriate for the task at hand, somehow.

He was not an indecisive man, not by any stretch of the imagina-tion, and so it was startling to have his mind offer up alternatives and second-opinions and double-thinks as he rode, nearly bringing him to the point of steering the whole damn column of them back home. But he persisted, as all men of firm opinions do, for even as his mind faltered, it bolstered itself too, fortified and re-fortified, shooting justifications like warning shots across the bow, so that he glared straight forward and pedaled without speaking, bent on their destination. He had not been under anyone else's employ for some time. More than anything it took courage, he was coming to find.

Jamal, who rode to his right, thought the woman was destined to do what she set out to do. And that was one quandary he'd swept around his mind. If she *were* to succeed, there would be a persuasion necessary for anyone—anyone with power—not affiliated. And he knew, he was now destined to be that persuader.

People on the street knew him. They stopped what they were doing and stared with wide eyes as the entourage passed. Some feared him. Some knew him as the grandfatherly Pop who rolled in with charitable funds. It was possible that she already had someone. That they might already be heading into some sort of confrontation. But no, Jamal had assured him.

As he pedaled he found his legs still had strength. Though on each upward pedal his knee bumped against his belly, his hands gripped the handlebars with, he imagined, his old bear's strength, a power natural to him, that age could not drain away. Perhaps he was not so old as he thought. He began to set the pace and drove his entourage forward.

The state of the streets saddened him, their previous vibrancy now thwarted and twisted by poverty, fire, and crime. What part had he had in this, he wondered. They passed a house that belonged to an old girlfriend of his, a tryst he'd had behind his wife's back. She'd had the smoothest skin he'd ever known. The house was a small two-story built in the nineteen-teens. The porch leaned sadly, on the verge of collapse. All that was left of the windows were a few shards of glass. It was clear she did not live there anymore, that most likely she was dead, and this caused his chest to quake as he rode. Why had he not reached out? It wasn't only the boy's prodding. He was doing the right thing. He knew he was.

They stopped at the end of the block, the headquarters just up the street. He caught his breath and watched people come and go. Bicycles streamed from her HQ at regular intervals, and people walked with purpose to outbuildings and neighboring houses that her organization must have gobbled up like a hungry wolf.

"Well," he said.

"Let's go, Pop," Jamal said. "I know where she'll be."

"We'll walk," Gregor said and dismounted from his bike. He would have preferred to have done this over tea, at his house. For not the first time that week he considered his desire for predictable patterns and routine. He had not always been this way. It is age that has brought it on, he thought, and here I am beginning entirely anew, beating back these habits with new, radical risks. He cursed quietly and briefly fantasized about turning the whole ship of them around again. What a relief it would be to re-enter his house, sit in his chair, await the next visitor, to ignore whatever impending chaos may come. But within him, at the very bottom of him, buried by time and loss and cynicism, was the seed of something whose existence he scarcely admitted to himself. She might pull this off. What she wanted, what Jamal wanted, was what he wanted. To separate from the whole rotten mass of the country, to carve the one good bite out of the rotten apple, to be free of their flags and rocket ships, their posturing and ignorance. Fuck them all. They could do better. He waved a *charge!* signal to Jamal, and they followed him into the compound.

Bea stood guard outside of Renee's office for nearly six hours as Gregor and Renee hammered out their agreement inside. At times the volume rose to a shout, and she winced, desiring to go in and kick the old fart out. She stood at least four inches over him, and she thought she could take him. She would be the panther against his bear. Go for the eyes, she told herself, punch his neck. He would be slow, but could take a lot of damage.

It was times like these when she fetched water. She held the glasses in her hand for a moment, facing the door, listening to the muted shouting from within. She knew why he had to join—they would be the mother and father of Sherwood, the good cop and bad cop, the leader and the enforcer. They would be parents to the hundreds that now worked for the organization. But Bea didn't have to like it. She waited until the right cadence in the argument, a moment she could not help but interrupt, just as a child might try to dispel a squabble between her own mother and father. Then she bustled in, as innocently and yet as noisily as possible, setting the first glass down in front of Renee. It wasn't until Bea had already turned away and was placing a glass down in front of Gregor's spot that she realized Renee had winked at her, and this made Bea happy. She amused herself with the thought that *mother must be winning this one.*

 Gregor paced and Bea asked if they needed anything else. He looked tired to her, exhausted even, as he hobbled stiffly back and forth across the room. For a brief moment she felt sorry for him, remembering how aggravatingly stubborn and strong-willed Renee could be.

Then she pictured his body as a crash-test dummy, and her karate chopping it, and felt better and left them to their work.

As she stood guard, Jamal dropped by and listened at the door.

"And?" he said. He rocked with agitation from foot to foot.

Bea shrugged. "They're yelling a lot."

"It'll work," he said. "If it doesn't, I'm counting on you, babe. Put them in a half-nelson, whatever it takes. Right?"

"I don't know," Bea said.

"It'll work," he said. "He wants this, she needs him. It'll work. But I can't stay to find out, it's fucking up my nerves." Jamal tapped her shoulder twice with his fist and left.

An hour later when she came back in to clear glasses and see if anything was needed, Gregor appeared to be telling a joke.

"A robber breaks into a house, right? It's at night. He sneaks his way upstairs to where they're sleeping. He points his gun at the couple in their bed. And he says, 'I'm going to kill you. I'm going to kill you both. But first I have to know your names, I don't kill anyone without knowing their name.' He puts the gun to the woman's head and says 'Tell me your name!'"

Bea involuntarily clutched the front of her shirt and wondered if some elaborate metaphorical threat were being made. She looked at Renee, who wore the expression of someone being told a joke, expectant and skeptical.

"She's half-dead with fright already, but she says 'My name is Marguerite.'"

"'Oh no,' the robber says, 'oh no! *Goddamnit.* That's my mother's name.' He's seriously put out here. 'I can't kill someone with the same name as my mom.'"

Gregor paused in his telling to take a swallow of water. Then he took his right hand, which clutched an unlit smoking pipe, and jabbed the pipe stem like a gun barrel toward an imaginary man's head.

"'How about you,' the robber says."

"The man is shaking, his teeth are chattering. 'My name is Eddy, but-but my friends all call me Marguerite.'"

Renee guffawed once and Bea felt weak, and like she had to get out of the room immediately. As she collected glasses and fled, she heard Renee say, "Exactly. See? Exactly."

At last they exited Renee's office together. Gregor had his arm across Renee's shoulders and to Bea it looked strange there, a powerful brown arm, Maid Marian and the local mafia. But as they chatted she watched them. If you didn't know who they were, she thought, you might consider them workers in a community center, or perhaps a government agency, co-workers posing for a photo.

"Tomorrow then?" Renee said.

Gregor pulled away and slapped his hand against a sheaf of handwritten paper. "Tomorrow we build," he said, and then he pointed his pipe stem at Bea, as if to say *you heard it here first*, or *be there or be square*, or *as the romans do*, or *you're tall, girl*, or some other pointless expression she was sure he'd intended.

When he was gone, Bea asked what'd happened. She saw Renee's eyes glow like close planets, each a shade different than the other, a trick of light perhaps.

Renee hugged her. "It went so much better than expected. He's perfect. An enterprise needs a partner."

Over several grueling days, Jamal, Gregor, and Bea interviewed every single volunteer that had showed up at Maid Marian's house on Going Street. The number had swelled to over three hundred. They listened to them explain why they wanted to be a Ranger, wrote down their experiences and skills, and put them through aptitude tests. Forty were singled out.

And this, too, Gregor and Renee argued about. Just as they had for the last three days about every detail that crossed their mutual paths, discovering in whose hands the power lay. They argued about the style of the uniforms being made, about how this new security force would be armed, about where water went or who would be put in charge, about how to deal with every other person of power in the neighborhood.

On the night of the second day of argument Renee realized she'd made a horrible mistake. A man who has spent his life in control cannot cede control to others. She should have raised someone else into

the role, made Jamal her general, perhaps, or not him either, forget
the whole family. She could not go to sleep. Under her covers she
shook with rage and wished she were done with the whole affair. It
was a stupid idea. Zach was an idiot, Gregor was nothing but a criminal. But Josh, she thought, thinking of his body in the grave in the
backyard, could have helped, or was she romanticizing the dead now?
Bea snored like a bear and she felt rage at her too. "Bea," she called out.
She stretched her foot across her mattress and onto Bea's and gave a
kick that woke her friend.

"Come on," Renee said, deciding in that instant what she must do.
She gave another kick. "Follow me."

Gregor had been sleeping in his office at HQ, sending his men to
his home for supplies. It was here that Renee went. She knocked at
the door with a hard, angry rap and the sound echoed down the quiet
hallway. She brushed her hair from her face and prepared to charge in.
She'd tell him what she thought of him. Tell him it was over.

When a sound came from inside she threw the door wide. He was
not in his bed. The bed was not even there, but stored still in the closet
where it spent the day. He was sitting behind his desk, fully dressed,
his pipe hand poised to tap. She wondered if he'd been sleeping at all.

He waved her in. Just you, he told her, signaling Bea should wait
outside, and Renee nodded her assent.

"I know why you're here," he told her. He lit a candle on his desk
with a match and signaled that she sit in the chair across from him.
He smiled at her then, a charming smile so devoid of anger it sapped
some of hers. He stroked at his beard, gray and black, and cut sporadi-
cally, she supposed, with scissors. The candle caught his eyes so that
they reflected the light, they glowed a reddish brown.

"Listen, I know why you're here," he said again. "I'm frustrated
too, but I've been thinking about it non-stop."

Renee swallowed and nodded. She felt like standing, and then did
so, pacing back and forth in front of the desk with her hand on her
mouth, her other gripping her elbow.

He stood and pointed at her with his pipe. "You're in charge," he
said. "I do not wish to run this."

She nodded again and felt how close they'd been to the edge of
it, and for a moment her intense desire to eject him from her house
reversed entirely, so that she suddenly wanted to embrace him, to
thank him for saving them both with his moment of graciousness.

"Look," he said, and pointed to the wall where a uniform was hung, in the exact style she had specified. It was beautiful and she loved it.

She knew what to do then. "I'll write us a contract," she said. "A document meant for you and me. The assurances I can make, what you and I each decide, everything. In the morning, we'll discuss and finalize it. Agreed?"

He nodded his head, tapping the stem of his pipe into his palm. "Yes. Do that." He smiled again and she realized that she had to make it work, that the relationship was hers to make or destroy.

The chosen forty would be specially trained and put in Jamal's charge. They would carry weapons. Several were assigned to Maid Marian guard duty—others would be a special task force for crime prevention, border protection, or to train other rangers.

The feeling of his new command exhilarated Jamal and made him—against all expectations—more afraid.

At night as he lay in bed a wash of fear would rise up through him, as if the ground had suddenly fallen away beneath him. With a conscious effort he'd try to get to the root of it. Of all the fears: the fear of going hungry or thirsty, of living like an outlaw, of command and responsibility, of his father, fears from the past—that sickening and thrilling fear when you've been ordered to kill someone, buried nonsensical fears, their origins deep in his childhood, it was the fear around his Going Street Brigade that caused him the most concern. It was like owning a giant cannon, he thought. At first you felt safe, protected by the giant, manly monstrosity, and then, because of that weapon, you knew you were seen, and the necessity to live up to the object's potential overwhelmed. At some point you would have to level its awesome firepower at something, and whatever you fired at would fire back.

He wondered if his father had ever experienced this. Perhaps this is what caused him to go to war in the first place. The simple ownership of soldiers necessitating their violent use.

In the mornings, he stood in front of them in the back field, training. They were always training, he thought, and it was his doing, his to control. He worried they would not be ready.

He was comfortable in front of them—he'd led the small gang of his father's in King neighborhood. In the Going Street Brigade there were twenty-eight men and twelve women, and nearly every one had more combat experience than he had. They'd fought in wars or had martial arts training or boxing or had been in a gang. One of the women had been a city cop, and it had been a difficult decision to bring her on. She lived nearby and the allure of Maid Marian and disgust with the city had pulled her from the force.

The newly formed Going Street Brigade ranged in age from twenty-four to sixty. The sixty-year-old, a man named Hugh, was slower and out of shape, and Jamal worked at him, curious to figure out what he was capable of.

"He's not an old man, Jamal," his father said. "I'm sixty four."

"Well," Jamal said and shrugged. "Join the elite force then."

"No," Gregor scoffed, "I hear it's run by some kid."

"A kid wonder."

"Mm. Kid blunder maybe."

"Yeah. Thanks, Pop. We'll be out here at six a.m., you old shit, if you can handle it."

"I could handle it."

"Yeah?" Jamal raised an eyebrow in challenge.

Gregor dropped the bundle of papers he held with a slap on his desk. "I've got real work to do here, son. Why don't you go play with your pals."

"Will do," Jamal said, and backed from the room, his arms flapping like that of a chicken. "Bawk, bawk."

Hugh, the sixty-year-old, had fought in two wars by the time he was twenty-six, both times against guerrilla forces in urban environments. Jamal prayed like hell they weren't preparing them for a war, but the man knew what he was doing. He had skills they needed. After the wars, Hugh had spent thirty years as a high-school chemistry teacher.

"You sure you want to be in the combat unit?" Jamal asked him in private. "I don't want to step on any toes, but we could definitely find you a different job."

"Yes sir," Hugh said. His face was hard and set but his eyes were complex, tree rings, Jamal thought, layers of previous wars and a new war. He was shorter, and his shoulders were big and hunched, his head sticking above like a turtle's from its shell.

Jamal thought of how he must have disciplined his students with chemical equations and repressed a shudder.

Hugh saluted, the motion brisk and all elbow. His fingers a poised karate strike against his cheek.

Not being from a military background, it amused him to see how they each showed respect for their superiors from whatever experience they had. Many soldiers fell into the comfort of military protocol, but others—say Preston, a big kid with hair scissor-cut to the scalp and a ring of tattoos around his neck, a black belt in Aikido and a fondness for practical jokes, bowed comically to Jamal. In some cases, Jamal enforced a formality, in others he was lenient. When bowed to, he bowed back.

Ten years back, when he was eighteen, Jamal had gotten his first action in the war between drug houses. Another dealer had tried taking over the east side of Gregor's territory and six of them had been sent to scare the other dealer off. Only Jamal and one other came back that day. They'd underestimated, and by the end of the month half of all of Gregor's crew had been killed, including his older brother. The neighborhood shuttered themselves in and locked their doors and the police cruised the streets in their cars, too afraid to set foot on a blacktop painted with blood.

To Jamal's surprise, Gregor showed up for six a.m. training wearing ugly teal sweat pants and a T-shirt, fitted tight over the Liberty Bell of his belly. Jamal could feel his troops tense. Those who had military training stood at attention, and the others followed. Here was their general, in his gaudy glory. Jamal wondered what his father was trying to get at.

"Sir," Jamal said, "do you think we could talk in private for a moment?"

Gregor trotted toward the back of the lineup, "No, I do not."

"But—"

"Proceed!" Gregor said over the heads of the Going Street Rangers. "Some asshole called me 'old' yesterday." There was nervous laughter among the troops.

"Pop . . ."

When Gregor was properly in formation, he saluted and waited stoically.

"All right. All right, people. Let's do this," Jamal said.

The mayor was home, finally, from a day that would not end, a series of meetings strung together like purgatory popcorn necklaces. The day had given him headaches that piled on top of each other, stood on each other's shoulders, achieving what before it no other headache had achieved. Mayor Brandon Bartlett limped to the sofa and slumped into it and did not move.

"Hard day, love?"

"Nnh."

"Sorry."

The mayor heard Christopher's progress about the room but could not be bothered to open his eyes, even as the footsteps approached.

"Fancy a diversion, then?"

The mayor opened one eye and observed Christopher's hand holding a slim, hand-rolled cigarette. "Is that?"

Christopher bit his bottom lip and nodded yes, his eyebrows raised.

"Yes," the mayor said. "Really?"

"Really."

The mayor stood up and pumped one elbow behind him. "Oh my god, yes. How in the hell?"

"He has his ways." Christopher shrugged. "He can get, when he wants."

"He is a savior is what."

"To the balcony, monsieur?"

"After you, my friend."

Like two high-schoolers, the mayor thought, with their hands cupped over the flame, a dusty wind scraping into the fourth-floor balcony. With the first inhale he had a coughing fit and could not stop, but it was a gleeful, barking cough, his lungs burning and the taste in his mouth pleasant. With his nose he chased the wispy trail of secondhand smoke, vacuuming it up, which made Christopher laugh.

When it was finished they watched a deep red lava-bubble where the sun descended from the sky. The mayor leaned into the concrete edge of the balcony and watched, looking over his city as its gray haze transformed first into a dusty golden cityscape, and then an umber quilt. He still loved it, right? The place he governed, and the job itself?

Pretty much, he thought. *Yeah.*

"There's this woman—" the mayor said and stopped. He could picture her face as if it were there in front of him. He closed his eyes and saw her, dressed inevitably in head-to-toe blue, blue blouse and blue jeans, or a long blue jeans dress, with eyebrows as if made of cat fur, long curly brown hair, a shade of lipstick that never seemed right—too brown or too pale. She and her husband manifested everywhere he went now. He, the husband, gray-haired and short, covered himself almost entirely in political bumper stickers and the mayor wondered at the mechanics of that. His whole body a collage of protest snippets. Was it the same outfit, or did the man have an unlimited supply? They were his heckling regulars, the oddball standouts in every crowd of impassioned protestors. The husband always the first to lead a cheer of *Heartless Bartlett*, or to call out in opposition to any bland thing he might take a stance on. But her: She never said anything. She simply watched him, and when he met her eyes, she smiled. Weirdly, he'd come to think of her as who he most wanted to please. The protester's wife, less shrill and more dedicated, dressed in blue; expectant. Waiting for him to do right. Perhaps she was his biggest fan, and her husband his most fervent detractor, the mayoral office the dividing battle line they'd chosen in their marriage. He wondered about sending an emissary right now out into the city to find her and bring her here. It would be nice for them to sit across the table from each other and she could smile at him, with her small mouth and big cat eyebrows. *Constituent*, he could say, *Leader*, she would reply. They would shake hands. On a piece of paper he would draw up all of his plans for her, they'd sprawl across it like mathematical equations that she would find brilliant. He would make changes for her, listen to her reasoned advice. Then . . .

Oh I am so stoned, he realized suddenly. He looked into the distance and smiled. For a moment, looking out over the darkening city he felt like embracing it, a man lonely on a platform, ready to hug the thing he stewarded. For that was what he was: janitor, nursemaid, protective father. It seemed entirely unfair that he was of mortal stature. He should be a hundred feet high, with a skyscraper-sized broom for housekeeping duties. He would walk the streets with great footfalls, *bom bom bom*, sweeping it free of drought detritus, sweep right into the Northeast where he could feel them plotting against him. Big dust blooms blowing out in front of his broom.

"You OK there?" Christopher said.

"Me? Hey, yes," the mayor said. He reached out and grabbed Christopher's hand and smiled. "Hell yes."

Somewhat later they went to bed and had sex and then in the dim moonlight lay on their backs, their eyes wide open, staring upward.

After a long period of post-coital contentment and silence, they had one more conversation that went something like:

Mayor: Mmbop.

Christopher: Beep beep.

Mayor: Mmbop.

(long silence)

Mayor: Please sir, may I go to sleep now?

Christopher: Are you talking to me?

Mayor: (Laughing.)

Mayor: I think I was talking to my brain.

Christopher: (laughing)

Mayor: Unless you're the one making it so noisy in my head I can't go to sleep.

Christopher: Me? (gasps, laughter relapse)

Christopher (finally): No, I'm looking at the walrus. It won't let me go to sleep either.

Mayor: Walrus?

Christopher: In the paint up there? I thought you knew about the walrus.

Mayor: Oh my god. Oh my god.

Christopher: Right?

Mayor: There's totally a walrus there.

Christopher: Every night, it watches us.

Mayor: Creepy.

(silence)

Mayor: Should I do something? About it?

Christopher: (chuckling, turning sideways into the mayor) No, he's OK. He watches over us.

Mayor: Could cover it up? Tape something?

Christopher: Mmm, no.

Rumor spread that water rations would be cut in half, and the rumor was posed as a question on the news. As dusk neared and the power went out, neighbors reeled from their houses, disoriented with outrage and thirst. They banded into menacing groups, full of rage and looking for something to blame. They were quick to argue and fight, bloodying themselves, and Gregor knew they would destroy each other for lack of a proper target. The only means they had, he thought as he watched the infectious violence roil down his street, was to destroy what was theirs. He checked his pistol again and spat out into the dust in his yard.

No riot would come to his porch. He would stay there to make sure of that. But he had a different task for Jamal. He put his hand on the head of his first born and mouthed quietly the closest thing to a prayer he could bring himself to say, and then pushed him toward the stairs to do his work.

Jamal grabbed his bicycle from the porch and carried it down to the street. He checked his watch. There were others, and they had to be in synch. Then he rode into the waning light. "Maid Marian is in jail!" he yelled out, his voice a hoarse wail that rattled into other people's houses. "They got Maid Marian at Killingsworth station!"

The Killingsworth station was the last, closest bastion of city forces. A small police station that mostly drove their cars toward the wealthier neighborhoods west of Martin Luther King Blvd.

The effect was immediate. He watched people sway as if from a blow, and then spring back, changed by the news. Rioters spilled from their own neighborhoods toward the Killingsworth station, the rage making the target only a general aim as the wave of them burned cars and ransacked houses en route.

A single squad car was swept up into the action. A cameraman intrepidly tagged along and filmed. The following morning on the news, after a severe warning about the nature of the content, the film was played in its entirety:

A policeman exits his car and strides into the rioters with a pistol in each hand. On his face there's a grim look, but pleasure perhaps, the sense that this is the moment he's been waiting for. He places his feet wide apart like a gunslinger. Around him is a scene of complete chaos—hundreds of people, a mixture of all races, but mostly black or Hispanic, breaking the windows of cars, exiting houses with whatever can be carried—water, food, TVs, stereos, furniture.

On the porch of one house a man is in a wrestling death-grip with another who appears to be stealing his unit gallon. The policeman nears the porch, puts his arm through the railing and shoots. The owner falls, the back of his head suddenly difficult to distinguish. There's an audible "Jesus Christ!" from the cameraman and the camera temporarily loses focus and control and during this moment there's a second bang of a gun. When the camera stabilizes, both men lie dead on the porch, the unit gallon resting between them.

The camera follows the policeman for a few beats more, wielding both pistols, shooting—sometimes at point-blank range. At one point the policeman turns back to look into the lens of the camera and smiles, much as the baker smiles as he watches his customers take the first bite of his best bread, as if to say, are you getting how good this is? Do you not see the rightness of what I'm doing? He kills a few more before a mob storms over the top of him. The camera angle jumps around, its angle upside down, the scene in rapid retreat as the cameraman flees for his life.

Police fanned across the city to quell the violence. Sixteen officers came to the defense of the Peninsula neighborhood, the upscale neighborhood across Martin Luther King Boulevard from the riot—they stationed themselves four to a squad car at strategic locations, hoping to contain what they could not stop and ready to flee. The National Guard did not show up, and this absence remained an unanswered question posed on the news. The police shot the occasional canister of tear gas into densely packed areas or to seal off a route. Until the riot simply burned itself out. No one came to the defense of the poorer neighboring King and Vernon neighborhoods; they were left for dead.

When the video of the lone policeman made it to the news and was played repeatedly in a hypnotic loop, the city turned upside down. The policeman was not found, presumed dead. That there was no longer anyone on whom to take revenge for such heinous brutality only fueled more destruction.

Indignation swelled all over the city. Inquiries and resignations were demanded. Marches were held with signs bearing the image of Maid Marian, or with the text *Free Maid Marian*, or *Down with the Sheriff of Nottingham* and a photo of the mayor's face or the police chief's.

More film footage aired. The few still sitting in their chairs rose up, went to their front porches, felt themselves getting swept into the one angry mind of the city. They were angry at the mayor, at the police, at the rioters, and perhaps more than anything, they were angry at each other.

The following day, the news anchors started by saying they had something very big to announce. They showed a still image of Maid Marian, as she was at the first water heist. Along the bottom of the screen it said: "Pre-recorded tape received from Maid Marian today."

In the first few seconds as she waited to begin, she stared slightly to the left of the camera and smiled, a little awkwardly, toward whomever she was with. She was dressed in a dark green collared shirt. Her black hair was braided into two long braids that lay across the front of her shirt, giving her a touch of a darker-skinned, and somewhat militaristic, Pippi Longstocking. The daughter of Fidel Castro and Pippi, perhaps, pretty and strong-willed. A black and green patch on her pocket bore an insignia of a long bow leaning against a unit gallon. There was a sparkling of wit in her eyes, giving one the impression that a joke had been made off camera. She certainly did not look captured by the city, as they had been led to believe. She was changed from the image of her they held in their minds. And in the briefest moments before she started speaking they all tried to reconcile the difference between the woman on the television with the one that was burned into their minds, handing out water. Before there had been a sort of otherworldliness to her. A divine, selfless creature come to save them from their pain. On her brow they saw the healing scar of that incident. Now, though, she gave them a smile. They could clearly see the edge of firmness to her, the unsettling sense of control and purpose. It gave them pause, and in living rooms across the city there was quiet as they waited, held by a tiny clutch of fear as they wondered if they were on the verge of losing the hero they had in their hearts. Would she tell them to behave? they wondered. Were they being chastised for the unrest?

"Ready?" she said to the person off-camera.

"Hello, Portlanders," she said and nodded her head toward them, and they felt how her voice had a pull on them, how their hearts lightened with hope as she spoke. "I would like to take this opportunity to invite you to meet my merry men and women." She smiled, acknowledging the wordplay. They had given her the name and she had used it. The camera panned to the side of her and faced a window. Beyond in a large brown field standing very still was a large formation of men and women in the same green uniform. There were easily hundreds of them, and the camera panned slowly across their length. "They are called Green Rangers," she said. Behind the formation there was another mass of uniformed people, each standing straight with one hand resting on his or her bicycle.

The faces of the rangers were not those you would see on a military lineup. Their ages spanned fifty years. They looked up toward the camera and blinked, dressed, as if taken by surprise, in their new uniforms, obviously sewn together from what material could be found. Their faces were not the cold, obedient faces of some nation's army, but appeared as if they'd just that moment stopped speaking, their heads tilted upward in hopeful anxiety toward Maid Marian's vantage; some smiled and one or two waved. They were mixed racially, reflecting the neighborhoods from which they came, and this certainly gave the TV viewer pause. In a mostly white city, the riot footage had mostly been of a similar racial mixture as this new, sudden army.

"Together, we are a new country. From Fremont Street to Columbia Boulevard, Martin Luther King to 205—if you live within those borders you are now a citizen of a new tiny nation called Sherwood." She paused and the camera panned back to her.

"Mayor Bartlett, I am taking your greatest problem from you, freeing you to care for the rest of the city. We are within your borders, and will respect the essence of the law. We are your good neighbors. Give us what is ours: the U.S. government water trucks may enter by their usual routes, but we will manage distribution. We will pay for our services, but no city police or worker may enter our borders without our permission. We free them of their duties here to attend to the rest of the city, where, I'm sure all will agree, they are needed."

"And to Northeast Portland—Sherwood"—she held up a small, clear glass of drinking water—"let us share water together. We will keep you safe and healthy. We will make sure that what water and food we have is distributed fairly and quickly. We are your government, and we will not fail.

"To those on the streets tonight, or with friends and family on the street, I urge you to go home. See your families. Be with the ones you love. This is your country now. Tomorrow we work. Tomorrow we build. Tomorrow is ours.

"To the rest of Portland, I invite you to consider Sherwood. Doctors and naturopaths, farmers and bikers, scientists and artists, we'll consider everyone. Come live in a new country. Your water will be delivered to your home. Your streets will be safe. Your children will go to school.

"Reporters and newscasters—you are welcome to come see us. Please do. Your press pass is your open passport to Sherwood."

"Sherwood is now a country within a city, an enclave. Our primary immigration office is at Ainsworth and Martin Luther King Boulevard. Please come visit us. Thank you."

The tape ended and the pretty blond newscaster came back on. "That was a recording from the so-called Maid Marian, sent to us earlier today. She's leading an effort to have Northeast Portland secede from the city. Is this heroism or terrorism? Robert, what are your thoughts on that?"

The view switched to a male newscaster. He waved the camera away, but in the briefest glimpse of him the TV viewers saw that he was visibly shaken, tears welling in his eyes.

Zach watched the news with his mouth open, his body in a state of semi-shock. It was really happening. At the top right corner of the screen they had placed a still shot of his girlfriend's face in a green uniform, below it the map of the new territory.

The news anchors scrambled to find pundits who could intelligently talk on the happenings. All other news stories were cast aside and all of the city sat in front of their televisions listening with hunger for anything the news could tell them, to help them make sense.

An older, weathered newscaster spoke: "As far as I know this is unprecedented in our history as a nation. The city will feel compelled to intervene. Whether they can afford the resources is another matter entirely." The newscaster paused and stared into the camera, unsure of his ability to predict any next outcome, and Zach could see him struggle to come up with something else to say. "Marcie?" he said and looked off-stage, "can we get a response from the city yet? No? Maid Marian is a popular figure and I think the level of her popularity is indicated by what's going on in the Northeast right now. The Sherwood Club that preceded this, as many of you may not know, was already providing security for a large section of that area, and so many of the people who live there might have a good sense of what they're getting. We're told the announcement has served to quell the violence almost entirely. That's something the city obviously couldn't do. James, how about we get a view of that?"

The view switched to a silent, darkened neighborhood presumably in the Northeast somewhere. "Not much to see there. Half an hour ago? An hour? This was complete chaos. There were looters and gunfire and massive property damage. You can see by this serene view that everyone must be inside, pondering Maid Marian's message and, we presume, the prospect of their new citizenship."

Zach scoffed with annoyance at the broadcast. The news had gone increasingly toward an on-the-fly, seat-of-the-pants production style, as if every event happened exactly at the time of air time and they were lucky enough to find a camera in their hands. It made the news feel sudden and amateur. Though partly driven by a lack of resources, it was obviously stylistic.

"OK, we've got Professor Marylin Carvat here and she's going to give us a history of secessions in America. Marylin? What can you tell us about other neighborhood secessions?"

"There haven't been any, Robert. We've got South Carolina, which seceded after Lincoln was elected. But that was by vote of their state congress. Which of those citizens living in Northeast Portland voted on a secession? Which of them had a choice? See, I'm not sure this is secession—it's more akin to an invasion, technically."

Along the bottom of the screen the word INVASION showed, in red with a line circling it, the font-style of a rubber stamp.

"But they live there already!" Zach yelled.

"An invasion," Robert said, and Zach could see the word was distasteful in his mouth. "But she has stopped the fighting instead of starting it, and the invaders do not normally provide a suite of services. You saw what those neighborhoods look like now?"

"Yes, and by what armed power did she enforce that? I would be very afraid to be living in that section of the city right now. She's there illegally—the city will have to respond with force. But we have to ask, where was the city's force during the riots?"

Zach yelled bullshit at the television and paced across his living room, his fists clenched to his chest and then just as quickly sat back down.

"But, Marylin—you've got to remember her popularity is terrible trouble for the city. What kind of issues might the city face if they went in and shut her down? Did she promise to dissolve her organization at the end of the drought?"

"Dissolve?" Marylin said with scorn, "To my knowledge, dictators rarely surrender power. We can't allow our cities to become subdivided like this."

"Come on, you motherfuckers!" Zach yelled and swiped the large stack of newspapers off the couch. Their speculative drivel was driving him mad. "What does the city say?"

"The other question is: does the city actually have the resources to handle this situation? I understand police and National Guard forces are extremely constrained. There are riots in Los Angeles again, and they've been flying National Guard out of here to help down there." Bob looked at the camera. "It's eight o'clock. Stay tuned, folks. This is KATU News and we'll have the story for you. Have a good night. Stay safe out there."

The KATU logo went up for a long second and then the television and house lights shut off as the power went out. The moment it did he tuned into the sound of the wind outside, wailing at the building, blowing mercilessly in great gusts. It carried with it a thick, unbreathable dust that worked at the window sills, trying to get in. He could taste it on his tongue and feel it in his nostrils

At dawn Zach climbed to the roof. He waited for the power to resume and the morning news to broadcast so that he could find out if Renee was still alive, and to see what the city's move had been.

With a sudden jerky hum the power came on and he listened as items sucked up the life in the wall sockets. On TV Robert narrated over what was essentially a very empty, calm neighborhood. Zach breathed a sigh of relief. No wars had sprung up in the night.

As he waited for news, they went through the entire recap again and Zach kicked at his old coffee table, the legs gnawed on by a Dachshund from his youth.

"OK, I'm getting something here . . ." Bob said and stared at the camera intently, Zach realized he was reading something on the teleprompter. It was disarming, looking the newscaster straight in the eye, without him talking, as if he were waiting for Zach to respond.

"What?" Zach finally said. "Come on, you dumb sonofabitch."

"I've learned that so far no water trucks have been seen entering Sherwood. All water trucks have already been to the airport and are on their way to the distribution points, except for the neighborhoods under Maid Marian's control. There have been no statements issued from either the mayor, the National Guard, or Maid Marian yet. That's all I have right now—we'll tell you more when we have it."

The camera angle widened to include another news anchor sitting a few feet away at the same long desk. She was a young and heavily made up woman who, to Zach's eyes, appeared as though she'd been dipped in some kind of liquid plastic.

"Are we officially calling it Sherwood now? Isn't that giving them some recognition they shouldn't have?"

Robert frowned. "Yes, that's what they call their country, I don't see why we shouldn't refer to it as it's named."

"Well, sure, a country needs a name, right?" the made-up woman said.

Zach turned off the television and spent some time fretting. He went up to the roof and paced across its length, eyes toward Sherwood. He fiddled around with making a telescope, but did not have the tools or glass to complete it. Then he slumped back into his TV couch downstairs and waited. The power was off again and would be for some time. She'd been gone a long time.

After the news a deep, unsettled quiet lay over the city as the mayor and the police and the new citizens of Sherwood tried to digest this unexpected turn of events. Arguments broke out at the policemen's union, some arguing that the territory was a festering cesspool of crime, prostitution, and drug use, and good riddance. Others argued that Maid Marian was the biggest criminal of them all now and must be crushed, and many others made muted comments of relief, that policing of the area was now in someone else's hands.

In the nation of Sherwood, where there had so recently been rioting and violence, people poured from their houses to take a new, fresh look at the place in which they lived, as if simply calling themselves a different name allowed them a new perspective, a moment of reflection in which they might emerge, chrysalis-like, as someone else. Their fear turned to curiosity. Everywhere they turned there was another Green Ranger standing next to his or her bike or walking along with a unit gallon of water, offering a poured unit to whomever held out a cup. To all questions they answered, "Maid Marian will make sure there is peace," or simply, "We haven't been told what's next." There was a tentative and heady feeling of being at the threshold of deliverance.

Nevel hid his family in the tunnel during the riots. While they were downstairs, he paced nervously from window to window watching for a sign the riot would turn toward their home. He'd purchased a handgun on the black market he had never fired, and he held it up as he paced, thinking that were some explosive branch of the riot to come toward his house he could at least wave the gun insanely in the air.

No, he realized with sudden clarity, when they came he would break his own windows. He would howl and thrash about as if he were the alpha looter. He would employ the coward's defense. He scanned about the room for the first things he might like to destroy, and after a moment he realized that to the last one they all belonged to his wife. The bland painting of a farmhouse, the strange statues, the knick-knackery. He thought about how he might crush the painting over the top of a gaudy ceramic vase she'd bought on a trip to Mexico. He picked up the vase and hefted it and realized he'd gotten it backwards—the vase would go into the painting. A far more satisfying crunch could be had there.

"Hi, Dad!"

Nevel spun to see his five-year-old Jason standing in the living room in his pajamas. Nevel quickly scanned the windows for signs of violence.

"What are you doing with the vase?" Jason said.

"You should be downstairs!" Nevel yelled, and then, after the downcast look his boy gave him, said, "I'll bring the TV down, it'll be like a movie party. When the power comes on."

"Yay!" Jason said and ran in place Road Runner style, and then disappeared back down the stairs yelling unintelligibly.

Nevel carried the television to the basement. He strung the cord deep into the end of the tunnel where, sitting on beanbags on a plywood platform, lit by the light of flashlights, his children looked thrilled and his wife miserable and anxious. He set the TV down in front of them.

"How are my stowaways?" Nevel said brightly.

"Lovely," Cora said. "Would you like a turn in the hold? I'm perfectly capable of waving a pistol around."

Nevel felt for the gun he'd tucked self-consciously into the back of his pants. He liked its presence there and admired its lines and hardness. The gun was his and he wanted the heroic job up in the living room. He switched on the television and found that most stations were already covering the riot happening outside at that very moment. It was a strange sense of alternate reality, where the faraway third world scene he watched on television was in fact a few blocks to the north. He watched with fascination and a detached compassion for anyone living in such a place where something like that could happen.

"That's Safeway!" He clutched his throat and watched the store get swallowed in flames. He feared at any moment he would see his own house, hordes of Molotov cocktail–throwing rioters at the doorstep. "I've got to get back up there." Nevel touched each of their heads and his wife emitted a tired, fearful sound.

Back upstairs he tried to place where he'd been. There was something about the tunnel that always reset him. There was a crash from across the street and the fear returned, but it was quiet enough through the windows that he wondered if people were rioting privately in the comfort of their own homes. Then he remembered where he'd been with the vase and the painting. He picked up the vase again.

There was a terrific yell from the basement and the vase leapt from his hands. He clumsily bounced it from hand to hand in a futile attempt to regain purchase until it rebounded off of the front door, through the grip in his hands, and clattered heavily to the floor, confirming his suspicion that the ugly thing was unbreakable. There was another loud call for him and he worried suddenly the tunnel had collapsed. He sprinted back to the basement.

The tunnel was lit blue by the light of the television like some strange route to the afterlife.

"Look," his wife said, "it's her."

Nevel saw Maid Marian on the television briefly and then the newscasters were back on, showing a map of Portland with a red outline around a quadrant of the Northeast. In the center they'd written, *Maid Marian claims Northeast Portland.*

"That's us," he said, pointing stupidly at the television map and feeling far from comprehending what was happening.

"No, it's across the street," Cora said. "She just spoke. Northeast Portland *seceded*, it's another country across the street now."

It had gotten late and the kids wanted to sleep in the tunnel. Nevel was thrilled with the idea. He could see it in their eyes already, how it calmed them, how their lids were heavy with the peace of it. His wife threatened to sleep by herself upstairs.

"It's a dirty hole," she said, and then, when she saw she'd genuinely wounded her husband with the comment, said, "I mean it doesn't go anywhere, you can't call it a tunnel," and then, in an attempt to patch things, offered to go get their sleeping bags.

She left and did her grumbling out of earshot. These were helpless-feeling times, and she understood how a man might fashion a project for himself in which he could feel himself a hero, no matter how insane or inconsequential that project might be.

She fetched the sleeping bags and pillows and camping tarps and returned to the tunnel where, she admitted, he had made significant progress. Wooden posts—salvaged from the porches of abandoned houses—lined the way in. The floor he'd covered with sand, from god knows where he got that—to the delight of the children. In spots, plywood lined the walls and the ceiling.

Jason now claimed he wanted to be a tunnel builder when he grew up.

She could not understand the motivation—were there the threat of a bombing, sure, a bunker like this could be useful, but it was a drought. It was like her husband hadn't been able to match the disaster to the defense. And yet, she did feel a calm upon entering. Once she quashed the claustrophobia its earthy silence relaxed some deep core of her.

She helped Nevel lay out sleeping bags for the kids and they nestled down into them. Then they made their own beds there, and she felt annoyed at him all over again for making her sleep on an air mattress when her own comfortable bed awaited empty, two floors up.

But once in bed it was more comfortable than she'd expected and so quiet, and because he was so thrilled to have them down here in his odd little space, he was extra kind. They talked about the new country that had opened up across the street, and about Maid Marian. He gave her a neck rub and told her how nice she looked in the candle-glow and then she saw what he was after and she rolled into him and they kissed. It had been a while—she couldn't remember. A month maybe? Only the vaguest memory surfaced of their last time, of awkward clumsy limbs and distance. It was a comfort to find there was genuine interest now, in her own body. In the emotional battle that waged in her about her husband's growing strangeness and his odd pet project, acceptance gained a notch or two in her mind. There, not five feet from their sleeping children, quiet and still as nocturnal animals, and deep in the earth below their house. Afterwards she stared into the deep black of the tunnel and for a spell the dread left her.

Zach toiled at his office desk, researching enclaves, when he felt the place go tense. One of the partners ran down the hall. The mayor, he thought. The mayor was here.

He stood and reflexively straightened his unstraightenable shirt. Be calm, he told himself. His mind was full of Northeast neighborhoods, of riots and secession. Then again, he thought, everyone's was.

One of the Patel & Grummus partners stood at the door looking haggard. "Come," she said to him and the others in the hive. She jerked her thumb in the direction of the conference room, then turned and walked with quick, clicking steps toward where the mayor and his inevitable entourage of sycophants would be stationed.

The mayor looked like he hadn't slept in a few days. His eyes were bloodshot and tired and he hung his head at an unnatural angle, bent as if he carried a weight on the back of his neck.

Zach extended his hand across the table. "Mayor Bartlett." Zach forced a bravado, deeply aware of his new project, assisting a different leader of a smaller country. By Morse code, he'd received a laundry list to research, of ideas to vet, and pleas for his presence.

The mayor clutched his hand in a steely grip. "What has happened to us?"

Zach searched for words, trying to cast them so as to set the meeting on the right track. It came slowly to him that the meeting, again, was his to control were he focused. He shrugged. "It hurts, but we have gained an opportunity," he said finally.

The mayor squinted at him and then with a suddenness slammed his fist on the table. "I have completely lost popular support. I can't maintain control over the city. Half of it is rioting, the other half—" he waved his hand vaguely toward Northeast Portland, as if there were not words that could describe what was happening there. "Explain to me how your agency has helped garner an opportunity!"

"Sir," the partner said, "I don't think this is something any of us could have anticipated." Her left hand trembled and Zach realized that the agency was at stake. This client kept the lights on. The one that granted them an extra allotment of power so they could even do their jobs.

The mayor turned his gaze to Zach and stared hard at him. "I would like to hear our boy genius explain himself."

Zach cleared his throat. He managed the mayor best when he was brutal and honest with him, when he treated him like a little brother. "To be fair, in the Northeast your reputation is deserved. Or do you disagree?"

The mayor seemed caught off guard by the challenge and did not answer.

"Those neighborhoods are a wreck. There is no fantasy we could spin that would salvage your standing there. You should know that." He could feel the firm's partner, a few chairs to his right, begin to work at an interjection. The way Zach talked to the mayor had always alarmed her.

"Everybody's bad off," the mayor said.

"Not equally," Zach said. "The news rarely even reports from there. They are scared. How many police do you have up there, what's the National Guard presence? They drop the water rations and run, right?"

The mayor's face had gone red.

"Cede the territory. There's no other way," Zach said. "Otherwise you dig your own grave." Zach let this sink in and the room was quiet. "Put yourself out there for comparison. This is your opportunity to make us understand why a democratically elected mayor and a city council, with you at its head, is the ideal form of government for these times. Effect the change that we all need to see. That's the spin control that's needed most. Action."

"Um," Nevel said, "if I could break in here a moment. Can't you withhold their rations? Smoke them out, so to speak?"

The mayor exhaled in frustrated disgust. "The rations are a humanitarian effort. I have no control over their distribution. Withholding people's water would be political suicide, and anyway that's the National Guard's ball of wax, and they—who knows what they're doing."

"So water trucks have gone there?" Zach said. "They've gotten their rations?"

The mayor threw up his hands. "I told you, I can't do anything about that. It's the Guard's pet fucking project, apparently."

Zach felt like crying with relief. They would have water.

"Well," Nevel said. "How about a pros and cons list, us versus them?"

The mayor turned to the firm's partner and held his hands out, as if to say *this is the best you can do?*

"Totally," Zach said. "Good one, Nevel. A pros and cons list. Pro: you are free in the city of Portland. Con: In Sherwood, you are at the mercy of a dictator's whims. I think a poster campaign that compares and contrasts you with this Marian character is a great idea." Zach, for himself, could think of nothing more damaging. What the mayor really needed was a bold action for the neighborhoods that remained, not the invitation of comparison. He could see the mayor on the edge of a decision. "Let's do another campaign and talk about what you've done," he said, "and in the meantime: do something. Let's play to your strengths. Now that the Northeast is out of your control, it's out of your responsibility. Someone has cut away your greatest liability. Use that liability unabashedly against her—point out the state of that neighborhood."

"Do you all understand the stakes here?" the mayor said grimly.

"Absolutely," Zach replied.

"I want three proposals immediately. We'll see where this goes from there."

Later that afternoon, as Patel & Grumus submerged deeply in the process of brainstorming, the creative staff breaking into mini SWAT teams, they received notice by courier that the city was no longer in need of their services, effective immediately. Zach smiled wryly at the news. The mayor was smarter than he'd thought and now the future yawned vast and frightening before him as he, too, would join the masses without a job. There was a flurry of panic; a few cried quietly at their desks. But since the city provided their power, there was no reason to come to work tomorrow. The agency was closed.

At the end of the day Zach packed up what belongings he cared about. The lights flickered once, and then went dark. He had done this, in part, he knew. He had cost them their jobs. He looked around at his somber coworkers with guilt as they shuffled a few belongings into boxes. He cleared his throat to say something, but for once, no idea came.

Nevel sat at home in the dark, freshly unemployed. He was like everybody else now. Perhaps, he thought, that was why he needed the tunnel.

Who else had a tunnel? But he could not go there tonight, to work on a project that, in the end, was probably for nothing.

The riot left in him a paranoia, and so he lay on the couch, the gun on his chest, and listened to the night outside and for the rapid patter of children's feet from the floor above, or perhaps his wife, unable to sleep, pacing about their room. But it was quiet. He turned the gun on his chest until the barrel touched the soft skin of his throat.

It was an idle fantasy, he knew. He was poorly engineered for taking the easy way out. Men who take the easy way out do not spend years building pointless infrastructure under their houses.

He rotated the gun back to pointing at the door and worried through a host of issues, chief among them: how he would provide for his family. It was time for him to claim the manhood that had always seemed far off as he integrated into cultured society, as he worked at an ad agency, as he planted an herb garden and raised toddlers. There was no manhood to be found in the purchasing of gas efficient foreign cars and eating artfully prepared foods. Now was the time where you grabbed the axe from the woodpile and went to hunt that hunk of flesh for your family. Kill or be killed.

He imagined himself wandering through the streets in the dark in. search of prey. The awful fantasy lasted no more than a few seconds, when his mind inserted a pack of roving men far hungrier and more manly than he, that tore his imaginary self limb from limb. For good measure, his mind taunted him with a scene of the men eating him on the spot. The thought rattled him.

There was a knock and a silhouette appeared in the door's window. Nevel jumped. He rolled off the couch and crouched, the gun in one hand, trying to make out who it was. He'd already been spotted through the glass.

The door handle shook. "Nevel? I have something for you," the figure at the door said.

Nevel tucked the gun into the front of his pants where it could be seen, then he tentatively opened the door the width the door chain would allow. The man on the other side slipped an envelope through the crack. Inside was a handwritten note: "Friends don't forget friends," it said. He knew the handwriting immediately.

"Open up, we have boxes."

Nevel unhooked the chain and swung the door open. A short queue of shadows waited behind the man who handed him the note.

"This is my favorite part of the job," he said gruffly, and Nevel stepped aside to let him in. He had a long mustache and a baseball hat, and looked capable of eating another man's flesh.

The shadows filed in and put down boxes, which settled onto the wood floor with heavy thuds. They quickly stacked up. There were twenty-five boxes, in all. When they were done, the man with the mustache held his hand out and shook Nevel's with vigor.

"Enjoy," he said, and tipped his hat.

After the door closed, he stood over the delivery, bewildered. He cautiously broke the seal on one. Inside there were four full gallon-sized glass bottles and an equivalent portion of food rations. Nevel ran back to the door, but the truck was already gone.

He sat back on the couch and his heart sank as he realized that *this* was how he stood up for his family. Did others in the agency receive the same? He thought not. It was he who knew the mayor's secrets, and secrets were worth something. Silence was expensive. This shipment was surely a pittance compared to what they were hoarding away for the wealthy, but to him it was a small fortune.

He stood and opened the door to the basement. He needed to get these out of sight before his wife saw them. The boxes were heavy, but in half an hour he had all of it deep in his tunnel, down a side branch, a cache of survival for end times.

Unpacked, they were gorgeous. In the beam of a flashlight he admired his glittering cave of rations. He was sullied now. Cora would be disgusted by these, by his acquiescence to the dirty work of the mayor. But he had a family to look after. He was the provider, and look at this. He swung the beam across the width of the hoard. He craved to fill the rest of the hole with them.

In a moment of sobriety he realized this hole would never stop hungering for its prize. He would have to keep filling it. He extinguished the light and fell to a crouch, each hand steadied on a gallon, and stayed in the dark for he wasn't sure how long.

After Christopher went to bed and his advisors shuffled off to their own lives, Mayor Bartlett played video games. He played first person shooters mostly, and he was good. He liked control. It was one of the reasons he'd run for mayor—to be in control—and it was to his great dismay that he realized that the job was constantly out of control, in free fall, like driving a school bus full of vocal citizens down a snowy mountainside with several other would-be drivers wrestling for the steering wheel.

His video game obsession was a poorly kept secret. The city council knew why he'd show up once or twice a week with deeply bloodshot eyes, speaking each sentence as if there were a hairpin turn in the middle of it. He'd received as gifts, over his term, nine copies of games—mostly those that in some way or another resembled his job, SimCity or Civilization—games where you managed a city or developed an economy, and these sat unopened next to his console. He promised himself he'd open them someday. In the meantime, he preferred to shoot things.

On the night that a coffee barista assumed control of approximately one fifth of his city, he decided to spend the night killing Nazis.

"Coming to bed?" Christopher said from the bathroom.

"You go," the mayor said. "I'll be in soon."

"No, you won't." Christopher lined his toothbrush with a toothpaste he loathed. The mayor insisted on purchasing it because it was made by a local factory and with local ingredients.

"Please don't do this," the mayor said.

"Think about what you've got to do tomorrow, that's all I'm saying."

"Chris." The mayor lay down on the couch and put one hand over his face. In his other hand he gripped the console's controller. "I have fought—screaming matches, really—with pretty much every person I regularly interact with over the course of my day. The only exception being you. And that's *all* I'm saying."

"I'm not fighting, " Christopher called from the bathroom, his speech fuzzy with toothpaste foam.

The last phrase hung in the air, awkward and only vaguely resembling the truth, waiting for one of them to push on it either way until Christopher, finished with his tedious routine of brushing, flossing, face washing, fluoride rinsing, fingernail clipping and face picking, came and stood over the couch where the mayor was collapsed. He put his hand on Brandon's head and caressed his perfect mayoral hair. The generator kicked on, filling the space with a comforting hum.

"OK," Christopher said finally, "but don't stay up too late. Don't hurt yourself."

"I might get shot."

"What?"

The mayor waved the controller weakly in the direction of the television. "Joke," he said.

"Ah. Do you want to talk about it at all?"

The mayor paged through a few on-screen characters, picking an Allied machine gunner, and then launched the game.

"Talk about what? About riots springing up like sewer rats? That I lost a quarter of the city to a bunch of people wearing pajamas? You know this Maid Marian chick is calling it Sherwood now. Yeah, I've talked about it all day and just can't get enough, you know?"

"Hey," Christopher said.

"I know, I'm sorry." The mayor's Allied soldier charged kamikaze-like into a bunker of Nazis where he dislodged grenade after grenade until they'd shot him full of holes. Blood erupted in a flowering mist, a geysering ketchup across the supposed screen's camera lens. "Fucking fuck," the mayor said, but his heart wasn't in it.

"I don't understand why you can't just go in and get her," Christopher said.

"Oh, Chris. You should play these games. You could shoot things. It'd make you feel better. Believe me, if it were easy and clean to go in and shoot things up, I'd give it some real thought," the mayor said. "And the council? Look, here they are—" The mayor called up the Axis soldier chooser on the TV and pointed at it: a huffing, serious German gunner swayed dully back and forth, some kind of coffee ground stain across his jaw, an apparent rendering of beard growth.

"You mean Nazis or game bots? Doesn't that suggest some kind of organization or evil intent or something? They're more like mangy koala bears. They need to be taken in and loved by you. They need to be persuaded to be civil. They're not leaders, Bran, they're followers, they just need to be pointed to your tail."

"Christopher, please."

"Isn't that why we have all these soldiers? To keep the city safe?"

"You saw her speech, right?" The mayor dropped the controller and held his fist in the air, counting off on his fingers, trying and failing to keep the condescension out of his voice. "Number one, she's cute. Number two, she looked insanely competent. Her voice did not waver. She amassed an army and put them in uniforms. They looked rumpled and retarded, but there were a lot of them and they were serious. Three"—he raised his middle finger—"she's a fucking folk hero. That's how she did it. That's the only way. I don't know what she's paying that army, but you can bet that the appeal of serving a Ms. Guevara is a hell of a recruitment tool. Four, the entire fucking city would riot if we took her out. Think about it. It's a rioting mood out there, it's like everybody's new favorite hobby, and she's everybody's new favorite person. And number five?"

The mayor held his pinky in the air. The huffing German soldier and Christopher waited and watched until Christopher could see there was no number five, and knew this would be one more irritant for the mayor, one more bit of imprecision lining up in protest against his obsessive-compulsive tendencies, and so he took hold of that pinky in the air with his own fist and kissed the end of it.

"Shoot some monsters, Bran," Christopher said. "We'll tackle it in the morning. Maybe she'll have lost control by then."

"Nazis," the mayor said.

"Nazis." Christopher patted the mayor's shoulder and left him to his violence.

The mayor stayed still in the empty room. The generator turned off, the batteries having filled, the bedroom door closed. The night was quiet outside, and there was an ache of fear and anger that lined his insides with the weight of lead. He kept his fist up in the air, his pinky upraised, unable to let it down until a number five came to him.

Out the window where there'd once been a sparkling night view, the city stretched dark and dull. In the distance he could see the yellow twinkle of a fire of some kind, a house fire or a car, or even a whole block. He was comforted to see the lights of an emergency vehicle, making its slow way through the unlit chaos. That's me, he thought, right there. Putting out fires.

"Number five," he whispered finally, shaking his pinky out toward the view, "she'll fail, because people revile and fear a foreign body. What she has built is more akin to a cult. Those around her will fear its spread like a cancer and the populace will focus on cutting her out." But he wasn't sure this was true. A cult, a trend, a fad—any radical change had its shot at becoming the new norm, shedding the skin of the old as it went.

He picked up the controller and reset his game and savored the thought that in the world he was about to enter he was unequivocally not the bad guy. He was an Allied soldier fighting the Nazis. His cause was just.

THE NATION

Friends:

My name is Maid Marian. You may have seen me on the news. If you've received this letter, you live in one of the following Northeast neighborhoods: Cully, Rose City, Beaumont-Wilshire, Alameda, Concordia, Sabin, King, Woodlawn, Vernon, Sumner and Madison South. All told we estimate there are between forty-five and sixty thousand of you. As you have probably heard by now, we have seceded this block of neighborhoods from the city. Together, we all make up a new country now: The nation of Sherwood.

Welcome to Sherwood!

Let's get to know each other. The person who handed you this note is your direct link to me. He or she will show up every day—why? As of tomorrow, your water and food rations will be delivered to your door. No one needs to trouble with a water distribution again.

Here is my promise to you:

Together we're going to make Sherwood safer, healthier, more educated and wealthier than the failing city that surrounds us. We would not have seceded if we didn't believe we could do this. Together we will steer this new territory into better times. We will staff our schools so that our children may freely and safely attend once again. We will set up clinics, so that those in need may have the care they deserve. We will re-establish libraries and create book exchanges. Together we will till land, so that we can

163

eat from the soil of our country. At night, you will feel safe walking the streets.

Here's what I need in return.

I need your trust, and I need your faith. It's not going to happen overnight. This is an extraordinary move. As they say, extraordinary times call for extraordinary measures. Give me a week of your time before you form judgment. I am not here as a seeker of power, but as a righter of wrongs. When the city can do a better job providing for its people than we can, I will quietly hand control back. The way I look at it is: We're running an emergency government. When there's no emergency, we will cede to democracy.

I need your time. Sherwood is going to require volunteers. Every week you will be required to put in some community service hours. We will have census takers visit you soon to catalog your skillset.

I need your input. Tell us how we're doing! Tell us what needs doing. Tell us what you need. Let us function as one great organism together. To do so, we need to hear from each of you. Tell your water carrier, your water carrier will tell me.

I will charge taxes. I promise to be bluntly honest with you, and here's a good place to start. In order to run this government, we need a small share of your water. Two units daily—one twentieth of your daily ration. This water will be used to support clinics and farms, to pay our employees, and to make sure no one goes thirsty. It will feel steep in the first week, but I promise that our efficiency programs will more than make up for it in the long run.

I look forward to running a marvelous country with you.

Yours,
Maid Marian

Rangers spread to every edge of Sherwood, their task to seal the border that surrounded the new nation. They had at it with everything in their disposal. Across some intersections barbed wire was strung, nailed to the sides of houses. In others, dead cars were lined up into walls. Couches, refuse, construction materials, dumpsters, trailer trucks, and so on. Most were still passable by anyone determined enough to get through. For now it was the best they could do, a psychological barrier. A separation, they hoped, between chaos and order.

Jamal had overseen a guard-booth building workshop the day before, attended by a mass of new volunteers—everyone they could dig up with building skills. It felt like months ago already. The guardhouses were simple structures made of plywood and two-by-fours and fabric, meant to give a full-time border guard or two some protection against the sun and wind and a place to sit, and to give some formality to the place, a watchful structure to ward off would-be city intruders. They built nearly a hundred of them, interspersed along the border and within sight of each other.

He worked with two volunteers and a ranger now at the corner of 21st and Fremont in front of a crowd of onlookers, Sherwoodians and Portlanders, staring across at each other over the ugly border of discarded couches. Most were silent. The riots had taken their toll, and after the secession the people of Sherwood had turned inward, with hope and exhaustion, to lick their wounds and begin to rebuild, wide-eyed at the prospect of the task they were undertaking together. They stood now and watched, some still clutching their Maid Marian letters in their hands. The volunteer office was swamped, with prospective recruits forming a line nearly three blocks long. All who could were put to work, most with only an inkling of direction. Many of the volunteers were recruited on the spot as Maid Marian tried to fill out the employees of Sherwood. Everyone wanted a job. Volunteers received fifteen units of water extra for their work, and that alone, besides having anything to alleviate the boredom-crush of drought time, was a motivating factor.

Across from Jamal the ragtag city residents stared and whispered, just as battered by the recent riots. They looked on and wondered if they were witnessing some terrible tragedy progressing before them. A youth called out and waved and was answered on the Sherwood side, a distance of sixty feet between them, shy now as they realized they waved between countries. They wondered: Would those trapped inside endure some kind of hell, their fates bound to some dictator's fancy? Should they fear for their safety? Or were they blessed?

Jamal squatted and dropped his hammer to the ground, letting his blistered hands have a moment's rest. It felt good to hold a hammer in his hand—but he had absolutely no skill here. Growing up in a drug family did not prepare you for carpentry, it turned out. A National Guard jeep drove slowly by, honking to clear the city residents who moved aside lethargically, emboldened by what progressed across from them.

The four soldiers stared toward Sherwood with stern, impassive faces. "Well, shit," Jamal said to no one in particular. A wave of unease passed through him.

The city government had done nothing but pace anxiously along the border, like a beast cordoned off from its prey. He knew Sherwood's nascent, petty army was nothing against real soldiers. Were they to storm in by force, there was nothing real holding them back. At the front line of that storm would be him, as captain of the armed Going Street Brigade.

Jamal blew on his hands to cool the blister burn. This was his third guardhouse of the day. He suspected a thousand or more had pitched in to create the border. It was a good feeling, despite the terror of change that lay underneath it. There was camaraderie and euphoria.

Tonight he would bear arms with the brigade, tailing Maid Marian to Irving Park, where a covert meeting with the mayor would take place.

Green Rangers were spread through the entire territory now— each of them within eyesight of another. Gregor had made up a series of hand symbols—help, city vehicle, news crew, and so on, so that a line of sight communication chain could pass a message along back to central.

The guardhouse was done. All but the painting. In great donation drives the territory had acquired huge stores of paint, gasoline, wood, seeds, and other useful supplies. And so tomorrow, provided they still had a country, a force of some hundreds would go painting guardhouses and border lines and the barricades. It would not be pretty, but a coat of paint would give it the look of a concerted effort, a thought-out plan, rather than trash piles at the border.

———

They arrived as an armed mass of bicycles, thirty strong plus Maid Marian and Bea. They shared sparse, giddy words with each other as they dismounted and filtered between the dead trees of Irving Park in the dusk-light, and wondered if they were going to their deaths. At the far end of the park the contrast between the two groups became clear. They wheeled their bikes toward a Lincoln Town Car surrounded by police cars.

The police were better armed and better trained, but in the dim light up close the Green Rangers were an unknown. To the police there was a mysterious and threatening quality about this new, strange army. They kept no formation and blended into the park. It was difficult to know how many there were. But most of all, they fought for something still mystifying and vague, under the guidance of *her*, deeply unnerving the mayor's force.

Beforehand, Jamal had struggled with a way to holster their weapons, and it'd made him feel like an asshole that in their first meet-up with another force, even this they had barely worked out. In the end they settled on a thigh holster made of a canvas sail scavenged from someone's garage and sewn into shape by volunteers. It worked well enough. As he squatted behind a dead tree he gripped his gun against his leg, steady in its pouch. He was close enough to put a bullet in somebody. He looked up into the tree cautiously. You never knew when one would spontaneously shed a branch.

The door of the Town Car swung open and from inside the backseat the mayor beckoned.

"Don't do it," Bea whispered hoarsely at Renee as they approached on foot with an escort of two rangers, while the rest took up positions.

Renee patted her friend's arm. "Don't worry."

Renee climbed into the backseat and closed the door behind her. Bea stood uncomfortably outside the car, huddled with the other two rangers, exchanging size-up looks with the police who stood nearby in the reflected glare of headlights.

In the backseat the mayor turned sideways and scooted backwards. The car felt unreasonably small with Maid Marian in it beside him. She smelled of sweat and dirt and looked at him now with intent, grim eyes and he could feel himself on the verge of sputtering, whereas moments ago his imagination had him dominating this encounter.

She held out her hand and he shook it. "Maid Marian," he said.

"Nice car," she said.

"Yes," he said, and then realized he should have brought her something to drink, or something, anything to put between them. You wined and dined foreign nationals, did you not?

"This can end without a fight," he tried. "You could run a volunteer force, a neighborhood association, and we wouldn't interfere and . . ." The mayor folded his hands in his lap, and then unfolded them and rested his elbow on the headrest, in a position of greater control but less comfort.

"It's already done," Renee said.

"Not at all," he said.

"Listen. We went through all of your options." She held up her fingers to tally off his detractors. "Between the U.S. Humanitarian Aid Act, my popularity, the riots, your forces which hardly have free time on their hands, the water grafting you've done—don't," she said and held her other hand up to keep him from interrupting, "—and the unrest in the rest of the city—you *don't have any* options. Cede control. I'm sitting on a time bomb."

For a brief moment he lost track of what she'd been saying as she rattled off his problems with easy fluency. It reminded him immediately of what it had been like to fight with his mother, who had battered at him with unending lists of data. As his mind came out of its anxious reverie he found her last phrase rattling around his mind like a marble in a tin bucket. "Time bomb?" he said.

She handed him an address on a piece of paper. "The trucks will enter here. Please make sure there are no city personnel nearby."

"The trucks?"

"Distribution, obviously."

"The Guard?"

She nodded, and he could see she was playing her ace.

"There's no way. The Guard is not going to be delivering water to your enclave-thing."

"Already worked out."

He took the paper and stared at it and was unable to read anything it said, his eyes blurring and his face burning. He didn't know what she was talking about in regards to the Guard and he realized the meeting had gone horribly off track. "You've got city government and the U.S. government to contend with. You can't seriously think you can run a country inside of a city. You've got twenty-four hours to—"

"The U.S. government?" There was a scornful sarcasm in her voice.

He'd known it was a bad tactic as he'd said it. The U.S. government was nothing but a provider of bare-necessities aid, much of it funneled from other nations. They had little influence west of the Rocky Mountains, only a moral duty, which they nominally fulfilled. They could give a damn about a micro-secession. Their local representation, the National Guard, he was supposedly in charge of, or in cahoots with, though he was regularly being reminded otherwise.

"Let's be clear." Maid Marian leveled her gaze at him. "It's me and you." She jabbed one thin, dirty finger in the air at him, attached to, he couldn't help but notice, a nicely shaped hand. "I plan to be a good neighbor. How about you?"

"It is not only me, the city council—"

"Don't even bring up the council."

"We're a democracy. You're playing with human lives!" the mayor protested.

She stared hard at him. "Spoken like a true glass house dweller. I'm heading to a news interview, anything else?"

"No!" he hollered. He saw a policeman's face loom large out his window and he waved him away. "Don't go." She had one leg out the car door and he grabbed her arm. "Do not split the population of this city. Why not be a whole unit, why not solve our problems together?" he said, finding his voice finally. "You don't want there to be a civil war, Maid Marian."

"I don't see us solving our mutual problems any time soon. I'm going to take this problem off your hands and run a tight, well-functioning nation in place of your chaos and shitty leadership."

"Don't go," he said. "Please."

"We'll negotiate for other services with the private enterprises that run them."

"Please—"

"Let go of my arm," Maid Marian growled.

"But aren't you scared?" he said. "To be doing this? To be in charge of this many people?"

He could see the anger in her face, how she would have liked to sock him in the nose. She dipped her head and studied the seat between them and he released her arm. It was quiet in the car. "If I were you," she said finally, "I would be terrified."

After a moment she left, closing the door behind her. It was dark now and he watched her shadowy form walk back into the trees with her people, her hair glistening in the headlight beams. Like some fucking wood nymph. He bunched his fist and punched the headrest. Then he opened the door and called his advisors back in.

The mayor had acquired a copy of Maid Marian's letter to the residents of Sherwood and the paper burned in his hands. The news channel had given it to him as a courtesy before they aired its contents. He circled his couch with it, waiting for Christopher to wake up from his nap. Christopher would know what to do. Together they could craft a response—he could go on the news—during the weather—with a brilliant speech. He would guffaw with scorn at their water taxes and her plea to give her a week of faith. *Faith!* Next she would be expecting them to sacrifice virgins to her.

He flattened out the letter on the table that overlooked the city and self-consciously glanced up toward Sherwood, as if she could see him standing there, obsessing over her letter. Then he looked toward the bedroom door again. Christopher was sleeping his fucking life away.

He eased open the door to the room and saw Christopher's form in the sheets. His lips parted slightly as he slept. The last few years had aged him. Drought years, years he'd been mayor, hard years on anyone. Still, the beauty of the man he'd first met was present, on his face, but also in the mayor's mind. Those first impressions of Christopher from years ago etched deeply enough so that when he looked at his partner's face, years of memories overlaid themselves on top, and he saw his partner in two worlds, young and happy, and older now, married to the mayor.

The mayor put his hand on Christopher's hip but he remained deep in sleep. The feel of that hip under the sheet, still sharp and interestingly contoured, lean after all this time, was arousing. That and, for some god-damn reason, Maid Marian's letter. Crumpled and flattened on the table where he'd left it. Its message bore implications of his own impending doom, so that all there was left for a man was carnal indulgence.

He stripped his clothes off and crawled into bed and pressed his lips to the back of his partner's neck and inhaled. The scent of his husband's skin was complex; it brought comfort and relief and lust and a welling up of gratitude. He clutched him and Christopher protested that he was asleep but it was no serious protest and he turned toward the mayor.

Later the mayor fetched the letter and Christopher read it in bed next to him in British-accented falsetto and the mayor laughed with happy relief and pretended she was someone else's adversary.

"But Bran, you have to go on tonight," Christopher said, all at once serious.

"Must I?" The mayor groaned, though he'd known it to be so.

"Of course. Let's get this done." Christopher fetched a pencil and a pad of paper and brought it back to the bed, and together, in the leavened moments of afterglow they composed a rebuttal: half rant, half reason. A plea to the thinking citizen. The mayor needed everyone to know he was serious about city changes. They would quickly dilute Maid Marian's message with progressive action of their own. He'd bring in new advisors, announce some new proposals, give everyone an extra bonus water day from city reserves.

"Do we have that? Can we do that without it going through council?" Christopher said.

"Fuck the council. Get Jenny on the radio and ask her to round up any serious activists from the Southeast neighborhoods. We'll—I don't know, tell them we'll have a town hall once a week or something. Let everyone know their voice is heard. It'll scare the hell out of them, and then we'll surprise them with our outreach."

A moment later Christopher came back to bed and told him that Jenny had defected to Sherwood.

The mayor leapt out of bed and ran to the sliding glass door in the living room and flung it open. "Fuck you!" he bellowed toward the Northeast, and then he leaned on the balcony and held his head in his hands until he became aware he was standing naked in plain view of passers-by below.

"Who do we have left there we like?" the mayor said from the bedroom door.

Christopher shrugged and tapped the notepad with the pencil. "Let's get in touch with the news. You need to be seen. You need to talk directly to the other neighborhoods. OK?"

"Would you call them? I—"

"Sure, love," Christopher touched the mayor's face briefly as he passed out of the room. "Hold it together, will you?" he said over his shoulder. "Now more than ever."

Smack in the middle of it the mayor lost track of his place. The tele-prompter continued to stream words he should have been saying out loud. From the sidelines someone waved at him frantically. Noticing he'd stopped, the teleprompter controller slowed it down, and then reversed the speech to where he'd left off, mid-sentence, something about solidarity blah blah, stronger as one.

She wanted their faith, he thought. He wanted faith too. Wasn't *he* their elected leader? As if she were some omniscient who would make everything all right if they only lived their lives justly. He was fucking up the newscast, he was going to blurt something out. The rebellious egg in his mind, that patch of renegade brain cells responsible for non-sequiturs bristled and bustled, waiting to be heard, raising an anxious class-clown hand.

Out of the corner of his eye he saw his newsroom handler signal-ing him frantically.

His lips parted and he held his mouth open as he tried to make out the next sentence on the teleprompter, the words garbling in his sight like some Arabic mash. Then he could hold it back no longer: "I want you to like me!" The voice that emitted from him repulsive, elementary-school indignant. "I'm honest too. She's no Robin Hood!" The mayor wiped his brow where a drop of sweat stung the corner of his eye. "Chris!" he yelled.

The television went fuzzy dark for twenty-two seconds, as if someone had slipped a sheet of black construction paper over the front of the camera lens, and then the mayor appeared again. He smiled hugely, with a touch of mania, made a joke about channeling the leaders of nearby nations, and continued his speech from where he left off.

The first couple days had gone awkwardly. Talk about fires, she thought, and the putting out of, but need everyone be a match? And reporters had been everywhere recording all of it. She'd granted three interviews already. Borders were still being sealed off, Rangers didn't yet have a feel for their attitude, and a handful of angry citizens gath-ered around HQ with their Sherwood letters in hand, wanting an explanation about what this nonsense was all about despite holding the explanation right there in their hands. Throughout the territory there were a dozen or so scuffles and a few fights, and at least one death that she knew of. The fights had been over the pettiest little shit—one Ranger had thought he could leverage his new position to get his old girlfriend back. There were a spate of robberies, in two of the cases her Green Rangers had actually apprehended the thieves. Finally, one gentleman in his thirties was killed. There was a head wound involved, but no one came forward to confess what happened and no family materialized to claim him.

She had no time for meting out punishments commensurate with the crime. When Rangers, to her surprise, started holding people prisoner at HQ, she realized she needed to set down some laws and consequences. After much deliberation with Gregor, they decided the penalty would be swift, merciless, uniform, and irrevocable: major crime offenders would get drop-kicked to the other side of the border and a wave goodbye. A special four-person escort service was formed to do the drop-kicking, and the "prisoner's room" at HQ was quickly taken over by Volunteer Coordination. Minor crimes—neighbor disputes, fighting, theft other than water theft—would receive double volunteer shifts, with no pay.

After a few lucky days of news coverage, the immigration office had begun to simply add potential new citizens to a long waiting list. The territory was growing at a rate that would soon be unsustainable. Out with the bad, in with the good. She'd mention the penalties in the next day's Sherwood letter, along with the good stuff that happened—as soon as the good stuff happened.

There were bits of respite, successes. Some days earlier she'd met with Commander Aachen of the National Guard, in the same park she'd later met the mayor. He'd sent a prompt reply to her written inquiry.

She had practiced her case before she'd met with him, citing passages of the Portland Water Act and the US Humanitarian Aid Act. She would appeal to his honor as a soldier. She felt certain of the rightness of her case.

He listened to her impassioned spiel in the darkness of the park, where they both stood away from the danger of trees. The moonlight etched deep shadows over his eyes. Far at the edges she saw the machinery that had delivered him.

"Hm," he said when she'd finished. The pitched tone of his voice was like that of a mother with a rolling pin in hand, at ready to use as a tool of punishment, as her boy explained how the window broke. He was not a large man, barely taller than herself. His white hair shone ghost-like under the moon as he stood still.

He did not ask any questions. As she awaited his answer, she sweated. It was not so hot, but her body overheated. Sweat leaked from her scalp and dripped its way down her nose, along her temples. She fanned her shirt to cool her armpits. She began to speak again but he held his hand up severely, and she stopped.

"I'm thinking," he said, a voice more like a train whistle than a man's.

The moonlight painted an ice sculpture of the commander, white and frozen stone-still. And as if on cue, her body temperature altered again. A breeze shifted quietly through the park and her brow felt a chill with the wetness there. She wrapped her arms around herself and shivered. This is one way to wield power, she thought, to make me wait interminably.

He clasped his hands behind his back and for minutes they did nothing. She felt the slow gears of his mind calculating. She gripped her fist and swore to herself that she'd get what she came for. He was just a man with toys, with soldiers to order around, and she would back him down. She prepared to speak again, but then he smiled pleasantly.

"Of course, our job is to execute the distribution of rations," he said and his smile stayed long on his face as she waited for what came next. "If you want to subcontract that job and take our payload, I am willing to trial the arrangement for a period of time. If you can do a better job than we can, and we expend fewer resources, what objection could I possibly have?"

"Thank you," Renee said, wondering if she had just sold away a portion of herself, without really understanding the implications.

"It's best not to tell Mr. Bartlett about our agreement," he said, and with that he turned and walked back toward his entourage of jeeps.

She watched him go, his pale head floating like a second moon in the park. As soon as possible, she thought, I will sever my agreement. In the meantime, the small nation would have water and rations.

Even so, water distribution was a clusterfuck. The trucks had shown up with extra National Guard, looking burly and paranoid and packing large weapons, and each of the many trucks that came in had its own ideas on how to conduct business, as if the commander had only suggested a rerouting but gave no formal commands to his troops. Or perhaps he wanted her to fail. Some drove to HQ and did what they were told: fill unit gallons for the water carriers. The water carriers stacked their unit gallons on bikes with customized trailers— some hacked together from grocery carts and other wheeled vehicles, others made from scratch—and then set off for delivery. The process was painstaking and kept a contingent of National Guard soldiers camped out in front of HQ all day, which made everyone uncomfortable. She smugly accepted the defection of one of the National Guardsman that first day, whom she installed immediately as a Going Street Ranger. Her mantra of those first days: trust first and completely; upon betrayal act mercilessly. Some of the water tankers drove to their old distribution spots, where a smattering of citizens showed up looking bewildered and scared, and their water carriers followed trying to usher them back to their houses.

Bea and Renee met at 5 a.m. and wrote down a list of items that Renee called her faith list. After the mayor, in a bizarre television appearance, had mocked her call for the citizens to have faith in her, it became the internal buzzword, the HQ joke, and the first week's agenda. Their job was to build a proof for faith. There were a thousand fires to extinguish, but the focus remained security and water delivery. When these were done she could point and holler justly: *Has the city got these? We are Sherwood!* (And the citizenry would raise their skinny fists in the air and cheer deafeningly, at least in her mind they would, no matter how hard it was to believe at the moment.) With each new item or diversion that demanded her attention, Bea stood at ready to pound the clipboard if the task did not help the faith list. At the volunteer office she spearheaded teams to build off-site water storage tanks, to research water cart vehicles, to lead donation drives for needed materials.

She and Gregor refined, and then refined again the ongoing Green Ranger training. They met with their small army of trainers—thirty in all—to build what they considered *the spirit* of the Green Ranger. Vigilant, warm, practical, ethical. Never standing aloof to one side, but intermingling with the people of their assigned block, always aware of the people they served, memorizing their names. They created a two-week partner system, so that Rangers could learn from each other, but not be tempted to collude with one another. As she watched the training from her back window, she bit down on her knuckle. So far, it was working.

Spinning up and sending out a decision was exhilarating, and she kept at it. In the mornings she woke with the thrill and terror of it. Now I am the boss of everything, she would think. Then the responsibility that came with the job would infiltrate her thoughts, suckerpunch her in the gut.

She had notecards created with the Sherwood seal stamped at the top of them and with the help of Chris made out the list of needs. Concrete sealant, rollers, tubing, fifty-gallon barrels, bicycles to power pump apparatus, various seals and silicone caulking, nails, hammers, wood. Solar cells or crank powered mechanisms to hook to computers and phones. At the top of the card she wrote: *If you have any of the following, Maid Marian requests that you donate them to Sherwood. Thank you.*

What a power it was when they loved you, when they dared not disappoint. At the end of a day she climbed the stairway upward, passed meetings in progress and went to the end of the hall where she shared her room with Bea. She was bone tired, as tired as she could imagine a person being, dead wood and ashes and dirt tired. There was nothing left to her. It'd been eaten out by the eyes that watched her as she passed, by the image she tried to project, by trying to be someone she wasn't, not yet. She climbed into bed, pulled the covers over her head and wept until she slept. In the morning, she told herself, I will be stronger, within me will burn a fire of certainty.

The mayor sat at his desk in front of the photo of 1950s Portland, which looked down on him now not only with disappointment, but with exasperation. He tapped absently on his field telephone with the tip of a number two pencil—not quite ready to pick up the receiver— and attempted pseudo-calls.

"Hi, this is Brandon. May I speak to the douchebagging double-crosser, calls himself a soldier, manipufuckulador fuck? Yes—Hello?" The mayor put his face in his hands and waited. Maybe it would ring by its own self, an explanation on the line.

"Hello, this is the mayor speaking, commander *asshole asshole asshole asshole!*" He stood up and circled his desk, following the track in the carpet worn there by himself and previous mayors. The desk was a perfectly stationed island in the room to circle in times of mayoral restlessness. He stopped at the corner, picked up the receiver and held it to his ear, but did not yet dial. "Hi, Roger! Oh it's good to talk to *you, too*. Sure, sure, sure. I have one question." Then he held the quiet receiver there for a time indeterminable to him, allowing the hard plastic to warm his ear and his mind to go soft with fantasies in which everything worked out in his favor, for once.

There was a soft knock on the office door and he heard Christopher say, "You make the call yet?"

"Working up to it," the mayor said and didn't like how it sounded in his voice. "Just about ready to!" he said, turning the tone at the end into a positive enunciation of the words, an *engine that could,* an *I think I can.*

There were no further comments from Christopher, and the mayor imagined that he had wandered off to busy himself until it was over, worrying for him, which the mayor appreciated. He yearned to be out there with him, doing some domestic activity in tandem, this whole business with the call finished.

He picked up the phone, and before he lost his nerve he dialed the number. There was always some subordinate who answered in succession, making the mayor feel as if he were dialing into the office of a swineherd in some high castle and had to work his way up the floors, scullery maid to chandler and so on. "Brandon Bartlett, calling for the commander," he said several times, and then was subjected to various silent hold-periods when he wondered if they'd simply disconnected him.

"Hello, Brandon," Roger said over the line. He had a high, stilted voice, and spoke with strained enthusiasm, i.e. as a root canal patient receives a gift basket.

"Roger, hello, good to talk to you. I'll get right to the point."

"Oh, I know what you're calling about!" Roger said.

"I see, yes, of course," the mayor said.

"I've been expecting your call."

"Ah."

"You understand that my job here is very clear, to provide humanitarian aid via the aid act. It's not my business to concern myself with city politics!"

It was entirely possible that the commander had some kind of old vocal box injury, the mayor realized, something acquired in a military exploit. So that what he himself interpreted as shouting was simply the commander's regular means of expression.

"Roger ... come on," the mayor said, "this isn't city politics. This is a secession in the city. This is a criminal warlord who has taken one-third control." It was absolutely impossible for the mayor to get a read on the commander's mental acuity.

"I see it as city politics!"

"Roger, for fucking ... excuse me, sorry. So you talked, you talked to her?"

The commander might have said something that was the equivalent of assent. *Er*, or *arj*, or *eur*, the mayor was unsure.

"Can we at least have a meeting to discuss this? Partners in the stewardship of this city and all? Or let me rephrase: this is my city, and the Guard works under my direction."

"I'm not really sure I see the point of it. My responsibilities, as I said, of course are to the city, but primarily to carry out the US Humanitarian Aid Act. We distribute water to civilians within the borders of the US. I intend to be very literal in these obligations."

"Ah ha!" the mayor said. "But they call themselves an enclave, they are not Americans!"

"To me, they are within our borders. What they call themselves is irrelevant. It's your job, if you don't mind my saying, to resolve the city's conflicts. Mine is to ensure that there is access to basic humanitarian aid!"

The mayor tried like hell not to bring up the situation in San Francisco, which weighed on him daily. "So you recognize their statehood, is what you're saying?"

"I do not recognize anyone's statehood!"

"—gah."

"Let me qualify that. It is not my business to recognize anyone's statehood but the government of the United States of America!"

"Whose side are you on, Roger? If you don't mind *my* asking." The mayor realized he really preferred not to have an answer to that question.

"I know what you're thinking, Brandon, but I don't take sides. This is not San Francisco. I'm here to do one job and one job only!"

"I wish we could establish some means of regular communication between us, beyond what we have? Twice-weekly meetings, say? I take my own stewardship quite seriously, and the performance of my job would be significantly enhanced were we to communicate and agree on our actions."

"As I said here, Brandon, this issue is really not my concern. Now, if you have any further questions?"

The mayor did not. He told the guard commander he appreciated his time, and there was an acidity to the remark that would have caused him and Christopher to fight for hours, but the commander did not seem to be keyed into subtleties of human language.

"Well, it's nice talking to you too, Brandon!" Roger said.

After they'd hung up the mayor struggled with the twin opposing desires of wishing to seek solace in Christopher's embrace, and the shame in having to admit to him he'd lost so much of his city and there didn't seem to be anything he could do about it, presently.

Nevel and Cora watched the evening news after they put the kids to bed.

"How would you like water delivered directly to your door? I'm not talking about in the pipes, I mean through your front door! Our KATU *citizen correspondent* Dan Barmann shot this film from his very own house in Northeast Portland—*Sherwood*—and we have it here to show you now."

The screen switched to a poor-quality video and in the center of it, presumably, was Dan Barmann. He was unshaven and holding his own camera pointed at himself. The camera jiggled and Dan went from the center of the screen to a tilting off-center. Nevel knew that were he to see the man coming toward him on the street, he'd give a wide berth, not of fear, but because of the need in his eyes. The man had the look of someone who would tail you around and ask for a favor or to sign his petition or maybe just a hug.

"Hello, citizens. This is Dan Barmann. I live up in Sherwood, and while this whole experience has been on the scary side, something happened yesterday morning that started to change my mind about it. It's about to happen again in a minute, and I'm going to tape it for you, yes, you, KATU watchers."

The video paused and lines of text overlaid the still image: "Recorded earlier today. Dan Barmann, citizen reporter."

The camera view spun to Dan Barmann's floor, and the edge of his door. "That guy needs some training, right?" Nevel said. "I mean come on."

"Nevel."

"Why are are we looking at the floor still?" They heard the sound of a doorbell and the view of the floor persisted. "I don't have time for this, right? Why can't the studio spend ten minutes editing the thing?"

"It's true, you're a busy man, you've got a tunnel to dig."

Dan Barmann opened the door and on the other side was a cute, bob-headed woman with long eyelashes. Two tattooed bluebirds were visible at her neckline, just above her T-shirt. "Hi," she said and then noticed the camera being pointed at her.

"Well, hi there!" Dan said.

"That guy is an idiot," Nevel said. "Right? Isn't that guy an idiot? She's cute though."

"Stop," Cora said in a manner indicating she was no stranger to, nor particularly troubled by, Nevel's commentary over the course of a decade and a half of marriage.

"Well, she is."

Cora exhaled. "Agh—it's going to be awkward if they don't start speaking."

The water carrier cleared her throat. "I'm here to bring you your unit gallon," the woman said. She held up a unit gallon for the camera and handed it over.

"And, oh, OK," Dan said, and while he talked the camera drifted into her hair and then sky, "tell me about this. Why are you bringing me water?"

"Maid Marian is running a water distribution network so we don't have to go to distribution. It's less dangerous, creates jobs, and saves people a lot of time. Also, it gives you a direct connection to Sherwood government. You get two units fewer, but it's delivered to your door."

"Now we get to it," Dan said. "Two units tax! That's a big deal—skimming from the top. That doesn't sound like robbing the rich to me. What's she doing with all the extra units?"

"Well it's just one twentieth of your take," the woman readjusted her glasses and explained patiently. "Extra units will go to clinics and the needy and be saved for future emergencies."

"I see, OK, and what about you. Do you want to come in?" Nevel could hear the note of hunger and a loneliness, and it roused the part of his body reserved for screaming "No!" at the television while watching horror movies.

"Thank you, but I've got other deliveries," the woman said, confirming for Nevel that in real life the hero is rarely ever innocently lured into the villain's house. "I'll be back tomorrow. Everything OK here? Anything you want me to pass on to Maid Marian?"

"Oh. Tell her good job from me, ha ha. Water delivery is nice."

The water deliverer almost, but did not quite, roll her eyes at the camera and then said see you tomorrow and Dan turned the camera back on himself. Nevel thought he remembered seeing the correspondent before, reporting with youthful bluster on missing dogs and odd little factoids, a sort of independent camera junkie that sent stuff into the stations. But he appeared to have taken a few wrong turns since then.

"A unit or two fewer is a serious deal, make no mistake about it. On the other hand, let me show you this." The camera seesawed as he made his way back through the house, past dirty dishes and piles of clothes and other domesticities Nevel would have preferred not to see, and out the back door. In one corner of the backyard was a large wooden box with sheets hanging from it. "That's my new outhouse. These are mandatory in Sherwood, and there are crews going house to house building them."

There was something about seeing this man's own personal outhouse that made Nevel shudder.

"They came and built mine yesterday. Sure, there are some inconveniences here, but I'm saving far more than the couple of units per day they skim off, water that would have normally gone toward sanitation control. And that's my report from Sherwood."

"Huh," Nevel said.

The anchors wrapped up and the power shut off.

"We could build that. You like to dig," Cora said.

Nevel stood up and looked across the street. Even in the evening his previously humble intersection was busy. In the moonlight he saw people queued there from both nations—looking to do trade or send messages back and forth. A Green Ranger stood half-in and half-out of her guard post. Everyone needed cleared for entrance.

He hated going to distribution. It was a hassle and sometimes frightening. "I want my water delivered," he said.

"By a cute lesbian," Cora added. She picked up a novel, folding sleepily into his vacated spot on the couch.

Nevel lit a candle for her to read by, but he could tell it wouldn't be long before she was in bed and then he'd go to work on the tunnel. "How about you?" he said. "You could be a Sherwood deliverer, stop by with unit gallons for me." And it sparked a desire. He admired her form on the couch and thought ahead briefly to the first fifteen minutes down in the basement, when he would lie on the floor of the tunnel and fantasize about his wife two stories up. Like many things, doing the job yourself was easier than asking for it.

"True. If *somebody* built us an outhouse, unusual things could occur."

It did not happen in a covert manner, not in any secret meeting exactly, though later Renee thought back on the moment many times and each time saw it in a new light. It happened in the hallway on the first floor of Sherwood Nation HQ, between their offices. Around them the employees of the small nation continued their business.

"I want you to take a look at something," Gregor said.

She was on her way to meet with the volunteer crew. Gregor seemed disheveled, or as if there was some kind of physical strain on him.

"You alright?" Renee said.

"Eye the list," he said and handed it over.

The list was written in pencil in Gregor's stunted, blocky penmanship, and surrounding the names were many other lead-gray marks as if the pencil had struggled with each line, tapping out time between letters written, or written and then erased and written again. There was no title and no other text on the paper, which appeared to have been cut down to fit exactly the five names it held. The edges of it were worn, as if it had been worried around in someone's pocket for a while. Seeing the names there all together gave Renee a terrible shudder that came on suddenly and then continued to reverberate through her body. Her teeth chattered and she gripped her arms about herself.

"Sorry," she said.

"It's OK," Gregor said.

"Can't we give notice first? Like to flee?"

Gregor looked pained at the suggestion and leaned against the hallway wall. "We can . . ."

"I'd prefer it that way."

"It's—it's more dangerous, you know, if they . . ."

"Of course," Renee said, "but some of them will."

She leaned against the wall and faced him, still battling her shivers into stillness. They didn't say anything for a while. People passed next to them, sensing something of gravity in progress that could not be interrupted. It was intimate, Renee clutching the paper, Gregor facing her, patient.

"Warn first," Renee said.

Gregor nodded and took the list back. "It's complete?"

"Yes, complete."

The nightly news reported on four gun-related deaths in a single night in Sherwood. The territory seemed to be arguing with itself. The news asked Maid Marian for an interview; the city wanted an explanation. An internal inquiry determined that Rangers had not been involved in any of them.

In the country of Sherwood, by order of Maid Marian, the second amendment was repealed.

"Fuck it," she said, deeply aware of the taking away of rights. In her mind marched a procession of Sherwoodians past HQ with signs and banners and the appropriate chants, asking what rights were next to go.

She offered a five-gallon trade-in program per gun and ten units per box of ammo, and that message was carried through the water carrier delivery network. They received four hundred and eighty-two guns in all, far more than she had expected to receive, and surely a fraction of what still remained hidden in the neighborhood. These were hard times for the giving up of weapons.

The next day, Maid Marian sent another letter: She began with an impassioned plea, to mothers and fathers, to the common sense of the people. Security was taking hold in Sherwood, and she would guarantee theirs. Anyone caught with a gun by day number seven of the new country would be booted out, back to live in the city, no matter what family or possessions remained in Sherwood. They received another two hundred thirty-three guns.

Sherwood was gun free. Or at least that's what Jamal told himself, as he steered his giant tank of a battalion through training exercises. They had ammo for a small war now. People had saved up for end-times.

He trained them in crowd control, emergency management, siege, sniper fighting, and survival tactics, making up most of it each night as he prepared for the next day, scrawled out on notebook paper. When one of the brigade knew more than he did, which was often, he put them in charge of that exercise. They trained for hours a day, but most of all, he trained them in restraint. As a shiny new country, a single entity in the sea of a greater city, they could not risk giving anyone an excuse to take back control. One death and one news exposé and the experiment could end.

"Someone gets trigger finger, you come see me," he said. "Your neighbor gets trigger finger, come tell me. We'll go down to the train tracks and shoot some dead freight. You want a brawl—be a Green Ranger, go on a water route, you'll see action. But nobody here shoots anything, *anything*, unless I say so. After you leave practice, you are a lamb, understood?"

Zach wanted to go north, and each day he toyed with a plan in that direction. But he believed what the news implied—that it was too dangerous to travel to Sherwood. Not Sherwood itself, which the news continued to portray as if they were on the personal payroll of Maid Marian, but the neighborhoods that lay between his building and Sherwood.

In some semi-suicidal gesture, someone would set his own house on fire, or in a feud, his neighbor's house. With the city as dry as it was, all it took was one fire before a huge swath of homes would become blackened holes. It'd already happened twice—great plumes of smoke made columns into the air. Fire trucks circled around the neighborhood looking for a place to make a stand. Their tanks contained precious fire suppressant—waste water and liquified sewage—that they dared not use on a house that could not be saved. Bulldozers lined up to build a dirt moat around the blaze. They cut down any tree that might be a bridge for the fire to travel along.

The daily death toll for the city stood somewhere between ten and forty, and yet he knew that much of this was concentrated into pockets of violence. And not just random violence; there were always small wars going on, gang vs. gang, neighborhood vs. neighborhood, for resources or control or just desperation.

Twice he'd packed up his gear and sat next to his bicycle on the ground floor until the light left the sky and darkness fell, but his house was a castle to him, it was his wizard's tower. It contained family history and secrets and projects and—he admitted it—his bed, which he liked very much. He wasn't like her. The physical unknown that might await such a journey daunted him.

And so he spent countless hours on his roof, his telescope trained on Cully neighborhood where she'd found refuge. A mere five or six miles away.

Seventeen days after he'd sent Renee and Bea into hiding in the north, a body slipped into bed beside Zach in the middle of the night. He leapt up, pulling whatever was at hand to him in defense. In this case the sheets, which he held in front of him now like a shield.

In the moonlight he could not see her face, just a long naked body, scars and moles and blemishes air-brushed away by the dim light of the moon, leaving a polished creature, a marble-smooth statue that lay there like some apparition come to love or destroy. Helix strands of intrigue and fear spiraled up his spine and he froze like that, his sheet bunched menacingly in front of him.

On the floor below, in his kitchen, he could hear what sounded like an invasion by a family of bears. Things rattled and bumped as their clumsy paws attempted to discover the subtle opening mechanisms of pantry and refrigerator.

"Hey," said the body on the bed, turning onto her belly—for it was definitely a woman—squeezing the pillow to herself in a hug, her face pressed into it.

He stared at this new topography of her.

"I'm not going to be able to stay awake much longer. Your bed is so much more comfortable than what I've been sleeping on." He could hear the sound of her grinning through her words.

He let down his sheet guard and got into bed beside her. "You shouldn't be here," he said. He kissed her back and let his head rest there, his head turned toward the hills of her buttocks in the dim light. "Now that you are, I'm going to tie you up, so you cannot leave again."

"I've had to argue with practically everyone about coming here, so don't make me do it all over again with you."

"Who's downstairs?"

"Oh—you know, Bea and the rest of my silly entourage. You'll meet them in the morning."

He climbed atop her back and kissed her neck, pressed himself into her.

"I'm going crazy up there, Zach," she said, her voice muffled by the pillow. "I had to get out. I have hundreds of people working for me now, and it's all on a sort of credit. I'm faking it, and the more I fake it, the more I become the person they think I am. I don't even know what I'm like anymore."

"Mm, queen of the north. Sexy queen of the north."

"Yeah, that's me."

He brushed her hair from her face. "Hey, I lost my job," he said.

"You? You seem like the last person who could lose a job. What happened? Why aren't you at my gig yet?"

"The mayor hates you. You probably know this."

"I sat in his car, you know. You would have been proud. I should have asked after you."

Zach stared out his window. The city was dark, powered down for the night. The loss of the electric hum made each sound outside an anomaly, a potential threat, a curiosity.

"So? What have you got holding you here then?"

He tried to imagine himself up in Sherwood and couldn't figure out what he could carve out for himself there. He did not join well. He could not lead and was a poor follower, and he couldn't shake the feeling it was all headed for catastrophe. "I'm—," he said.

Renee's body bucked up against him. "Come on."

"I have a building, I need to . . ."

"You got me into this mess, buster."

"I, *hardly*—anyway, you rose perfectly to that mess. You went way further than I imagined. I'm the quiet ref on the sidelines, the old man on the park bench, I don't play."

"I don't know what you're talking about," she said. "You don't see what you are." To make her point she bucked against him again. "You see yourself as some uncommitted futzer. Come up to Sherwood and be an architect, do something big."

"Architect?"

She wasn't listening, she pushed into him, pivoting her hips upward.

"You don't mean houses."

"Nope."

"You're not going to tell me?"

"Oh," she exhaled. "No. Shush. This is what I think about at night."

He reached out and clasped a hand in each one of hers.

"I have big plans for you," she said. "I've been waiting to steal you away from the mayor. Brain drain."

"Shh," he said. "Go slow."

By delivery to his front porch, tucked into the old mailbox, Martin received a piece of paper called "Notice of Exile." "Fred!" he yelled. "Fred, come here!" What load of tarring bullshit was this?

"Yes, boss."

"Read this to me, will you? I read it and got it all wrong."

Martin's cousin Fred took the paper and studied it, listing slightly to one side, as if one foot were shorter than the other. He straight-armed the paper away from him, at a distance he could read it. Martin hadn't realized Fred needed reading glasses. They were getting old.

"Here," Martin said. He held out his own reading glasses and shrugged. "I've got extras."

Fred took the glasses and fiddled with them and smiled with them on, ridiculously.

Martin sighed impatiently. "And so? Ain't that many words on there."

"It's from that chick. You didn't watch the news last night?"

"No, I didn't watch the fucking news last night."

"What are you on my case for?" Fred said.

"Give me that. I know who she is. She can't do this."

"Boss, she got a army."

"But come on. What do we do? Just pack on up?"

Fred shrugged.

"I'm not going anywhere." He was no longer welcome? He had twenty-four hours to move out of "Sherwood"?

"Lots of houses we could set up in," Fred said.

"Really? It's that easy for you? This is our home, Freddy. My da' lived here, your uncle."

He started to carry around his little Heckler & Koch KH4. It'd been his father's, but it was in good shape. He didn't like to carry one; it felt uncomfortable and there was never the right place to put it. He tried wearing a suit jacket so he could wear it inside, and for a moment he thought he might be fashioning himself a new look. He had to admit it looked pretty fucking good. But the boys all laughed and started calling him Mr. Boss, so he went back to wearing it in his pants, where it made an imprint in the aging flesh of his back. He wasn't supposed to be packing anyway, that's what irked him—*that's what you had men for!* But he was feeling a little less sure of everything these days.

Suddenly the streets were full of green dudes and it was getting a little aggravating trying to run the business. He had employee issues. All they ever wanted to talk about was her and the *country.*

"It's the same fucking place it's always been, assholes," he yelled at them, but he could see they took the conversation elsewhere.

Second, everybody was so distracted that business was essentially dead. Patience, he told himself. Everybody would come back after they got bored. Everybody always got bored, and they always came back. He'd let them take a little vacation in their minds, visiting the new country, but they'd be back.

Still, he sent Jenko down to her office to see what the fuss was about. Get an explanation, maybe a little leeway. Martin could play nice. He didn't see why he couldn't play under the radar, beneath the covers. He wasn't greedy.

Jenko never came back! Just disappeared. Probably never even presented his case. A day later Fred saw Jenko in one of the green suits. Martin wanted to strangle the skinny little son of a bitch, and he had his men run a few messages over to Jenko's house to let him know, one after the other. The more he thought about it, the more pissed off he became and so he piled on with the abuse.

He needed some alone time after that. He went down to his place in the cool basement and poured himself a small bath. It was heated by a wood-fired stove, and he took great pleasure in stoking the fire, imagining while he did so that it was her big wood house burning.

Turns out he'd left the Notice of Exile next to the bath. Must have needed to relax in a hurry last time. A little warm water kept the steam from getting all built up in his brain, so he didn't have aneurisms, blow his top like his old da'.

She even had her own letterhead. That gave him an envy-pause. Why didn't he have his own letterhead? "Fred!" he yelled toward the stairs. She had a logo too. The notice was printed on a third of a piece of paper. He could see the cut line jagged, like they'd printed three notes on the same paper and cut them apart. *Who else got a letter?*

He'd thought it might have been his rude little visit, some little vendetta she had. Now he realized she was purging. She was shitting all of them out on the other side of the line she'd drawn. They were all casualties in her war with the city. But the city didn't like them either.

He had to talk to someone. Maybe that spic German, have a meet-up and compare notes. Just bring it up casually, you don't want him knowing you got a notice if he didn't.

Martin turned the letter over and to his surprise found something printed there.

Presenting the Sherwood Anthem
Composed by Jayla Williams of the Sabin neighborhood.

As if a myth from greener times
Maid Marian carved us a country
Drew twelve miles of righteous lines

Oh Sherwood,
you stand small but tall
Like the last matryoshka doll

Now life is good to us
She took the helm
Of our happiness

We make, we build, we farm
we teach, we bike, we love!

Oh Sherwood,
you stand small but tall
I hear your worthy call

I will defend you with all I have
So that others may love you too
Where life is our right and water our due

Oh Sherwood,
you stand small but tall
My favorite enclave of all

"What in the holy name of fuck is this?" Suddenly the paper felt weirdly contagious in his hand. "Fred!" he yelled. He didn't like people seeing him in his bath but this was a disturbing revelation. He poured a little bubble bath in and churned it up to hide his privates. Where the fuck was—"Fred!"

He heard some noise on the stairs. "I need you to go talk to German"—he pronounced it *hair*-mun—"pronto. His English is not so good, you know any Spanish?"

But it wasn't Fred on the stairs. It was like a ninja or something, all dressed in black with a black knit hat and a black handkerchief tied across his mouth. Martin stared at him and tried to figure out why Fred would have sent this dude instead; maybe a new hire? And then he startled into understanding. He threw himself over the side of the tub, a burst of adrenalin making him limber, splashing a giant eruption of bubbles and water, and ducked down on the other side. His KH4 just had to be in his fucking pants, didn't it.

"Hey now, hey," he said. "This isn't a robbery, is it? This about that notice maybe? I—ha ha—was just reading that."

He crouched naked on the other side of the bathtub. Humiliating. "You going to say anything first?" Martin tried to reach his arm around the tub. "Sir? About that notice. I was hoping—Fred!" He was going to have a few things to say to Fred, that was for sure. His heart thumped in his chest, a bass line of a rap song in a cheap car. "Tell me your name. Who you're with at the very least." He took inventory of the places he could hide behind in his basement, the man-hole, as he called it. There was a pool table, the bath, a bunch of couches. He had done some work on a dude's skull with a pool cue once, but that was a ways back. "Say something!" he yelled and felt like weeping and pissing all at once.

Then the ninja-fucker leapt in front of him and Martin's head whipped back and hit the concrete.

When he woke they were dragging him up the stairs, and he had a headache to end all motherfucking headaches. One eye was all worked over. Through it he could see nothing. Through the other the world was a hazy film. They'd put a plastic bag over his head! The ninja shot him in the head and he wasn't dead. It was a miracle. The bag was to keep blood from getting all over the place, he thought, which in the back of his mind he was appreciative of. Professionals.

The good eye began to go dark and he struggled to get a hold of himself. *Come on, Marty.* Outside it was night and they were talking about him.

"Rose City?"

"Yes, thanks."

"He's naked."

"Well, I wasn't going to dress him. He was in a bath."

"A water bath?"

"What else is there?"

"Son of a bitch."

They loaded him into the back of some kind of bicycle-pulled contraption and began to pile stuff over the top of him and he tried to call out. Rose City was a cemetery. No way he was going there, but as he struggled to keep his remaining eye from going dark, he began to feel a hunger for sleep.

"Where next?"

"Twelfth and Prescott."

"Oh man."

"We're nearly done."

The other eye wouldn't stay open now. Maybe Fred had let them in. He wished he could tell his cousin it was alright. He understood. Fred could take some of their reserves and do OK for himself. He wasn't going to need the reading glasses back.

"You get the other one?"

"You mean Fred?"

"Ha ha, the dude was screaming for a dead man the whole time."

A few days after Renee's one night visit, and after spending the morning packing and then changing his mind, hanging out in various doorways in a state of pre-nostalgia for the building he'd not yet left, Zach put on his backpack, swung his leg over his bike, and started pedaling north.

In the end, it wasn't a big deal. Several blocks were burnt utterly to the ground and the air was filled with a choking soot, but there was no human threat. On other blocks the residents ignored him—they sat on their porches or carried water rations back in protective groups or wheeled along, possessions piled high in shopping carts.

At the border he approached an outhouse-like structure and was hailed by a large black man dressed in green with MM's insignia on his shirt: a bow and a unit gallon.

"What's your business in the Northeast?" the man asked.

"Ah," Zach said and tried to figure out how to say he was the boyfriend. "Do I have to tell you?"

"If you don't live here, you need to be issued a permit." The guard took out a piece of paper and Zach saw that the heading read Temporary Visiting Permit.

"On whose law?"

"Sherwood law," the guard said with obvious boredom. The guard's gaze wandered up the street and as he prepared to ignore the ignorant city peon.

Zach nodded. "And you work for Maid Marian?"

The Green Ranger looked briefly uncomfortable. "Of course."

"It's hard to get a regime off the ground," Zach said. "You're doing good work, I'm sure."

"Do you want a permit or not?"

"I have a friend I'm visiting."

"Location? If you don't have the exact number, I can retrieve it for you." The guard gestured up the block where Zach could make out another ranger dressed in green. "Visitors have to have sponsors within the country. We'll send a message to your sponsor."

"She's on Going Street near Fifty-Second."

The Ranger frowned at him. "Your friend doesn't live there any more. That section is closed. No one lives there. Your city ID please and the name of the friend."

Zach handed over his ID card and made up a name for the friend. The Ranger wrote them both down. "Come back tomorrow. I'll have the location of this person if they're still in the territory and confirm that she's willing to sponsor you."

"So I can't get in?"

"No."

"Is there anything I could do to get in?"

"No."

He wondered why the hell he'd made the journey up here in the first place. He looked back the way he'd come and desperately didn't want to return. He rode away in disgust—across the street and up a ways and pondered the territory. He passed a city police car going the other way along the border. He imagined they were always there, waiting and watching to see what this new entity would do next.

On a block with no guardhouse he rode up a bank, climbed a short fence into a backyard and pulled his bike after him, and then he was in Sherwood. He found his way to an alley and skirted round the Green Ranger who watched the intersection.

Above him the sky was gray with clouds and all at once a pattering of rain came down, moistening his head and arms as he pedaled,
and he stopped momentarily to look up. It was a tease, as it always
was. It would not stay or last. The dots on the street quickly dissipated. But nevertheless, he took it as an auspicious sign, and proceeded with hope.

He rode hard toward Cully neighborhood and saw that things
were buzzing. There were people dressed in green outfits everywhere—whether they were employed by Sherwood, some volunteer
force, or simply in solidarity with, he couldn't tell. People were out on
their porches, removing trash from their homes, talking with neighbors as if no riots had taken place. About a third of the houses were in
a state of permanent garage sale, with items laid out on their dry front
yards. Everywhere he looked people were packing things—bundles
on their backs, loads in bike trailers, duffel bags over shoulders—he
couldn't imagine where they were all going. Perhaps this was simply
the sign of a makeshift, functioning economy he thought. Trade and
barter and the occasional sale.

At Nineteenth and Alberta he noticed that he was being followed
by two women on bikes. He accelerated, and the moment he did they
went into chase and rapidly caught him, pulling alongside.

"Stop," a woman said.

Zach pulled his bike alongside a curb and feigned indignation.

"You snuck in. What's your business in the Northeast?"

"I did not," Zach said.

"Don't even try," the other woman said, wagging her finger at
him. "You're the third dude today. It's such a hassle when you deny it."

"I'm going to visit a friend."

"But you were told to wait."

Zach shook his head and wondered at how he'd been caught and
how word had traveled about him already. They didn't seem to be
employing any kind of communication device.

"You work for the city," the other, a heavy-set, blond-haired
woman said. Her hands bore word-tattoos—*Fire* on the left, *Ice* on
the right. The two women shared a striking resemblance and Zach
spooked at the thought of the law being enforced by a great army of
tattooed twins. He realized he was answering too slowly.

"Spy," one said and the other nodded. "OK, you're coming with
us. Come on, back on the bike."

Zach biked toward the Cully neighborhood escorted by his twin enforcers, relieved that they didn't simply toss him back over the border but alarmed at being deemed a spy.

They took Zach to a house he remembered, a behemoth of a craftsman, as if it were built for a race of people of greater height and girth, and he saw how it had morphed into fulfilling the needs of a government building. In a backyard the size of a small schoolyard field there were construction projects on one end and troops—the fabled Green Rangers, he assumed—being run through drills on the other. They stepped into the house and into a waiting area, walled off from the rest of the house with seats containing several anxious looking individuals. Perhaps they were waiting for her audience, he thought, or job interviews, or criminals awaiting punishment.

One of the women steered him in, her hand firm on his shoulder. They went into a back room where an older black woman with a tall maroon hat was seated behind a desk.

"What's your business in Sherwood?" the woman said without looking up.

"This one snuck in." The girl had his shoulder like a dog bite. "He's a spy."

"Mm."

Zach told them he was here to see Maid Marian, and that she was expecting him.

The woman with the maroon hat squinched up her eyes at him. "I've heard that one today already."

"He works for the city," the biker with *fire* tattooed on her hand said.

Zach told her Maid Marian's real name, and said she would know him.

An older black man dressed in a black sweater and blue jeans appeared in a doorway at the back of the room that Zach hadn't seen. In his right hand he wielded the bowl-end of a smoking pipe. He eyed Zach with cold authority.

"I'll take this one, bring him back."

They followed into the back room where the man seated himself behind a great desk. He wore a black baseball cap and the Maid Marian emblem was safety-pinned to the front. He was in his sixties, and from the moment Zach entered the room until he was seated in front of him, the man locked eyes with him. There was a professorial air about him and, from the way the escorting Ranger treated him, Zach knew he was in front of someone important. He sat and waited for the man to talk but he said nothing for a few moments. Zach fidgeted.

"You work for the city?" the man said.

Zach felt flustered and his face reddened. "How do you all know that? I work—worked—for an ad agency—we did work for the city sometimes."

"You crossed the border without permission. What are you here to find out?" Zach didn't know how to answer and so they said nothing. "We are specifically looking for someone to make an example of to send a message to the city. Are you that person?"

"No, sir," Zach said hopelessly, his mind gone startlingly blank.

"This would be an appropriate time to explain why you're here, then."

Zach glanced at his woman captor, hanging back to see what their captain would order them to do with their prisoner. "I'm in a relationship with Maid Marian," he said, and after no one made a response he felt like he ought to clarify. "I'm Maid Marian's boyfriend," he said, and it came out meek and uncertain. He wasn't sure he knew this woman who had closed off the borders and flooded the streets with a green army. Any longer, "boyfriend" seemed such a small, pedestrian word. Unfit for a warlord. A warlord had a wife, or *wives*. He glanced again at his captors, who were at full attention now, surprised at this new, dubious news. Or perhaps she's not here at all, he thought, this is just some great coverup, and it's this man who's in charge.

"Maid Marian?" the man said, one eyebrow raised and ready to crush the absurdity of the claim. He tapped the desktop with his pipe.

"I mean Renee," Zach said.

The gentleman pointed his pipe at him like a pistol. "Prove it," he said, and then turned to his Rangers and made a gesture. The two soldiers left and before Zach had formulated a proper reply they returned with a small wooden table and two chairs. Then a teapot and two cups were brought. The older man rose from his desk and sat with him.

Tea was poured and Zach felt disoriented, but grateful to be momentarily relieved of the glare of the man's eyes. He fought the impulse to grab the tiny cup and down it in one gulp, a desire to quench the thirst that disabled all mannerly sipping. He sampled the tea and found it some kind of green. That was fitting, he thought, the tea, the uniform. Diuretics were heavily discouraged by the city and common sense—the man seemed to be indicating to him he was above these concerns.

"I don't know how to prove it," he said. "She worked at a cafe close to my house in the Southeast. I went every day for many months." He gulped another swallow of tea. "I'm not particularly forward."

He saw the man pull his chair close in, lean in so that he could speak in a quiet voice, the skepticism turning suddenly to curiosity and—perhaps—disappointment. So this is her boyfriend after all, Zach imagined him thinking, no great warrior but a bespectacled, uncertain fellow, with a slight stoop, shaved head, and arms that seemed extra long.

"After a while I asked her out and—and, and she laughed." The amazonian warriors who'd brought him in chuckled appreciatively at this, and he noticed that they had leaned in to listen too. "One night I was in the cafe at closing. She locked the door while I was still in there. I was the only person in there. She pulled a bottle of wine from behind the counter and she took pulls from it. She sat down at my table." Zach couldn't help but smile at the memory, feeling proud and lucky and singled out. "She slugged me on the shoulder and said, 'where are we going, old man?'" Zach remembered how he'd treasured that phrase, how it had made it into their lexicon, the intimacy of "old man," as if they'd been married for years.

His interrogator nodded and looked up at each of the Rangers in the room with him for confirmation. "Sounds like her." He held his hand out and they shook. "I'm Gregor, formerly of the Woodlawn neighborhood, and general of the Green Rangers."

"OK, nice to meet you," Zach said and took the man's hand, the adrenalin still a skin-prickling fear in him.

"You suppose Maid Marian will still think you're her boyfriend? Or is this stalking?"

"Well, I think she thinks I am," Zach said and looked at each of them helplessly. So much had changed in so short of a time. "She told me she had a job for me."

Gregor nodded at one of his soldiers and she left.

Zach finished off his tea and stared at the tabletop. He'd like to ask him about the Green Rangers and riots and governing and water distribution, but after you have just narrated in some detail your inadequate courtship skills and as you wait for your prospective girlfriend to show up and claim—or not claim—you like a soiled scarf from the lost and found—well. Zach felt it a bit of a challenge formulating a question that wouldn't bubble out like some anxious gas and float in the air between them.

"It's going well," Gregor said, answering Zach's unasked question. "Touch and go, I suppose. We're calling this Faith Week. We're working on borrowed confidence from the citizens." Gregor put a weight of seriousness behind each word, so that one felt comforted by the inherent veracity of what he was saying. "What are your skills, Zach?"

Zach looked Gregor in the eyes and realized the implication. Any boyfriend of Maid Marian was a public figure, or else ought to stay in the shadows.

"I'm not sure," Zach said.

"He's my strategist."

Zach and Gregor looked up to see Renee in the doorway. Zach stood. She was dressed in green too, and the emblem of Sherwood was embroidered over her heart. They must have a team of full-time embroiderers and uniform-makers, he thought. Her braids flowed out from under a boxy baseball cap that said "Magnetic."

"Tea time with Gregor, eh? We drink a lot of fucking tea around here."

"Says he knows you," Gregor said.

"Yeah," Renee said. "Come on, Zach. I want to show you the map room."

Gregor offered his hand to Zach again. "That's a lot of clearance, boyfriend." There was a warmness, and a warning, in the phrase.

Zach turned to follow Renee.

"If you want to put on a uniform—" Gregor said.

Renee shook her head. "No, he doesn't. Come on, Zach."

Halfway up the second flight of stairs Renee turned and embraced him. "I'm glad you're here," she said. "We're barely keeping it together. People are dead."

"I'm sorry," Zach said, not knowing what else to say and feeling the joiner's angst well up in him. Every cause he could ever remember being a part of had failed. He returned the hug until she released him.

Everything changed for Zach when he came into the map room. In the center of the room was a large round table with hundreds of scrawled

notes. There were crumpled scraps of paper on the floor and a truly
huge and impressive hand-drawn map that split the territory and its
borders into several sectors laid across the wall and overlapping onto
the ceiling and the floor.

"Hey, Zach, you made it." Bea stood at the table inspecting a pile
of notes. She waved noncommittally and went back to her work.

Zach traced his finger along the wall. Each house in the entire
country was drawn out as a tiny square on the map. Inside the houses
there were tiny scrawled messages, or just ID numbers. Along the
streets, routes for water trucks and trash trucks were traced. There
were dotted lines for bicycle delivery routes and little sentry box symbols for border guards.

"I want you to meet Leroy," Renee said and steered him to the far
side of the room, her hand on his lower back guiding him.

A wiry black man turned around from what he was working on.
He had a fistful of white paper in one hand and a Sharpie in the other.
Zach held out a hand to shake.

Leroy looked down at his two occupied hands, then back at Zach,
and nodded, and then Leroy started from Zach's feet and scanned him
up. It was a naked feeling, as if his whole body lay atop a photocopier
glass. When Leroy looked him in the eyes again, he could see at work
on his face a sincere struggle to fabricate some idle talk or perform
some other leavening social convention. "The weather . . ." Leroy said
and then held up the hand that bore the sharpie, waved it dismissively
in the air as if to scratch out his comment. He turned and went back
to his work.

"He's busy," Renee said. "This is his map."

Zach spent the next while going through the pieces of the system. He learned how the notes arrived, how directives were given,
how things were balanced and issues dealt with. He watched Bea and
Leroy argue over whether an outpost ought to be written as permanent or temporary and he drank in the room; the immense amount
of information induced vertigo. He was euphoric.

Renee sat down in a big leather chair in middle of the room and
pulled out a bottle of some kind of hand-labeled alcohol from a hidden
drawer in the side of the chair. "The perks of being in charge." She
poured them each a glass several times larger than Zach felt comfortable with. "One of the very few. We're starting up a distillery. This?"
She swept her hand toward the room. "This is not my specialty." She

patted his hip. "I was hoping you—well. Take a look around, sweet thing." She took a deep swallow, grimaced, closed her eyes, and leaned her head back. "See what you think. And then later, maybe you'd go on a date with me? I need a date. I'm glad you're here, Zach."

While her eyes were closed he rested his hand on her forehead and studied her. There was something mortally tired about her. He supposed that transitioning from running a cafe to your own empire could do that to a person. He wished they were in a dark bedroom alone together. How many warlords went back to managing cafes? How many lived to a ripe age? He bent and kissed her lips and then inspected the room.

Bea and Leroy squabbled about another section of the map. There was shuffling at the door and a man dressed in uniform stepped in and put a three-inch stack of notes in a basket there. Incoming data, Zach realized. He wondered if his own note, generated in his exchange with the border guard, lay in the bin and he went to inspect the incoming. There were notes for everything—the Rangers wrote down all interactions in Sherwood. "The swing set in Alberta park is broken." "Mrs. Homes is too unsteady to carry her unit gallon from her front door to the kitchen counter." "National Guard has two jeeps and six soldiers parked at MLK and Fremont— they're setting up some kind of structure there." "Jahrain suspects his neighbor of taking an extra ration for someone he claims lives there but doesn't." They collected everything. Zach looked up at the wall and at the carpet of discarded messages and the diagnosis came to him easily: information fatigue. The data crashed like a great wave into the room each day, inundating them. With no proper analysis of the data, no sense of trends, and no indicators, they would never understand the effect of their actions.

After he'd read several dozen notes and made the rounds of the rooms, he realized he'd done this before. I've played this game, he thought. He had burned thousands of hours playing Command & Conquer, Age of Empires, Settlers, and other strategy games, and he'd done this for clients, too. Here was simply a massive real-life version. He found some scratch paper and began to sketch out plans for status meters. Indicators of the empire. Information was not power, it was the ability to synthesize data where the power lay, and he could give them that. He could give *her* that, he thought, and he hummed to himself with pleasure as he worked.

He took all of the stacks out of the incoming basket and began to sort them across the floor.

"Zach!" Bea said.

"Don't worry! I know what I'm doing!" he said.

"Let him," Renee slurred, her eyes still closed, "he's a smartypants."

Martin came to splayed out in the wooden wheelbarrow-bike contraption in time to hear a shit-storm of swearing from the two dark forms digging a hole, *his* hole, in the dim moonlit graveyard. He couldn't quite follow the gist of it, but one of the assholes had apparently hit the other with his shovel.

He could feel death hover close. A rotund, corpulent, drought-fed reaper, scratching its ass and waiting for him to close his eyes that last time so that it could slaver away over his soul. His da' would be there, wherever this reaper took him, and Martin regretted not for the first time how rusty he'd let his Russian get. Martin wriggled one arm free and tore a face-hole in the plastic bag they'd put him in. A cool wind blew grit into his eye socket. Martin sighed *"fuck"* in a long, despairing exhale, in pain and tired to be alive. He was going to have to do something about it now. In the chaos of the argument, he quietly tore open the rest of the plastic bag and then levered his naked, lumbering form over the edge of the contraption and rolled himself away into the night like a little burrito.

When he was far enough away, he stood and walked toward the border on the far side of the cemetery. He'd be a real fucking horror for any accidental bystander, he was sure. He found a hole in the chain-link fence and squeezed himself through it, scoring his middle with scratches. Then he stood and held up his middle finger at the territory. Oh he would be back all right, he thought, answering the unasked question, motherfucking right he would.

Zach scratched out a to-do list, remembering all the citywide campaigns they'd pitched to the mayor while working at Patel & Grummus. Inevitably there was something written on the back of the paper he used—this one had a fragment of what looked like someone's insurance policy from a decade back. All the scratch paper in HQ had been acquired in a donation drive, much like everything else: printers, computers, office supplies, paint, tools, lumber, odd items here and there. All Maid Marian had to do was put Needed for Sherwood on any outgoing correspondence and it poured in.

On the list he put:

Marketing objective: *Instill sense of unique Sherwood culture by manufacturing cultural artifacts and pop-culture events*

- Hire for internal marketing agency
- Refine logo (bow and quiver of water vials is functional, but has no personality—possible mascot wearing these?)
- Create first Sherwood holiday (Parade!)
- Water freedom day?
- Give something to your neighbor day?
- Show and tell-a-thon?
- Craft Sherwood slogan
- "Sherwood: Steal from the rich give to the poor"
- "Sherwood: FU PDX"
- "Sherwood: surrounded on all sides"
- "Sherwood: Forward!"
- "Sherwood: Vice Versa."
- "Sherwood: Enjoyable Enclave"
- Brainstorm methods for helping rangers propagate culture
- Free concert and permanent concert venue—in which every band plays its rendition of the Sherwood anthem
- Create Sherwood fact sheet

Zach leaned back into the couch in the middle of the map room and stared at the ceiling, wondering if one day other neighborhoods would be drawn there.

"How we doing, Leroy?"

"Mm," Leroy said.

"Awesome. We're doing awesome."

Leroy didn't answer.

"How much do you think people know they're being governed by a dictator? Does it cross their mind that there's no vote?"

It was him and Leroy, and he hadn't exactly managed to have any involved conversations with him yet. Though there was no denying that, though the man was reticent, he was highly attuned to the system.

A memory like a Swiss watch. Exactly the type of person you wanted in the nerve center. At the corner of his list he penciled, "LR happy? Something we could do?"

"It's in the news, but I think we need to bring up the subject of dictator before it hits the street too much. I'll write a letter." Zach loved writing letters. Had there ever been a more personal way to reach people? He grabbed a fresh sheet of paper.

"Instead of introductions, considering how many of us there are," the mayor said, "could you all introduce yourself before you speak?"

"Should I . . . then?"

"Yes, thank you." The mayor adjusted his reading glasses and stared down at the paper in front of him, and then looked up at the small, nervous man across the table. Around thirty people, he estimated, sat around the four large conference tables they'd fitted together in order to house this particular task force.

"My name is Ernest Weatermeyer. I run—ran a small company that creates pet supplies. In Beaverton. We, you know, there was like for fleas and other pests, and also other chemical-based products to control animal smell and—I am still not quite sure why I've been asked to come here?"

"I can explain that, Ernest, and—"

"Please introduce yourself, Margaret," the mayor said.

"Household Efficiency Task Force, Sellwood Lead. You're here because of the smell issue. You fabricate urine—what do you call it?"

"Odor removal?"

The mayor noted that Ernest was beginning to look alarmed, as if invited to his own inquisition.

"How much can you make?"

"Sorry, I—we haven't been in operation for some time now and—is there something, is something wrong?"

"Let me give you some back story," the mayor said, holding up a hand in what he hoped was a friendly, sliding sort of wave to deflect Margaret who, being part bulldog herself, might need some urine odor removal afterward for her own use. "Did you not get the task force mission statement?" The mayor gestured to his economics development advisor to hand Ernest the one-pager. "Thanks. Read it on your own time, but essentially we're looking at ways to improve household efficiency. One possible solution we've been looking into which would work in concert with our new simultaneous flush initiative is for—for, well, men *specifically,* and anyone who cared to take it on, to urinate in the back of the toilet tank."

Ernest held the one-pager and nodded eagerly but, the mayor could tell, uncomprehendingly.

"You see where you might fit in, then? No. OK." The mayor quickly rounded up facial expressions around the perimeter of the table, taking a quick read. Postures appeared dug in for an extended meeting. Unit gallons stood like small sentry robots in front of each participant. "Limited water resources puts an enormous strain on the sewage system, you understand. Wastewater needs to be recycled."

A hand was raised at the far edge of the table and the bearer spoke: "Anthony Brinestone from St. John's, former corporate defense lawyer. They call it Savewater in Sherwood."

"Yes," the mayor said and with his left hand he pinched the thigh of his own leg hard enough that his eyes watered, "thank you, Tony. Are you with us here, Ernest?"

"You have a smell issue? Sir but—"

"How much do you believe you could produce, and does it neutralize or can you describe what happens, on a chemical-level, I mean? You're a chemist, correct?"

The mayor watched it click in for Ernest, that a market opportunity had presented itself the likes of which he had not seen before. They were making progress now. But as with any thought of progress, the progress arms race with that *other nation* emerged, a race in which they were impossibly behind.

As others took on the substance of the meeting, the mayor slouched subtly into his chair, letting his face swivel from speaker to speaker, in the oft-employed expression of attentiveness of which he was a master. It was difficult not to shake the sense that it was meaningless progress. He felt he understood more clearly than ever before how a country might go to war, envious of another's prosperity, its citizens defecting or becoming restless. The urge to invent a mythology of evilness around that other, more successful nation compelling. Ernest, it appeared, had decided to fully capitalize on his supposed expertise and was now pontificating grandly and with self-importance. The mayor sighed and shifted a little more deeply into his seat. The phrase *Task Force,* to him, once noble with the ring of super-heroes, now felt more akin to an army of tortoises, wandering slow over the desert, aimless.

For task forces, god love them, were full of *citizens*. He tilted his notebook so that he might sketch the three citizen archetypes, putting each in a heroic stance. There was *the aging, inflexible do-gooder*, who when pressed spoke in indignant barks, fervent and jaw-clenching, never satisfied, constipation incarnate. There was *the unselfconscious rambler*, whose thoughts littered the sea of her mind like flotsam, and who could be persuaded into nearly any viewpoint, provided the right eloquence. And finally *the shiny-eyed optimist*, usually young and idealistic, whose energy matched only her/his naiveté and who would, in time, morph into one of the two previous types. Once sketched he appreciated his work—he'd always been a decent doodler. He drew a *TF* emblem on the character's chests, and gave them *TASK FORCE* boots and Zorro-style masks. And lo, he was their leader, surely manifested out of one of the types drawn, driven a touch further by ambition. This, then, was what made the world turn! Behind them, he sketched himself, his cape blowing in the wind. There were other ways to win, besides a war of progress.

He looked up from his work and scanned the room and noticed that all eyes were on him, waiting expectantly.

"Yes exactly," he said, "an excellent point, and thank you." He could see he hadn't hit the required response yet. "Sorry, I was having an interesting thought—" he smiled absently, "—and so where were we, Margaret?" For a moment he'd given them complete control, his mental absence ceding the decision process to the citizen committee—and he could feel them all biting into the responsibility at hand more deeply for it.

THE BEGINNING

Hello Sherwoodites!

Times are hard and we've inherited a mess here. Let's not delude ourselves: things will be a mess for some time to come. The intention is to get Sherwood to a level of self-sustainment so we can transition to a more moderate form of government. You should never have on your lips the question: "Who's in charge?"

I'm in charge. Will I always be in charge? No. I've sketched out below the stages I would like to follow for transitioning the government. Help me achieve these tasks, and let's move Sherwood forward!

Governmental Transition Plan

STAGE 1—CRISIS
Dictator

STAGE 2—WEAKNESS
**Maid Marian President
with elected council**

STAGE 3—STABILITY
**Consensus Government
with strong leadership**

We're in the dictator stage! That's a terrible word, right? Why do we need a dictator? *It is nearly impossible to make radical change through consensus.* The democracy—and I

use that word in the loosest of terms—beyond our
border is prone to corruption, ineffectual at real change,
an instrument for keeping the status quo. It cannot
handle an external crisis of this magnitude. But this is no
ordinary dictatorship. You have a direct line to my office,
via your water carrier. Use it! Your voice will be heard far
more clearly than in the current "democracy" of Portland.

Stage 1 "Crisis" goals

- Establish independence from the city
- Establish security
- Establish water distribution
- Establish clinics
- Establish farms/begin intensive gardening
- Establish schools
- Establish central bank based on water
- Begin to generate revenue through sale of water
  (excess water acquired through efficiencies, tax
  revenue and trade)
- Country-wide skills and education training

Stage 2 "Weakness" goals

- Successful harvests
- Expanded trade
- Minimum balance of 500,000 gallons of water
- Country charter
- Elect council

Stage 3 "Stability" goals

- Governmental transition based on work in stage 2
- The gradual reduction of my role
- Erect gargantuan statues of yours truly (joke!)

How long will all this take? Considering the substantial
progress we've made already, I believe these goals to be

attainable within a year or two. We are currently estimating a 200–300% drop in crime rates. *One week in.* I am enormously proud of this.

Pin this letter to your walls, my countrymen, and help me stay on task!

Thanks for your attention,

Maid Marian

Normally, it was dangerous not to ride your bike, Jamal thought. Best to be getting from one place to another quickly. Walking was something you did in your house, or within view of your house. Jamal considered this as he held the saddle of his bike in the morning. If you were walking, your slowness subjected you to all kinds of possibilities. Bike gangs could circle you like flies around a cow. You could pick up hangers-on, people the drought had made not right, their neuroses honed to single weird obsessions that they shared relentlessly with you as you walked, trailing along at your elbow, always within a comment's reach of rage. You could be ringed by child beggars, gangs of four or five or six who pecked at you for a sip of water and waited for you to show a weakness. Your route might radically lengthen by some impassable obstacle: a block fire, a wall of cyclone fence, fighting.

He looked up his block and saw trash blowing along the street, but the wind was mild and didn't carry enough dust to sting the eyes. The summer was at its height and he could feel the heat start to swell into the air, an itchy sweat in his scalp. In the old days before the drought he'd sometimes walk a day away. At thirteen, fourteen, fifteen—if you had nowhere to go and were desperate to leave the house, there was no better way to leave it all behind. He'd steal a pinch of dope from the stash, plug into headphones, and take his body elsewhere.

He was curious, mostly. For the feel of it. They were an island now, ringed in by a sea. In a handful of days there'd been a dramatic change to the street-level safety in the neighborhood. At least it felt that way. He was due for work—what a foreign word that was to him—and he knew it was idiotic to walk from King to Cully neighborhoods with no escape vehicle. There'd been plenty of times he'd cycled hard away from a hail of stones or down a side street dodging pursuers. And he was no easy target.

He gripped the saddle of his bike and pushed it along and decided to walk a ways. It was a little past dawn and the streets mostly slumbered still. He knew nearly every burnt-out house, and he planned his route to avoid them. They depressed him—permanent decay, like teeth lost to cavities. In the world they lived in, they would stay charred hulks. No house got rebuilt.

But in the yards of many other houses, he observed the hole and tarp setup that marked a condensation trap. Another Sherwood project implemented via the volunteer force. Like a nation's factories, he thought, there was industry there.

A few blocks up, Jamal stopped in front of a house with blankets laid over their dust lawn. The habitants smiled cautiously at him as they scurried in and out their front door, bringing objects of every kind and laying them out in patterns on the blanket.

"Everything OK?" Jamal asked a woman in her twenties in army cutoffs and a tank top.

"Hello, Ranger! Yard sale, open everyday now." She smiled. "Come on in." She gestured with a sales flourish and a wink at their collection.

Jamal wandered among the items, some on tables, some laid out on the ground in organized piles. For the most part it was ordinary garage sale fare—from the old days—for white roommates in their twenties: books and records and electronics, toasters and silverware, trinkets, movie posters, a spattering of unlikely furniture, cables that no longer had a place to plug into, semi-used art supplies, clothing of various discarded fashions. There was a heap of greenish cloth with a sign that poked out: "National Pride!" In it he found a pair of children's army-green walkie-talkies, the price marked both in US Dollars and water units, but the batteries had been robbed from them long ago and the chance of obtaining more was slim. He hovered over a handsome accordion with shiny ivory keys and a case with purple velvet lining until a bone-skinny man with a thick beard called out from the doorway that it wasn't for sale. The bearded man, shirtless and dressed in some kind of—Jamal didn't know, circus pants?—brought out a lawn chair and parked it next to the accordion, and then began to play a mournful tune. Jamal felt a brief nostalgia for an old Portland, or rather not his old Portland, rife with dime bags and family power, but the city's self image. With its sea of whimsical musicians and artists, bike shops and gluten-free bakeries, living up to the nation's stereotype of them, at least on the surface, before need and fear had either driven them away or made them serious.

There was a whole spread of makeshift weapons, fashioned largely from broom handles, duct tape, and nails.

"Very cheap," the girl said.

"You made them?" He'd seen the style.

"Yeah, we made them, we used them," she said quietly. She pointed up the block where a woman dressed in Ranger green sat in a lawn chair at the intersection. "But, you know? Somebody is there all the time. We don't need so many anymore."

Jamal stared up the street and wondered if he knew the Ranger. Cops had inspired scorn and hatred in him before, but here he was, dressed same as her.

"They'd look good on you, Mister," the woman said about the weapons. "I could strap one to your back like a samurai. Very handsome," she said wryly.

Jamal chuckled. "How much?"

"For you, a unit each. You could strap them to your handlebars like horns. It's in style, big time."

"You're a hard sell," he said.

She curtsied. "I'll go get a measure."

He picked out two and talked her into finding some more tape in order to attach them to his bike. She took the job seriously, and he could see that in the way she'd worked, she'd once done this scared, that at one time they'd huddled in their basement fabricating weapons. After she finished, she admired her work. They were tightly holstered there but could be pulled off in need.

"Thank you," he said. He pulled out his canteen and poured two units into her unit measure and admired the enterprise.

At Alberta Park he stopped and watched the farming operation. The fields were tiny, using as little water as possible, and he couldn't imagine that they would do more than provide a slice of carrot to each. It'd be one proud carrot, however.

A sign asked for unit donations and for the second time he pulled out his canteen and, after being directed by the gardener, planted the two seeds that were given to him and split a unit over the seeds once they were in the ground. He admired the dribbles he'd made over each of the plantings. The gardener placed small plastic bottles cut in half over each of the seeds. These were his to care for now. I've got a stake planted down, he thought. Roots here.

He shared the road with many other walkers and bikers. There was a new feeling everywhere, an industriousness, as people looked up from their misery after a few days straight of peace and began to pick together scraps of their lives. There were goods to be sold, projects to work on, Sherwood volunteer work to be done, water to be delivered.

By the time he arrived at HQ, his body was vibrating with hope.

Zach made a paper representation of their water supply. On a piece of paper he drew a large box with a Sharpie and labeled it "Water Supply (100,000 gallons)." Then he placed a piece of paper he'd colored with blue crayon inside of the box, adjusting the level by sliding the blue paper up and down through a slit in the bottom of the paper. He pinned the thing to the wall and he and the two Rangers who'd been assigned to help him admired his work. It was about as rudimentary as it came. Each morning he instructed his employees to check the supply in the various tanks throughout the territory with a bamboo pole.

He made indicators for money and the number of Green Rangers. He created an arm-span-sized map of all Sherwood that he outlined neighborhood by neighborhood. Over these he pinned colored indicators that he fashioned out of construction paper. Fire, gunshots, death, sickness, news van, rioting, city, unrest, party, miscellaneous. He could use the stream of incoming news and pin a visual representation to this map, so that a quick glance could show where the trouble was. He wanted them all to know exactly where they stood, and he was assigned the manpower to tally and change his meters. Over time he would graph them all and compare them to a history of policy decisions.

He quickly realized they took delivery of enough extra water per day in taxes and through other sources that they had an excess, and so he advised that they sell water on the city's black market. A single unit of water fetched between twenty-five cents and a dollar, depending upon the news and whatever crisis was in vogue that week. At forty units per gallon, this made an excellent ongoing base for the economy, but it was not enough.

As Zach fretted over the figures at the big table in the map room, other Sherwood Rangers and officials busied about behind him.

"We need taxes, Renee," he said as she sat down next to him. "That's how all governments work."

"We have taxes—"

"I mean more than two units—we need them to pay. You can't run clinics and farms and schools on nothing."

Gregor leaned into the table and crossed his arms. He still made Zach uneasy. In the transition from drug lord to general of the Sherwood army, very little seemed to have changed. He wore the same V-neck sweater most days and never donned a uniform. He moved like some great, lazy cat, languidly carrying his belly weight. When they'd had a conflict on the western border with the city, Zach had been startled at the speed with which the man could jump to action. Gregor served tea often—pulling off of the water bank liberally to do so. Indeed, tea ceremony, and more simply water ceremony, had become a part of Sherwood culture.

"Can you imagine?" Renee said in agitation. "We go from robbing from the rich to give to the poor, to charging them double taxes all in the space of what, a couple weeks? The irony would cause riots. Nottingham!" she called and raised her fist in mockery.

"The Rangers need money if they're going to stay on," Gregor said. "An idea only gets you so far. When that runs out, you have mass defections."

"Sure, hey, let's draw their blood too. We'll arm the water carriers with syringes."

"Renee—" Zach said.

"Marian," she said.

He was allowed to call her Renee in private only. He exhaled and they all stared at the center of the table for a moment.

Somehow the thought of paying her Rangers had been a blind spot. There was something distasteful about the whole affair, and not for the first time that week did she long for the simplicity of being outside the law, fighting with a small band of believers. But admittedly, the sight of the Rangers out her window in the morning gave her a sort of happiness, a power and comfort. Dressed in green, like the yard of grass that ought to be below her.

"We can't pay as we would in non-drought times," Zach said, "but they've got families and bills. Some will drop out, others will join. How about we start them at thirty dollars a day. I can make a budget for that."

"Forty," Gregor said.

"Thirty-five," Zach said. "We can't hamstring ourself with more. Thirty-five with a potential weekly bonus. Put them on four-day work weeks. Depending upon the size of the force, that's eight to twelve thousand dollars a day."

"Every day?" Renee said. "Is that even possible?"

"Every single day. That's why we need taxes."

"Absolutely not," Renee said. "Can't they pay to get out of mandatory volunteer work?"

Zach snorted, "Every time you say mandatory volunteer I feel a little sick. Wait, what?" On paper he began to work through the math. "Say it costs, what, fifteen dollars? To get out of your one volunteer day?" Zach bounced his leg and scratched out the plan on paper. It was a massive number of potential volunteers, even after removing children and elders. Management of a fresh workforce of six or seven hundred volunteers on a daily basis was going to be an immense and interesting problem. "The percentage who pay will be a minority, but still I'd guess those would be decent revenues. With that alone we could hire one to two hundred Rangers a month. And I don't think we let them opt out every time."

Renee nodded, satisfied. She'd learned to move quickly on after decisions, and to rely on others to implement. There were so many systems to create. "Then we do it. Zach, draw up the policy. Gregor, put someone in charge." She pounded her fist once on the table and smiled. "You people are geniuses. Progress, people!"

As she departed, on to the next task, she let her hand trail along Zach's back and hoped he would feel in the caress an apology.

She was of two minds now, and one tinkered on in the background, observing what the other did, while the other commanded a country. She took to carrying a knife around. It was a thin-bladed fish boning knife, sharp as a razor. It had a subtle curve, like a miniature saber, and a solid plastic handle. The six-inch blade locked into a plastic sheath, and she wore it attached to her belt. She wore the knife parallel to the belt, in place of where a belt buckle would be, so that it took a moment's observation to see that she was indeed armed. She did not wear it for show or to deter; she wore it because she was afraid.

She woke that morning out of a dream where soldiers stood around her bed—US Marines—shooting into her, and she'd looked up at them calmly, as she felt the blood drain from her body. It'd been a surprise to feel along her stomach after she'd woken and find nothing. No blood, no unnatural holes she could dip her index finger into. She lay in bed and let life return to her, trying to push away the feeling of impending doom.

"These are no end-times," she whispered into the room. It was a mantra she'd taken up since her first night in Sherwood. A poem of sorts that had taken shape in her head, the words reeling out of her. "These are no end-times. This time is simply a tunnel, from one time to the next. I work here to see us through. The darkness is a passage."

It was with great strength that she blotted from her mind the end of the mantra, a new addition: "I do not seed the violence." The last part began to show up on her lips, materializing there out of deep subconscious, tacked on to the end of the mantra unbidden.

"Who said anything about violence?" Renee said aloud. Bea was gone, her bed meticulously made. A single shaft of dawn from the east made it through her north-facing window and burned orange against the west wall. Water, food, security, health, education. That's what she did. And yet? She leaned up out of bed and looked down into the backyard and saw, as always, the small army there, rifles on their shoulders, pistols on their belts, Jamal in their midst, and she shuddered.

Renee divvied her own water share. Her Ranger-delivered unit gallon—minus one tax-unit—had been left at her door. The remaining 39 units—each one fortieth of a gallon of water—were divided between six task-based gallon jugs, old glass apple juice containers. Water to drink: 18 units. To cook with: 10 units. Cleaning: 4 units. Hygiene: 4 units,. Miscellaneous (a plant she had on her window sill, a luxury, the occasional wetted handkerchief to wipe her brow, etc): 1 unit. Charity: 1 unit. Savings: 1 unit. She stared at the portion she'd parted away for cleaning and it looked trivially small. Just over twelve ounces of water. She hungered for a shower and a way to properly wash her hair. But above all, she thought, she must live as she asked others to live.

She breathed in the smell of the water, taking pleasure from its many mysterious sounds, the way a quantity of it sounded in a glass jug, *glunk, glunk,* or the way the glass rang with the water inside when touched with the blade of her knife. She could delegate this, but divvying water was a vital ritual, a uniting one. She imagined herself performing the task in synchronicity with everyone else in Sherwood, like a morning prayer.

Today she would work on the clinics. She'd find doctors and nurses who understood her, who knew that these were not end-times, who may be persuaded to work locally and not in the hospitals. In her entire territory there had not been a single doctor's office, and so she would need to find and pay for equipment and medicine. Nearly every day they carried bodies to the Rose City cemetery. People who had died because of dysentery or bloodshed, dehydration-related symptoms, old age, or the relentlessly boring pace of an apocalypse in slow motion. Fewer died than before she'd come, she reminded herself. They dug holes where they could find the space. She'd been to more than a few of these, wielding a shovel and talking to families and drawing off some of the hate and grief and taking it into herself. Afterwards the survivors told their friends and family that Maid Marian had come to the funeral and wept, and her renown deepened. *Time is simply a tunnel,* she told herself, *from one time to the next. There is no end, there are no end-times.*

Even without her, with her personal end—say, a marksman's bullet taking her down—there was no end. She was only time's helper, a temporary worker.

She ate the breakfast a Ranger brought her in the map room. No one else was yet in the room and this was when she loved it best. When all of Sherwood was only hers. It was in the early morning when she composed her notes to Sherwood. Later they were printed by her team in a fury in Sherwood's computer room, so many to a page, in the hour of electricity, or when their batteries were charged, or hand-lettered en masse when technical difficulty made it necessary.

Her breakfast plate was divided into sections, rations on one side— a mottled piece of tinned fish and a clumpy bit of bulgur or something of its ilk—and on the other a fried egg, given to her by some grateful citizen and cooked with reverence by some other Sherwoodian. She tore into the egg. A surprising number of chickens were found in the territory, and they were also on her list. They needed roosters. Surely there was at least one lucky rooster in the territory. They needed a flock. *These are no end-times. This is the beginning of time.*

And then it hit her: This *was* the beginning, and time needed to reflect that. She pulled the calendar off the map room wall and stared at it. She would make July 17 the new independence day, the day when the nation of Sherwood rose up. But the year bothered her, sitting at the corner of the calendar with its four ungainly digits, its two-thousand-year baggage. She didn't want that tacked onto any Sherwood holiday. She grabbed a marker from their meeting table and scratched a black patch over the year. Beside it she hesitated: was it the year zero or the year one? How does time begin?

In binary numbers, she remembered, 0 was off, 1 was on, 1 was *yes*. And so she wrote a big, chunky 1 on the calendar. Yes.

Dear Sherwood, July 24, Year 1, she wrote. *Welcome to the end of week 1, in the year 1, of your new country.*

She doodled in the margin for a moment as she thought back on her week of faith. She had nailed it. She had so nailed it. She fidgeted at the edge of the paper there trying to figure out how to word things, in the way an A-student futzed with the margins of a perfect essay before turning it in. A moment of reflection to delay the praise that was sure to come. Informally, her approval rating was in the nineties. Water delivery and street safety were now a given—*in a single fucking week.* There's no way the citizens of Sherwood would go back.

As security issues began to resolve, Zach set in on Renee's second wave of projects—clinics, schools, and farms—and he finished the last of his indicators. They were fine work, if he did say so himself. There were indicators for water level, Rangers, money, crimes, and food. Because he loved the numbers, he searched about for a few more he might add to the mix. He hit upon one that he thought might be a perfect indicator of Renee's popularity: immigration versus emigration requests. At the time of his first tabulation they were 19 to 1.

Using the water carriers to query citizens, Zach put together a skills roster for the nation, and he developed a symbol system so that bikers and Rangers could quickly mark up each message with metadata, which greatly enhanced the efficiency of the information processing. This would not, he thought, be a nation that took its data processing lightly.

Among his other pet programs was something he called the "research department." He'd tried to remember all the water-saving projects he and Nevel had come up with over hours freighted with the knowledge that the mayor would shoot down one after the other. Each of the department projects hung from the wall of the map room on a single clipboard. Some of them he got the official OK to put together a team to pursue, and some languished there. Along the top of each clipboard was the initial proposal:

- Garden techniques—plastic sheeting and water drain-off, high density gardening, water recycling via elevated, cascading beds. Build series of greenhouses.
- Urophagia (drinking urine)—issues: salt danger to kidneys, marketability for mass consumption, instructional manual for population. Benefits: extreme recycling! Or: Urine filtration for other uses (boil + steam runoff?).
- Rain dancing—Seriously, why the hell not? Needed: team of four to hunt down anthropological books mentioning the subject for possible techniques. Seek out any elder Native Americans in the territory that might have a connection to traditional rituals. Evidence of efficacy? Mass institution? Ritualize it? Dance party?
- Well digging—secure location closer to Columbia River. Previous attempts moderately promising, yielding a trickling amount of water after substantial digging.
- Cloud seeding—(i.e., rain making through chemicals!): in need of silver iodide or dry ice.
- Employment metrics—guarantee that every citizen works for pay at least one day a week.
- Independent Press—crucial, but govt. hand must be absent. Suggest meetings w/ former journalists?
- Distillery—Improve upon ration-distilling techniques, consult gardener. Make some small portion available. For sale? As part of distribution?

In the meantime he began a surveying project, sending a dozen or so water carriers off with questionnaires in order to measure the satisfaction of the citizens with their new government.

It was not at all unlike a small village, Zach thought, one in which the populace's survival dangled by a thin thread of interconnectivity.

The slightest of tension and that thread breaks, and people die. All of them were hyper-dependent upon each other, and upon outside forces.

Pulling down a sheet of scratch paper he penciled **SHERWOOD** at the top, and then spent a half hour idly drawing trapezoids below it. In a village, he thought, much of the security and functional nature was dependent upon its small size. The smallness led to an increased familiarity and mutual dependency and thus trust. With their nation, much larger than a village, he set out to duplicate these aspects of a village, while attempting to keep some of their scale. The government must feel as though it is familiar and known to its citizens, humanly recognizable, the arms of it going deep into the citizen's lives, or conversely, the sensation that each citizen holds a marionette string straight to the top.

Below the trapezoids, he wrote:

Cannot exceed the level beyond which citizens are human-processable by the government.

On the side of his unit gallon he stared at the phrase he'd asked them to write on the side before they went to mass production. "That which is measured improves." It was more true now than ever before.

On Saturday, August 18, Jason helped his father with the tunnel while his sister napped upstairs. His mother, Cora, was talking to a neighbor across the street. His job was to take loads of dirt up to the backyard. There were great mounds there now that he knew his mother didn't approve of, but his father had promised to make a series of raised beds from the dirt. Step gardening, he'd said brightly, as if it were a feature she'd always wanted, as if any sort of gardening was possible. For when the drought is over! He'd managed to get grudging approval.

Jason had two plastic beach buckets and he took them to the end of the tunnel to be refilled.

"Ready for another load, sir?" Nevel said. His tunnel had at first snaked its way toward the street in front of the house. It was the way the wall faced and digging straight out felt right. Then the tunnel took a subtle bend to the right and Nevel knew it was because of the highly attractive woman who lived across the street and one house up. There were no definitive plans—none, other than, Nevel had justified, if you are going to tunnel, tunnel toward beauty. He liked the idea of sitting in the tunnel below her house, the feel of her sleeping up there somewhere. Obviously, he knew, this was deeply perverted shit to get into. It was not a fantasy to share with your family, who could scarcely understand your motivation for digging a tunnel in the first place. But he was nowhere near that destination yet and had kept himself from thinking about it in too precise terms. Lately, however, a side tunnel had made some marked progress in the direction of Sherwood. He looked down from shoring up a wall. His son Jason was contentedly embedding a toy car into the dirt at three feet high.

"All right, let's get you another load."

"Do other houses have tunnels, Dad?"

This was a startling question and Nevel froze for a moment, listening to the earth, wondering if just beyond any of the walls he worked on there were the ends of some other neighbor's tunnel. Perhaps all men dug beneath their houses. Perhaps he was simply another victim of some mental illness epidemic brought on by the drought that turned fathers into moles. Perhaps the beautiful woman in 3416 was working on one and their two tunnels would meet. A tunnely tryst may await him already!

"Huh . . ." Nevel said, gripping the tunnel wall in a brief moment of vertigo. "I don't know. We should ask your mom, wouldn't she know?" After a moment he said, "No, let's not ask her. I'm going to guess no, right?"

It would be a beautiful thing if it were so. He liked the idea of a secret shared closeness with his neighbors. Some mutual passion they could not speak of.

"What about your friends—do you know if any of them have tunnels?" Nevel asked. For not the first time he fretted about which other parents might know of his tunnel, none of whom he spoke with personally, but from whom he received news via the arcane facts gossip network of their children.

Jason shook his head and Nevel wasn't sure if it was a "no" or "I don't know."

"Well, our tunnel is a secret, eh?"

Jason nodded automatically. He'd heard his father repeat this in one way or another often enough his lines were memorized. Still, he couldn't resist asking of his father the question that evoked a different answer every time. "But why is it a secret?"

"Oh," Nevel said and sat down in the dirt, coming closer to eye level with the boy. "We have a lot of reasons for our secret. Sometimes it's nice to have a secret. It's like buried treasure. You keep it inside your mind and know it's something special that's just yours, as long as you don't speak of it." Nevel worried his simile was going to work against him, for there *was* a pirate's treasure in this tunnel, hundreds of bottles of water, squirreled away in an obscure side-hole. He didn't want the boy down here digging by himself. "Also, the parents of your friends all think I'm a relatively sane person, right? Digging a tunnel under the house might be seen as somewhat *ha ha*."

"Somewhat what?"

"Let's say quirky."

"Calden thinks you're weird."

"Yeah, well, Calden, right?" Nevel gave Jason an elbow nudge and Jason smiled.

"When will we be finished?"

"Digging the tunnel? December seventeenth, around four thirty in the afternoon, just in time for dinner."

"Dad. Tell the truth."

"Hell, I don't know. Maybe when we discover what it's really for or find something at the end of it or maybe when we get tired of it or reach some kind of digging satori, you know, like uh, higher consciousness, like a super power. Maybe we'll build a giant robot over our house then. Maybe we'll be done when we've taken it under the length of the city and we can stroll underground into the forest. That'd be nice, right? When do you think we'll be done?"

"We could really build a giant robot?"

"Sure—but, you know, *after* the tunnel is done. All right! Back to work, soldier." Nevel filled Jason's buckets and handed them back. "Careful now."

Jason gathered the buckets and set off back up the tunnel. Nevel watched him go, feeling honored that the boy would help him on the tunnel voluntarily and happy for the company—good father-son time, he told himself. And yet there was a guilt at sucking the boy into his mania, of making a five-year-old carry buckets of dirt out a tunnel.

He wished, for the boy's sake, that a clear purpose as to what he was doing would reveal itself. Something the boy could learn from. Remember all that hard work, boy? *But look what we've built!* For now,

and for him, the reward was in the process, to be doing something—
anything—active with his hands, a forward momentum in a time
when everything else remained mired in the doldrums.

There was a clattering and then a large crash from the front of the
basement and Nevel jumped to his feet.

"Dad!" Jason yelled and there was a trapped scream in his voice.

Nevel sprinted the length of the tunnel and to the basement stairs.
Jason was in a heap of dirt and buckets at the bottom of them, his left
arm bent underneath.

"Oh, bud," he said, failing to keep the anger out of his voice, the
strange presympathetic emotion, for being clumsy; for the toil and
derailment a child's wound took. He picked the boy up and Jason's
mouth opened and no sound came and the boy's arm swung loose
and odd, like an appendage attached in afterthought. There was dirt
in his teeth and hair, at the corners of his eyes and nose. Nevel rushed
the boy upstairs, despising every molecule now of his own lazy, greedy
self, that would load his son up with dirt for the basement stairs. He
heard himself repeating "Oh no! Oh no! Oh no!" and realized with
his parent's third eye that that was particularly not what was required
of him now. He took him to the car, which he thought might have a
gallon or two of gas left, and laid the boy down in the backseat. Jason
cried hysterically now. "It's going to be OK," Nevel said, "it's going to
be OK, we're going to fix you up." He stood and turned and let out a
panicked bellow into the neighborhood. "Cora!"

He peeled out of the driveway, holding the horn down, looking
for his wife, but she did not come out of whichever neighbor's house
she was in. He remembered his daughter sleeping in the upstairs of
the house and cursed and honked again and then saw that everyone
at the small border crossing was turned toward him. There had to be
a closer clinic in Sherwood, he realized. He'd seen their new clinics on
the news. He pulled forward into the intersection and a city officer
came to his driver's side window and a Green Ranger to the passenger side, each of them dutifully enacting their made up border-patrol
duties, as if they were actors in some local drama. He rolled down the
windows and they both looked at Jason, who continued to howl in
the backseat.

"His arm is broken, let me through, for god's sake."

"You have a Sherwood permit?" the city policeman said.

"No!"

"City won't let you enter without one. Or a Sherwood card? Do you have one of those?" said the Ranger from the opposite window.

"Fucking fuck the Sherwood card!" Nevel yelled. "Look!" He jabbed his thumb backwards at Jason. "I'm going to the clinic!"

"I'm very sorry, sir, the closest city hospital is on Williams," the city policeman said.

Nevel revved the engine. "Come to your fucking senses," he yelled.

The city policeman rested his hand on his rifle. "I cannot let you pass. The hospital is that way."

Nevel eased up on the brake pedal and stared forward. His face was burning up and he was having trouble thinking about anything except ramming through the makeshift barrier. He thought he could race through it. He knew what awaited them at the city hospital. The crying stopped from the backseat. Jason was staring fixedly at the ceiling.

"Jason!" he yelled.

"It looks like shock, sir. Get him to the hospital. If it's just an arm they can patch it up," the Green Ranger said.

Nevel nodded at them, acquiescing, hating them both. He backed the car up. In his rear-view mirror he realized Cora was running toward him.

He yelled out the window, "Luisa is asleep, Jason broke his arm, these fuckers won't let me through!" Then he put the car in first gear and tore off, leaving Cora standing in the street, and that was something else to hate himself for. The car dissatisfyingly gripped the pavement without fishtailing or leaving burning smoke in the air, as a father desperately trying to do the right thing might hope, leaving a show of super-heroic dramatics in his wake. He studied the right side of the street for an alley or intersection to veer off into, but each was blocked. Cyclone fencing covered half the entrances, Portland Police and Green Rangers like chess pawns from either side guarded the others. Which side doesn't want you to come in, he wondered. At each crossing the car was slowed to a crawl as people milled about it, looking in, curious to see what an automobile was up to. They stared at Jason with vacant eyes. Nevel was in a full sweat now; his eyes stung as it dripped down his forehead. He beat on his steering wheel and honked his horn and felt like an orangutan among the walking dead and wished he had a gun to fire into the air to scare off these monkeys made slow and dull and bored by thirst.

He turned onto a city thoroughfare and raced toward the hospital. The wind kicked up a great whirling cloud of dust in front of them and before he had time to roll up the windows they were in it. He heard Jason cough from the back seat and croak out "Dad."

"We'll be there soon, bud, we'll get you taken care of, you just close your eyes."

Renee sat with her tea to meditate—meditation being a practice, she admitted, she found completely inane, the antithesis of action, just this side of comatose, but Zach had teased her about being all action xand no premeditation and with her new sense of obligation came a nagging feeling of the necessity to be wise and to make non-impulsive decisions. Whether meditating helped with that, she had no idea— mostly she found her legs ached while some scrap of song echoed hollowly in her mind.

Afterwards—or rather, after she'd given up—she sat at her desk to go through the affairs in this, week four of year one in the country of Sherwood. She filtered through the mound of correspondence from all quarters: there were notices from the city and the daily press release, there were notices to write and notes distilled from the map room, there were inquiries from other impromptu organizations up and down the coast, some formalized but most asking for advice or writing in admiration or hoping for alliances or even stewardship. She did not want to grow, not yet anyway.

Their census had tallied 39,647 citizens in Sherwood territory, down from the last official census's claim of 58,785. Some twenty thousand people had moved or died since the drought took hold.

The territory lines at the eastern reaches were in flux, and she was trying to put an end to that. She'd sent out teams to clearly demarcate the land with a six-foot-wide swath of mud-green paint, a mottled ugly color, the combined mixture of thousands of donated cans of paint from the territory. They painted it on with push brooms. If your house was in the territory, on this side of that snot-green stain in the road, you were in her protection; if you were outside of it, you were the city's problem.

The territory was beginning to hum into its morning action. Outside her window down in the big grass field there was, in addition to the soldiers, a ration cooking class for all citizens over the age of

fourteen, held daily for fifty people at a time. Next to it, the mandatory gardening class. All families were asked to keep a garden with
low-water crops. Out front, she knew, volunteer forces gathered to
work on various projects: trash services, community farms, school,
and childcare. There were beautification projects, new classes to be
given, and construction projects to complete. And at the center of it
all: her. Queen of the year one.

Zach and Renee sat on the back porch in the dark and watched
the Sherwood volunteers unwind after a day's work. A great bonfire burned out in the open, under the stars. It's strange, Renee idly
thought, that the wood of empty houses and dead trees might bring
such warmth as they turn to ash. That a dead thing might seem so
alive. She shivered and scooted closer in to Zach. For a moment firelight reflected off his teeth as he smiled.

"Thanks," she told him, and then wasn't sure how to piece together
the rest of the clauses that might attach to that. Thanks for coming
up, thanks for your work, thanks for your ideas. She had told him
she didn't want to be seen together as a couple, so as to maintain the
image of Maid Marian that the public knew. And because of this there
was a bundle of guilt that propelled the thanks out of her. Thanks for
sticking with me, even though I can be difficult. Even though I aim to
keep you a secret, it is not because you're not appreciated. She leaned
her head against his shoulder.

He waited to see if she was going to say more and when she did
not, he said sure.

A couple of Rangers passed out the door behind them, but this
far from the ring of fire Zach and Renee were cloaked in darkness and
were not seen.

As for Zach: just then, with the crackling of firelight beyond,
and the sparks spiraling a wild dance toward the stars, so that as they
rose one twinkling light was lost in the other, just then he thought
he loved her. He held her hand and let her head rest on his shoulder
and he was genuinely happy. For a moment he pondered this, but
at a distance, worried that any study of his happiness might suc-
cumb to its analytical observation. But there it was, this happiness
that arrived at last in a new trembling nation born from the worst
of times.

He had spent some weeks there now, building the systems in the map room and enjoying these few quiet, secret moments. Hating her sometimes, too, yes. There were endless slippery facets to her. Despite his job as the director of information, he felt there was a subcurrent that he couldn't quite grasp. It was the same with her personality. The longer he knew her, the less certain he felt of what he did know. If he could save this instant, freeze them both here staring toward the bonfire, a simple moment, he would.

"Chilly?" he said.

"A little." She scooted into his embrace.

"What are you thinking about?"

She laughed. "Frogs."

"Really?"

"Yeah."

The image of his building across town came to him then, with its little projects and familiarity, with its promise of solitary pursuits, and like a little ping of sonar a tiny homesickness sounded in him. Here he slept behind the couch in the map room and lived among swarms of people, and shared his girlfriend with the world. He gripped her hand more tightly and she reciprocated. He didn't want to think about this. It was as he'd feared, his happiness diminished with focus.

"They must have been the first to go."

"Frogs? Were there even frogs here?" he asked.

"Well, everywhere, I mean."

"Don't think about that."

"All right," she said. And then after a while: "Are you doing all right?" She stroked his leg.

"Yeah. I'm good," he said, but her query focused the lens further and he felt the sonar ping grow strong until it was a bugle-horn of sadness in him, like a hunter lost deep in the woods calling toward a distant home. He cleared his throat and palmed her knee. "Yes," he said. "Frogs. They would have lasted a little while, right? Just moved in closer to their waning ponds? Rain-dependent plants were first, I bet. But they have seeds. The seeds could grow back."

"You don't want to talk about it?"

"Let's just sit here."

There was a commotion at the fire as a round of cheers broke out. Another log was put on and a storm of sparks whorled skyward.

She leaned toward his ear and he moved in to hear what she wanted to whisper.

"Ribbet," she breathed. He laughed.

"I want you to be happy here," she said.

"Yes," he said, "thank you." He kissed her. Afterward he wished for the sound of a single frog in the distance, at a puddle's edge somewhere, croaking hopefully into the night.

The bullet was removed from Martin's skull.

"A terrible shot," the new surgeon observed jovially. "But if it'd been that much over?" The surgeon held up his fingers to show how close he'd been, and Martin observed a thin centimeter between the gloved finger and thumb with his remaining eye. "Hoowee, I'm sure you don't mind my telling you I was sweating bullets working it out. But here you are!" He patted Martin firmly on the shoulder.

He'd lived with it long enough to have a certain meditative relationship with it; waiting in the hospital queue, waiting for an AWOL doctor to show, building his strength again in a hospital bed. And now with the pocket memory of it, the niche it'd hollowed out of him, and the canvas patch that covered its entrance, he felt like they'd pulled a metallic seed of hate from him, the thing that turned him like a compass needle toward Sherwood, with the crushing mallets of his hands wound up for pinwheeling.

Now he stood swaying. Outside the hospital trying to decide where he would go.

It turned out there was enough hate left over without the bullet there to guide him still. He walked slowly in the direction of Sherwood in his hospital-supplied clothes. Dug up from the morgue, he suspected but did not ask. His gait was slow and unsteady, pain a dull bloom in his eye. He kept his right hand half raised to protect his blind side—a lesson learned from having rammed into objects in the hospital whose proximity had befuddled him.

He'd heard incessant rumors of Sherwood's progress. The patients talked of its clinics, how life must be tolerable there. The very surgeon who failed to show up to operate on him had disappeared, they believed, to a better life inside its borders. His fellow patients in the cesspool-hospital, even the nurses, had spoken of Maid Marian until his eye socket burned with lava rage.

It was not far. Two blocks north, five blocks east to the outer edge. At the corner across from the border there was a burned-out gas station, and he squatted in the wreckage to allow himself a moment of rest. The streets were quiet. His one eye spotted the roving of people down the length of the border, but not vehicles. The image of his hands around her neck played with a lusty pornography in his mind, and after each vision he found his breath ragged and his face hot with sweat.

Martin walked up Fremont, his right hand raised in front, his left hand out to the side trailing along the wall, as if to sense for her presence in the border debris: cars and furniture and detritus, all painted an olive green and blocking entirely one lane. Guardhouses demarcated every block or two, manned by young acolytes.

The inside of his mouth tasted like the leather of old books and the thirst craving was deep. He stopped at a guard station. Inside was a big-boned, brown-haired woman with a flattened nose. She looked at him distrustfully as he leaned into the tiny guardhouse's window.

"Can you help a one-eyed fellow out with a drink," he said huskily.

"No, I'm sorry," she said and scribbled something on a small stack of papers in front of her.

"I'm dying here. Sherwood supposed to be all good people, right?"

"You have a Sherwood ID?"

"I used to live here."

"Migration is back up that way." She hooked her thumb. "See about getting in with them. I don't do that."

Martin shrugged and hobbled further along. The old dress shoes the hospital gave him were uncomfortable, and he could feel the heat spots of future blisters.

A mile or so up Fremont there was an official crossing. Several police officers and a few more Sherwood guards stood on opposite sides of an opening in the barrier, and a dozen or so people milled around performing the shady under-dealings that border leeches perform the world over. He looked for someone he knew. A man with a beard down to his chest and no shirt offered him something in a whispered garble of syllables and Martin elbowed past him. Even the drugs were unfamiliar to him now. How could so much change in so little time?

A car roared toward them and came to a screeching halt in front of the border. During the conflict, a passel of border-junkies faded quickly toward the crossing and Martin joined them, pushing across the threshold nonchalantly. Once through, they burst apart like dandelion seed, separating into the citizenry of Sherwood as best as they were able. The illegal border crossing was noticed and an alarm was sounded. Rangers began to spill in from side streets to round them up. Rather than run in his blister-inducing shoes, Martin sat down heavily on the curb of the busy block and took off one shoe for inspection. The pursuing guards ran right past him.

Martin smiled into the leather of his shoe. Too smart for management, he thought. After they'd passed, he limped up the sidewalk to the house he'd sat in front of, and barreled through the front door.

What a shitty father he was. If they could get through this without Jason having a permanently bent arm, he thought, grown into some strange hook or backward-facing appendage, he'd close the tunnel, live right, get a new job, pay attention to his family.

After he'd parked at the hospital, he picked the boy up in his arms and Jason groaned and passed out. The arm slipped out of his hands and flopped backwards, hanging down, at a new joint above the elbow. "Shit shit shit," Nevel said. He used his knee as a table to hold him and grabbed the errant arm before setting out.

On the other hand, he thought, maybe he would take his tunnel deep into Sherwood. He could run an underground railroad—*literally underground*—transporting injured children to Sherwood's clinics.

Thirty or so people stood in front of the entrance, in a queue. They were quiet, shuffling from foot to foot. At his feet the pavement was stained and still slick with repeated paintings of blood, the trail of it actively reapplied through the day as patient after patient added their own Pollock contributions. There were too many emergencies to treat, and far too few working hospitals. A nurse came every few minutes to catalogue the newly arrived, whisking, when she could, any life-or-death cases to the front.

When it had first become clear that the city—the entire west— was in for a hard haul, hordes had left. They migrated east or overseas. The wealthiest, and especially those whose skills were valuable everywhere—doctors, dentists, nurses—had to consider the well-being of their families over that of the city. Who could blame them, Nevel thought. And why hadn't he gone? When he still could—before the east had closed its doors to most immigration. They could go nowhere but here now. Just stay where you are, the world told them, hunker down, do not move or squirm, consume nothing. Someday it will be over.

Several places in front of them a man passed out and fell, a hard and solid sound. The line continued its glacial pace around him, their guilty, self-pitying eyes making awkward glances until paramedics came for him. Nevel noted the way in which they carried him, exhausted and callous.

Inside the crowded waiting room he spoke with a kindly nurse. She put her hand on Jason's head and said "poor thing" and then he found a seat on the floor and waited, with Jason still in his arms, until his muscles burned from the effort. Jason woke and cried until he'd cried himself out and still they waited. They talked about the tunnel and giant robots in hushed tones and tried not to speak about broken arms.

Nevel told him every single detail he could remember from the first three *Star Wars* movies. The fellow patients around leaned in close, with their own broken bones or bleeding wounds or cancers, adding a missed line or detail here or there, until it became a collective retelling, with side commentary and trivia and the occasional sound effect by a wild-looking, bushy-bearded gentleman with a makeshift bandage across his neck.

Jason was transported by it. He held the broken arm across his lap like a dead eel and did not move except to ask for clarification, "What do the sand people eat?", "Which is faster, an X-Wing or a TIE fighter?", "What if you have to go to the bathroom and you're in a battle?", "Did Luke ever get a broken arm?", "Is Maid Marian like Princess Leia?"

The last question caused laughter and interested debate in the patients around him. Nevel paused in his telling as he thought again of the mayor's gift. He had slipped some into their own rations. He topped off bottles at night, taking advantage of his wife's absentmindedness to make their life a little easier. But now, as he framed it in the black and white universe of *Star Wars,* he realized his son would interpret his actions as belonging to the dark side. Right? Remembering his attempt to use the clinic in Sherwood earlier, he gritted his teeth in anger again. His boy had a glazed-over expression now, in his lap unable to sleep. He whimpered from the pain and held very still.

Deep in the night they moved on to the prequels until a little before dawn they were called in. As the doctor set Jason's arm the boy screamed. By ten in the morning they left with a plaster cast and a weak chorus of "may the force be with you" and headed home.

Cora met them on the porch. The night had been hard on her. She embraced Jason and steered him into the house and Nevel knew they would argue later. He sat down on the first step and looked across at the border, busy as always. He was exhausted. Nevertheless, he'd taken care of things. It may have been his fault, but he'd taken responsibility, and there was some satisfaction and relief there.

When the children were asleep he grabbed hold of Cora's arm. He would show her his water stash and tell her the truth. He would free himself of guilt.

He led her into the tunnel, his flashlight's beam absorbed in the dirty brown of the walls. Finally he came to a small grotto, against one wall of which he'd leaned a number of flattened cardboard boxes.

"Nevel," she said. In her voice there was a tinge of fear. She didn't like being in this far.

"No, come on," he said. He pulled away the cardboard boxes, revealing a four-foot hole behind. "In we go," he said. He crouched down and stepped in, taking the light with him.

"Nevel, please."

She was in the dark on the far side of the hole now. He skimmed over the tops of the bounty in his cave and the light reflected marvelously along the walls, warped and brilliant through the glass. He gave the bottles a tap with his shoe so that the light danced. "Cora," he said. He leaned down and went halfway back through the small tunnel and put his hand out. "Come now, it'll be OK."

She took his hand and followed behind. When she saw the bottles she stopped, her mouth agape, and he watched the light play over her face now. He couldn't remember being more in love with her.

Mayor Brandon Bartlett stood at his balcony window and watched the commander of the National Guard drive away. His vehicle, a black armored SUV, was accompanied by an armada of similar vehicles which traveled everywhere with him, so that when you saw him he seemed to be part of an angry swarm of metal, all protecting him.

The whole lot of them continued on below his balcony, and the mayor raised his middle finger to send them off properly.

The mayor hated himself just then, as the last of the SUVs rounded the corner and Roger retreated toward their airport base.

The commander, he remembered, had even brought his own water with him. When the mayor's assistant offered the commander a drink, one of his own tight-buttoned underlings swept forward with a glass and filled it for him from a canteen. Did the commander think the water from the office of the mayor was undrinkable?

He sat on the couch and waited for Christopher. It was intensely sunny out and dry as a goddamn bone. The whole city out the window was a baking hot desert. There would be unrest to deal with, amid the normal schedule of concerns. He closed his eyes to ward off the sun glare on the television set. Christopher abhorred the commander, and had visited friends close by while the meeting was in progress. He wished he'd return soon.

The only explanation that he could think of—it came to him suddenly—was that the commander suspected that he himself, Mayor Bartlett, might try to poison him. He held still, in mid-motion, his head tilted in revelation, as the discovery dawned on him, surprised at its implications and its possibilities. And then he laughed for a long time afterward.

They'd never officially started sharing a room together—perhaps because of the foreboding, serious, and protective presence of Bea. Or perhaps they'd never shared a room because Renee was too preoccupied, or wanted to keep their relationship a secret, or because Zach had never demanded it.

So he lived in the map room. He worked on the project obsessively and Renee would find him asleep at a table at one or two or three in the morning and take him to his makeshift bed, a ratty sleeping bag in the corner behind the couch, there she'd strip him down. Or she'd be wandering around the house early when all was still silent and slip into his bed and they'd fuck.

An appropriate word for it, Zach thought: fuck. The word had its sexiness, but there was mostly a utility to it, a violence even. There'd always been a sort of violence to Renee—an unpredictable, usually charming suddenness, a physicality, but the job was changing her, he thought.

The time he spent here was straight out of his teenage geek self's wildest dreams. Sex at all hours with a wild girl, and a game-like puzzle where he was actually making a difference in the world. The chief of intelligence, the conductor of information. But as was the case with all teenage fantasies, he supposed, things turned out to be more complicated in real life.

Of the nights they'd been together—and he had to sift back through his mind, through the string of late nights and early mornings, through the behemoth project, for the few nights they hadn't been together—there hadn't been any variation to them. There were no moods in their relationship anymore. There weren't intimate, slow nights or nights of idle sex or much talking at all. She came to him and he could see how deeply preoccupied she was, transported and unreachable, exhausted beyond measure by the day's work and the night's nightmares.

At first it was nothing. He held her while she slept, though he longed for a moment of slowness or tenderness with her. But more and more he felt he was only the object of a cold, endless hunger.

He enjoyed it some, sure. But it haunted him, flustered his concentration when he should be working, made him pine for the early days of their relationship. It created a mass of sorrow in his ribcage, so that every time he saw her it ached and throbbed like some small animal living there, awake only in her presence.

After, when she fell asleep finally against him, in the times where he could reach above his own self, he felt sorry for her. Her time was no longer hers, she was getting used up by the country she gave everything to, and so of course this was a sort of recourse, and he tightened his grip around her.

They fought fiercely and often.

He told her the new clinic was in the wrong spot, that she was too hasty.

She told him nothing would ever get done if it was up to him.

He explained how it wouldn't have to ever get redone once it was done.

She told him he was stubborn and that he never got out in the neighborhood, he was a goddamn homebody and it was leading to incompetence.

He told her she was arrogant and regal, running a dictatorship like some queen, that her aggressiveness would lead to violence, that she was trying to build everything in a day and it would end in ruins.

Is this about Sherwood or about us? she said.

Sherwood, he yelled.

You don't have any idea what you're talking about, she said.

Yes I do, he said, but you're too megalomaniacal to see it.

Then she threw her mug at him and struck him in the forehead.

The two Rangers in the room disappeared through any available entrance like a wind.

When Bea finally came in, Zach was sitting on the couch tentatively mapping out the new bruised terrain on his forehead, and Renee was standing at the window looking at the giant dead hedge that sat like a castle wall at the front of the house.

"You OK, Zach?" Bea said.

"It hurts," he said honestly, rubbing the swollen spot. "She threw a cup at me."

Renee turned and walked from the room. Her footsteps retreated loud and angry down the stairs and out of the house.

"She's under a lot of stress," Bea said.

"I know! That's what we argued about. More or less."

"I'm sure she didn't mean it," Bea said.

Zach spread his hands and stood up, not caring who heard him. "She threw a cup at me."

"But Zach, you've got to understand."

"I do understand! I totally understand." He started to pack his few possessions, stowed behind the couch, into his backpack. How long had he been there, waiting for a change? A month?

"What are you doing?"

"But you know what? I don't have to be cool about it. She doesn't get a special exemption. You don't resolve arguments by throwing shit at people." Zach winced as he saw Bea try to make some kind of rebuttal in Renee's defense and come up with nothing. "Anyway." He put his hands over his face. "Maybe she'd be better off with some solo time."

"Zach, please."

"Why are you in here making her case—I'm flattered, honestly. Not in a million years would she ever do this."

"Because, goddamnit—" Bea gestured to the walls covered in maps, to all of his work. "I'm not making her case, I'm making this case."

Zach looked up and felt an immense remorse, but he knew he had to leave, that he could not back down. It was devouring him, the house, the map room, Sherwood, Maid Marian. "I need to check on my house, Bea. I need to reset. When I hang out around her I feel like I'm a subject, like I'm competing for her love with forty thousand other people."

"So do I," Bea said quietly.

He put his hand on her shoulder and squeezed. "You know what happens here, the Rangers do."

"Zach," Bea said, and he was surprised at the tone of her voice, so often toneless. There was an edge of panic to it. She was afraid he'd leave. He wondered again if there was something he didn't know, information he didn't have. He looked at the walls, studied the trouble maps and resource indicators and realized that of course he didn't have all the information. He'd been privy to the primary channel, the main floodgate of information, but there were other channels that went over his head. Renee could easily have her own spy network without his knowledge. She could be bribing public officials, could be bringing in weapons, operating with the government, anything. Would she do that? Perhaps there was even another map room. It was his shortsightedness that led him to believe his data was *all* the data. He stood there for a moment, stunned by this possibility.

"What do you know, Bea?" Zach whispered.

Bea looked taken aback. She turned away slightly, as if ready to flee. "I know you can reach her sometimes, that's all."

"Is something else going on in Sherwood I don't know about?"

Bea shook her head at him, her eyes steady and complex, and then she shrugged.

Zach looked around the room again and tried to memorize it. No, he thought, this was an information minister's paranoia, wasn't it? This was only about him and Renee, that's where the complexity was. It was too late for him to back down, he thought, for his own self. He realized that deep down it was tantrum instincts and pride that made him go. He wanted her to realize she needed him. The system here was delicate and finely tuned, and he didn't know to what fate he left it.

Looking at the resource indicators he saw they were all near the top. As a whole they said: *The nation is thriving!* At least according to the scale in which he'd drawn the indicators. They said: The government is rich and powerful. They said: *We're winning.*

"Bea," he said, "do me a favor—redraw the scale on those indicators. All of them. Double or triple them. Understand? Like for water—draw it up to, I don't know, a half million gallons."

"But we don't have that much storage."

"Exactly—perfect. We don't control the data, we control the data's perception. It's important, OK?"

Bea nodded and Zach stuck out his hand and she awkwardly shook it and he pulled her into a hug.

"Please. Are you sure?" she said.

He nodded. "I'll probably be back in a few days."

Zach turned and left, leaving Bea alone in the nerve center. His head hurt but it felt good to be outside. The dust was light in the air and the sun shone. A slight cold edge to the air was pleasant and he had to remind himself that autumn brought no rains any more.

If you didn't count the backyard, he'd been away from the house very few times in the last couple of weeks. He'd poured too much into the job, and he felt the knot of sorrow contract upon finding one of Renee's arguments already turn to truth. He found his bicycle and set off for home.

As he rode through the streets of Sherwood toward the border he observed the depth of the changes. There were no burnt automobiles or piles of garbage in the streets. Children played in their yards. At one corner ten people with paintbrushes painted a giant mandala, one of the beautification projects. But most of all there was a changed feeling in the air. A month was a long time.

Jamal received word that his father wanted to see him. He wound his way through the big house to Gregor's office and stood outside of the door for a moment in the busy hallway.

"He's in," a Ranger said as he passed.

"Thanks," Jamal said and still did not enter. Being called into the office was rare, and there were only a few reasons for it. Jamal knocked once and then entered.

Gregor sat behind an oak desk that had come with the house. He gripped his tobacco pipe in one hand, though he'd given up smoking cigarettes a decade earlier after heart surgery, and tobacco was difficult to find anymore. He liked having the pipe in his hand. The curvy bowl of it fit the circumference of his forefinger and thumb perfectly and he enjoyed having an object to point directions with, as if the pipe itself held some share in commanding the armed and unarmed forces of the government of Sherwood. Conductors had their batons, cowboys their pistols, professors their pencils, and so he felt justified in taking up a rod of some sort with which to execute his business.

"Sit," Gregor said, and with his pipe end pointed to the chair in front of the desk.

Jamal's relationship with his father was complicated, but his wholly separate—in his mind—relationship with the same man, as his general, was not. There were two separate tracks this conversation could ride on. One train was simple, direct, its compartments clean and uncluttered by familial ties and a mutual relationship with his mother. In the other train, each car held a different chaotic story, in which no clear understanding of the train as a whole could be gleaned. In that train his mother and older brother entertained court, aunts and uncles barbecued or fought, and in each played out a scene from the last thirty years that was on permanent archive in his mind.

In one, he is walking through the living room, bearing a small bag of groceries his mother tasked him with carrying. There is a white woman lying facedown on the floor, her small skirt hiked up to her waist and nothing else on. She is asleep or unconscious or dead, and Jamal stares at her, wondering if perhaps she was a neighbor who had accidentally gone home to the wrong house. Or was this something white people do? She was pretty, but her mouth was open and the drool at the corner of her lip was unsettling. Mom? He called but she was still out at the car. Dad? There was a sound from the bathroom and in there he found his father, naked and in the tub. In the toilet there was the rank sloppy jumble of something thrown up. Dad? He said again. He remembered his father opening one eye falteringly, and then his eyes rolled back into his head and Jamal screamed.

There was a whole era of drug addiction and infidelity to contend with, until his mother's death straightened his father out.

In another car he walks through as a grown man, serving tea to his father and his father's enemy, a man named Barstow, as they finally agree not to fight any more. In this, he is angry at his father for not reaching out and snapping the man's neck, the man who by proxy has been his own enemy for seven years, since his exit from adolescence. The man who had taken his brother's life. Barstow was a wiry snake of a man, his hair in cornrows, his teeth full of gold. After surgeons had opened up his own heart, Gregor had had a change of heart about war, even as he'd won. He brought Barstow in for a truce, for peace in the neighborhood. Gregor's presence—and that's what Jamal remembers most, the presence of a man who could straighten out the most curved of wicked sticks—made his enemy trust him. In Gregor's presence, a man became different, better. You wanted to please Gregor. And you did not want to be his enemy.

Gregor tapped the bowl of his pipe on his desk, making a solid knocking sound. "Three Rangers have disappeared," he said. "You know anything about that?"

Jamal scooted in his chair, understanding which Gregor he was talking to, and feeling a nervousness over his charge. "When, from where?" Jamal said.

"All three were working in the Woodlawn neighborhood. Two street watchers and one border patrol."

"What do we know?"

Gregor waved his pipe in a dissatisfied, dismissive gesture. "They're poorly trained. Who knows, they could have gotten lost. They didn't come back yesterday and didn't show up this morning."

Jamal waited for instruction with uneasiness. They, his father and he, had a history with Woodlawn.

"They could be sleeping something off." Gregor glanced then at Jamal, eyeing him over the top of his reading glasses, and Jamal saw the subtle concession, knew that they'd just seen through the train's window a vision of that other chaotic engine running up the mountainside, as if to say, "some day we'll ride that one."

"I need you to go find them. If we're having defections, I need to know immediately. If someone is disappearing us, we need to know even sooner."

"Yes, sir," Jamal stood up.

"Take two of your own with you." Gregor tapped his pipe on the desk and Jamal reached for the door, musing that he could never tell his general his pipe habit looked ridiculous.

"And Jamal? Don't go falling under some fantastic notion that this is happyland, OK? Everybody else here has gone all dizzy off their own self-satisfied euphoria. They are grudges out there. We're recent from violence. The reflex runs deep."

Jamal went to the map room to pull the last week's notes on Woodlawn before he went to investigate.

When he entered there was a squabble going on between Bea and another woman about, as far as he could tell, handwriting legibility.

"Everybody," Jamal said in greeting and was roundly ignored. The map room was a place of wonder for him, but as far as he could tell it made everyone batty who worked there, down to the last man. Zach was a nice enough guy, but sometimes he felt like he'd have better luck talking to a bear, were there any bears left and were one inclined to speak on national security issues. The man's brain was turned inside out.

He asked where Zach was.

A quiet spread over the room.

Jamal approached Leroy but the man moved away as if there were a pole attached to each of them, and Jamal's forward motion pushed him an equal distance away. "Leroy?" Jamal said, one finger up in the air, but Leroy turned away again, as if he'd not spoken at all. Jamal stood awkwardly under the Woodlawn map and wondered if the map room had taken an extra dose of crazy.

Bea continued to reprimand the Ranger, and Jamal waited his turn.

"—but nobody uses the symbols. They don't make any sense to me."

"Don't make sense to *you*. Exactly! I don't care if they make sense to you, just fucking use them. Can I help you Jamal?" Bea said, sounding like a diner waitress on the 3 a.m. shift.

"Hey Bea—yeah—is Zach around?"

"Zach is gone."

"Like disappeared?" Jamal said and a sudden shiver of fear went up his legs.

"No no no, gone. He left, went home, quit."

Jamal noticed for the first time the changed demeanor of the room. The massive box of unprocessed notes, the chaotic work table, the floor covered in a coat of discarded data. "These?" he pointed at Zach's dashboard of resource indicators, which he took much comfort in.

"Hey now, listen. You wouldn't believe how busy—"

"Not accusing!" Jamal said. "Trying to scope the situation here is all. And Maid Marian?"

"She's in her office, business as usual."

"But you're not giving her reports?"

"Leroy and I are doing the motherfucking best we can here, Jamal."

"I'm not on your case, Bea. My father know about this?"

"He knows."

"I didn't realize it was so—"

"It's complex, trust me."

There was a sound at the door and a Ranger dropped off a stack of notes in the incoming box. "Woodlawn," he said.

"Ah! I'll take a look at those," Jamal said, very happy to have some direction other than the conversation he was having with Bea. He knew Bea well enough from practice with the Going Street Brigade a couple of times a week. She did firearms practice, obstacle course, running, fighting. She was driven and hardcore and would make an excellent soldier, though she ran a little hot. He'd thought of her as uncomplaining, if a little hostile, until now.

He retrieved several disordered stacks of notes from the Woodlawn section and made his way to the couch.

There were about eighteen hundred houses in Woodlawn, twelve hundred of them occupied, and to him it seemed as though they'd received notes from about a third of them. He flipped through, trying to make sense of the handwriting and somewhat cryptic nature of the notes.

6241 14th—O.H. collapsed middle of night, needs repair

"What's O.H.?"

"Outhouse," Bea said.

6255 14th—Wants to knw when school will open

6311 14th—has 5 gal gas 2 donate. He will talk ear off.

6322 14th—Thinks she has poison oak..??

6331 14th—Complains man in 6311 left garbage in his yrd.

"This is ridiculous. Why are we getting so much information?" Jamal said. "Do we take care of this crap?"

"Renee wants everybody to feel heard."

Jamal had a better sense of how the job might make you feel like that 3 a.m. diner waitress. He flipped through each one until he found a note that said, "Wants me to tell M.M. Charles is in charge now—? Was insistent."

Jamal thumbed the edge of the note and reread it. 6722 12th. Close to the park, which had always had a dark edge to it. Charles in charge. Did he know any Charleses? He slipped the note in his pocket and put the rest back in *incoming* under the hot glare of Bea.

"Is he coming back?" he said.

Bea put up a hand. "Fuck if I know."

Jamal took a step out the door. "Weren't he and Maid Marian?"

Bea frowned and shook her head no and then appeared to change her mind and nod yes.

Jamal and two of the Going Street Brigade rode down the once tree-lined Ainsworth Street toward Woodlawn neighborhood. They carried handguns only, tucked away inconspicuously. Jamal didn't want them spotted carrying rifles. They wore no uniforms. They were just three men on bikes.

He'd chosen the two men based on their competence, though he knew they didn't find terribly much to like in each other, though at one time they must have appraised each other's skills and come to correct assumptions. You really didn't know a man's true skills until he was out and under fire, Jamal thought. Rick was a white guy, an Iraq veteran. He was gung-ho and fleshy—beefy—in that US soldier way, though reduced water and food intake had certainly pared him down some. He felt decidedly American to Jamal, with a corny sense of humor, oafish veneer, and a firm sense of what he believed to be right and wrong. He was quick to deduce a situation and, when a situation turned serious, he became someone else entirely, subtle and professional.

The other man, Carl, was a defected police officer. He was in his forties and hypercompetitive, a not entirely stable man, given to holding silent grudges or making unwarranted hostile remarks, but over time Jamal had found him one of the most competent of the brigade, who, because he'd been born and raised there, had a deep understanding of the issues of the neighborhood.

As they rode they passed the work of the territory. A crowd of people were gathered at the grocery store on 33rd and Killingsworth, repairing the windows and cleaning the place up—quite inefficiently, from the looks of it. As with any project there were probably four times the needed number of workers. Maid Marian wanted people busy, he knew. She wanted them all to feel wanted and useful and to have a stake in things, even if it meant a mob showed up to build an outhouse. The dead trees that lined Ainsworth Street were being cut down to provide firewood for the winter ahead. Jamal spotted water carriers and the occasional Ranger.

Woodlawn neighborhood was quiet as they weaved their way through its blocks, looking for a place to start. They spotted a water carrier team, and Jamal pulled them over. He wondered about two white girls in this, of all neighborhoods, mostly black and with its history of violence. Or perhaps this was only *his* history. He told them they were Rangers, and saw that they recognized him.

He saw their own Ranger come into view at the end of the block and start walking toward them—water carriers were supposed to be under line-of-sight protection at all times. "We're out of uniform," Jamal said.

"Obviously," one of them said. She was tall and thin, like a length of board. "Have you got the password?"

As a security precaution, there was a daily password haiku displayed at Sherwood headquarters. Rangers were required to speak this to each other. If you had not been through HQ on that day, you had no authority. It was not a tremendous security measure, but it gave a sense of formality and dignity to interactions and reminded them all to be vigilant.

Jamal leaned in close to the thin girl and whispered that day's pass-phrase haiku into her ear: "There is only one, for which all life does depend, the sun is a fire."

The closeness made him desire to lean in further and kiss her neck. And he saw a similar reaction in her, namely: in a whispered pass-phrase something sexy, but mostly weird, had happened deep in the territory of each other's personal space. Perhaps he should have said it aloud, he thought.

She signaled an "OK" up the street to her Ranger.

Jamal asked her about the route and if she'd felt or seen anything unusual.

"Everything is fine," she said, "unless you say it's not."

Jamal showed her three photos, each with a label bearing a name, and asked if she'd known them. They'd already been to each of the Rangers' residences to make sure that no inebriation was being slept off, and it was there they'd obtained a photo of each, but the three— all black men in their twenties—were unaccounted for. One of them had a family and two children and the wife was justifiably worried.

"I know all three," the first girl said. "They're Woodlawn Rangers. This one"—she tapped a picture of a wide-smiling boy, barely twenty—"he's our Ranger sometimes: Robby. What's up?"

Jamal shrugged. "We're looking for them—you seen them recently?"

"Sure, last day or two."

"Which is it, one day or two?"

She shrugged. "We don't always see them up close." She turned to her partner.

"Two days," the second girl said. "I noticed the shift changed up. Some of the other water carriers have new Rangers. And that Ranger"—she waved in the direction of their ranger, a block away— "isn't our normal."

"And there's been no rumors or talk?"

"I assumed HQ switched things up. We don't talk to them much on the job."

The first girl pointed to the photo of the man who was a father. "I talk to him sometimes," she said. "We talk about kids. He cycles back with me sometimes. We live near each other."

"And the last place you saw him?"

"Crossing Woodlawn Park, probably."

Jamal swore. That goddamn park would be the end of him. "Thanks," he said, "we'll nose around there." He smiled at the first girl whose ear he'd recently whispered a haiku into, and she smiled back. "We'll catch you around then," he said. For him, as of yet, the Sherwood revolution had been an utter failure on the sexual front. Rumor was, everyone else was fucking like rabbits. He'd noticed all sorts of sly, lingering looks and unintelligible jokes passing back and forth in his Going Street Brigade, where he spent the majority of his time, but as captain he was kept in the dark.

On 12th near Woodlawn Park the streets were silent. They got off their bikes and walked and Jamal felt spooked. There was something not quite right but he couldn't place what. He had memories of trick-or-treating in this neighborhood, and later of the war he'd fought up here with his father's people against Barstow. The memories unnerved him. Maybe no one lived in these houses. He studied them and they looked like others everywhere—dead trees, a coating of dust and grime covering them. There were many broken windows; the riots had been intense here.

"Quiet," he said.

They stopped and Jamal dug out his canteen and passed it around. They each took a swallow. He opened a US government rations nut bar and divvied it in thirds and passed it around.

They stood with their bikes under the wiry skeleton of what was once a great tree, the kind which he could no longer identify.

Jamal remembered the water carrier notes and he pulled out the note that read *Charles is in charge here now.* The house was at the end of the block, up on a rise, with a commercial shop butting up against it.

In charge of what, he wondered. The house? The block? The neighborhood? He looked around for Rangers or water carriers or citizens and saw none. It struck him as unsettling. Jamal pulled out his phone but there was no signal. It was an old habit from another time, though he still kept it charged, when he could. The time read 1:19.

Zach lay on his back amid the dried ruins of his rooftop vegetable garden and stared at the wispy clouds passing overhead. They were like great ships passing by, refusing to stop at their lonely port. They danced about up there, the tendrils of water vapor curling about in the atmosphere, doing their own rain dance.

It was vexing to watch all that water pass by above. What need did the sky have while the land went without? Perhaps they were simply a victim in someone else's war, a feud between the earth and sky.

On the street he heard a couple of quick gunshots in succession and his hair prickled and he thought of Renee.

He watched the cloud dissipate. In order to function, he thought, in order not to come entirely undone, you need to have faith that the Earth will not stop spinning. That the sun will not quit. That gravity will hold you down. You stake your existence on their working. You rely on those around you to believe that the cash you hold in your hand is worth more than just the paper. You become used to running water, and electricity, you base your existence on the premise that there will be air to breathe, night to sleep by, and water to drink.

He felt he understood how civilizations of the past might have believed they'd angered their gods when a system failed that was beyond their understanding. You cannot remove the foundation from a house and expect the house to stand. How far away were they from sacrificing their own virgins? Certainly, he thought, we're all asking the gods: Why? Why this, why now, why us?

Zach made a square with his fingers and looked through it, wishing he could cut the rooftop's profile out of the cloud above him, so that a square slice of moist could nourish his plants.

He made his way to the roof's edge to take a look down the street, hoping like hell that he wouldn't see a dead body down there.

There was a man in the street on his back next to a station wagon with its driver's-side door open. He was struggling to get up on two elbows and Zach could see he'd been shot. His clothes glistened darkly at the hip and there was a slickness to the street at his waist. At the back of the station wagon two water raiders quickly and precisely removed gallon after gallon of water from the back. So they'd caught a hoarder. Zach ran for the stairs.

By the time he got there the raiders were gone. The man had a thick beard and he was in a state of shock. His eyes didn't track well and he asked Zach several times about the location of a gas station. He was shot in the thigh. Zach couldn't think what to do—he yelled out for his neighbors, for someone to contact an ambulance, but there was no response. The streets had gone scary calm.

Zach helped pull the man to a one-legged stand and the man went limp in his arms in a noodly faint. Zach embraced him, holding him upright in a tight hug, his own clothes becoming doused with blood and his body shaking with the effort. He started to inch his way toward his front door until the man came to and then they weakly hop-hobbled into his house.

He laid the bearded man out on the floor of the kitchen and took a pair of scissors to his pant leg. There was a hole on his upper thigh the size of a nickel, and an exit wound at the back of his leg. What the man needed, Zach thought, was a thorough cleaning of the wound, antiseptic, antibacterial, stitches, weeks of bed rest, and whatever else a hospital could offer. What Zach had was a bottle of hydrogen peroxide he was loath to use. Exposing hydrogen peroxide to air formed water and in turn would become drinkable.

He settled on a battlefield medic cocktail of one unit of hydrogen peroxide, salt, honey and turmeric. Then he duct-taped a wad of clean dish towels tightly around the leg. Amid moans, the man fainted again, giving his head a solid whack on the kitchen floor tile.

He wished Renee were there. There was a reassurance in her taking charge, a comfort in her command. You trusted her. But Renee wouldn't have pulled the man in, a water hoarder, invited danger into her house like he had, would she? She drew limits, made rules, created policies. He didn't know anymore.

He had no way to get the man to the hospital, and no way to contact emergency services. He could go flag down a rare car or the police, he supposed, and he pondered the likelihood one might stop for him.

Inside he fussed around the kitchen. The injured was laid out like an island on the floor. After a while he came to and groaned. When Zach leaned down to understand what the man said he clutched Zach's shirt front with snake-like speed and whispered "thank you," and then put his hands over his face and cried.

His mother's old bedroom was closest, and so he helped him there.

"So?" Zach said.

Zach fetched him a no-spill sip cup with two units of water and some pain killer. After the man had hungrily consumed both, Zach tried again: "What's your story?"

With a weak, halting voice, the man told him he'd driven here from Oklahoma.

"To make some quick cash?" Zach guessed the station wagon could have carried a good eighty or so gallons of water. A small fortune on the right market.

The man gave him a wary glance. "I grew up on my grandfather's dustbowl stories. I sold a few gallons to get by, that's it."

"To the wrong people, I take it. Now you know what the populace thinks of hoarders."

"I told you already. Not a hoarder."

"Well," Zach said. "Everybody hoards a little, that's basic, it's human, but you can't go round with that much in your car."

Zach took some glee in the analytical aspect of having a patient. He found a clipboard and sketched out a set of statistics to track the progress.

Patient Name
Time of arrival
Minutes lying down
Units of water consumed
Grams of food taken
Pain killers

He had a quick bout of homesickness for the map room and Renee. There had to be other measures he could use to track. Wellbeing? Words spoken? Or better: Verbosity. A subjective measure to track a subjective statistic. Answer range: Silent, reticent, inquisitive, chatty, verbose. It was a rough scale, and he knew that a "normal" wouldn't be set until he'd gotten a feel for the average.

He drew each of these statistics on a ten-day chart and began to fill out day one.

"Name?" he said.

The man groaned and opened his eyes and said, "More water."

"Yes, but what's your name?"

"Nombre."

Zach hovered over *Clarity,* readying to mark negative and somewhat surprised that they'd already spiraled into this. "I'm asking your name," he tried again.

"Nombre—means 'name' in Spanish—dad thought it was funny. Last name White."

Zach frowned at how it looked at the top of his patient statistics. Nombre White. Like first grade Spanish homework, he thought. It diminished the sex appeal of the chart significantly. He erased it, and wrote: "Mr. White, Water Hoarder."

He inspected his chart and saw that the patient had gone to sleep. A feeling of disappointment came and went. He wondered what was happening in the map room in Sherwood. On his chart, he made an extra column for sleep and marked the time with satisfaction. He hung the chart on the wall and it felt like adding a title on a painting, a still life. *Wounded water hoarder, asleep on mother's bed.* It was a perfect moment.

Upon closing the door to the house in which he'd hid, Martin jumped at the sight of the behemoth, lifelike painting of Jesus in the entry way, looking down on him with stern, agonized, compassionate eyes, blood seeping from his forehead crown.

A short, older woman appeared directly in front of the painting, her head at Jesus's neck height, so that in the dim light it briefly appeared as though the giant Jesus head had grown a diminutive, wizened body to carry it around.

"Que?" the woman said with a volume and severity Martin had not thought possible in such a small person.

Goddamnit, Martin thought, she's just an old lady and standing in front of Jesus to boot. But there was nothing to be done. He stretched out his hands for her neck.

But she moved like a jackrabbit. Before he could get his hands around her neck, she grabbed a baseball bat at the foot of the painting and swung it into his blind-side knee.

"Jesus fucking Christ!" Martin hollered in pain and dropped to the floor. He gripped the damaged knee and she stood over him with the bat raised. "No no no, please," Martin yelled. "Holy shit, lady! Yo soy buena gente, buena gente!"

She left him then and he stayed where he was on the floor feeling sorry for himself. He was thirsty and damaged. For a moment, as he lay there, he had occasion to consider his current trajectory. A few deep thoughts shuffled through him as to the meaning of his own life. And then he decided that when that lady shitbird came back, this time he was going to wring her little old leathery neck, without fail.

He wasn't sure how long he lay on the floor of the dusty entrance-way, breathing in the smell of old people house. The bloodied Jesus looked down on him, now with less compassion and more spite. A man of fifty-three, he thought. This is kid's work. Lying on the floor with a busted knee.

After a while she came back. In one hand she had a small glass of water, in the other she gripped the baseball bat. She offered him the glass.

"Gracias," he croaked. He gulped the water down and leaned his head back against the floor.

Her name was Celestina Angela Romero. She was seventy-three years old, under five feet tall, and widowed. He sat on a flowery couch underneath another painting of Jesus on a cross, this one scantily clothed. Across a room cluttered with religious knickknacks Celestina sat in a chair and talked to him unceasingly in Spanish, a fraction of which he understood. He rested his hand on his swollen knee and prodded at it carefully. Nothing was broken, but she could deal a hell of a blow. In his mind he phrased and rephrased a way to ask for more water without angering her and then gave up, leaning his head against the couch. His tongue sat in his mouth like a dried cat turd. He got the feeling she didn't get too many visitors. In fact, he supposed she'd harbor a rabid brown bear, if he'd only sit and hear her out.

As dusk began to darken, the house the lights came on. Celestina got up and motioned for him to follow, which he did with great pain. Along the way she pointed out the house's salient features in Spanish. One window featured a view of an outhouse in the backyard. They passed a kitchen he hungered to rip through for whatever rations remained. Halfway down a hall she stopped and motioned for him to enter a room. Inside was a tidy, spare bedroom with a twin-sized mattress. She gestured insistently. He was too tired to argue.

"Gracias, Doña." He nodded. He closed the door behind him, killed the lights and was asleep shortly after.

In the morning, his knee was improved but he walked with a hobble. She fed him at the table like he was an errant son who'd returned after many years. He wolfed down several corn-sweet breads she worked up during the short power-on, and then she listed through the tasks that needed doing, and like that errant son, he obeyed. He patched up a broken window with cardboard and Elmer's glue, dry-dusted everything over five feet high, including the tops of the Jesus paintings, hauled trash from the basement that had sat for some decades, and, in the remaining bits of daylight, re-affixed the ailing door to the outhouse. He didn't know what the fuck he was doing.

It was there on the inside of the outhouse door that he found side-by-side artistic renderings of the Mother Mary and Maid Marian. He sat over the shit hole, attempting the impossible, for he was no match against the vengeance his intestine wreaked on him, and spent a few moments inspecting them. The one with the halo, the other with her gritty rebel hue. The rendering made her pretty, he admitted. With her twin braids lying across each shoulder, her vague Hispanicness, dark eyes and large eyelashes. He longed to deface her image somehow without evoking the suspicions of Celestina. He drew his thumbnail across her neck so that a crease was made there. "On guard, puta."

She glared back at him, righteous, and he swore. Enough motherfucking dallying. It was a toxic oven in the outhouse. The weather had turned vicious hot. He finished the outhouse door with muscular irritation and then stomped back through the house, favoring his good leg. Celestina picked up his trail, clutching a handful of lightbulbs, doling out his next chores. But he had made up his mind. He grabbed the baseball bat from where it leaned under Jesus and walked into the dusk toward Sherwood headquarters. He was going to take care of this bullshit right now.

She'd taken his home, shot him through the head, and killed his cousin Fred. He tested the bat and found he could wield it like a spry stick, the anger giving him strength.

The air outside had the smell of an approaching dust storm. There was an electric nosebleed burn to the dryness, and static shocks bit his finger when he grazed his hand along a chain-link fence. Martin clasped the bat to his bad-knee leg so that in profile it would not be noticed and limped toward headquarters. There were many blocks to walk, and he began to grunt in pain with each step.

Two blocks in, a fellow who stood in the middle of the street called out to him. A Ranger, he saw now, as he drifted closer. The man had called him "countryman" and had asked him to state his business.

"Ahoy, countryman," Martin said cheerfully as he approached, and then Martin socked him in the balls with his bat.

The Ranger collapsed to the ground, wheezing an unintelligible retort. And then Martin saw him start futzing around with a light, and so Martin hit him again, somehow missing his head and hitting him on the shoulder.

Martin stepped on the Ranger's hand that held the light. Looking down the line of sight, he saw a far-off light reply and realized the alarm was sprung. Martin snatched the light and frantically blipped the button on the little gizmo back toward where the light was coming from, hoping he'd sent some kind of message back.

"You little bastard, what am I going to do now?" Martin spotted the Ranger's bike leaning against a stop sign. He tenderly threw his bad leg over the seat and then pedaled into dark. He returned the way he'd come, wary that at any moment Rangers might come pouring from the night like in some third-rate horror movie.

Back at Celestina's he stashed the bike behind the outhouse. Then he put the baseball bat back where Jesus could watch it. In the quiet, dark kitchen, he fumbled onto a small plate of food she'd left for him. It was still warm. He had done enough damage tonight, he thought, and chuckled to himself about the poor bastard he'd left in the street. He would be more careful next time. He pulled out his new Ranger light, a little LED thing, and scanned it over the food. Sweet breads and beans. He could kiss her. She was the most wonderful woman in the world.

———

Zach felt a hollow fear bang around his insides and knew it was time for distribution. Every morning contained a growing thirst and an expectation of that fear. He missed Sherwood. He had been at his house too short of a time and had no savings. With the two of them, he and his patient, to look after now, he could not afford any mistakes.

When the time came and his tongue felt coated in ash he tucked a knife—a small but easily opened blade—into his pocket and set off with his unit gallon. He watched his neighbors walk toward the same destination like wolves toward a kill, and he stayed close in with them, familiars by sight. Most of them were in groups, and he knew that those who walked alone were not to be trusted. In times like these, people who have the disposition band together and watch each other's backs.

The day was burdensomely hot and the heat pressed on him, made each footfall toward his destination feel like a herculean extra effort. There was no cloud in the sky, just a mammoth bowl of blue sky that crushed down on them. As the temperature had increased over the last week, his skin had dried up, so that the subtlest of facial expressions caused his lips to crack and bleed.

Distribution was at Oregon Park, a few blocks from his place. The truck was already there, white and bulbous, like an egg waiting to be cracked, darkened by dust and the grease of human hands that reached up to touch its cool belly. He stood in a line that wound its way along the dusty park, its once great trees all cut down in the winter previous. There were patterns rutted deep into the ground for this daily ritual they all performed. The standing in line, the truck parked in the same spot, the National Guardsmen roving their eyes back and forth across the lot of them.

After a long wait Zach made it to the front. There were some moments of confusion as the guard checked his identification with its water code and noticed that he'd had his card registered in Sherwood recently. Zach responded quietly that he'd moved out of Sherwood, as he'd explained many times already, and he could feel those behind him lean in to listen. When he was cleared he hooked the nozzle into the top socket of his unit gallon and heard the relieving sound of it being filled. But as it came to the top the nozzle sputtered and the tone changed. Behind him someone yelled and he quickly disconnected his gallon. The truck was out of water and there were at least a hundred more in line behind him. The murmur of the news made it quickly up and down the line, and the ragged-looking man directly behind him called out in protest.

"That's enough," the Guardsman said and held his hand up to calm the crowd behind him.

Zach gripped his bottle to him and eased away from the line as the crowd began to go amorphous, transforming from order to mob. "There'll be another truck," the Guardsman yelled out.

"I stood here an hour! An hour!" the man who had been behind him said.

"It will come," the guardsman said.

"Hey, Sherwooder!" he yelled as Zach retreated. He followed after Zach and then reached in for a hold on Zach's bottle and for a moment they wrestled it like a football on astroturf, pulling and scratching at each other. The man's furry, tangled mat of hair was sticky from grime. They fell together and struggled for the prize on the ground and then Zach pulled away enough to get a foot up and kick him. The blow landed in his face and there was a sickening pop. Zach rolled backward and then to his feet and fought a gag reflex. He snatched the bottle from the man's clutches. "Sorry!" he yelled, catching a last glimpse of him on the ground, his head reared up, blood and dust mingled into his mustache. "Sorry!" Zach turned and ran.

A warning gun shot rang out and Zach turned to see the National Guard jeeps circling in close. The crowd huddled angrily. They were promised another water truck would arrive sooner rather than later. Zach hurried his bottle out of the park toward home. He needed to meet someone. To pair up. Perhaps his patient. Walking the streets alone with a bottle was a risk he didn't want to take often.

Back at the three-story building, he went to the roof and looked out at the city. Soon the people would be getting ready to settle into darkness, gathering ration candles, if they had them, the coming power outage about to dim the landscape.

He opened his unit gallon and drank three units off before he could stop himself, and when he did, he felt as though he'd only wetted his lips, mere drops in the dry well of him. He found some empty canning jars, retrieved his permanent marker and sat in front of his unit gallon and concentrated on distributing a portion from each to a jar before he would allow himself another drink. Sherwood habit. He labeled the jars with their intended purpose.

Jamal saw a young boy of nine or ten at the end of the street. He walked with a heavily practiced gait, swinging his brown arms aggressively and with flair. He wore a black sweatshirt and white sweatpants, negating entirely, in Jamal's mind, the effect of cool the boy sought. But what did he know? He was already too old for street fashion. The boy was thin and looked like he needed a bath, three square meals a day, and the care of an attentive mother to set him back on some forward-facing track. None of which Jamal felt he'd turn down himself.

The boy crossed the street toward them and his swagger faltered once as he made eye contact with them, and then intensified as he got close.

"Y'all be looking for yo Rain-Joes?"

"You've seen them?"

"Check da house." The boy pointed to the same house where the note claimed Charles was in charge.

"Oh? Hey wait—" Jamal said, but the boy turned to walk away. Jamal called after him, "Who is Charles?" and he thought he saw a noticeable jerk in the boy's walk, as if a marionette string had been yanked violently, throwing one leg in the wrong direction. The boy quickly regained his stride and was gone.

"Somebody sent him," Rick said.

"We're being watched," Carl said.

"Yep," Rick said.

"It's a trap," Carl said.

"Yep," Rick said.

Jamal fought the desire to cut and run, fifteen-year-old memories running ghost-like over his anxieties.

"My spidey sense is tingling," Rick said.

"Don't say spidey sense," Carl said, "just don't say it."

"What? Why not?"

"There's no such word as spidey."

"It's from—"

"I know what the fuck it's from," Carl said. "But listen to it. There's 'spider' and 'spidery,' there's no 'spidey.'"

Rick deepened his voice and gave it an English accent, "My spidery senses are causing my fancies to tingle."

"Where is everybody?" Jamal said.

They locked their bikes to a stop sign and kept watch on the house at the end of the street.

A cloud passed over the sun and Jamal stared into the sky, seeing great clouds there like the front line of an infantry passing by. They would bring no rain, he knew, only dust.

"Does anyone have a plan?" Jamal asked hopefully, feeling that the proper thing to say was: *I have a plan*, seeing as how he was in charge, and realizing that he was relinquishing some morsel of authority simply by asking the question.

"Check out the house," said Rick. He was digging in a flesh-colored fanny pack—which Jamal noticed for the first time was actually a pack and not part of the man's flesh. He came up with an extra clip, which he put in his back pocket.

They were so not a real army, Jamal thought, not the Going Street Brigade, and especially not the measly three of them. He wished he'd brought another fifty soldiers with him. He looked up the street for a Ranger to signal with, but the streets were dead empty in all directions.

"You think they're still alive?" Carl said.

"I'm not thinking anything," Rick said.

"We can hope," Jamal said. But he couldn't imagine why anyone would go taking hostages. Life was cheap in the drought. Who would waste the water to keep a hostage alive?

"This is going to creep me right out if we don't start doing something right now," Rick said.

They fanned out and walked toward the house at the end of the street. On the right at the end of the block was what appeared to be a micro junkyard, with high fences and several dozen old junkers. There used to be big, angry dogs there, Jamal remembered, who would throw themselves against the fence to get at him as he walked by.

Jamal signaled for Rick to go up the stairs of the house and knock while he covered him. The house had a tall porch with broad steps. It was built in the twenties, before the shop behind it had blocked off its backyard with a big concrete wall.

Next to the door was a large, intact window that led to the living room, covered by a full curtain.

Carl eased around the right side of the porch and managed to find a vantage where he could keep an eye on Rick.

As Rick turned the doorknob, Jamal watched Rick's body jerk with gunshot impacts and then fall against the door, which swung wide with the pressure. Jamal ducked and looked around wildly—the shots were coming from elsewhere, though he could see no gunmen. There was nowhere to run, except into the house. Jamal leapt up the side of the porch, nearly colliding with Carl, and felt one leg twitch away from him, an icy coolness there that began to yield pain. And then he was inside, dragging Rick's body deeper into the house.

After Jamal had been gone for ten hours, Gregor paced around the map room, blisters of anger and worry erupting from him in sharp bursts.

Maid Marian sat on the big orange knit couch and observed how quickly the system had fallen apart without Zach. She was angry at him for not training others well enough. He'd become irreplaceable. And yet she had spent time with that convoluted brain, knew the feeling of irritated bafflement that came over her when he tried to explain how the system he'd created worked. He'd trained a horse only he could ride. When Zach was gone there was nothing left but to shoot the horse.

"Tell me again where he is?" Gregor said, pointing at the piles of notes with his pipe.

She'd not seen Gregor like this before. He went to his knees and began rummaging through a box, making an utter mess of the notes, reading them at random and then throwing them aside. He'd lost a son and a wife already, she remembered. "Zach is not coming back," she said quietly.

"Yes, but *why*? Where is he?"

She didn't want to get into this with anyone, especially not her general. Dictators don't have spouses. Dictators have low-level, disposable concubines. It should be easy, like a toddler's passing interest in a toy. You find a Ranger. You pick him up and then you set him down when you're finished. Were these different times Zach and she might be together, but she couldn't worry about the feelings of anyone else, especially not her chief of intelligence. And yet, she did, and it was her complex, conflicting emotions that'd finally been too much for him.

"Zach has gone home to the Southeast," she said.

"We need him here," Gregor said, he held up a crumpled wad in each hand. "He's left a shithole."

Renee shrugged dismissively. She wanted this topic to end. She picked up the handful of notes she'd been reading through and began filtering through them; her eyes had trouble with the words, her mind unfocused.

"I'll go get him," Gregor said. "He can't abandon post."

"How?"

With irritation Gregor said: "We'll slip through the border and bring him back."

Renee watched her general pace back and forth in front of her. She realized it had been a mistake to allow him to appoint his own kin as captain of the Going Street Brigade. The same kind of mistake as appointing your boyfriend to be information officer.

She thought about kidnapping Zach. Could they hold him here as a worker? She wasn't sure. She told herself she needed to make the decision for the nation. If fetching Zach was something that could right her general and keep security from collapsing, then it was necessary.

"He's somewhere in Woodlawn," Gregor said, speaking of Jamal. "This makes six disappeared in forty-eight hours. We need a force to go raze the neighborhood."

"No," she said. She got up and began to pace on the other side of the table, their pacing like two pendulums working in opposite synchronization.

There were two Rangers under the charge of Gregor waiting for his orders. Leroy hovered close and tried to reassemble the various messes Gregor made while Bea read notes from the pile. Renee could see Bea work studiously at the notes, ashamed for being the last to see both Jamal and Zach.

"There's nothing from Woodlawn here," Bea said. "Only today's notes. Last week is gone. Jamal must have taken them."

Gregor walked to the Woodlawn neighborhood map section and tapped on it with the end of his unlit pipe. To her he looked stooped and suddenly aged. Renee waved one of Gregor's Rangers over. "You know Morse code, right? I need you to go to the Vernon tank, that old water tower on Twentieth and Prescott. You know it?"

"Yes, sir."

"Take a friend and this." Renee handed over the green laser pointer she fingered in her pocket.

"I have one of my own, sir, if you'd prefer. I'm a semaphorist."

"Of course you are, fucking Zach," she said. "Well, that's what I want you to do. Stand on the south side of the tower and aim high enough on the tank with your pointer. He used to watch that tower for messages in the early evenings from the Southeast."

"What should I say, sir?"

"To get his ass back up here, right now," Gregor said.

Renee shrugged. "Please. Tell him Jamal is missing and . . . you probably won't even get him, he's not going to be out there anymore. You know what? I'll go, you come with me."

Bea stood up quickly.

"Goddamnit!" Gregor said. "I don't know what to do with this crap." He threw down the pile of notes he'd been shuffling without reading. He felt he was reliving a nightmare from his past, when he'd been willful and arrogant and at war with Barstow. Except then he knew who his enemy was.

"Gregor," Renee said and signaled for him to leave the room with her. In the hallway they whispered. "What don't I know about this," she said.

Gregor briefed her on his Woodlawn history. He spoke in a hoarse whisper, an aura of defeat about him.

"But we're not drug dealers," Renee said, "we're the government of Sherwood. This is not Zach's fault. It's not Jamal's or Bea's fault. This is a situation. We handle situations. Get with Leroy, pull a month's worth of notes, read them all. If a note is odd, ask Leroy if he knows the address. Do your work, remember who you are. I'll work on Zach." She pressed her hand into his chest and said, "We can totally do this. We're not going to fall apart."

Gregor straightened. "Yes, sir," he said.

They held each other's gaze and she felt like she was staring into a mine the depth of which was unknown. "We're OK?" she asked.

"We're OK," he said.

She could not read him, but his demeanor seemed free of resentment. It was the first time she'd ever seen him lose focus and she couldn't help but want to apologize for giving him—a generation older and a leader for decades—a lecture.

"OK then," she said.

THE TROUBLE

Jamal sat on the living room floor and stared out into the street through the window. For a moment he'd lost his shit and now he was getting it under control. Rick was laid out on the wood floor in the next room with a couple of bullet wounds that would down a polar bear. He could hear his ragged breathing. Carl was checking doors and windows, looking for vantage points and escape routes, gathering supplies and whatever the hell else the man found it necessary to do in a situation like this. Carl hadn't been shot.

Jamal removed his clenched hand from his calf muscle and tried to figure out what was going on there besides a whole lot of pain and blood. He unraveled bits of his jeans, removing them from the center of the mess with a substantive uptick in negative sensation.

"You hit too, buddy?" Rick said from the other room. His voice was wet and croaky, a forced whisper.

"How are you even still alive?" Jamal said.

"That's not very reassuring, boss," he croaked.

"Just—stay that way. We'll get out of this."

"There you go."

Jamal heard Carl cussing from the back of the house.

"He hit too? We could be blood brothers. You do that when you were a kid?"

"No, man," Jamal said. "What do I do?" If this was one way to keep him alive, he thought, to grant strange last wishes, to appease and by appeasing to leaven, he would do it.

Rick indicated that Jamal should touch his leg to Rick's wounded arm.

Fuck it, Jamal thought. If this is what was expected of him as a leader, this he could do, as meaningless as it felt in the moment. They were out of sight of the window and he could hear Carl scuffling around in the back of the house. He assented and overcame a moment of squeamishness. They awkwardly touched limb to limb, a light brush of wounds, exchanging some microscopic bit of blood. They did so before they each died, he thought, and dying was alone, and with this tiny bit of blood he took a weird superstitious comfort.

He inspected his leg. There was no bullet wound on the other side and Jamal wondered if there was a bullet inside his leg still, hidden there like an Easter egg, a little metal bit of treasure he could carry around. His leg felt heavy, like it had an anchor tied to the end of it.

"I found our Rangers," Carl said. "No one else is here." He crawled into the dining room, keeping out of sight of the windows, and sat next to Rick. "You look like shit."

"You're not reassuring either," Rick groaned. When he'd caught his breath he said: "Nobody teach you fuckers can-do attitude?"

"They're all laid out neat in the back bedroom," Carl said, "one strangled, the other two—they're all dead."

"Not going to be any help in a firefight," Rick said.

Jamal looked back out at the street but it was still and quiet, as it had been moments before a hornets' nest of bullets fell upon them. His calf had bled in a solid stripe down into his shoe before he'd sat down and he could feel the wet stickiness at his heel. The wound looked like an eye, and he stared into it. For a moment he again considered the possibility that he would die here and he felt a fearful excitement about it.

"Got grazed, did you?" Carl said. He'd crawled across the floor without Jamal noticing.

"Grazed?" He inspected his leg again, tenderly wiping away the blood to get a better look. He saw how the wound was a mark across his calf. It had taken a small chunk of flesh as it passed. There was no bullet inside, and he felt lighter and more able and a little disappointed upon learning this.

"I'll be at the window there." Carl pointed. "There's a concrete wall in the backyard. The only way out of this is through that front door. Not a bad spot to hold off a siege. Tie some cloth around that." Carl nodded at his wound.

After Carl crawled to his post Jamal began to come back to himself from an altered state. The adrenalin receded, his breath evened, and his mind cleared. He thought of his Going Street Brigade, divvied into duty and rest, some home with families, and wondered how he could get word to his father.

He used his knife to cut off one of his sleeves and this he tightened around his calf.

"Ask them to hurry up," Rick said.

From behind the big window's curtain—the glass all shot out—he tried to search out who had attacked them. It had been a great number of bullets. Quantity over quality. Though they'd done fairly well with Rick.

There was no indication of anyone living out there. Two of the houses on the block looked like empty shells, the windows gone and the insides stripped out. The micro-junkyard on the corner had a tall fence and he couldn't see any visible gun ports. For his part, he didn't plan on doing anything that would draw their fire. He supposed they would wait.

It was an unsettling feeling. Siege was such a medieval word, with archers and catapults to fend off. And time itself had to be fended off as well, as the castle defenders cut their rations and waited, and cut their rations again. He suspected that madness was the primary weakness in the walls and gates, that and a fear that screwed its way into you.

He needed to check on rations, but he couldn't bring himself to leave the window. He stared out at the houses and tried to decipher shapes in the shadows, until the images were burned into his eyes and boredom and fright ached in him. He readjusted his legs and found one had gone asleep. The pain of unraveling it and the movement of his wounded calf made him call out.

"Carl, how much water you got?"

"Just shy of a liter. Nut bar."

He and Rick had the same, minus one nut bar. He laid them out in an orderly fashion against the wall and tried not to think about them there.

"Are we cool?" Carl said from the room over.

"We're cool," Jamal said. He repositioned himself and stared back out the window and waited some more.

He needed something to do with the time and so he emptied the contents of his pockets and backpack and arranged it on the floor in front of him.

He had a clean handkerchief, three paper clips—likely the result of his trip to the map room—his pocket knife, his Sherwood ID, a hat, and paper.

"What's in its pocketses," Rick hissed, watching him with half-lidded eyes.

"Sadly, no magic rings or tasty fish for you." There were keys to his bike lock, his home in King neighborhood, and a key to the stolen water truck he'd neglected to return. His phone indicated it was 2:47 p.m. He had the stack of neighborhood notes he'd stolen from the map room and a pen.

"But if you feel like composing any poetry," he said to Rick, "I'm all set up for you."

Rick didn't say anything and Jamal watched him, wondering if the man had any chance at all. When Rick died he'd be in the room alone, and a terror gripped him.

He scurried across the floor. Rick didn't seem to be breathing and held stone-still. He shook his shoulder.

"Yeah?" Rick opened one eye and blinked. "I was taking a quick nap, blood brother. I don't feel very well."

"OK there, man," Jamal said, "everything's cool."

"Maybe I'm coming down with something," Rick said and Jamal couldn't tell if he was serious or delusional or joking.

"Well, don't die," Jamal said; was that the best he could do? "Can I get anything for you?"

"Hunky dory."

If the shots had been heard, he believed enough time had passed that a message would have made it to HQ and a response made. Jamal began to resign himself to the possibility that no response would come.

"Carl?" he said. Carl had sequestered himself in the room on the other side of the entranceway, and he hadn't heard anything from him for a while.

Carl said something that ended in "gun" that Jamal couldn't understand.

"Think they aim to starve us out?" Jamal said.

"Just one little shot," Carl said. "I've been deducing which house to shoot at."

"Could last a couple days. They'll know we're missing before that, they'll send people, right?"

"Maybe the yellow house," Carl said, "that's the one I got a bad feeling about. Sending off some serious vibes."

"Yeah, hmm. They want some kind of war here, but who even is it."

"I bet they've been watching us this whole time," Carl said.

"Charles, I guess," Jamal said.

"They're hoping we'll bleed to death, but they didn't even hit me. I'm not bleeding one bit."

"They hit Rick pretty good," Jamal said.

"I'm not going to bleed to death."

"Carl!" Jamal shouted, trying to get the man's attention, realizing their conversations were only loosely connected.

There was a long pause, and then Carl said, "Yeah?"

"How's it going, man?"

"You already asked that."

"Think we should make a run for it? I am bored out of my mind." He kicked at the edge of the wall with his non-wounded leg.

There was a deep sigh and the sound of objects being moved around in the other room. "Nah," Carl said. "That'd be crazy. They want us to bleed to death, but they didn't even hit me."

It was glorious to be out on her bike going fast at night. She felt as though she'd left her new identity behind. Outside she was just Renee. Someone who'd once been a coffee barista, who had a boyfriend, who was a decent enough welder when called upon. Someone who, upon getting high, inevitably spent ten solid minutes laughing uncontrollably.

They tore down Prescott and she realized the last time she'd biked in the dark was their first night in the territory. There were no cyclone fences sectioning off blocks now, and she took relish in listening to the peaceful hum of the neighborhoods.

Power was out and people sat on their porches in the dark and talked. She wondered how many times they uttered her name just now in all of Sherwood. She repressed the thought. That was Maid Marian, and she was Renee. They shared a body, but she wanted to be only Renee tonight.

At the tower Renee looked up at the underbelly and then south toward Zach's house and had misgivings about the whole thing. There were only three possible outcomes here. 1) He wouldn't answer, 2) he'd say no, 3) he'd say yes. Now that she was out and had shed a layer of Maid Marian, she felt anxiety that he might say yes and come back expecting it was she—Renee—who was asking him, when it was the territory who needed him now. She wasn't sure where she stood in the matter.

"Let's go," Bea said, impatient. She stood lookout and waited for Renee to begin.

Renee pointed the laser pointer and toggled the green dot back and forth there on the underbelly of the empty tower. She waited for his reciprocal dot. She liked the idea of filling the tower with water again—a sign of ultimate power—though it'd be a brazen display of wealth and a security pain.

For fun she traced the shape of a heart with the pointer and then quickly changed its shape when she came to her senses. It was a lonely dot there, a sole green point of light in a blanket of blackness. She stared down the hillside across all the somber houses into city territory. There were stars out above the city like a shining phosphorescent sea.

Her arm began to get tired and she broadened the arc of her pointer, making sweeps along the tower, wondering if he was there watching but refusing to answer. Come on, she said. She turned and pointed it toward his house, out there somewhere, wishing for some kind of brute force communication, a trumpet blast, a rifle shot, rather than the passive communication she played at.

She sunk to her haunches. He wasn't going to answer, she realized, whether he'd seen it or not. It was for the best, his only reasonable course. Leave her behind, move on, start something new.

"How long have we been here, Bea?"

"Twenty minutes?"

She swore. She hadn't sent a single message, only laser-carved the tower with bland, distracted desire. She pocketed the laser and said she was going down there.

"Renee," Bea said.

She was not making decisions for the territory, she was making them for herself. Perhaps they—she and her, her two selves—were falling apart, a schism growing. She didn't care, she wanted to see him. She was fastened on the idea now and couldn't let it go. It had to be done.

"I'm going down there," Renee said.

Gregor's Ranger looked back and forth between Bea and Renee. Renee said nothing to ease the woman's mind.

"That's a really bad idea," Bea said, "a really stupid one." There was anger in her voice which Renee had not heard in a while, and she felt a twinge of aggressive excitement at hearing Bea rise against her.

"You stay here, Bea. Help Gregor, tell him he's in charge for the night."

"Bullshit," Bea said.

"Yes," Renee said.

"I'm coming the fuck with you," Bea said and Gregor's Ranger compulsively stepped back a pace.

Renee looked out over the city and felt elated and relieved and wanted to hug her or punch her and she tried one more time, her voice notched into Maid Marian's, the voice of one who commands an army. "You stay here. You have a job to do."

"No way. I'm coming with you, that's work enough," Bea said and mounted her bike and gripped her handlebars as if she expected Renee to jet off without her.

Renee hid her smile and turned to the Ranger and instructed her to tell Gregor to take charge until they returned. "We're going to get Zach. Keep him steady and focused if you can. Here, give me your water." Renee reached for her canteen. "You got all that?"

The girl nodded and stood there. Renee could see she was afraid to leave with the burden of such awful news and for a brief moment Renee felt like hitting her too, taking it out on this young innocent Ranger, such an easier mark than Bea, straddling her and beating it into her, for her slowness to obey, for her sullen terror. What was it she was becoming?

"You say, 'yes, sir,' and then you ride," Renee said, finding Maid Marian's commanding condescension come to her and the girl snapped "yes, sir," hopped on her bike and road toward headquarters.

"Well," Renee said. "What the fuck, right?"

Bea laughed the tension off and told her she was an asshole and a dumbass and Renee agreed.

They both knew the border section on the map well. There were border crossings and smuggler's crossings, some she'd created, others she monitored. One she'd known about but never seen. They headed for this one. It was imperative no one see them, not her Rangers or the smugglers, not citizens of either side. The spirit of her country depended upon her, she knew. She was the air inside its balloon.

Gregor's Ranger rode two blocks in the dark, her heart racing for the news she had to bear. On 28th and Prescott, under the boughs of a barren oak tree, she barreled her bike headlong into a large man in the dark, his impact grunt a thing she heard but did not ponder, before she hit the ground herself.

As the night went on Gregor's pacing became more pronounced. He became violent with the notes, digging through them at a frantic pitch, handing out stacks carelessly to Leroy and the Rangers. They were sitting among thousands of notes now and he pulled notes archived in storage.

One of his Rangers asked what they were looking for and he wasn't sure. That was the problem. Any single statement could be a clue. Suddenly every note seemed turned against them, each one a carelessly veiled threat.

"2216 Going St—wants a baseball bat. For baseball. Mentions it every time I come."

"4411 Ainsworth—fresh signs of many holes dug in the yard. When asked what they're for, acts confused."

"6212 15th—burned her own house down on purpose, then moved next door to 6210. I'm not even sure what else to say about this."

What do these mean, he wondered. Were each of these a clue into nefarious activities or were they the idle motions of a citizenry going about their business? Did they all add up to a whole?

"Please," Leroy said. "Please put them back in the same order. These are all filed." Leroy clutched his head as he watched the room he'd helped create erupt into chaos. He hovered over the top of Rangers reading through stacks with brutal carelessness and then discarding them, as if they'd memorized them and had no further need. He elbowed in and re-sorted, grumbling and shaking.

Gregor wondered where Maid Marian was. He checked his watch—four hours to bike to a water tower and back? On the outside it might have been an hour-long task.

"6747 8th St—thinks she saw Batman."

"6411 Grand Ave—many people coming and going from this house."

Gregor crumpled a handful of notes in his hands and stared out across the room, trying to make his eyes focus. There were ten Rangers in the map room now. Each sat on the floor, an archived box of notes cradled between their legs, which they dug into with Christmas fervor.

He'd had enough. "Stop!" he barked. Everyone stood abruptly, the tone of his voice compelling them up. He signaled to two of his rangers. "I need the entire Going Street Brigade awake and in the yard and twice that many Rangers. Get them there and lined up in forty-five minutes, no matter what you have to do. These orders override everything else they may have going. Pull them off the street if you have to. Everyone else, out. Wait in the yard."

The Rangers quickly fled and he was left in the room with Leroy, who fluttered from box to box, trying to repair the damage done. Gregor tossed aside his crushed fistful of notes. He'd give Maid Marian one more hour.

Gregor stood in front of his Rangers, a third of them armed Going Street Brigade troops, and rehearsed his orders in his mind before he spoke them.

They stood, lined up as best as able, in the failing battery light of the backyard, looking bedraggled and off kilter, most pulled from their beds.

"Take a minute to straighten yourselves," Gregor said. He needed a moment before he introduced panic into the territory. He walked a rectangle around them, counting them again and doing his best to memorize the dimly lit faces of those he did not know by name.

He returned to the front and cleared his throat. Jamal's absence was conspicuous, he knew. This was his job. And they were all aware of the possibility of her presence there in the house, the bedroom where she slept; he could see their idle upward glances, and none would know yet that she was not there.

"This morning," Gregor said, "we are doing searches. You will be in groups of five. Two Going Street Brigade and three Green Rangers to a group. Eleven teams in all."

He selected a leader of each group and brought them into the map room—lit by candles and windup flashlights—for instructions. Leroy nodded, manically, Gregor thought, to the soldiers and moved stacks about as they came in, so as to keep them from trampling the piles on the floor.

"That's enough, Leroy," Gregor said with irritation. "Leave it be for tonight." He had no power over him, not really, but it didn't mean he had to wade around some obscure filing system when they had an emergency.

Leroy raised a long bony finger and pointed at him and said something unintelligible and Gregor wondered if he'd been scolded. He steered the Rangers over toward the Prescott Street map where the water tower was.

"Maid Marian and two Rangers went missing between here and there." He tapped the map. He'd said it now, and it could not be unsaid. There were gasps and questions, and he silenced them fiercely. "I want six teams here. Houses searched and questions asked of everyone along this line. Stay in view of each other at all times. Two Rangers and one Going Street Brigade enter a house, one man at the open door, and the last Ranger standing in the street with an LED. Two teams to a block. Work fast, be courteous but direct, ask questions. Search the entire house." Gregor estimated they were roughly an hour before dawn. "Do not say who or what we are looking for. Do not tell your Rangers. Tell them you're looking for a fugitive. Did everyone catch that," he said, his voice lowering to a hostile growl. "Do not. Do not tell them what you're looking for. Get going."

After they'd filed out the door he turned to the remaining four, who shuffled their feet nervously and wondered what was next.

Gregor sighed and closed his eyes. He pressed his fingers into his eyebrows. Eyebrows that had suddenly followed the rest of his hair into grayness. Then he moved the remaining four Going Street Brigade to the Woodlawn map section of the room. One of the men he knew well. He'd served under him in the wars. The man studied him carefully now, and Gregor avoided his eyes.

"Jamal is missing," he said.

"What's going on, sir?"

"Jamal is missing," he said again, the voice hushing out of him with venom, and then he waved the question and response away. An epidemic of abductions seemed to be sweeping across the nation, and he feared for every Ranger he sent out. "We'll take five teams here. Be careful." He jabbed his finger into the map near Woodlawn Park and wished his finger could crush the whole lot of them, every last house in that neighborhood.

As the bassoon-sound of Celestina's prodigious snoring began to rattle the house, Martin tiptoed out of bed, put on his clothes, grabbed the Jesus bat and headed back onto the street for another inning against Sherwood Nation. Rangers generally kept to the middle of the intersections, so as much as possible he walked the back alleys or just along the porch line. With all of Sherwood in power outage, there was only the light of a three-quarter moon to be seen by, wispy cloud-haze slug-trailing across it now.

At the mouth of an alley he heard the approach of bicycles along the street, and along with them Maid Marian's voice in Doppler as she went past. His dead eye throbbed at the sound of her. Does she do that? he wondered, go on bike rides in the middle of the night? If he were in charge, he would do no such foolishness. Nevertheless, the night felt suddenly lucky. He was too slow to leap out and home-run one of them off their bikes, but he hobbled along in a hurry after them.

After some blocks of this, the futility began to wear on him. He was slow. His feet were wedged into cheap, dead-man's loafers, made more tight by blister swell. They were fast and long gone. He should have taken the bike he'd stolen. He trudged along with the bat on his shoulder, his limp exaggerated as he favored the bruised knee. Tiny pain grunts rose up out of him with each step, *unh, unh, unh,* so that he sounded like an ecstatic pig at the trough.

At 24th and Prescott, walking down the middle of the street under the eerie skeletal night shadow of dead trees, a biker rounded a corner and aimed right for him. He could see a glint of its chrome in the moonlight, and he wondered if it bore Maid Marian. It was moving fast and he stepped to the right to avoid it but it swerved into him. He called out and shielded himself with the bat but it was too late. He heard only the crunch of their forms, wood bat and bicycle parts and his face colliding with the rider's chest, the handlebars with his stomach. The breath was stolen from him and he was knocked flat. From the ground he gripped his gut and searched about for his weapon, sure that a second round was coming. She had attacked him, alone and single-mindedly.

"Motherfu—horror of god, you crazy bitch," he hissed when his breath came back. But under the tree shadow instead of the bat his fingers found the slick topography of a human face. He yelped and recoiled.

He crawled on his hands and knees until he located the bat and then he stood over the form on the ground. "Get up," he said. He prodded her with his foot. He swung the bat and it thudded with the form's thigh and there was no stirring. If this was the end of her, what a sorry end it was.   .

"This is for you, Fred," he said into the dark, and it spooked him.

He reached down and fumbled around until he found the front of the rider's shirt. It was a woman, he ascertained, and it was not yet a corpse, if he read true the soft pulse at her neck. A moment of exultation passed through him. "Ha ha!" He lifted her shirtfront enough to raise her head off the ground and dragged her slowly across the street, out of the shadow and into the light of the moon.

Only by the short length of the hair could he tell it was not Maid Marian. "Jesus Christ," he said, feeling disgusted with himself. What the fuck was she doing riding in the dark? It was hard to gather much more without light. Her forehead was wet with blood where it had collided with the bat or him or the blacktop. There was gore on his fingers and his conscience nagged at him.

Could he leave a woman to bleed to death in the street? He cursed his luck.

He gripped her shirtfront again and dragged her laboriously back across the street and onto the front porch of the closest house. He beat on the door with his bat and then backed off the porch and hid in the dark. No one answered and he dug his fingernails into his palm.

Finally, he returned to the porch and picked her up—she was not overly heavy—and slumped her over his shoulder. In the other hand he carried the bat. For a moment, before the knee pain of the grueling walk home set in, he felt like the manliest of cavemen, hunting for a wife in the night.

At Celestina's place he slumped her against the wall, under the painting of Jesus, and leaned the bat in the corner. He fumbled around with a candle there, cussing each faulty match-strike until one lit. She was a young black woman with her kinky hair scissor-chopped short and a head wound. She was muscular and her thinness gave her a youthful gangliness. He went to wake Celestina.

"Accidente," Martin said as he steered Celestina in to look, "por bicicleta."

"Ranger." She pointed at the girl's clothes.

Martin jumped. How could he have not noticed?

Celestina directed him to carry her to his bed in the spare bedroom. She began to care for the wound in a businesslike manner.

Between the two of them, they stopped up the bleeding and got her situated, but she did not wake. His hand shook when he touched her skin, which was cool and marbly smooth to the touch. Celestina, too, impulsively reached out and touched the woman's face. They acknowledged this with a look as they fussed over her. Celestina indicated she was going to undress her for bed, and so Martin retreated to the kitchen. When she was finished and covered, he retrieved his paltry possessions and moved to the couch in the living room.

But he realized he wanted to see her one last time. Celestina was still there, hovering over her in the candlelight, though he couldn't see what work she might be attending to.

"Ranger," she said again.

He didn't know what she meant by it. That they should turn her in, like some kind of lost-and-found Ranger doll? That she was not theirs to toy with? Or that perhaps they would come for her, a favorite possession gone missing. Strangely, the sight of her caused a zealous protectiveness to rise up in him. She had been fleeing in the night. He was responsible for her.

Celestina put her hand on his shoulder. It was a surprise to him, and he stayed frozen where he was until she removed it, not wishing to interrupt whatever feelings she may be having. Until, he thought, he began to feel it too, something. Whatever it was, the three of them in the room.

Renee and Bea rode block by block west along the territory, one block in from the border. At 26th they turned and walked slowly toward the guard station at Fremont. The street was quiet and lined by wide, spacious houses. The people here, at one time, had done well for themselves. Bare bones of giant trees, or the remaining stumps, were prevalent. Even now Renee couldn't see a burned house on the block. She led them to a few houses from the border station and walked quietly up the driveway of an abandoned house with its windows gone. Zach had told her of the tunnel's existence ages ago. He'd tapped the map. "This guy," he said, "just on the other side. I used to work with him." His finger covered a house right on the border. "He says he's digging a tunnel under his house."

"To where?" she'd asked.

"I'm not sure he knows," Zach answered. And so Renee had assigned Rangers to monitor the area. Recently a Ranger noted that the man had been spotted on both sides of the border and that he appeared after the border closed. Then a Ranger saw him manifest, his head rising from the ground like a prairie dog. At the back of a long-abandoned house there was a strange opening in the concrete driveway, covered with sticks and garbage. The tunneler, the Ranger reported, had wandered around for an hour without any purpose in particular that she could deduce, and then went back into his hole.

"You're fucking sure about this?" Bea whispered. It was the first she'd heard about it. They stood over the hole, a broken concrete opening into blackness. "You're sure there's no man living underground there?"

"Yeah." Renee smiled. "I'm sure. Don't be a sissy. You got your gun, right? " She relished the tease and chuckled. It was craziness to climb down into that dark shithole but nothing could stop her now. She shone her penlight down into the opening but it was weak and revealed only an amorphous gloom.

She lifted her bicycle and tested the dimensions of the opening— it would fit going wheel first. She got onto her knees and put her head down into the mouth of it. There was an earthy smell and she caught something else she hadn't smelled in a while—a wisp of dampness. The smell of dirt from deep in the ground, deeper than the graves at Rose City cemetery, deeper than the water tank holes.

She put her hand in and felt around for some means to climb down but there was nothing and she got spooked, imagining spiders and cave dwellers and who knew what else. "Fuck," she said and stood up. She pulled out her drinking flask and took a drink and passed it to Bea.

"We could go another way," Bea said. "If there's a man there with a gun, nobody is going to hear it go off. Look, this guard station—the Ranger is probably asleep."

"Might be city police on the other side."

"Yes, but—"

"I'll go first," Renee said. "You hand me down my cycle."

Bea looked at her uncomfortably and Renee took pleasure in being allowed to take the risk first.

She levered her body over the edge of the hole and dangled her feet. She hung there—there was nothing solid upon which to gain purchase and she panicked. Perhaps she was dangling her body over a hundred-foot well or some forgotten urban mine shaft. Perhaps Bea would hear nothing except the fleshy thud of her body as it collapsed into itself at the bottom. She held on there for a moment, grappling with the fear and her knowledge of the hole, which told her a man's head had emerged from it, birthed from the earth.

Then she let go and immediately hit the top of a stool, which tipped. She crashed sideways into the bottom of the tunnel, the wind knocked out of her.

"Renee!" Bea whispered as loud as she dared.

Renee tapped on the side of the wall as she attempted to get her breathing back. "Oh," she groaned. "I did it all wrong."

The floor of the tunnel was hard-packed dirt and rock and she felt like lying there for a while and contemplating the opening above, with the silhouette of Bea's head and stars beyond, a sort of moon in the black sky of the cave. She wondered if she'd cracked a rib. It had not been such a long time since her last injuries had healed. She stood and put her arms out to get a feel for the cave and found wood supports and clay-like earth. The floor of the tunnel sloped downward, as if the opening were the end of a teapot's spout.

It was deeply quiet in the black openness that stretched before her in the tunnel.

"All right," she whispered, "hand down the cycle, then I'll set the stool up for you."

"There's a stool?"

"There's a stool. It didn't work out for me."

"You're OK?" Bea asked, but it didn't really sound like a question, more like *you got what you deserved, hopping into a fucking hole.*

The tunnel moon eclipsed above her as the bike was lowered in. It was tight and she pushed it down the tunnel and rested it against the wall. Then Bea's bike and then Bea.

Bea turned on her pen light and began to inspect where they were.

The tunnel was not simply a means of getting from A to B, Renee saw. It was cared for. There were pictures hung at intervals, the occasional rough relief carving in the wall. There were pockets and shelves cut into the dirt, and in some of these odd trinkets and other miscellany were stored. Someone had put in a good deal of effort here. They pushed slowly onward, speaking in hushed voices and following the tunnel floor down until it leveled out.

They passed under several narrow, four-inch shafts that went up to the surface through which fresh air trickled in. She guessed these were for breathing or perhaps tests to see where the tunnel was.

It was pleasant inside. Perhaps it was only that it felt good to be shedding her other self, to be on an adventure, but she felt anxiety melt away from her, even as Bea pulled her gun out and breathed raggedly with fear.

"You claustrophobic?" Renee asked, and in the dim pen light Bea gave her an irritated look.

The tunnel wended and they passed several branch starts, as if the digger had not known which way he was going and tried out other paths.

Deep in, far enough so they'd resigned themselves to the completion of the journey, the way back in the dark too far now to consider, they heard a man yell *stop* and they both jumped. Bea killed her light and they stood silently.

"Don't come any closer, I'm armed and I'll shoot."

Bea reached out and grabbed Renee's arm, but they said nothing. After a while, Renee said, "We like your tunnel."

"I don't have any water, and—" There was some shuffling about in the tunnel. "Go back to Sherwood. I've already killed lots of people down here. All of them are dead. It's no problem for me to kill you two."

They were talking to a citizen of Portland, Renee had to remind herself. She'd watched city news and reports and correspondence came in regularly from other neighborhoods. Water crimes were frequent.

Bea whispered, "I don't believe him."

"We're passing through," Renee said. "May we pass through? My name is Renee and I'm with Bea, who is also armed, but we're not here for water, we're just coming to the other side. You sound like a good person. We don't believe you about the bodies."

"Then go back and use the border," the man said. "Believe whatever you want about the bodies! You'll see if you come this way! They're all stacked up here!"

"We can't use the border. We do not wish to be seen."

"Oh, for Christ sake!" the man said. "This is my tunnel." There were a few moments where the man made shuffling sounds in the dark and sighed. "It's not a freeway. How many people know?"

"Only us. We could put in a word with Maid Marian, give you Sherwood privileges."

"You don't even know her."

"We work for her."

"You're Rangers?"

"No."

"Then what?"

There was a long pause. Renee listened to the sound of Bea's breathing and realized meeting a stranger in a dark, earthy tunnel was a sort of nightmare, and wondered why she felt so calm. "This and that," she said, "administrative."

"Will I get clinic access?"

"Are you sick?"

"What about school?"

"You have kids?" Renee didn't know why she was so surprised, maybe building an elaborate tunnel under your house and having children seem antithetical, and then she remembered her own father and his time down in his wood shop, a two-liter bottle of wine always open on the table saw, tinkering at some project while he quietly sorted and railed against his various demons.

"How do I know you're not bluffing?" he said.

"Goddamnit!" roared Bea. "We can't hang out in the bottom of this fucking tunnel having an idle fucking conversation all night!"

"Bea," Renee said.

They heard a woman's voice faintly from somewhere deeper in.

"We have trespassers," Nevel said. "Call Bill and Bob downstairs."

"Who?" came the woman's voice and then they heard whispering.

"Well?" Renee said to Bea. "What the fuck, right?" and then she walked out in front, slowly, toward the sound of the voices. Once she was a few strides beyond Bea's pen light, if she closed her eyes it was no different than having them open. She wheeled her bicycle forward and stretched her other hand out to steady herself on the walls. "I'm walking forward," she called.

She heard Bea cursing her in a whisper behind.

Renee walked another thirty paces around a curve in the tunnel, until she could sense the couple in front of her somewhere.

"Who are you?" the woman said.

"My name is Renee. My friend Bea and I need to come into the city for a little bit. It's just us and our bikes. We need secrecy. In exchange, we can promise you clinic and school access in Sherwood."

There was the light of a flashlight now and Renee followed that to the end of the tunnel. She let them shine it on her, lowering her eyes against the glare.

"How can you promise that?" the woman asked.

"You'll have to take my word on that," Renee said.

"I know who you are," Cora said.

"You *know* this woman?" Nevel said.

"Yes," Cora said quietly, "I do." Cora put her hand to her mouth. "Are you in trouble? Can we help?"

"What?" Nevel shouted. "Who the hell is she?" Nevel squinted at them in the dim light but saw only two women covered in tunnel smudge.

"Thank you," Renee said, "we need to find someone in the city."

"Come upstairs," Cora said. "Nevel, you get her bike."

"But—but the other girl is back there, with a gun!"

"No, I'm here," Bea said, "and hands-off." She grabbed the bike that had been left against the wall. "You can put your gun away now, tough guy."

"This is my tunnel," Nevel said.

"Wacko," Bea said as she passed him. Bea struggled both bikes up the basement stairs and huffed loudly.

From around his neck, Jamal removed the charm his mother had given him—a tiny metal Guan Yin figure, a small symbol of the disparate paths his parents chose. As his father tread deeper into being a junkie, his mother sifted through religions, thumbing through each as if browsing albums to buy. In the end, she adopted Buddhism. It was no wonder in his mother's absence Gregor had turned to tea ceremonies, the ritual a sort of communion with his dead wife.

"Here," Jamal said, "I brought you something." He uncurled Rick's paw-hand and recurled it around the figure of Guan Yin. "Hello?" Jamal said. He nudged Rick's shoulder. "I put something in your hand."

Rick opened one eye and brought the tiny figure in front of it for inspection. "It's a lady, right? She's a little lady?"

"Yeah."

Rick brought her closer to his wide bloodshot eye and inspected Guan Yin's features. "She's cute," he said.

"She's the Buddhist god of compassion. And mercy."

"OK," Rick said, and closed his eyes again.

"Hold on to her, you know, for, just hold on to her for now." Jamal nodded and then the sound of a shot made him jump.

He crawled back to his window and inspected the street for signs of activity, and then asked Carl if he'd seen anything.

"I got that yellow house," Carl called back.

"You see someone?"

There was no answer.

"Carl likes to shoot at things," Rick said.

"It's a house," Jamal said.

"That's a thing."

"You hang in there, Rick." Hours had passed and the strain of it was audible from the other room where Carl had begun to talk to himself in an unceasing whisper. There was no sign of their attackers and Jamal began to fantasize about simply walking out the door and biking home. His calf ached and he was hungry. There were three dead Rangers in the house and he hoped they weren't going to add a fourth, or more, to the number.

He pulled out the stack of neighborhood notes and, hunkering in a squat, began to arrange them on the floor according to where the house was positioned in the neighborhood.

A terrific bang sounded from the room over and Jamal started and lost his balance and disrupted the system of notes he'd laid out.

"I got the house," Carl said.

"Carl?" Jamal said. "Why don't you take a nap? We're going to be up all night here."

"I resent that."

Jamal waved his hands in the direction of Carl but couldn't think what to say. "Why are you shooting the house?"

There was no answer and after the adrenalin seeped from him he turned back to the task at hand. He straightened the notes until he had nine blocks laid out, three blocks square, filling the room end to end. There were many missing squares from empty houses or where no message had come, so the blocks were patchwork. He started with the house they were in, a concrete building away from Woodlawn Park, with its charming playground and play-fountain, and the inevitable horde of boys who wanted to kill him—or at least him of the past, and now it seemed some of them were back at it. This neighborhood was a cesspool of anti-Jamalism, he thought. He wondered if this was the same war. Perhaps it'd never ended, just gotten drowsy for a few years. Perhaps his father's enemy had respawned. He remembered Barstow had died some years back of a heart attack and a younger member of the gang had taken the lead. "Charles is in charge now," read the note for this house. Who had lived here, he wondered, who had answered the door to relay the message to the water carrier? Where was their water carrier?

There was not much left of the house. Some broken furniture, and small heaps of discarded junk.

He had a note for the yellow house across the street: "Wants conference with M.M. about security." And now, Jamal thought wryly, Carl is shooting up a justification for her. He read through all the others, thirty-three in all, some of them stacked several deep on the same house. There was only one other note on their street. "Says she saw a city cop in a regular car drive through. She's old."

He crawled back to the window and spotted where he believed this house to be, up near the top of the block, and pondered what a city cop's business would be here.

"It's not the blue house up the way, Carl," he said, feeling fairly sure they weren't being shot at by the old lady.

No answer came and he thought, not for the first time, that the man might have a pretty low sanity threshold and that perhaps, all corny humor and movie references aside, it might have been better, circumstances provided, to have switched one comrade for the other. Though there was a hell of a lot to be said for a wounded man who did not complain.

"How you doing, Rick?"

"Are we there yet?" His voice was barely audible.

"Don't go anywhere without me."

"I'd like some ice cream, vanilla is fine, or whatever."

"When we get out we'll get some. First thing."

Jamal sat and watched the street. It'd be sundown shortly and he dreaded the night and felt certain Rick wouldn't make it through. He crawled across the floor into the kitchen and beyond, into a large pantry, or perhaps where a washing machine would go, where the three Rangers were laid out next to each other, their bodies touching, their faces ashen, the smell of death not yet fully on them. He looked at the father; his face was swollen with bruises and his head tilted in a subtly odd manner on his neck and Jamal felt anger surge into him. Like a gasoline fire it raged out of nothing and burned hot and then was gone. Maybe they were fighting the city, he thought, maybe this was the frontline of a quiet war none of them knew had started. Then he wondered if the rest of the territory was all right, or if small invasions were happening everywhere. He steeled himself, knowing that to search the man's clothes was something that must be done in the dimming light before nightfall.

They were complete, each one of them. Like Ranger action figures, with their full outfits minus the baton. They bore the standard tools: a whistle, pen, a small stack of note paper, an LED pen light, pain killer, baseball cap, semaphore cheatsheet. They'd been freed of their standard weapon: a fighting baton made of a thirty inch length of steel rebar a half inch in diameter, with a duct-tape handle. Also missing were their drinking flasks, and that was robbery enough. He wiped the sweat from his eyes with the back of his hand and noticed how dry their skin looked.

He put the items in his own pockets, then did what he knew he ought to have done long ago. He was not actively religious, nor did he actively believe in ghosts, but a lifetime's exposure to the devout and superstitious required him to go through the motions of blessing them, and freeing the house of the possibility of haunting before nightfall. He touched the top of each of their cold heads in turn, one whose head was crusted with blood, and told them he was sorry. "We're here now and we'll try our damnedest to get you back to your families. If you see the need to do any haunting or spooking, please keep in mind we already have quite a few problems of our own and we are, after all, on the same side. Please consider the people who did this to you as a perfectly good option for haunting, if you can leave the house, or whatever, and all that," he said. His voice reverberated eerily in the otherwise empty room and then went silent.

"Especially leave Carl alone, and don't let Rick die," he added. "Our Father in heaven and in the name of your son Jesus I ask for you to come get these men and to take their spirits up to heaven, without any lingering, and so on." He felt touching their heads once each to be sufficient but then he wondered if it'd been too hasty and he touched each of their cold foreheads again and said amen each time.

There, he thought. It'd gotten dark quickly and he wanted to leave the room immediately. His knees were sore from crawling and now that it was dark he stood. At the doorway he wished for some kind of barrier to close them in for the night. He walked through the darkened house to the living room window.

"What'd they say?" Rick said, his voice appearing apparition-like, omnisciently, from a body lying as if dead in a pool of its own blood.

Jamal had to grip the wall for a moment to let his heart calm.

"Can we not—personify them?" Jamal said, and then felt like a total asshole. "They didn't say anything."

"I heard you talking."

"Yeah, well, I did all the talking."

"What are you mad at me for?"

"Nothing. I've got more painkiller, you want it?"

"Does the pope eat french fries?"

"I really don't know, Rick," Jamal said, and then because he was talking to a dying man he felt he owed him an answer. "Does he? Eat french fries?"

"Can you get my water?" Rick said. "If I move everything's going to leak all over the place."

"Jesus," Jamal said.

"Jamal," Rick said as Jamal fetched the water, "there isn't nobody who doesn't eat french fries."

Afterward, Jamal went to see Carl. He had not moved since he'd last seen him. He sat on the floor, his gun resting on the window sill, pointed toward the street. He peered outward from behind the curtain.

"Well?" Jamal said.

"Shh."

"We've got to figure out how we're going to do the night."

"I said shush. I'm watching them."

Jamal leaned down to get a look out the window, thinking perhaps Carl would take the whole night's watch either way. "You do stakeouts much in the force?" Jamal flicked a corner of the curtain aside and at that moment he heard a great rumbling and the house vibrated. Then out the window he saw a big tanker truck with its lights off drive up the street and turn the corner.

"Hey," Jamal said.

"I saw it!" Carl whispered irritably.

"That was a water truck."

"Goddamnit, I saw it. Sit down and keep your voice down."

Jamal slowly sat and then realized the dim shapes he was looking at were men on the porch of the yellow house. At least three of them, but the light was low enough so that one shape melded into the next or split apart. "What are they doing?"

"They're waiting."

"For what?"

"I don't know."

They sat and watched until a biker came keening down the street, swerved into the yard and ran up onto the porch.

"Maybe for him," Carl said. "We're going to need to do some shooting." Carl sighted down his gun. "For which I am very happy."

Carl was one of the best marksmen of the Going Street Brigade. "Can you hit someone from here?" Jamal said.

"Not well enough in this light to be worth it. Better to wait until they come for us."

Jamal stood. "Tell me if you see them move."

He searched around the house for anything that could be of use to them and began to pile it in the living room. He unscrewed several broomsticks from their heads and tried out wedging them against the front door.

He found some dish soap and, looking out at the yellow house, eased himself out the window into the darkness of the front porch. "It's me," he said toward Carl's window, hoping the man wouldn't shoot him. He squirted dish soap on the wood stairs, on the doorknob handle, and as far toward the sidewalk as he dared. These seemed like great defenses for fending off a few spear-toting barbarians, not gunmen. He did not feel like Robinson Crusoe. He had no bombardment of logs to free, no mountain of stones to unleash, no boiling oil to pour.

He hesitated on the front porch and crouched. He could hear talking across the street but could not make out the words.

He pondered what it would take to run up the hill and be gone from here. He could hop the side of the porch and climb across the next and the next after that, then hit the sidewalk running and be rid of the whole nightmare. There was sound from up the street as well but he thought one person could slip by in this dark. He could unlock his bike at the top of the hill and ride through the neighborhoods like a falcon, he could head toward that girl into whose ear he'd whispered a haiku, to whom his thoughts had turned several times as a small piece of hopeful adventure that he might undertake were he to free himself whole from this nonsense. The darkness beckoned to him warm and accepting, ready to take him into it, to conceal and squirrel him away.

Or he could die trying. He was the captain of the Going Street Brigade and he had to stay with his men. Getting killed trying to

escape would doom them all, if they weren't doomed already. Back in
the drug wars he'd left a man. He'd been scared and run and a friend
had been killed. The impulse to flee was fully quashed by the memory
of that regret.

Nevel and Cora sat at the kitchen table and talked quietly after they'd
left. The kids were asleep, and the leader of the independent nation
of Sherwood had shown up in their basement earlier. His tunnel
was officially that, now, no longer just a cave but a portal to another
nation. He felt unease about where their house siphoned off to, out-
gassing across the border.

His wife was electrified. Cora had chatted for ten minutes with
Maid Marian before they'd left and they had liked each other immediately. There was a feeling in the room like they'd had exotic visitors
from a foreign country. Do they shake hands like normal people or do
I kiss an ear or something else?

In a moment of insane fervor, of good will and charity, he took
Maid Marian down to show her his cache of water deep in the tunnel,
thinking to turn it over to Sherwood, to prove the mayor's misdeeds.

While Cora and Bea stayed in the kitchen, he walked her slowly
back into the tunnel, pointing out salient features with the flashlight
beam without naming them. Something ancient and unspeakable
made him build this tunnel, he thought. Or hoped, rather—his conscious mind was not entirely clear on its purpose.

At one point he turned and looked back at her. In the confines
of the passage she could have been a Vietcong soldier, the tunnel a
perfect fit around her. "Does any of this make sense?" he said, and she
smiled. He wished the passage spanned out much further, that they
could walk on and on this way.

"Is this the end?" she said.

He stared at the flattened cardboard boxes that covered the hole
to his water treasure and his stomach ached with what he was about to
do. If he showed her this she would have another piece of solid proof
against the mayor. Perhaps he would be on the news. They would
move to Sherwood. He extinguished the light to go through the hole.
In the darkness he could hear her breathing; there was fear in the
heaviness of it, but she kept it steady. He pulled away the cardboard
from the hole and felt his way in. He whispered a *hello* to them, lined

up as they were on the floor. This is what he had. These were the cards you held close to your chest. In some future history of his family that his grandsons would read, a single line descended through time to him now: *This is how Nevel saved his family in the time of the drought.*

He grabbed a single unit gallon and pulled it back out with him. When he turned on his light he shone it through the container so that it glowed.

"Oh," she said.

There are hundreds more in there, he thought to say, but the words did not come out. Finally he said, "For your journey."

"You have children," she said.

"We want to help."

"We can't accept that," she said. She reached out and touched his elbow. "That's my job, to give water out." She smiled at him, her eyes joyful despite the rathole he'd dragged her through. He thought he'd follow her anywhere.

Back upstairs they found Bea and Cora at the table. He placed the unit gallon on the table and stole a glance at his wife. He did not know what she would say. When she met his eyes he gave a quick, subtle shake of his head. He had not given their ill-gotten wealth away to a better cause.

"Nevel and I would love for you to take a gallon with you," Cora said.

Nevel sat. His wife was keeping the secret, he realized, and he felt an immense love for her suddenly. Together they were doing the wrong thing. They could keep the treasure, they could harbor the little hoard for their family.

The mayor was playing Battlefield 1942. He lay on the couch, playing aimlessly, past the time where the game still felt enjoyable. He'd killed all of the Nazis and then he'd killed all of his teammates and then the citizens.

At the other end of the long couch Christopher sat, an open book on his lap. "What will you do when the drought ends?" Christopher said. He had owned a sushi restaurant before the economy broke it.

"You've already asked me that," the mayor said irritably.

"I know, but it's a fun question. I'm going to drink a beer, for one. I so miss beer."

The mayor stepped into a bunker with the last remaining enemy soldier on the island and drew his knife and hit the buttons frenetically on his joystick, *Uh! Uh! Uh!* The soldier grunted with each stab wound, until the mayor was shot, and the game ended. "Fuck," he said. "I thought I had him. I had him, right?"

"And then I'm going to wash all of my clothes. Maybe by hand. Just for the enjoyment of it. And I'm going to sit in the bath and watch the water drain out. You know those little whirlpools that dance above the drain, when the water is draining? Think of that. I mean—we could do that now"—Christopher tilted his head and tried to judge to see if the mayor were paying attention—"but I'd feel guilty. I'd love to wantonly waste it, just for a little bit. Like drinking water from a garden hose."

The mayor switched sides and restarted the game as an Axis soldier with a sniper rifle. He climbed on top of an Allied bunker outside of a small compound and knocked off everything that moved until a grenade blast exploded him back to reset. "Fuck," he drawled.

"And going out to eat. I want to go out for dinner and eat a burger, doesn't have to be fancy. I mean sure, fancy would be good too, but a burger—bacon, bleu cheese—fries—how about a milkshake? Rations, right? I mean hey. And to go to a restaurant where it's buzzing and there's a line—'well, of course we have a seat for you, right this way, mayor.'"

"What are you talking about?" the mayor said.

Christopher held up his hands defensively, "I'm passing time, same as you."

"You know what I'd do?" the mayor said. "I'd run the city, that's what I'd do. Something besides water use restrictions, police cuts, systems reduction. I'd govern a city that could pay taxes, *united.* I'd spearhead transportation initiatives, add another light rail line, I'd make sure schools had funding. I'd revel in the news that our city was growing, a desirable destination. There'd be art, I'd fund new arts organizations and set up city grants for local artists. I'd create a motherfucking monument—you know? Why not? Like say we raze that annoying lot on Second and Pine, and put in a water park—recycled its own water and shit and commemorated the drought."

"With a statue of you?" Christopher nudged the mayor with his foot in jest but there was no response.

The mayor restarted the game as a pilot and climbed into a fighter plane and was silent while he got the plane in the air, a process that, Christopher knew, had taken him some time to master and for which he still had to concentrate.

"I haven't heard you talk like that in a while," Christopher said.

The mayor sighed. "You want me to be idealistic in this shithole? You want some kind of citizen's hero out of me?" The mayor was being tailed by an American fighter and after a *thwok thwok thwok* his plane began to trail smoke. "Well, don't, this is a new era and you better drop that fanciful shit. I am not the mayor of that city. My job is to feed and water these miserable shits, and to make sure they don't kill each other."

In an evasive maneuver the mayor took his plane on a loop but he was losing altitude and halfway through the loop the plane nosedived into the water. "Fuck!" The mayor leapt up and threw the controller down and Christopher watched the screen. The water washed over the wing as it dipped below the surface of the ocean.

Christopher drew his feet up to his chest. "This is getting pretty hot. Like maybe there's some part of this conversation I missed."

"You're always trying to lead me into talking about some issue or another."

"Well."

"Like you think I don't realize it, I'm some child that you can set on a 'happy subject.'"

"I like it when you talk about what you'll do. It did used to make you happy."

The mayor left the room and Christopher could hear his movements through the house. In the kitchen he rough-handled a few cupboards and then he was back, yelling.

"I can't be your project. You need something to do. Find something else to fuck with."

"I just realized something's happened," Christopher said on a daring whim, knowing the trouble he was making for himself.

The mayor paced back and forth in front of the city view.

"What did you do?" Christopher said.

"This is about you, not me. I'm running a city."

"Are they in Sherwood?" Christopher saw the mayor's body angle away, as if deflecting a blow.

An outhouse program, farming initiatives, and a fledgling volunteer program were all new city initiatives, inspired by Sherwood ones, but they were weak, watered-down in comparison. Christopher knew the mayor spent far more of his time plotting up ways to splinter or destroy Sherwood than anything else. And his hate for Maid Marian had created a network of paid informants through the territory.

Christopher felt bad for him. Maid Marian could get things accomplished the city had no hope of. He was but a politician with low approval ratings. "Come on," he said, "tell me what you've done."

After a moment, Christopher patted the couch next to him and the mayor gave in. He sat down and sank into it, hunching his shoulders up. Then grabbed the controller instinctively, his fingers twitching over it. He clutched it to his chest and then, pre-empting criticism from Christopher about how they were talking, and not to play when they were having a real talk, he tossed it to the floor and sunk deep into the leather couch again.

"You captured Maid Marian," Christopher said.

"No."

"Is this going to be twenty questions? Did she do something? Is there a riot somewhere?"

"No. And I had no choice." The mayor started to speak and then petered off again.

"We could be here all night. Tell me, we'll talk it out. It's going to be all right."

"We're seeding a rebellion in one of the Sherwood neighborhoods. Guns, water, money. So that it looks like they're trying to secede back to the city. We're funding a drug dealer to do it."

"Huh. You and Roger?"

"You think I could get his help? There's no way I can run this city with it all fucking splintering apart. We paint her as a nasty dictator, and take all the wind out of the other potentials, get the news back, and make real progress here. It's the only way."

"How many dead?"

"I don't know."

"It's a pretty smart plan," Christopher said finally, and he tried his best to sound like he meant it.

"Fuck you," the mayor said. He leapt up and resisted the urge to throw the controller again, but a burning aggression was in him now and he strode from one side of the room to the other in big, exaggerated strides. "It's a smart plan. It's a smart plan. It *is* a smart plan, OK?"

"What ever happened to good governing? You can't beat her with politics?"

"No."

"You can beat her with ideas and programs."

"No! I've got to fend off Herr Commander Aachen, who approaches problems like a chipper shredder. Any good idea that goes through the council process comes out a turd on the other side. She has won the progress war."

"That's not true and you know it."

"Christopher. It's too late for this conversation."

"Well, I think it's depressing."

"Stop it, it's too late."

"This is who you want to be?"

"Christopher, shut up!"

"You're turning into someone you'll despise."

". . . —No"

"You should self-reflect."

The mayor leapt up and got his hands round the other man's shoulders and forced him to the ground. He was easily stronger than Christopher and he shoved him down hard. Christopher struggled, kicking at him and grabbing at his face but the mayor kept his hold. Then the mayor lifted him again and shoved him back down, knocking Christopher's breath out in an *oomph*. Brandon throttled Christopher's neck and felt the desire for completion.

"Don't," Christopher said in a whispery breath.

The mayor collapsed in place. His head fell on Christopher's chest and he sobbed, clutching him. "I'm so sorry," he whispered, and then whispered it again.

Christopher put his hands on the mayor's head and took full breaths, and they stayed frozen like that for a long while. A whole new fear had oozed into Christopher, a breath-stealing fear, a dread he'd never experienced.

They thanked Nevel and Cora and rode slowly in the dark, wary of what they might find lurking there. Crime in the city was several times the rate of crime in Sherwood, according to the news, and that was the statistic for reported crimes. Who knew what transpired in silence.

Trash littered the streets. Renee knew it was a matter of perception, but the dust in the air felt more intense in the city, a presence you breathed in and out. She stopped to tie a bandana around her face, to hide themselves and filter out the dust.

"We're out of water," Bea said. "We should have taken what they offered."

"Zach will have some."

"If he's there."

"He'll be there."

"If he let's us in."

"He'll let us in."

A block behind them a car's headlights bore down on them, the glow diffused by the dust. They raced around a corner, rode up a driveway and hid behind a garage. They heard the car accelerate and turn, saw the strobe of the car's searchlight bounce up and down between houses.

"It's a cop," Bea said.

"Is there a curfew?"

"I don't know. If they spot us, we have to run."

It was quiet behind the garage and felt safer than being on the road. She wished she could lie down there and sleep off the night.

"Come on," Bea said.

A few blocks later they rode headlong into a mass of people, their bodies lit in the moonlight, grappling and fighting. There were fifteen or twenty or thirty—in the dark it was hard to tell—brawling in the middle of an intersection. They were serious, intent on settling some score, the only noise grunts of pain and the brute sounds of violence.

Bea and Renee were riding too fast and became aware of them too late. In the moment Renee was upon them, adrenalin took over and she found a hole between the grappling bodies and sailed through. Bea followed and was knocked off her bike. She toppled over someone and fell heavily to the ground. A man lunged at her, landing on top, and a second later there was a gunshot and Bea rose up and her attacker didn't. A circle quickly widened around her and someone yelled "No guns, we said no guns!" Bea turned toward the voice and shot again and in the moonlight Renee thought she saw another figure fall.

"Bea!" Renee screamed.

Bea turned in a circle and the figures scattered outward, some running, yelling threats over their shoulders, stumbling into the dark.

Renee watched Bea stumble and she heard the stony thud of rocks and realized that they were stoning her from the safety of the dark.

"Bea, come!" Renee yelled.

One of the men on the ground was screaming. Bea stumbled again, and felt around for her bike. Renee dropped hers and ran the quarter block back and grabbed Bea's bike from her. A stone the size of a fist hit Renee's shoulder and she called out and pushed Bea in front and ran with her bike.

They ran half a block and mounted their bikes.

"I'm sorry," Bea said, and Renee watched her sway. She was aware of the crowd coming from behind, of the man still screaming in the intersection, bleeding from some hole. Bea fell forward, jerking her bike with her, and clattered to the ground.

Renee dismounted and pulled at her, but she was unconscious. She searched her body and found Bea's gun in a duct-tape harness under her arm. She couldn't tell if she saw shapes advancing in the dark or not. She kicked Bea in the back, furious now. "Bea, come on!"

A moment later Renee felt an iron grip on her leg. "Renee?"

"Get up right now," Renee whispered. A stone hit Renee in the chest and she put her elbows up around her face. "Get on your fucking bike."

She clutched the handle of the gun to her handlebars, mounted her bike and looked back to see Bea followed.

They rode fast for a dozen blocks. Behind them they could see a car had arrived at the fight scene. Renee pulled over and handed the gun back to Bea. "Fucking crazy bitch," Renee said and then gripped her in a tight hug.

"He was on me," Bea said, and then bowed her head. "I was scared."

Renee could see a dark stain of blood on Bea's forehead where a rock had struck.

"You shot two."

"I know," Bea said.

"Why? Goddamnit, Bea!"

Bea didn't answer. They studied the glow of light behind them and then rode on.

The plan was to grab Zach and bring him back the same night, but by the time they arrived it was near dawn. They were exhausted and thirsty, Bea was bleeding, and Renee had two big welts that made it painful to ride.

They stood in the door's alcove outside of Zach's building and took turns knocking while the other watched the street. After a while they heard shouting from inside and it was clearly not Zach' voice.

"Get your gun," Renee said. She put her ear to the door and listened. Someone on the inside was yelling, "Knock! Knock! Knock!" back at them.

"What the fuck?" Renee said.

"Should I shoot the lock out?"

The *knock knock knocks* had taken on the tune of jingle bells. They stood in the door well, the street spookily quiet behind them, and listened.

"Do you think he's—he's lost it?" Bea said.

After a moment Renee said, "I doubt it."

"Maybe we should go."

"No way—we have to be inside before it's light."

Renee looked up the street, hoping no one else heard the hoarse singing coming from inside. There were a few two- and three-story buildings around the intersection and up the block, and then it went back to typical residential.

The knock-knock singer went fully hoarse, the voice dissipating into wheezy radio static, and then disappeared altogether. Renee steeled herself and pounded on the door.

There was a loud crash behind them and Bea swung her gun around wildly. On the sidewalk they could dimly see a broken flower pot, a skeletal stem rising from the shapeless mound of dirt in the wreckage.

"From above," Renee said.

Bea leaned out of the doorway and pointed her gun up. "We'll shoot, asshole!"

"Shhh," Renee said, "for fuck sake. Don't do any more shooting. If he's not here we leave."

"Unless he's tied up in there."

"Bea?" came Zach's voice from above. "Is that you?"

"Yeah! Zach, damn it—let us in."

"Who's us?"

"Me and—Renee is with me."

"I see." After a moment he said, "I'll be right there."

The door opened and from behind Zach they heard someone say, "They're here-er!"

"Who in the fuck is that," Bea said and pointed her pistol around Zach and into the house.

"That's—" Zach waved his arm at Bea's gun. "He's my patient. Why are you here? Put away your gun, Bea."

"Not until I see him."

"You're not coming inside with a gun out."

"Put it away, Bea," Renee said.

Bea emitted a defeated growl and holstered it and then pushed past, leaving Renee and Zach standing in the doorway.

"We've had a hell of a night," she said.

"Oh? What's going on? Don't you have a country to run?"

"Can I come inside? Can I—" She gestured toward him. She spontaneously leaned in and gripped him in a hug, clutching him tighter than she meant to, tightening her grip on him when she felt the familiar feel of his back. The smell of his neck. The hug returned was light and impatient, and so she let him go.

"Come in," he said flatly. "I have to check if Bea has my patient in a half nelson."

"She's good that way."

"Matter of opinion."

Zach lit a candle and cared for Bea's head. After, he poured them a little water, and a dim light filtered in from dawn. They told him about their ride and Sherwood and Jamal's disappearance and asked if he'd come back.

"I'm not here because I don't believe in Sherwood," he said.

"Oh," Bea said. "Time for me to leave." She downed the rest of her water and stood uncomfortably. "Zach—can I—we didn't sleep—"

"—Of course, Bea. Why don't you take my room."

Bea caught Renee giving her a quick head shake *no* and Bea said she'd be fine with the couch. She turned and gave them a back-handed wave and edged her way around the sleeping patient and was gone.

After a while Zach said, "I wasn't sure I'd ever see you again. Borders are tightening and the city is getting rougher. At water distribution, people talk about how to sneak across, but they say it's hard. One man got beat senseless trying."

"Probably the city," Renee said, "afraid of losing important people. My people aren't authorized to use force at the border."

"I don't know . . ." Zach said. He ran his finger around the rim of his water glass. "I'm thinking about opening my own clinic here, seeing what I can do. I don't know. I've been restless without—either of my jobs. You ever hear of seeding rain clouds?"

"You haven't changed one iota. Let's go talk in your bed." Renee put her hands over his and smiled up at him and knew it was the cheesiest of smiles but she couldn't help it. He could rattle on unceasingly. She felt incredibly happy to see him, more so than she'd expected. But she was aware of the division of personalities within her: Maid Marian had a country to run and an agenda. Renee wanted to take Zach upstairs. And in this, Maid Marian's and Renee's desires were not mutually exclusive.

A shaft of sunlight like a golden rod traced out an area of floor in Zach's room and she could see that there were many projects at work here. On top of his dresser there was a baby food jar of clear red liquid, and when the light hit it, it glowed bright. She tapped the jar and raised her eyebrows. He started to explain but stopped when she began taking her clothes off.

He was wearing green-plaid pajama bottoms and looked down at them as if to take them off, but did not. She could see that he was not ready to do this.

"It's OK, weirdo," she said, "you can keep them on." She pulled him into bed and wrapped around him. She pressed her lips against his neck and after a while said, "So here's the deal. I'm sort of like two people."

"I guess."

"This one would really like to be with you. I'm not sure the other one can."

"How do I work out which one I'm with?"

"I don't know," Renee said.

With her toes she grabbed the cuffs of Zach's pajama pants and pulled, lowering them a few inches.

"Will you come back with us?"

"I have a patient here."

She lowered the pants another notch. "Maybe we could take him with us."

"He has a leg wound."

"Are you talking sexy to me?"

"He's from Oklahoma, his great grandparents lived through the dust bowl. Static electricity was so intense that nobody shook hands or touched. It could knock you flat."

"You *are* talking sexy."

Early the next morning Martin donned Celestina's dead husband's clothes. They were tight on him and fashioned after a different era but a suit and hat and a rolling suitcase allowed a sort of disguise. He set off into the streets to find water carriers to rob. He felt driven to provide, by some deeply buried instinct to protect those in your tribe.

It was odd, he thought, watching a woman sleeping like that. Unsure where her unconscious meandered, toward death or away, while you stood next to her bed. Her lack of participation in the relationship so far had allowed him a level of intimacy that would not have been possible otherwise. He had touched her skin and studied her face. And he enjoyed caring for her with Celestina too. She could be his daughter, if he'd had one, and Celestina his mother, and the trio of generations he found comforting. His eye-hole ached severely, and he jammed the palm of his hand hard over his patch. He hadn't figured any of it out yet.

He found a couple of water carriers to follow. Each served a side of the street, and they fell into a synchronous pattern now, meeting at the cart for water, and then knocking at houses on opposite sides, occasionally taking the time to jot down a note at their front doors. They were quick, fleet of foot, and he was a middle-aged, one-eyed hobbling bull in an overly tight suit from the 1950s, the pant legs of which exposed his ankles.

When they were both at houses, he barreled forward to their cart, grabbed two unit gallons, struggled with the suitcase, got the bottles in and hobbled on.

"Hey, man." A water carrier had his hand on his shoulder. "Come on, now. Wait your turn. Where do you live?"

Martin turned and mimed remorse and the boy smiled.

"You don't want to be caught doing that. Give 'em back now."

Martin saw the other carrier approaching now too. Martin leaned down to open the suitcase and then rose hard with his fist, catching the pup in the throat. The water carrier fell and writhed on the ground, making choking sounds while the other erupted in a heap of cussing.

"You tell her the cyclops is here. The cyclops is hunting her," Martin growled. "That he's back from the grave she dug for him. You got that? You tell her that."

Martin turned and walked away. He counted his steps. At one hundred he turned to look back. He was not being followed. All for *two fucking gallons* of water, he thought.

Back home he rifled around in the old woman's garage until he found some sturdy twine. *Cyclops.* That had come out of him by surprise, issued from some Greek myth. He touched his eye patch to make sure it was in place, a habit he'd picked up. Inside, he set the newly won gallons on the dresser in the Ranger's room like a trophy. Celestina hovered in the doorway, watching him.

"Hello?" the woman said. Her voice was weak.

"You're awake." He smiled at her.

"Where am I?"

"I found you on the street last night with your head open."

"Oh," she said meekly. "Is this a clinic?"

Martin took the twine and cut off four long lengths. "In a manner of speaking," he said. He took two of the lengths, positioned himself at the end of the bed and proceeded to tie her ankles to the bed posts.

"No," she said with alarm. She looked at Celestina in panic. "Please, god, no." She tried to struggle weakly but he was fast and no stranger to rope.

"Don't worry, we'll take care of you, Ranger." He patted her legs after he'd finished.

Celestina had her hand on his arm.

"No te preocupas, Celestina. It's temporary, for a little protection, so this one doesn't go getting us in trouble."

He tied her wrists as she fought him. When he was finished, the Ranger turned her head toward the wall and wept.

"Está OK?" he asked Celestina and she nodded. "Vamos a cuidar. Somos medicos! Agua." He pointed. "Mas agua por mi doctor." He patted her on the shoulder. "Doctor Celestina!" They were in this together. He cursed himself for not relieving the carriers of some food rations too. He would do that tomorrow. He had to make a plan.

He sat down on the side of the bed and dug his fingernails into his leg. The fuck was wrong with him. Revenge was not meted out by an oaf with a baseball bat in a street, two gallons at a pop. None of this was fucking planned, he thought. This Ranger was not a substitute for the other. He resolved to get together with a pencil and paper as soon as possible. He was bigger, smarter and luckier than the average bear. It had taken him this far, which, in the end, was pretty much nowhere.

"Your Maid Marian did this to me." He pointed to his eye patch.

The woman studied him sullenly.

"Listen, hey, I'm not going to hurt you. We saved you, right? But look—she sent her fuckwads for me." He lifted his eyepatch and showed her, and when she recoiled, he wished he hadn't. It made him feel sorry for himself all over again. "They shot me in the face and tried to bury me. I was still alive! But I got away!" he said. He put his hands up in the air. "Ta-da!"

"What did you do?" the Ranger said.

"Nothing. She didn't like my business. I'm just saying, she's no saint. She's going to bleed your little country dry. Evil queen bee. What's your name?"

"Rachel."

He patted her leg again. Maybe she'd come in handy somehow.

Rachel turned her face away from him and stared at the wall. "This place would be hell if it weren't for Maid Marian. She's saving us."

His temper took control of him for a moment and he crossed the room and brought his fist down on the dresser.

Celestina jumped and fled the room.

"Sitting in a tree, k-i-s-s-i-n-g!" he sung, briefly overwhelmed with hatred, and then he slammed the door behind him.

Celestina kept a pile of scratch paper on the counter and he grabbed half a dozen sheets and a pencil and sat with his head in his hands. In his gut boiled the same shameful feeling he'd felt as a nine-year-old playground bully. He was going to make a plan. He was going to be a hero, for once.

With a limped gait Jamal paced back and forth in the dining room, striding alongside the body of Rick, who had not made a sound for some hours. The wound in his calf was keeping him awake with its dull ache.

He didn't have it in him to check Rick for a pulse and didn't care whether they spotted him from across the street, through the ragged

holes in the curtains, pacing back and forth like some wooden doll in
a shooting game at the carnival.

He was sick of waiting. Carl remained where he was, as if made of
stone, a gargoyle watchman looking out into the darkness, mumbling
his demon curses.

If Rick was dead, they could run and for this reason Jamal couldn't
help but hope a little that the man had passed into the aether. Through
the night they'd talked on and off in quiet tones, about the war and
the drug wars. Rick had been cogent about half the time.

"Carl!" he hollered. Eighteen hours in this tomb and he could feel
madness at the periphery, an option that he could take if he were the
sort of man that had the inclination. His adrenal glands were spent,
he was sure, and the fear nagged on him like some old, foul sweater,
an itch and a weight around his neck. Thirst and hunger and the dead,
trapped with a gargoyle. Certainly there were those who, faced with
the choices of death or an indeterminate stay, might eventually choose
the easy detour of insanity. Who might burst from the light bonds of
reason and lash out into unknown territory of the psyche. "Carl!"

"What."

"Let's shoot at them."

He couldn't for the life of him figure out what their assailants
were waiting for, other than the inevitable passing of their opponents
into madness, or passing from thirst. Jamal's mouth tasted like he'd
chewed and swallowed a medium-sized doormat. The physical craving of water dominated his thoughts.

Jamal repositioned himself at his window, which showed signs of
eighteen hours of anxious living. Scraps of paper were spread around
and neglected. Wrappers from the rest of his meager supply of food
and all of his possessions formed a sort of nest.

He looked out the window again and saw the first traces of dawn
coming and that cheered him, for he knew whatever was going to happen was destined to happen now during daylight. The house across
from them was quiet and still.

"Ready when you are. I'll take the first floor and you take the second." Jamal had appropriated Rick's gun for Carl and between the
three guns they had seventy bullets. They agreed to shoot two bullets
each.

Jamal fired one in each window on the first floor, on either side
of the door. There was no glass and so he couldn't honestly be sure if

he'd hit his mark. His ears rang from the pistol shots and he looked up and down the street for any sign of activity, trying to keep out of view as much as possible. There was no response and so they set to waiting again.

An hour later Jamal saw what they'd been waiting for. An armored SUV with four police pulled in at the end of the block, around the corner from the micro junkyard. They ducked low as they exited the vehicle, their rifles in hand, dressed in helmets and full gear.

He watched the police advance on their house and felt hope leave him. They were not there to apprehend the occupants, not in Sherwood. "You watching?" he said, but there was no answer from Carl. Woodlawn was under city control, he was sure now. These were captured lands. He was over the border in enemy territory. The city was going to take him hostage.

The police took positions. They had scopes on their rifles. One drew near, taking cover behind a burnt-out car. He sighted through his scope and then moved forward. Jamal heard a double-blast from Carl's room and saw the advancing Guardsmen's shoulder jerk and then he fell to the ground. A few seconds later he heard a barrage of bullets rip through Carl's room.

He yelled for Carl but there was no answer.

Jamal leaned back from the window and used the reflection on the blade of his knife to try to see where they were, but the blurry distortion seemed what horror movies were made of.

"Where's my gun, blood brother?" Rick whispered.

"Rick—oh god," Jamal said, surprised the man was alive and grateful not to be alone, even if it was his last minute. "We're really fried here," he whispered.

"Where's my gun?"

Jamal quickly crawled to Carl's room and avoided looking at the man's body, which had fallen much farther from the window than he'd imagined possible. The wall around the window was riddled with holes. He gathered both guns and scrambled back to the dining room.

"It's the like SWAT or something," Jamal said. "They have scopes. They'll have to come up on the front porch to get a shot."

"Drag me into position," Rick said.

Jamal dragged Rick through his own blood to the small section of wall that jutted out between the dining room and the living room,

in view of the window and the door, and he took up position on the
opposite side, and they waited.

Jamal tried his best not to shake as they waited for the first trooper to
mount the stairs and come into view. Even then, Rick and he would
only get off a shot or two. The soldiers may just wing in tear gas or
burn the place down.

Across from him Rick looked horrid. Blood had managed to
spread to just about everything—his face, the gun, and the great
swath of it that trailed from the big stain in the middle of the floor.

"I thought you were dead," Jamal said. He faced toward the window with his gun aimed but needed to talk to calm himself. He could
sense them out there, creeping nearer like swamp alligators.

"Takes a lot to kill old man Ricky," Rick whispered, "Won't be long
now." And Jamal wasn't sure he preferred this new cogency. He could
have appreciated some optimistic delirium.

The first helmet bobbed into view. Just above the window sill they
could see it. They trained their guns on it, Jamal mouthing wait, wait,
wait, wait, to himself to keep from squeezing the trigger.

He watched the helmet bob there for a moment, its cargo indecisive, and then turn around and descend from view. "Fuck," he whispered, "did he see us?" His body was overtaken with fear and he placed
his hands on his knees to keep them from shaking. He waited a split
second more for some projectile to fly through the window. Then he
eased forward, walking in a squat. The helmet was retreating down
the steps. He heard shouting now.

As the street came into view he stood in disbelief—there was a sea
of Green Rangers. Green Rangers were running into the yellow house;
others stripped the National Guard of their weapons. "The rangers
are here!" Jamal opened the front door and saw his father standing
behind the four troopers who were on their knees. Rangers were pulling men from the yellow house and lining them up. There were Rangers retrieving weapons and confiscating the SUV. He called out as his
father fired the first shot, shooting one of the troopers in the back of
the head, execution style. Jamal jumped, sickened by the raw violence
of it, by the way the man jerked and slumped forward. Immediately
two of the men in line on their knees came to their feet and ran and
Gregor shot them down in mid-stride with blazing precision. A silence

emanated out from the act and the world slowed down to a snail's pace as he watched his father raise his gun to the last trooper.

He yelled *no* but it was absorbed in another gunshot. Jamal saw how the Rangers fanned wider with each shot. One bent over and threw up into the street; others stood grim where they were.

Jamal sprinted down the stairs and ran into the street and chaos. His father shot another and the men farther down the line were wailing and begging. He put his hand on his father's shoulder and spun him around. Gregor turned with his gun, an animal violence in his eyes, a blood lust, and for a moment Jamal thought his father might shoot him too. There was no recognition there.

"Dad," Jamal said, and he watched his father's face come back to itself from a great distance.

One of the men in the execution line fainted and keeled over.

"I thought you were dead," Gregor said, his voice a flatline. "We've been finding bodies."

Jamal pointed back up to the house and then couldn't find any more words to say. He was acutely conscious of interfering with his commanding officer in front of others. He wanted to embrace the old man, a boxer's hug, and the rest of him wanted to run from this horror. "Do not do this. Please, Dad. Bind them and take them back," Jamal whispered. "We'll figure it out from there."

Gregor shook his head no. He turned and held his gun to the head of a young man who wept openly. There were five men left on their knees and four dead on the ground. Gregor held the gun there and Jamal whispered please and held his breath, forcing himself to keep his eyes open. Finally Gregor pulled his gun up and holstered it.

"Bind these men and take them back," he said.

Jamal slowly let his breath out as the world snapped back into motion and the Rangers began to move again. He stared at the back of his father's head. He was nauseous. He wondered if the executions had been for him, in retribution for his own supposed death. Jamal shuddered and turned to find two Rangers to help him put together a stretcher for Rick.

Renee and Zach slept until the sunlight was harsh in the room. The
world outside was aglow with dust and it filtered through the air in
the room. When she woke, Renee rolled onto him. She could feel the
weight of responsibility coming back, the urgency to return to Sherwood as soon as possible and so she sought that which could take her
mind away from it for a moment. Her country was falling apart and
she needed him there to help her decipher the data, or she needed to
leave him. She could not waver in a limbo of escapism and responsi-
bility-dodging any more, and with these thoughts on her mind, she
did him as Maid Marian, so that Zach felt as if his hip bone were being
ground into a thin powder, like she was mixing him up as some salve
to be applied to her country. Her hands were like talons that cut into
his wrists.

She understood that she'd gone to sleep next to him as one person
and woken up as someone else.

When they were done, she breathed hard next to him and then
quieted.

"So," Zach said, feeling how radically things had changed in a few
hours. "Where do we stand?"

"I don't know," Renee said. She sat up on the bed and faced away
from him. "I have to go back to Sherwood tonight. You have to come
with me."

Zach marveled at how she had adopted the voice of command,
how she rarely asked for opinion or preference. "No," he said. "I can't,
Maid Marian," he said.

He watched her turn toward him in anger. "Don't call me—" she
started, and then she turned forward again and was quiet.

They sat silent for a long while. He heard a siren drone by and
then shouting in the street. It would soon be time to go pick up his
ration. He stared at her naked back, lithe and strong, accustomed still
to hard work, a back used to being the first to pick up and wield a
shovel. Hair that fell past her shoulder blades, out of braids for once.

"Yesterday night, before we arrived, I signaled on the water tower.
Did you see it?"

"Yes."

"You didn't answer?"

"No."

"But you were watching for it?"

"I was."

"Do you still love me?" She turned to look at him.

Zach didn't expect the question and he didn't know who was asking it. "Do you?" he said.

She was still, and as she paused tension gathered into the room, each additional moment he desired to get up and flee. Then she nodded subtly. "Yes, I do."

"OK," he said, "OK." He felt flustered and sat up quickly. He pulled his knees to his chest and drew the sheet tautly down over them. He toyed with saying he loved her back but he didn't know. He was afraid of showing any soft spot that might get crushed. She glanced once back and turned away and then he knew he'd let her question lapse. He'd waited too long.

He wished he could reel back that moment when he could have said "I love you too" easily and without the complications of justifying or proving or explaining. He thought he did—the woman who arrived the night before and came up to his bed—he'd been happy to have her there. Happy—such a foreign word, such a mysterious contraption relationships were, of which he'd had as many as could be counted on one hand and leave enough fingers for going about their own business.

Renee dropped her head and began to do her braids. When she finished she put her palms against her temples. He wished she'd turn around now.

A wave of impish adolescence overtook him, a handy last resort for fleeing adult troubles and difficult emotional situations. He kicked her, landing a nudging insistent blow to her flank. She turned and gave him an irritated and disgusted look and he kicked her again.

"The fuck?" she said. She looked hurt and insulted and he kicked her again and then she pulled back and socked him in the thigh.

"Oh!" he called out and grabbed his leg, which convulsed with pain and then he kicked her again with both feet, strong enough to dislodge her from the edge of the bed.

"You fucker," she said and stood up, and before she could walk from the room he leapt up, got his hands around her shoulders and pulled her down on top of him. She struggled to get away and he had to clutch at her back and hold on. She punched him in the side and again in the rib cage but the blows had softened. She took a bite of his shoulder and bit until he hollered out and then she let go and kissed him there and they were still.

It felt good to have her on top of him, a human blanket.

"I used to be able to hear birds out my window," Zach said.

"Really?" she said, the statement obvious enough to her that she wondered if he was mentioning it as a symbol of some kind in their conversation, or just being nostalgic.

"Yeah." He wrapped his arms around her lower back. "It's complicated, Renee. I would like to be together. But I'm not sure there's any room for that."

She turned and put her head face down on his shoulder, her eyes an inch from the red bite mark there.

"You know?" he said.

"I'd like to try again," she said.

"But is she up there? Is there a Renee in Sherwood?"

"I'll figure it out," she said. "I'll make room for it, this relationship. That is what I want. I will make it formal. And in the quiet moments, it will be just Renee and Zach."

He didn't say anything and they lay there until they heard Señor Nombre call out and Bea clunking around and then he said OK.

Nevel and Cora sat down to watch the morning news with excitement. They had access to Sherwood now and there was a feeling of sudden dual-citizenship, of being able to travel to a paradisiacal island any time they wanted, and so with an extra thrill they sat to watch for any mentions of their new country.

There was a full-time Sherwood news crew now, a journalist and cameraman. When that night's Sherwood segment showed, in the microsecond before the journalist spoke, before he knew the camera was running, you could see the grimness of the news on his face.

They watched and held hands as they saw live footage of Rangers searching houses. Sherwood citizens stood on the streets in their bathrobes as rangers went through their houses, house after house.

"They searched my house," a woman who appeared disheveled and agitated said into the camera, and then turned to the journalist who interviewed her uncertainly.

"And the reason they gave you for the search?"

"They said they were looking for a fugitive. I had to stand outside while all these green goons went through my house."

"I'm very sorry you had to suffer through that. Was anything damaged or taken?"

"No—" she turned to the camera—"can I take the green goons part back? Can you cut that?"

After the interview the journalist said they had contacted Maid Marian's office for comment and received none so far.

The view switched back to the news anchors, who wanted to know what had happened to the people who were detained.

The journalist's picture from a time past appeared in the upper right hand corner of the screen, looking plumper and more innocent, and the anchor faced toward that. "I haven't heard about anyone detained," Brian said, "but if there were—there are no jails. So these people would be pulled in to forced labor for the territory, or simply exiled. Sent to live in Portland."

"But she wasn't even there," Cora said, "right?"

Nevel sunk into the couch, sensing that their hole into paradise was like a whirlpool in the center of their house, sucking them in. It was their escape hatch there, or their line to the underworld.

When they got downstairs Señor Nombre and Bea were cursing at each other and suddenly Renee didn't want to go back. She sat at Zach's table in his building and let herself be waited on, and zoned out all talk. She played out what leaving the territory for good would feel like.

Was there a president or king in the history of the world who just walked off the job? Surely a few. Ones who went back to waiting tables and making espresso? Gregor would assume control and that felt all right with her. It was his territory. She'd been flaky in the past, losing interest in school or projects or boyfriends and dropping them mid-way through, but the scale of this flakiness was monumental, standing-on-a-building's-ledge huge, with the vertigo swaying you sickly, back and forth.

She pressed her forehead against the hard wooden tabletop and rested it there. She didn't want to solve conflict after conflict, to provide for them all, to have in opposition the mayor and the Guard.

For a moment, in her mind, Renee lived in Zach's house. She helped turn it into a micro-clinic, where good works were done and a difference was made. The stakes were so much smaller and she could be unequivocally good. There would be no punishments to mete out, levels of freedom to permit, and at night, each night, they could be alone together.

But everything changed after watching the morning news. Renee pounded around Zach's house in a fury of preparation. The footage of Rangers searching houses burned in her mind.

Renee set Bea to work building a mobile stretcher out of a hand cart, a sheet of plywood, and a lot of rope, cursing the necessity to take the incoherent patient for the time it would cost.

Gregor had crossed her. Had he so quickly gone crazy with power? Perhaps she would return to find the Rangers all turned against her. She wrote a list of items she wanted Zach to work on:

- Coup d'états, preventing
- Military allegiance
- Insights into data collected on informal power structures within the Rangers
- Jamal.

Would Jamal stick with her over his father? She worried what an allegiance either way would do to him.

Upstairs in Zach's room she punched his pillow until her anger had worn down.

In the hallway she cornered Zach. "Are you ready?" She could feel the power of Maid Marian returning to her. Her doubts had been trivial. She would return and run her country, she would do the job justice.

Zach looked at her with exasperation. "That thing that Bea is making—I mean on a bike—"

"Oh, he'll survive, and then we'll be in Sherwood."

In watching the news he'd remembered how miserable he'd been there, and he told her so.

"Yeah, I know," Renee said and did not want to have this conversation. She backed away from him, the guilt and pressure of her multiple personalities making the hallway feel claustrophobic. She wanted to promise Zach again it would be different.

"But it won't be. You know it'll be the same," Zach said.

"I don't know that—"

"For me," Zach said, "Renee—you—will always take precedence over that fucking country." He felt remorse for having cursed it, the feel of blasphemy to it.

Renee looked down the hall and could hear Zach's patient arguing fiercely with Bea. Señor Nombre had become garrulous in the face of his personal involvement in their trip north and ranted about the safety of hand carts and how he'd wouldn't be getting in one any time soon and shouldn't she use some wood glue there?

"What can I do?" she said. "Give me some options."

"Come here," he said. He pulled her to him. "Fucking Sherwood," he said again. He thought—for probably the hundredth time—that perhaps she needed a man who might pick her up and take her to bed, a solid muscular man who didn't emotionally bruise so easily, who stood straight and exuded confidence in interpersonal relationships and, sure, was a bit on the daft side. A figurehead of a man. A wooden dude to be mounted at the prow of her ship, a man who was not clear he was even mounted there.

He grabbed her ass and pulled her in closer and told her what he wanted, as if he were that man.

"I want to sleep in your room. I want one night a week with Renee—alone—where we don't talk about Sherwood, I want your country to know about our relationship, and I want you to be monogamous."

Renee seemed to cool and slip in his arms; she held very still and he knew there was a surf of guilt and indignation and righteousness that washed back and forth and he wondered which side of her it would reveal.

People had relationships, she thought. I am people, and thus . . . but it was difficult to picture pulling Zach up front of the Sherwood citizenry, to imagine his secondary public face, too. How many people would they be then? Did she protect him as her secret, or only hide him? Still, it was a nation for humans, and she was first among them. "I'm sorry," she said finally, meaning, she thought, to apologize.

He clung to her, already regretting making any demands, but these things, he told himself, were not unreasonable. He deserved them.

He thought of the map room and the systems he had created. I am the architect, he told himself. He dropped his arms and stood straight and she leaned into him. This is mine to ask. He prepared to say he would not return.

"No, you're right, I will promise those things," she said. They were both quiet then in the agreement, but he couldn't find the embrace they'd had, couldn't get her back into the angle of intimacy. They kissed and she asked if he was coming now for sure and he said yes and she said thank you and unraveled from him and walked up the hall. He wondered if he'd broken it, if by merely stating what he wanted, he'd destroyed what he'd had, which admittedly had not been much in the first place.

He went to his room and sat on the edge of his bed feeling wasted and empty and began to think dully of what he'd need to pack.

END TIMES

The news churned out two sensational stories on how Woodlawn neighborhood wanted to secede from Sherwood back to the city. In the first interview a blubbery soft black man in his late twenties eloquently railed against the tyranny of Maid Marian and specifically called out the cruel tactics of her general. The man spoke animatedly, a fine perspiration covering his body so that he glistened and shone with each verbal thrust.

"Her general has raided our neighborhoods, entered our homes, dragged out our men to the street and executed them. To him we are another class of people, to him it does not matter if we live or die, only that our land stay within his grasp, and for that reason we secede."

The interviewer seemed flustered by his heavy accusations and his eloquent manner of speaking and paused, the camera on her. "There have been city truck sightings up here. Have you spoken to the city?"

"Of course, the city has kindly offered us its services and our rightful place."

"I know him," Gregor said. He watched the news up in the map room, which felt bare without Maid Marian's presence. A few Rangers sat on the floor. Leroy and Jamal sat tense on the couch and Gregor stood behind it, in his usual spot, fiddling with his empty pipe. After the shootings he'd idly toyed with how else to hold his pipe so that it didn't feel as though he always held a gun in his hand, like a baby's pacifier in place of the real thing. There was talk, he knew.

"He saw?" Jamal said. He felt certain they'd searched and apprehended every person who would have witnessed Gregor's executions— something that still rattled Jamal deeply, that opened a new and deeply troubling facet to the clouded ruby that was his father.

"Barstow's nephew," Gregor said. "He's a year or two younger than you. These are old grudges. For the losers, a war never ends."

Jamal studied the sweating man and pecked away at his memory for some frozen still from the wars that would reveal a younger face under the puffy flesh of the man on the television who was poisoning them, had poisoned their country with his interview. He could feel the dread burn in him as the news infiltrated homes across the city. The worst of it was, much of what the man said was true, albeit only very recently.

Jamal was under-slept and his head reeled. He thought again of Maid Marian. His heart ached when he let his mind imagine the worst. Then again, if she were lying dead on the wood floor of an abandoned house in Woodlawn—why wouldn't this guy say so? And if she lived, if she came back—he wondered if they would need to turn his father over to the city for the Guardsmen executions in order to avert a war. The country was too fragile to appear anything but just. He stole a look at his father whose face was unmoving and calm, as if his head were plucked from some Roman statue, and a rush of fear and shame came to his face. He hoped like hell his father wouldn't try to fight Woodlawn's secession.

"Have we been asked about an interview?" Jamal said. "We've got to tell our side."

"That's Maid Marian's job," Gregor said. "I can't go on there—people know me."

Know what you've done, Jamal thought.

The interviewer asked the man how they'd built consensus in the neighborhood to secede, and his look was dull and unchanging. "We have gone from door to door and heard story after story of Sherwood. Consensus was clear."

"We need an interview," Jamal said.

"No," Gregor said.

"Leroy—you recognize that house?" Jamal said. "Know where they are? This is live. I've got to find that news truck."

Leroy studied the background of the house and shook his head. "I have never been there."

"Damn it." Jamal held his head and stood. "Pop—I'll find them, I've got to go find them, I'll send a signal through the network."

"There's nothing to say, Jamal." Gregor was obviously tired of having the conversation. "We have nothing to gain from an interview. You'll lose your anonymity. Actions speak louder than words."

"We've had enough action. Now, we have damage control to do."

"You're head of the armed forces; what will you tell her?" Gregor pointed at the interviewer.

"The truth? How about that."

"Absolutely not." Gregor turned to one of his Rangers. "I want everyone out of Woodlawn. All services stop, no water, no clinics, no volunteers. Close anything we have there. Immediately." The Ranger nodded and left to give the order.

"And so that's it?" Jamal stood and began to pace. "The city did this, they're undermining us, and we let them?"

"We cannot risk the fight," Gregor said.

"I agree, I'm agreeing with you—not on the ground. But the fight is in the news," Jamal said. "We can't risk not fighting there."

"We're fucking criminals, Jamal, that's how they see us. You know that. We can't be on the news. They'd slaughter you."

"Then we send someone else. What about that guy?" Jamal motioned toward their sweaty adversary.

Gregor shrugged. "He has the city's backing."

"But what's next? We lose King neighborhood? All because of some asshole on the city payroll?"

"Jamal." His father pointed the barrel-end of his pipe at him with a clenched fist. "The answer is *no*."

Jamal paced furiously along one side of the large map room and then left. The way things were going, they were going to lose the country by the end of the night. His father couldn't see it.

Downstairs he found one of Gregor's assistants. "Did the news contact us?"

"Yes."

"About an interview?"

The Ranger nodded.

"Fuck." Jamal felt like the ground was spinning under him. His father was fighting an old war. The stakes and the way the war was fought had changed. He made his way outside and to the street, not knowing what to do, just needing to get away from the house.

A communications Ranger pulled up in front of headquarters and dismounted from her bike.

"Stop," Jamal said. He grabbed hold of her handlebars and bowed his head for a breath. "I need you to send a message, right now." He pulled her into the middle of the street, in view of the Ranger on the corner. Jamal checked his watch. There were fifty minutes of the newscast left before the city was plunged back into darkness.

"Send, shit, OK, send a message everywhere, every single Ranger gets this, OK? This is what I want—every Ranger look for a news van—it's in Sherwood somewhere, there's definitely one in Woodlawn, oh Christ." Jamal sunk to his haunches and clasped his head. "Yes we've got to go in there, this is important."

"What's going on? What's the message?" the Ranger said. She watched the captain of the Going Street Brigade with alarm.

"I need an interview with the news tonight! Right now! What should I do?"

The Ranger asked what happened, dread spilling across her features.

"Never mind, help me, quick. Get everyone to look for the news van—have the van meet me in the clinic on Thirty Third and Killingsworth, near the grocery."

"Yes, sir." She used her LED to send a message. She repeated it several times and Jamal could see the answering flashes.

"And now—fuck, I'm sorry, can I have your bike?"

She looked down at her bike. "I—I'm just off shift. That's my neighborhood, can I ride you?"

Jamal climbed onto her bike rack, custom-made to support a heavy load of water. "OK, but please god, please ride fast."

The Ranger mounted her bike and he held onto her, finding himself in intimate contact with the second Sherwood employee in less than forty-eight hours. His hands burned on her hips. As they rode through the darkening streets—still lit partially by the lights of houses—each house flickered with blue light as everyone tuned in, as each house processed this new evil in Sherwood, the combative floating island of Woodlawn, as it drifted its allegiances. But as he stared into her back, he forgot everything. He couldn't figure out her race. She was a mixed-up affair, black or Indian maybe, or some of both, and he fantasized about seeing her in a dress, rather than a green uniform, which for him had begun to epitomize the opposite of sexuality. A red dot painted on her third eye. Dancing over him in some faraway bedroom.

As the wind blew he caught brief flashes of her neck, where a small black beetle was tattooed. Her black hair whipped into his face and he closed his eyes and let it. As general, Gregor had forbidden him from having any relations with another Ranger. As general, he had also forbidden him to give an interview.

He desired to say to *hell with it* to the whole enterprise then, to embrace this girl, let his desires consume his job and his thinking and his everything, to go home with her and spend the night in her bed, forgetting and forgetting over again, until they were exhausted with forgetting, and then to sleep.

He thought: Sherwood is the only place I've ever wanted to be. He would tell the camera that and they would see it was true.

The ride was spine-jarringly bumpy on the back of the bike and he used it as an excuse to hold on to her more tightly. When a surge of dust kicked up in the wind he pressed his face into her back.

When they arrived he dismounted reluctantly. The news van was not there and she studied him. "You're going to be OK?"

He saw in her look she'd been aware of how he'd held on to her, an expression of soft surprise, as if the stone she'd plucked from the ground was instead a seashell where no seashell should be. There was no malice or irritation there. He felt embarrassed and aroused and smiled and said thanks and jogged toward the clinic.

His watch said thirty-one minutes until blackout. He paced in front of the clinic, the jittery anxiety of impending calamity returning to him, and then sat on the curb. As time ticked toward blackout he despaired that all was lost. This new country was home now. He'd been built for it. Looking back at his life, his family, the drug wars and everything—it became clear that that his history was a product of living in the wrong nation. The city outside felt like a disconnected chaos, a war zone; inside they'd built a fabric. Inside he had a purpose. Inside he was right, his true self. Take that away and he was just a henchman for a drug lord.

Jamal took off his T-shirt and used the inside of it to clean his face and smooth his hair as best as he was able.

He saw the Ranger circling back around. She pulled up in front of him.

"Here," she said, "let me help." She took his T-shirt from him and wiped it along his neck, and being touched caused a chill to run through him with a sudden shiver, making his teeth clatter *klak klak.*

"I hope they come," he said, looking up the street again.

She put her hand on his shoulder in a passing gesture and said she'd gotten a message back. They were hurrying.

"Oh fuck, great," he said, the fear moving into stage fright. "Thank you," he said. And then smiled at her a beat too long. He would be on live television shortly, defending their country, and in his brain hummed a bees' nest. Mostly, he wanted her to talk, to keep talking. To give her some reason to stay a while and so he could keep watching her and not think. "You talk," he said, "I'm going to sit here and not freak out."

She smiled and sat with him and talked about her family and roommates and about being a Ranger and in his anxiety it all blended together into a compost heap of random details until at seven minutes of blackout the van screeched around a corner, followed by its security car.

She handed him his shirt back and he put it on. He stood up as the van pulled up. A news crew spilled out of the truck—the interviewer, a cameraman, and the driver.

"We've got to be quick," the interviewer said. She looked from another world, with a clean, pressed business skirt and a layer of makeup. Her hair, frozen in place like dried pasta.

Jamal opened the door to the clinic—which at one time had been a box store pharmacy. Inside were ten beds and in one of them was Rick.

"Rick!" he said and clasped hands.

"Blood brother," Rick said.

The news team picked a camera angle, with Jamal sitting on the foremost bed and Rick and several other patients in the background. The interviewer leaned against an adjoining bed.

"We film in five seconds," the woman said and Jamal sat on the bed just as the floor dropped out from under him and an immense vertigo took him.

"I have with me Jamal Perkins, captain of the Green Rangers, is that right? Of Sherwood. Jamal, can you tell me quickly what your job is?"

Jamal nodded and looked at her and then once toward the cameraman, where facing him like the eye of some great beast was the glossy dark lens of the camera. It had infinite depth to it and he stared into it and felt himself looking suddenly into thousands of eyes, looking at them in their living rooms, his image appearing dirty and frightened and half-cocked, and he could feel them staring back, several hundred thousand eyes, seeing deep into him, their collective power pulling his soul right out of him, holding it up for analysis and dissection, wispy and dark, the bruises of his history pockmarking its fabric. A million of them, each taking a piece of his insides out to chew on, the billion tiny bits of his being chewed thoughtfully in the mouths of the people, pondering, digesting him, obliterating him completely.

"You can answer toward me," the interviewer said.

Jamal turned back, the wormhole thrusting him through its turny tunnel, warping him along and spitting him out again as a single human being, sitting on the edge of a bed, across from a smartly dressed and exceedingly clean white woman who was asking him questions in a businesslike manner, a look of concern on her face that their live interview was slipping out of her grasp.

When the interviewer of the "Woodlawn Rebel," as they called him, came on, Bea and Zach monitored Renee for reaction. They sat tense on the end of the couch. Renee gawked at the television, frozen in a half-stand. Incredulity turned to anger. When the interview was over, Renee walked into the dining room, picked up a chair and against Zach's cry of protest smashed it over the top of the dining room table until the chair had splintered into an unsatisfactory mallet and the table leaned, partially collapsed.

She picked up another and proceeded to do the same until Zach had hold of her middle and Bea had hold of the chair and still she fought them, cursing and kicking and clawing at them.

They sat her down on the couch where she grumbled and talked to herself, until she stood sharply and yelled, "Fuck!"

"We finish the news." Bea pinned her shoulder against the couch and talked inches from her face. "We finish the news and then you make a plan."

Zach nursed a bruised rib and complained about his table and chairs. They watched the weather report. They listened to a city worker speak about water supply and the slow progress of a new desalinization plant. The news anchors discussed the Sherwood situation. Then an anchor said that Jamal Perkins of the Green Rangers would be interviewed at the end of the program, so stay tuned.

"Oh no," Renee said. "Oh fuck. I've got to get back up there!" She got up and paced around the house. Bea tailed her to prevent any new violence.

At the end of the show, minutes before the power went off, they held their breath as Jamal came on, looking sleep-deprived and strung-out, a dirty-looking clinic set up as his background. He turned and stared into the camera. His eyes were wide and for a moment he looked like the most fragile human being Renee had ever seen.

He seemed to be staring straight at her. She clutched her fists to her mouth. "Oh god," she said, and Jamal stared for a fraction of a second more and then turned to look at the interviewer. He smiled and his voice came out strong and confident. He sounded measured and reasonable. He talked about the progress Sherwood had made, the clinics and schools and farms. He turned to let an injured man wave from a bed behind him.

"The secession has come as a sad surprise to us," Jamal said. "Sherwood is an active citizen-participant government, and we solicit feedback constantly. With every daily water delivery we make, in fact. There has been no indication that Woodlawn residents were displeased, and we have thousands of recent comments from the citizens there. Several days ago several of our staff disappeared in the neighborhood and we became concerned. Rick and I"—he gestured behind him again—"were fired upon and Rick was injured when we went to investigate. And, more telling, we saw city trucks in the neighborhood. It's my belief that the city is seeding a secession and arming the power-hungry in the neighborhood."

"We're running out of time here, Jamal. But quickly—what is Maid Marian's response and why hasn't she appeared for an interview? We had an interview request turned down earlier today."

"Yes, good question. As always, Maid Marian is—"

At that moment the screen went dark and the lights went out and Renee exhaled and said oh my god.

"Go Jamal," Bea said, "I think he's my new hero."

"He did really, really well," Zach said. "Why is he on and not Gregor? He could have done more city versus Sherwood. Could have mentioned the schools, how Woodlawn's children will return to lawlessness, et cetera, but all things considered, that was pretty exceptional. I mean, yeah."

In her mind, Renee continued to see Jamal look at her, as the day darkened and with the power gone. "It felt like he was looking right at me," she said. "What the fuck is going on up there? Can we go now? Zach," she snapped, "shit. What can I do to get you ready?"

The mayor obsessively watched every weather report. Much as one troubles a zit beyond the point of bruise, the weather was a bane he wheedled over. Besides, both he and Christopher agreed, the weatherman was cute. And so they watched the weather like a soap opera, never missing an episode. The weatherman was a nice extra perk, the cherry on top of the mayor's madness for the subject. The weather had ruined his term, and he studied it for any sign of change.

The man who did the weather was emotional, and for this he was adored. Several times he'd tentatively predicted a change, a condensation or a spring shower, and when it didn't come to pass he wept during the broadcast. And the remorse, whether real or fabricated, was appreciated. People talked about him like a celebrity. He calmly explained why rain would not come this week, explaining fronts and systems, while tears made their way along the beautiful skin of his cheeks. He really cared, you thought, about us, about delivering to us what we wanted. He tried his best. But unlike the rest of the news, he had nothing under his control. The other reporters could spin an article, create a sensation, put an angle on something, but the weatherman had his reports backed up by hot, dry, incontrovertible facts.

Today's episode was much like the previous hundreds. The weatherman smiled and spoke his trademark opening: "Ladies and gentlemen, we've got some weather today." It was, by now, a complex smile, one that belied what they'd all been through together, but which also said: We can still do this, we'll never give up hope. Christopher sat down on the couch sideways with his back to the armrest and the mayor rubbed his feet idly as they watched.

The mayor had been exceedingly tender yesterday with the guilt of his violence still uncomfortable in the house. He'd fixed Christopher breakfast, invited his advice on issues, and in all things he'd been optimistic and kind and tried to act like a mayor ought to act. Dignified, decisive, tuned in, empathetic. Christopher had been gracious about the incident and they'd studiously not spoken of it since.

The weatherman showed satellite imagery of great clouds coming in off of the Pacific. A huge weather system like some foreign invading army on the march. They'd all seen this before. It meant dark days, but the invading army was meant for some other foe. The rain they bore would land east of the Rocky Mountains.

The weatherman got flustered by a computer glitch that showed him moving his hand over a blank green screen. He made a joke about how they'd all memorized this weather anyway, and to just close your eyes and imagine it. Christopher looked over at the mayor and smiled, and there was warmth there and the mayor felt relieved.

But when the mayor's Woodlawn rebel came on, the evening fell apart. Christopher faced forward, leaned in toward the TV. He could not bring himself to look at the mayor. Before the interview finished, he got up and walked out of the room.

The mayor stayed. After the interview, there were a few how-I'm-surviving-the-drought stories, depressing shit with ridiculously sunny commentary by the newscaster. Next, a police officer talked about a downtown robbery that'd been prevented. There was news on a controversial housing-assistance program, and a teenager weighed in with some sort of home-school essay the mayor couldn't make heads or tails of.

In the air the weight of an argument that hadn't yet happened lay heavily upon him. He sat on the couch and clenched his teeth and felt sick about it, wishing he were ten thousand miles away, in some swampy, drenched country.

The one thing that eased his mind was the lack of a Maid Marian interview. He would have the last word for tonight, at least in the airwaves if not the bedroom. His Woodlawn rebel's speech would sink into the minds of the populace. They would talk about it, the word *Sherwood* taking on a darker, crueler connotation. They would dream of the terrors that awaited them in that strange country. They would think well of the city for taking Woodlawn back in, for making the city stronger and bigger and slightly more whole.

But then, midway through, the news announced that Jamal Perkins would be interviewed on behalf of Sherwood.

"What?" The mayor stood up and wondered what new trick was this. "*Who?*" The mayor self-consciously glanced out his window. It was twilight and from his window at the far expanse of city he could make out Sherwood. He yelled for Christopher. The mayor pointed to the TV where they were showing some story about "a company that was making a difference."

"Who the hell is Jamal Perkins?" the mayor said. "They're going to interview him for Sherwood."

Christopher and the mayor sat on the couch and waited through several more stories and the irritating chit-chat of the news anchors.

The news cut to a clinic hospital–type place where, the mayor couldn't help but notice, there were several empty beds, very much unlike their hospitals.

"Bastards," he said. "I bet they shoveled some people out of those beds for the camera shot."

The journalist explained she would now interview the captain of the Green Rangers.

"But that's Gregor Perk—" the mayor said.

"That's Gregor Perkins's kid," Christopher said.

The journalist asked the first question and the cameraman focused on Jamal's face. His hair was unkempt and wooly, and there was an obvious stain of dirt around his collar. But most stunning was the look he gave the camera. A full five seconds of emptiness, with no sound and no movement, as though they'd slapped a picture of him up on the screen. His subtle movements, and a single startling blink, made it particularly queer and jolting.

"Whoa," Christopher said.

The mayor didn't hear anything for the first minute as he recovered from the shock of that look. He had looked right at him, addressing the mayor specifically, looking straight into his morality, willing him to do right by the world, to steward the city by the highest standards. "Did you see that?" the mayor said stupidly.

"Shhh," Christopher said.

The mayor tuned back in and saw that the man was an eloquent bastard, like his own Woodlawn rebel, the difference being that you believed what this one was saying.

"Where the hell is Maid Marian?" the mayor said, uncomfortable with this new enemy, another public face to the country. His Woodlawn rebel would stick in the people's minds, he knew, but the message was vastly less powerful by this dude's appearance.

The mayor wished only to go to bed now, a tiredness at the whole fight overwhelming him.

The newscaster asked for Maid Marian's response. Jamal started to answer but the screen went dark, the lights turned off and the house was quiet. The mayor and Christopher sat in the dark staring at the TV, and then the hum of the generator sounded and the lights came back on and Christopher stood up and stretched.

"I think I'll turn in early tonight," he said, and the mayor could hear the false notes, the strained syllables, the eagerness to disappear into sleep as quickly as possible, and he knew that they must each stake out their own outposts tonight.

"I'm going to finish up a little work," the mayor said.

They nodded and smiled and Christopher reached out his fingers and the mayor touched his fingertips to Christopher's and then Christopher was gone.

The mayor sat on the couch and stared into the TV where Jamal had so recently stared back out at him, seeing only his own distant reflection in the dark screen now.

At what Nevel guessed to be around three or four in the morning he woke to a great banging in his house. He listened to it from bed with a half-conscious fear, as the sound morphed itself out of his dreams—his body being slammed into a wall—*oomph oomph*—to a great creature's footsteps—*blam blam*—and then finally to the horrible realization that someone was actually pounding at the front door.

"Cora," he said and shook her arm. Cora was, and always had been, like their kids, the type of sleeper who could sleep through a meteor impact. He shook her again but she kept at it. There was no way he would answer that door with her asleep. The banging got more insistent and he wondered if he could wait them out. Who the fuck knocks at this hour? Someone committing a crime would go through a window, no?

Finally, Nevel grabbed his gun and tied a towel around his waist and descended the stairs.

Through the door's front window he saw it was Zach and he realized something terrible must have happened with the agency or perhaps they had a project due he'd forgotten about. Suddenly he feared this was a far larger nightmare than even his subconscious mind could spin.

"What do you want?" Nevel said through the glass.

"Open the door, Nevel," Zach said and gave it one more bang to emphasize his point.

Nevel worked the locks and pulled it open. "Sorry, did you—were you here for a while?"

"Yes, a very long time."

"Is there? What is there?" Nevel blinked rapidly to try to get his eyes to work properly.

"You're not awake yet, dorkus." Zach pushed sideways through the door. He was very aware of the slumbering border guards at the corner and of talking to Nevel in close quarters with the man only wearing a towel and a gun. "Nice outfit," he said.

"Why are you here?"

"Renee's at the back door."

Nevel looked at him with exasperation. He put down the gun to scratch furiously at his scalp with both hands. "Am I supposed to know what that means?"

"Your back door? Maid Marian?" Zach shook his head with disgust. It'd been a long, unpleasant night of crossing the city at a snail's pace, taking turns riding the bike that pulled his patient.

"Ah!" Nevel picked up the gun and they walked to the back of the house. "Just her or is that big girl with her too?"

"I heard that," Bea said when Nevel got the door open.

Bea pushed past him and Nevel wondered aloud if anyone was going to ask if they could come in, and then he remembered Maid Marian out there in the dark.

"I'm sorry," he said out the back door and into the dark. "Maid Marian?"

"I'm here," she answered. "Zach, I need your help with your dude."

Behind him Bea had opened the refrigerator and pulled out a pot of something. "I'm starving," she said. "Hey, rice."

Zach and Renee hoisted what appeared to be a hand cart up the three back steps and into the house. Tied to the hand cart was a snoring man.

"What's going on here?" Nevel said. He gripped the front of his towel tightly.

"Maybe it was made a little too well," Renee said.

Zach took the end of it and wheeled the man into the living room and then tipped the cart into the bed position.

"You guys—I? My kids are asleep upstairs—"

"Cute," Bea said. "Can I see them?"

"Can you see? My kids sleeping? *No*," Nevel said, "what? Why—"

"So you actually made the tunnel all the way through?" Zach asked. They stood around the island in his kitchen. Nevel clutched the towel at his waist, which was coming loose but which he could not retie for the gun in his other hand. Bea ate rice out of the pot with a spoon.

"It's crazy," Bea said. "It has decorations and everything. He's crazy."

"Can I see it?"

"Yes. No. I don't know," Nevel said, becoming increasingly alarmed by the slippage of his night from sleep into kitchen party, attended by people he barely knew, including a man tied to a hand cart.

"Sorry to wake you," Renee said. "We need to use your tunnel for passage back."

Nevel nodded and suggested they could use it right now.

"How are we going to get Zach's guy through the tunnel?" Bea said. She held the pot out. "Anybody?"

"Is there another spoon?" Zach said.

"It'll work," Renee said. "We got him this far."

"And that was awesome fun, a real hoot," Bea said.

"It's been kind of a long night," Renee said to Nevel. "We don't want to disturb you—maybe we ought to—we'll replace that by the way." She pointed at the pot. "They—" She pointed at the others and then shrugged. "We're all sharing Zach's one ration."

"Sure, sure." Nevel sighed and wished again that his tunnel were a secret. It felt to him a little like loaning out a favorite toy. "Cora will be sad she missed you."

"Come on over then," Renee said. "Join us for water ceremony at headquarters tomorrow. Bea, you get Zach's bike," Renee said.

"Aw!"

"You get what's-his-name, Zach."

Zach wheeled Nombre down step by step, handcart-style, pulling back against gravity to keep the man tumbling down all at once. Nevel stood at the top of the stairs behind him, struggling with a flashlight, gun, and the hastily retied knot of the towel around his waist. And so Zach descended mostly into darkness, with only the dim flickering of light behind him to pull out and tease the shadows in front of him, reminding him quite suddenly of how much he abhorred basements, dark places, and anything vaguely resembling a tunnel.

At the bottom of the stairs he wheeled slowly forward into the dark. "Anything in between me and the tunnel entrance?" Zach called up the stairs.

"Straight shot, straight ahead," Nevel replied, lighting the way for Renee and her bike and then Bea and her two bikes.

Zach ran directly into some large solid object that clanged loudly. "Gah! There's something here!" He tried to repress a panic that some foreign malicious object unbeknownst to Nevel was squared off in front of their escape.

"Maybe there's a washing machine down there?"

"Maybe?" Zach said. Nombre continued to buzz along in sleep, and Zach decided the man was either seriously disturbed or on death's door. He hoped he wasn't doing permanent damage to him. He asked for the flashlight.

"Come on, Zach, we're all backed up here behind you," Renee said.

"Fuckety fuck fuck," Zach said. He fiddled the dolly forward, touching the edge of the washer in small taps until there was no resistance. After a few more steps the stairway was unblocked and Nevel, towel, gun, and light came to lead them forward.

As Nevel passed, some pointed object caught his towel and instantly stripped him down to nothing, except his implement in each hand, a gun and flashlight.

The light was trained forward, and so they only saw a sort of shadow puppet show of him dancing about naked, the beam of light jagging about as he attempted to tie the towel on with gun and flashlight in either hand, and then the light went out and they were all left in complete darkness. "Just um. So that, just while I get adjusted, here," Nevel said.

"I've just figured out what my own personal version of hell would be like," Bea said. "If you shoot me while trying to put your towel on—I don't know what I'll do to you."

"I for myself cannot think of a sin commensurate with the size of that penalty," Zach said.

"Come on, guys, I won't," Nevel said, "OK?"

"I'm just saying my night couldn't get any better," Bea said.

"I guess I should have dressed," Nevel said.

"You guess that, do you?"

"Wasn't like I was exactly expecting visitors, right? You want me to lead you or what?"

"Not really, no," Bea said. She hustled the bikes forward to get around him.

"What? No! It's my tunnel. I'll lead." Nevel blocked off her route. He stepped into the tunnel and listened and Zach shuddered at the idea there might be anything inside there that one might listen for. He imagined a spice-worm rumbling along the passage, its spiked maw ready to devour them. Instead the faintest dankness seeped from it, which immediately eased the dry burning sensation on his eyes and his nasal passages.

"Water," he said simply, and a great thirst overtook him. He touched the leather strap which held his canteen, long ago emptied.

"If you go deep enough, the earth is still damp. That's why a few trees are still alive after all this time, the ones that can grow the deep roots," Nevel said.

By the end of the tunnel Zach felt that he did not know his work colleague at all. He had seemed a lazy, boisterous, and somewhat annoying manager whom he tolerated for his appreciation of quality, because he often took Zach's side in creative disputes. But he couldn't understand a man who would make such a thing.

It was spooky and oppressive, this thing, and yet thousands of hours of work were apparent. A side, dead-ended tunnel became a shrine of some sort. All of the jewelry in the house had apparently been raided and hung artfully on the wall. At one juncture, there was a low table with a tablecloth and on top of that a bell.

Farther on they passed a communist design nostalgia section, Soviet era posters adorning the walls.

"What—?" Zach started and then wasn't sure where to go with it.

"Right," Nevel said, "right. I don't know!" He flung his arms out and the light skittered about the tunnel. "It just, you know, happened."

"I mean don't get me wrong. I think it's completely fantastic, some wild outgrowth of your mind, like a tumor, a second brain you're growing in secret, a whole other side of you. I love it, really." Zach could feel himself getting choked up suddenly and so he cut himself off. A meaningless pursuit of this magnitude was one of the noblest things he'd ever come across. "And you started it before Sherwood?" Zach said.

"Yes."

"Where were you going?

"I don't know."

"Prescience," Renee said.

Like the Earth's intestine, Zach thought, and he wondered how everything changed when your meaningless project developed a use. Certainly if the tunnel had not been made, another connection to Sherwood would have been forged, but still, there was a divine madness here.

Back in Sherwood, Renee burst into the map room with her entourage.

"What the hell has been going on here?" she said.

Gregor and Leroy and Jamal and a few Rangers were standing at the Woodlawn section of the map. "Ah, the white people are back,"

Gregor said and smiled. Leroy strode across the room, an expression of relief on his face, and embraced Renee and gave Bea and Zach stout pats on the shoulder, as if to verify that they really existed, and Jamal queued up to do the same.

"I thought you were—" Jamal said.

"I saw you on TV." Renee gave a low, approving whistle. "We should talk about that." Renee went and stood next to Gregor. "Well. I saw the news. What the fuck?"

Gregor regarded her, the look on her face containing elements of anguish and disappointment, and a new coldness. "We had a crisis," he said simply. "Where were you?"

Renee pointed at Zach. "You know where I was, solving the crisis."

"No, I didn't know where you were, except AWOL. You weren't solving anything." Gregor turned to the map. "Ten of ours have died. We found their bodies in empty houses in Woodlawn. Rangers and water carriers, snatched from the street and strangled or—" Gregor mimed a knife across the neck. "I've pulled everyone out of the neighborhood. We think Barstow's people are here." Gregor circled a Woodlawn block with his finger. "But I would recommend that we let Woodlawn go, at this point."

Renee's face burned with the implied accusations and she felt like slugging him. He had been taking over, she realized, he'd been planning to run Sherwood. She stared at the map, her eyes unfocused with anger.

She thought of the Rangers and water carriers who had died for her, her country, her charges. "Ten?" she said, wondering if she'd known them, the word coming out loud and ungainly and indignant.

Gregor nodded.

She jabbed a finger at him. "You lost Woodlawn in the twenty-four hours I was away." She knew it was unfair—she had left him control, and that alone was her decision, and she had fled, but she felt like slinging shit back. The territory had been horribly mishandled, and he should suffer for it. She was aware of the room getting very quiet behind her.

"You were gone. Jamal was missing, Zach was gone. I squashed a city-funded rebellion. I executed four and took five prisoners. But they attacked via the media. Woodlawn is lost."

"Executed?"

Gregor held her gaze, "Outside, in public."

"Oh god," Renee said.

"Would you have done the same?" Gregor asked.

Renee was startled by the question. She stammered and searched his face and then turned to look about her and saw that the room was tuned in to their conversation, openly eavesdropping, their stances as if preparing for some impact, gripping tables and floor and pencils so as to keep from falling from the ship. She looked at Gregor again and realized this was their showdown. He was waiting for her to openly challenge him, to relieve him of duty. In which case he would do what? she wondered. The man had executed four people. The word had to be dragged up through the outhouse floor from the past, a word covered in evil and shit, it damaged the whole meaning of Sherwood and she wondered how she could possibly let him stay. Who would take her side? The Rangers? But the city had killed ten of theirs, and in a moment's rage she desired to pull another four off the city streets to even up the score. But: *executed*—it belonged to only the most horrific of times, not Sherwood. Gregor wore a gun and she saw him shift his hand away from it, as if they were each running along the same path of chess moves simultaneously and he wanted her to decide without its influence. The city was playing dirty and Gregor had executed four people.

"Who were they?" she asked.

"Three city police, one Woodlawner. All men. The Woodlawner was black. The officers were white."

There was a subtle sarcasm to his voice now and she realized that she was evaluating the execution, weighing the need for such violence against the specific personalities and backgrounds, evaluating the act as the citizenry would. She regarded the man in front of her. How he'd built her an army and in so doing had brought security and peace to the nation. He had given them the water ceremony and was her friend besides. She had ridden her bike to the Southeast, while a secession was taking place, while Sherwood was in a crisis and Gregor had been in charge. They were Sherwood leadership; his actions were her actions and vice versa. She nodded to signal she understood. The city had knocked to find out what kind of game they were playing, and Gregor had told them.

"I would have the done the same thing," Renee said, making sure her voice carried the length of the room now. Her throat hurt and she found it hard to swallow. She could feel Maid Marian coming back to her, the power and authority of her. Gregor straightened, his arms at his side, and she saw that she'd surprised him, that he'd been ready for fight or flight, or possibly to accept whatever fate she meted out, but least of all this. As the confusion dissipated, he saluted her and she saluted back. It felt awkward and odd and hugely relieving to lean on something like a salute to put a period on an argument that had run deep and unspoken.

"Release the prisoners back to Woodlawn and seal the border tight. No one passes into Woodlawn. Ainsworth shall be our new border in the north," she said.

"I will see to it," Gregor said.

"And then we shall show the city how this works." She wandered along the map until she came to an empty spot on the wall. "Leroy, I want you to draw Irvington, Lloyd, Beaumont-Wilshire, Hollywood, and Sullivan's Gulch. We expand to the south. We'll take the border to I-84." She tapped on the wall hard, her finger a woodpecker's beak.

The room shifted and erupted. Zach stood up from the pile of notes he'd surrounded himself with.

"What the fuck?" Bea said. "Are you serious?"

Renee snapped her fingers angrily. "Of course I am. Someone get me on the news. Leroy—maps; Jamal, Gregor, Zach—to Gregor's office. Let's go, people." She clapped her hands and walked from the room, gripping the stair railing fiercely as she descended.

There was no end to the preparations. In two days' time a fury of activity beat through Sherwood. Renee holed up in her room with Zach for an hour and hacked out a letter to her citizenry:

September 15, Year 1

Dear Citizens of Sherwood:

As you know, I have sworn to run a truthful and straight-forward government and, according to the government transition plan, leave my post when my work here is done.

For this reason I would like to take a moment to apologize to you for the strange turns of events in recent days. The city of Portland gave military and financial resources to a few individuals in the Woodlawn neighborhood in exchange for secession back to the city. Ten of our Rangers were killed—their names are listed on the back. I am horribly saddened by their deaths, and take responsibility for bringing the perpetrators to justice.

There will be a memorial tomorrow at nine in Rose City cemetery.

We did things we regret. In order to prevent Woodlawn's city-backed secession, some of your houses were searched. I apologize for this. We were looking for a fugitive. I would like to state that I strongly feel that these actions are out of character for Sherwood. We will immediately begin drafting a document akin to the civil liberties act that will give you rights and protections against these sort of actions. As always, we solicit your feedback.

People were killed by us. The city subversively waged war on us. Our brave little utopia was besmirched by the wantonly irresponsible actions of the city. These actions prompted us to fire back, and one Woodlawn citizen, under city pay, was killed, as well as three city police. Their names are also on the back, for your inspection and processing. The dead, even our enemies, shall never be anonymous.

However, Sherwood is stronger than ever, and a safer and better functioning government than any in the area. We have stores of water and food, space in our clinics, improving schools, an active, supportive community and a number of impressive public works projects in development.

Because of this, the neighborhoods to our south have been pleading for our help. As of this morning you will notice borders shifting and the small but feisty nation of Sherwood will expand to Interstate 84. This move will broaden our territory significantly, and I hope that when you've finished this letter, you will consider joining us on the streets as we welcome our new compatriots in peace and friendship and solidarity.

Please give us a few days of leniency as we get things settled. If need be, we may call on your listed volunteer skills during this transition.

Your support has been invaluable to me as we move through our drought crisis into a better country. Together we have done far more than I thought possible.

—Maid Marian

The letter was sent on the morning of the invasion. Down each street to the south twenty armed Rangers surrounded each border station, quickly overwhelming the city police that were stationed there. In all, nearly fifteen hundred Sherwoodites moved in to squeeze the city out. Several hundred Rangers, the day's volunteers and other forces, surged into the eighty blocks east to west and walked to the new border, purging all city employees as they went.

There were three deaths. One Ranger, a policeman, and a volunteer, when a brief fire fight broke out, but the overwhelming number of Rangers and Sherwoodians quickly quelled it. More deaths than she would have liked, marring an otherwise perfectly implemented maneuver. Their names would need to be in a letter.

Rangers and volunteers spread quickly through the new neighborhood, cataloguing resources, reassuring citizens, delivering water, setting up borders and developing permanent guard stations. They'd done this all before. She felt unstoppable.

Renee mounted her bike, and along with Bea and a small entourage of Rangers went to tour the new neighborhoods. Leroy rode with her, his mind forming the internal map of the place, cataloguing every house and street name. Renee particularly wanted to see the defunct Rose City golf course. She would convert the entire thing to farmland, all one hundred and fifty acres within her nation.

It was obvious the neighborhoods had suffered—there were signs of violence and instability; people stood on their porches and looked out at them with fear. Their children were hungry and underfed, their houses dingy, their attire poor. But it was also clear that these had once been thriving neighborhoods, containing far more wealth than her initial Sherwood holdings.

It was a proud day and she rode through the neighborhoods slowly and with her head up, speaking to whomever wished to speak to her. The people greeted her with varying warmth, unsure of how they were supposed to behave in front of her, many still gripping their welcome packet containing a note she'd written: "How things are done in Sherwood." News over the past week had shifted, and so while they welcomed Maid Marian the hero, it was with excitement and uneasiness that they saw Rangers ride through their streets.

The entire day the border moved outward until it finally came to rest. This gave Sherwood a solid chunk of I-84, a squirrely freeway that plunged into the heart of Portland from the east and then ended.

They acquired building and shopping districts, grocery stores and gas stations—most of them defunct, but a few persisted. The neighborhood was a far larger and richer resource than Woodlawn, though the thought of that lost neighborhood came as a sting to Renee. She wondered how it felt to be in city control again. Did they feel forsaken? Or had they despised her? For now, the border was sealed and heavily guarded.

Recruiting centers were formed to solicit new Rangers and water carriers, doctors and nurses, teachers, builders, and farmers. What busy ants we are, Renee thought, and felt the satisfaction of industry and momentum. She toured an unused movie theater and on a whim ordered funds allotted to ready it for showing films again. She felt unstoppable.

A news team followed Maid Marian all day. They were given exclusive access to her. She joked with them and played her part, empathetic and reasonable, decisive and optimistic. *These are no endtimes*, she said to herself as she shook hands and squeezed the shoulders of children, as she absorbed resource reports and coordinated her Rangers with Gregor, *there is no end. This time is simply a tunnel, from one time to the next.*

The city had not expected this. While they were still in chaos, Renee turned to her media crew and put out an open call for Portland citizens. We have space, she told the camera. Move your family here, come be a part of Sherwood, live with a government that works. There are empty houses and there is real work to be done. Several hundred made it across the border, carrying meager possessions or idling in vehicles piled with belongings before the city closed off the new border. *The darkness is a passage. I do not seed the violence.*

Gregor straddled the border at NE 37th and the freeway, the new edge of their world, and felt a vast satisfaction at the work he'd done.

Evidence of his work was everywhere. He tried not think about how thin they'd spread themselves, how much they depended on every little system working flawlessly, and how the city could not leave this unanswered. He feared the revenge would be quick and hard.

Night after night Martin walked the streets, driven by an unflagging desire for revenge. He searched for a gun, and hoped for a chance encounter with *her*. He risked visits to old contacts, but most were gone or wore Ranger garb now. He broke into houses and rifled all the places he would keep a gun were he to live there. A plan needed a man with a gun. Or perhaps: a man needed a gun when he was not clever enough to plan.

He used to keep guns locked in a cabinet in his den. He stood in front of his house now in daylight, wearing one of Celestina's many wigs, his suit covered in the fine dust that blew in the air. His former front yard bustled now with young children, and he watched in amazement.

It's a fucking daycare, he realized. She'd taken it and converted it. He stayed for some time watching the young nannies make up games for the children to play. He wondered what his old contacts would say were they to happen by, a satchel of dope tucked under their arm, or some piece they needed smuggled, asking a nanny his whereabouts.

In lieu of a gun, he carried a couple of screwdrivers, the tips of which he'd ground down to points with the grinder in Celestina's garage. The handles of these he pinched between his middle finger and palm, the points hidden up his sleeves, until the occasion arose.

He came out of his reverie in front of his old house and realized something was happening. Hordes of people were in the street, all of them walking south. He adjusted his wig and mingled in with the flow of people around him.

They were jovial and didn't seem in a hurry. He heard the word "invasion." Finally, he thought, the city has taken back control of this piss-ant little experiment. But these were not the victims of an invasion.

He walked with wonder over the spot of the old border as it was being disassembled by Rangers.

He followed the crowd deep into the new neighborhoods, disbelieving what had happened. How could the city have let this happen?

And then he saw her. She rode a bicycle with an assortment of followers and made her slow way through the street, waving and greeting her new constituents as she went. Kids and adults alike trailed behind her.

She looked older. Everything about her movements had changed, or perhaps these movements had been there but were now refined. From a distance he watched her touch the head of a child, shake a man's hand, embrace a woman. Her hair spilled in braids from a black Ranger cap. She wore a green workman's shirt, the sleeves rolled up to her elbows, and thigh-length jean shorts. Hardly an appropriate outfit for the queen, he thought.

Martin hobbled along behind, keeping his one eye fixed on her, held her there in his cyclops death grip. More than once he was slapped on the back by a fellow walker, a look of exuberance on the man's face. "How about this!" one said. They believed they were being delivered to the promised land. He wondered how many would get a "notice of exile."

He huddled in closer, pushing to get past those in front. In the inner circle of her progress a ring of Rangers kept the new citizens from turning into a mob, and one of these Rangers impartially blocked his way. He was only feet from her now. One lunge away. He squeezed the handles of his screwdrivers until his palms ached. *This is for you, Fred.*

A woman holding a young child yelled out a question. It came out in a confused blurt, the pressure of so many other questions behind it: "When the water—will?—how does it work?"

"Hello," Maid Marian said, and though she must have been asked the question fifty times, she made her way toward the questioner and the crowd opened in front of her. She put her hand on the child's back, and the child laid her head on her mother's shoulder. Maid Marian smiled. "Water will come right to your front door. Your first delivery is on its way, it will be there today so stay close to home. Your Sherwood water carrier will have many answers for you, ask as many back as you want." Maid Marian smiled again and the questioner dipped her head.

Martin saw the woman nearly shrink, caught surprised in the glow of her. Maid Marian laid a gentle hand on the woman's shoulder, and then went on to the next.

Martin pushed around the inner circle of Rangers to get in front. He would give them even more. He would make her a legend. A martyr.

He pulled his wig off and jammed it into his suit coat pocket. Look at me, he willed. In her magnanimousness, would the queen now forgive him? Would she accept him into this homeland, give him a home? He wished his hands were free of the screwdrivers so he could raise his hands into the air like the others who asked for her attention, but his hands were not free. He squeezed them, prodded the points into the crook of his elbows, piercing the skin. One for the heart and one for the lung.

He trailed along with them, jostled by the friendly crowd as it grew. When he was in front, he hollered out, not six feet from her, "I want to work! I want to volunteer!" His voice boomed from his chest, husky and virile, and around him people cheered and clapped for him. It felt exhilarating.

She turned toward him and made her way closer. Her smile on him now like a tractor beam. He felt his knees go weak. He saw that down the inside of her right arm she bore a tattoo that said: *There Is No End,* and it disoriented him. She came closer; she was going to come right to him, to embrace him. Did she recognize him? Her face was complex. There was warmth and power there, yielding and crushing. She was their mother, he realized suddenly, who gave them life and whose word was law.

She leaned in and put her arms around him and he reflexively embraced her, the screwdrivers gripped with shaking hands against the small of her back. He closed his one working eye, the other burned in its socket. He freed the points and heard someone behind her gasp. He shuddered once in her embrace, euphoric and conflicted, and she gripped him harder. Now, he thought. Her mouth whispered into his ear, a quiet shush of words he heard over the din of the crowd.

"Do it," she whispered.

He steadied the points against her back and willed himself. But in his mind, instead of a well of violence and revenge to draw on, he saw the faces of Celestina and Rachel, waiting at home. It paralyzed his hands, the intensity of the screwdriver grip causing them to ache. He was unable to do what he'd come to do. He let his arms fall slack to his sides then, all the energy gone. She turned and maybe she said something else and maybe not and then she was with the crowd again and they were chanting something and he did not move.

He stood where he was as the crowd pulled away. He was alone in the street, far from home. His hands hurt from the feverish clutch.

He put the screwdrivers in his coat pocket next to the wig. Across his front was the pressure-memory of her embrace, her shoulders against his chest, her breasts against his solar plexus. He felt weak and bewildered and began the long walk home.

Cora wept at the sight of Sherwood Rangers and citizens streaming into her street. She stood with a hand on each of her child's heads, feeling like they'd made it home safe. She'd steered her family through the disaster until help had come. And boy, had it come. Faced with an overwhelming number of forces from Sherwood, their city police border patrol quickly surrendered.

They watched cautiously out their window as the city police were marched westward along the old border of Fremont in a great line. They were pushed out without their vehicles and weapons onto the corner of Fremont and Martin Luther King Boulevard, ejected back into the city.

When the police were gone, Nevel and Cora and Jason and Luisa sat on the porch and watched. They waved to their neighbors and received ecstatic waves back. Nevel struggled for how to record this, the feeling of time rushing into the point of a pin. Like a moon landing, he thought, or some deliverance from disaster—everyone held their breath in the collective excitement and trepidation, united by its momentousness.

Jason wanted to know if the policemen being marched out would get shot. He sat halfway down the steps and banged his cast against the top stair to relieve some of the itch within. Nevel had heard Sherwood enter their play—whether it was cars or spaceships or dress-up, Sherwoodians were the good guys and their powers, were you to take it from Jason, were enormous and unstoppable.

"Oh heck no, they'll be fine. But we'll have to get fancy green outfits like these people," he said.

"Really, can we?"

"I don't see why not."

The main contingent of frontline Rangers moved on and they watched as people from both countries eyed the border that was. Sherwood citizens worked on it now. They removed items that had blocked the way, cleaned up trash, and shooed away the border bloodsuckers that always lingered on the city side—bewildered vendors and smugglers and coyotes that did not know to which country they belonged now. The Sherwooders looked up at Nevel and his family on their porch and waved, stepping lively as they rolled up the cyclone fencing and removed the wood structures that held it in place.

"Well. The tunnel is—" Nevel said.

Cora patted his shoulder. "It's all yours again, deary. You were a hero there for a little bit. I liked that."

"Really, you did?"

"Yeah, it was funny."

"Funny?"

"In a good way."

"Like an action comedy? With the quips?"

"Yes, you were funny with the quips. You were quippy. And very dramatic." Cora leaned in close and wrapped her arms around her children, and then pulled Nevel into the circle too.

They sat and watched the goings-on, as a steady stream of workers from Sherwood crossed over the border.

"Look." Cora pointed as four bicycles rode by their house. They were water carriers. Each pulled a wagon behind with a stack of thirty or forty unit gallons. It was a truly glorious thing to see, those translucent bottles trailing behind them, the most precious of cargoes out in the open and out for delivery.

"They're going to get robbed," Cora said. "I don't think the people here are ready for that yet."

Nevel followed their progress down the street and saw all of his neighbors on their porches, like foreign exchange students at some function in their honor. Hesitant and out of their element, certain they'd confused some vital message. Some wandered off their porches and followed along, trailing the Rangers or water carriers to see what happened.

"What do you think the city will do?" Cora said.

"Will we get bombed?" Jason said and made a whistling sound and subsequent explosion.

"Would you like that, buddy?"

"Nevel," Cora said.

"No! Of course not!" Jason said.

"Sorry—I really have no idea, but the important thing is that we'll be safe. This is forcing the city's hand. They'll have to become even more like Sherwood. And that's a good thing." Nevel thought of the mayor, his already-enraged heart pumping angrily away in his chest. "I would not want to be running things in either place."

"What? Why?" Jason said earnestly, wanting to dip into par with the conversation. Nevel grinned at the boy and thought how someday, provided they all lived through this, he would make a fine person.

"Remember everything Princess Leia had to do? With telling people where to be and in charge of things? And how people were always shooting at her? Well, I wouldn't want to be Princess Leia right now."

"I'd be Luke Skywalker!" Jason said. "Who would you be, Mom?"

"Luke's mom."

"And Luisa can be Darth Vader," Jason said charitably.

"Douf Vado!" Luisa hollered with a pitch and proximity that made Nevel's ears ring.

A woman biked up to the bottom of their steps, a great load of water bottles stacked up behind her, and wished them a good morning.

Nevel and Cora stood, wondering if there was some protocol or secret handshake they should know. This was their moment, that which they'd talked about for months. The iconic water carrier.

Cora descended the stairs and shook the woman's hand. She had a pretty face and black hair and tattoos of what appeared to be gears and bicycle wheels and ships' helms up both muscular arms. Jason and Luisa followed Cora down and stood, awed and interested, openly inspecting the woman as she chatted, looking for signs of her foreign Sherwood-ness.

"It all happened so fast, right? Here—" She pulled a sheet of paper from the back of her trailer "—this is the Sherwood welcome letter." She handed the sheet to Cora. Nevel could see his wife wanted to devour it on the spot, to hug and kiss this alien woman, to hop on the back of the trailer and begin delivering water.

The woman ruffled the kids' heads and said to Jason, "Hey, chico, how many people in your family."

"There used to be five but our cat died."

She made a sympathetic noise and encouraged them to come look at the Sherwood chickens. Then she handed each of the kids a unit gallon from her trailer. "These are for you. Careful getting up those steps."

"There's lots in there." The woman gestured to the paper clutched tightly in Cora's hands. "But for us, you and me—" She wiped her brow. "Phew, going to be a beautiful day. For you and me the most important part is the note system. You've got a sick kid, you tell me, you need some help or have some concerns or have an idea, you tell me. It's not a democracy, Maid Marian is in control, but you've got a voice, and participation is recommended."

"So I can write, so say I write I want to work on the farms?" Cora said.

"Great, yes—though here, I need you to fill this out to catalog your skills and interests."

They took the skills sheet and Nevel had a moment of anxiety over how many blanks were under the question: *Skills in which you have some proficiency.* "Can I send a note now? To tell her—" Nevel said, "uh, write 'tunnel' question mark."

"Maid Marian herself won't necessarily read it."

"That's OK," Nevel said, "let's try it out."

She shook their hands. "I hope you like Sherwood as much as I do. See you tomorrow."

Cora and Nevel bickered about who got to read the welcome sheet first. They sat at the top of the stairs, each clutching a side, and read it together. Nevel admired the logo—a bow leaning against a unit gallon quiver, full of water vial arrows. Even in the use of whitespace and formatting, he knew they had someone competent running what he supposed was their marketing department. Perhaps he could work again, he thought. And then, with clarity, he realized that Zach would be a big part of that marketing engine.

He skimmed through the various headings, which included items from farms to outhouses, water ceremonies to weapon exchange, and finally he paused on "what system of government is this?"

> Sherwood is a non-democratic temporary micro-govern-
> ment whose intent is to dissolve upon the cessation of the
> drought and drought conditions. It is a rational, intelligent,
> fast-acting emergency government for extreme times. We
> felt we could do better than the existing power structures
> and we believe that we have been proven right. Our citi-
> zens enjoy a substantially lower crime rate, more active
> government participation, and higher levels of health. Our
> children receive better schooling and our volunteer-run

*public works projects have no equal. While currently you
cannot choose who is in control or what programs are run,
we actively solicit your advice. Pending less severe circumstances we will continue to evaluate our philosophy. Why
not enlist as a Green Ranger, water carrier, or in one of our
many other positions and take an active role in this historic
government?*

The mayor paced the living room, circling the couch where Christopher sat, like a shark around a boat.

"What's to stop Sherwood from expanding again tomorrow?"
Christopher said.

The mayor went to the window and stared, Sherwood's front
line stood radically closer to him now. He could clearly see it, like a
tidal wave, consuming everything before it. "The Southeast is making a plea for her to take over there. They're throwing a rally today
in order to get on the news. Fucking *asking* for a dictatorship!" The
mayor wanted to crush her, to kill her. Without her, Sherwood would
die. Governments need leaders, dictatorships need them absolutely. "I
can't take control here. I need people loyal to me. Herr Commander,
in his infinite wisdom, could go in there now and stop her, maybe, but
who knows what he wants. Who do I have loyal to me?"

"You have me."

"Yes. Yes, love." The mayor turned to see if there was any face-
tiousness in Christopher's expression, but he stared toward the dark
TV. "We implemented some of her programs and some of our own,
but we're losing the popular war. And now we're losing the land war."
He wondered how long it would be before some crazy fuck slipped
past his faltering police force and put a bullet in him. Some fanatical
Sherwoodian acolyte who wanted to prove himself to *her*.

Christopher remembered his original suggestion from when she
had just come to power. That they should pull up with a couple of
tanks and take her out. He feared the mayor was thinking this now,
letting the options and possibilities of it rattle around his mind. He
grimaced and knew that if he didn't say it out loud it would turn
and rot and fester there, the violence replaying in a hundred different
fashions, the mayor hitting this game's virtual reset button so that he
could play it out again and again.

"So?" Christopher said. "What will you do?"

The mayor made a sound like a bear and slammed his fist on the sliding glass door, pulling the punch at the last second. The door thudded satisfyingly.

Christopher knew the unsaid topic was already in discussion between them then. They were discussing it and the irony pained him, that the mayor had taken up his early, naive suggestion while he now loathed the idea. There was a time some years ago where the roles of Maid Marian and Mayor Bartlett could have been switched. When the mayor was idealistic and charming and ambitious, when he could have run his own country and the people would have loved him. Before running a city had stifled him and tempered the idealism and made them both soft. Christopher knew that once the mayor had come to power he'd immediately begun to worry about losing it. It had altered them both. Power being that which wraps one in a blanket of security and specialness, boosting ego and privilege, pride and desire. He knew at times it became all consuming for the mayor, constantly reevaluating his position, seeing where he stood in relation to others. They could be happy without it, he thought, they could go back, but he wasn't sure he could convince the mayor of such. The mayor continually made micro-adjustments to guarantee his position; favors granted to those with means, deals arranged with those with sway.

"What if," Christopher said, "what if you offered to join her? What if the city combined with Sherwood? With the borders down you could joint rule. Perhaps she could—" Christopher was unsure how power could be shared and this, he thought, was the crux of it. "You could adopt her working policies, and obviously your working policies, and the entire city could be run that way. You're not that different, right?" He searched his mind for some formation that made sense and finally an example from history came to him. "The Romans, they had two consuls, one for east and one for west? Similar policies and shared power?"

For a long time the mayor stood with his hands pressed against the glass door looking out over their balcony and the city beyond and did not move.

"She would not have me. They would not have me. She invaded! I was elected and she invaded."

"What will you do then?"

"I will go in and get her," the mayor said. "The Guard and I will. I have talked to Commander Aachen. She is a terrorist and a criminal. She will go to jail and there will be a trial."

"If she is not killed."

"We will try not to kill her."

"Don't you think it's too late? To call her a criminal? She's been operating for what, nine weeks? Three months? In the minds of the citizens of this city, there would be few that think of her as a criminal now."

"Nevertheless." The mayor stood still, his head pressed against the glass, pointed toward Sherwood.

"And how do you expect it to play out?"

"I expect to assume control of the entire city. She'll go to prison. There will be chaos until we clarify the history of Sherwood, call out her crimes. Then favor will come back to us. After we have told our story and reestablished control, most will remember it only as a bad dream. They'll remember what we tell them to remember. That it was a sad, desperate period in the history of our city."

"If you do not kill her."

"We will try not to kill her."

"You want her to die."

"I will not let my feelings get in the way of what must be done."

"She'd become a martyr. There would be riots. The idea of her would become even more powerful."

"I'm willing to take that risk. But you overestimate her, Christopher. She's a coffee barista–cum–dictator. Besides, I don't care about martyrs. I care about running the city."

She felt sore from biking the entire day, up and down nearly every street in her new territory. Bea and her Rangers had followed along doggedly and Bea had been anxious with the tension of traveling through uncatalogued neighborhoods where they had no sense of the danger level. But these were her people now, and Renee wanted them to know she was theirs. Maid Marian belonged to everybody. She was their prize, their hope. She was their own personal army. Girls and boys between the ages of six and sixteen fell in behind her all day and followed along. People pumped her hand and gushed. She was bringing water and peace and a new way of life, she was welcoming them as citizens to the promised land.

She developed a honed sense of their expectations. With every Maid Marian response, with her eyes and speech, each action was a promise to those expectations.

But back at HQ she felt lost inside the cavernous personality of Maid Marian. She and Bea had fought: Maid Marian had given Bea an inviting hug in a moment of quiet, intuiting the need that was ever-present there and answering it, as she had done all day and to everyone, with Maid Marian's desire to provide, to be all, to be adored.

She made a victory tour of the map room where acquired bottles of champagne and other alcohol were opened and drunk. She shook hands and cheered and realized that she felt like a great, brilliantly colored beetle whose insides had been eaten out by ants.

She chatted with everyone, her words spilling from her, empty as styrofoam, and then she excused herself and went to her room and stood looking out the back window.

"I'm just tired," she whispered into the window glass. This part of the job, the part that was showboat, wore on her. There was too much work to do to waste so much time on it. But ironically, she thought, you could not get the work done—you could not empower the people to see the vision of the work—if you did not do the other.

Zach opened the door and came and put his arm around her. He had things to say, she could feel it.

"I'm going to go to sleep, Zach." She wanted to be alone. She wanted to get a foothold on who she was. She feared she was failing at the promises she'd given him.

"As you should. And so—it's just that—"

"Zach. I need to be alone right now."

"Yes, but—" Zach looked around the room and out the window into the dark backyard and stepped in close to her. He could see she was frayed and exhausted but he had more important things than her sanity to worry about. He gripped her arm hard to focus her. "I need to discuss something with you," he whispered, "and we have to do it right now."

The National Guard arrived at 2 a.m. There were four trucks of soldiers, a tank, and a small fleet of jeeps. The soldiers quickly spread out and secured the block. Rangers were easily taken out if they chose to fight, but most quickly surrendered to the superior armed force.

The tank's first shot, from fifty yards up the street, obliterated the map room. As if a comet had taken it out on its way through, it was nothing but a gaping hole, leaking fragmented paper and dust and smoke and the sounds of human terror.

The second shot took the back bedroom completely off the house so that the roof slumped. The teeth had been taken out of the house— the roof sloping nearly to the first floor—its bite full of gums. After the structure finished settling on itself, the National Guard moved swiftly into the house and collected the remaining few who held out. Stretchers entered the building then and pulled out the wounded and dead, and finally the great house on Going Street was empty again and Sherwood HQ was no more.

The mayor sat in the back of a Lincoln Town Car on a runway at the airport. He'd had his driver move there from the warehouse so they could get better reception. Two of his advisers sat with him and they chatted over the top of the constant stream of National Guard chatter on the military's open channel. They passed a bag of roasted peanuts between them. Bodies had been removed from the building and people taken prisoner, but he'd not heard any names yet. It was nearly 4 a.m. and he leaned himself into a corner, exhausted from several days of planning and the lateness. He felt shame for allowing it to come to this, and exhilaration. When the hell would they get the names?

His driver, an assistant to the National Guard's general, refused to take him there, citing area restrictions and the danger involved, but he desperately wanted to get a look at her, for them to lock eyes and for her to see how things had changed. He wanted to see her defeated with his own eyes. When he heard they'd used the tank on the building, he was aghast.

"You fucking brutes," he yelled into the leather-upholstered car. He got on the line with one of the commander's men.

"The commander, please," the mayor said, knowing there was no way he'd be able to scale the wall of phone transfers required to talk to Commander Aachen in the middle of a battle.

"Sorry, he's indisposed at the moment."

"Come on. This is the mayor. Have you found her yet?"

"I'm told they're still sorting through bodies, sir."

The mayor had a physical revulsion at the remark and had to pause while his throat worked it out. "No—how many? And they'd see fucking Maid Marian, right? Everybody knows what she looks like."

"Yes, sir, apparently there are a few that are somewhat difficult to identify. But I'm told we haven't see her."

This had gone wrong, he could see that now. He should have never trusted the National Guard.

"We're ceasing operations until morning upon your earlier recommendation, which the commander agreed with."

"Fuck the commander—find her! I don't care how many homes you have to search."

There was silence on the other end. "Hello?" the mayor said, "Hello?" In violent frustration he shoved a handful of peanuts into his mouth.

"Hello, sir, we will continue to search homes for another two hours, but efforts need to be taken to secure the country—neighborhood, area sir."

"Thank you—" he mumbled around his mouthful "—two more hours. If you hear or see any sign of her . . ." The line went dead.

The mayor gripped his hair. From the backseat an adviser leaned forward and rubbed his shoulders.

"We've gained a lot here tonight," the woman reassured him. "Sherwood is gone. We can run the whole city again."

The mayor wondered why there was no pleasure in it. He ran his tongue across his teeth—one of the peanuts had been bad, and he could not rid his mouth of the taste of rot.

It was the only place he could think of that felt really safe, and so they stumbled madly toward it, passing people erupting from their houses as they heard the crackle of gunfire or the boom of the tank gun.

Zach had gone over every detail he could piece together, holding the two notes in his hand for what felt like forever on the night of their victory, as the party raged about him, their meaning dawning on him slowly. Even as they celebrated, here was the end. The city had decided to risk everything to destroy them.

She had wanted proof of what he'd said and then they had argued.

"Look," she said and swept her arm across the room and toward the back, meaning the enormity of what she'd built. "I cannot leave."

He could see in her then a willingness to die with her nation, and it angered him.

"You have to go! I won't let you stay. You die here, then everything dies with you. There is no fight."

"Then we evacuate."

"Yes, OK, but have you seen them in there?" He could hear the fight in his voice, just under a yell. "They're all drunk. The music is blaring."

He agreed to announce what they could, to shout out into the room, but he worried about every second that passed. And so the moment they'd finished attempting to broadcast the message, this time shouting at the stunned, blurry-eyed crowd, he pulled her from the room.

They struggled against each other, arguing still as they left. She turned to each person they passed: *The Guard is coming!* And then they sprinted into the night. Across the back field they barely eluded a National Guardsman in the chaos of the first tank blast. The top half of Zach's head felt like it had been jarred loose and filled with gravel. The map room was gone.

In the dark around him he heard the sound of panicked running as others escaped too, boots in the field.

She didn't know who else got out and as she followed Zach she wept. She knew somewhere behind them the Guard was spreading out across her country, taking it back. It was over, she feared. The guard had betrayed them.

He clutched her hand and would not let go. They ran for blocks before they stopped. Jeeps passed and they cowered in the shadows. The National Guard was spreading outward into the neighborhood behind them. He could hear their engines and the cries of people pulled from their houses as they probed for her.

They crouched down on the porch of an empty house—coughing up dust and bile, their run having winded them. He put his hand on her shoulder to steady her as they listened to gunfire, farther away now. He wished they'd grabbed bikes, though he was unsure he could trust her on one.

They ran from one empty house porch to the next. Many Sherwooders would have taken them in, but there would be searches and he did not want to leave a trail of any kind. Past the perimeter of National Guard activity they avoided perplexed Rangers standing in the middle of the street, their eyes trained in the direction of Sherwood HQ, unsure if the sounds they heard were joyous celebration or something else. Warning signals flashed out into the Ranger message network, warning the Rangers away, or the conflicting message, to come fight. The many new gaps in the network caused messages to dead-end.

On 37th and Prescott Renee wandered off the porch and toward the lights of an approaching jeep.

"Renee!" Zach yelled. He ran into the dusty yard and tackled her around the middle, pulling her to the ground. They lay flattened there until the jeep passed. Zach held her down, gripped her to him, trying to squeeze some awareness back, some urgency.

"I'll turn myself in," she said. "They'll stop if I turn myself in."

"No!" Zach said. "No, you can't."

He pulled her up and forced her to run again. He could see the glow of fire reflected against the smoke in the sky. The sound was building from the direction of Sherwood HQ, the chaos radiating outward toward them. He gripped Renee's arm tightly around her bicep. Her head dipped, whether in grief or sleep or resignation he didn't know, and so he pulled her firmly along like a rag doll.

At Prescott and 33rd a line of jeeps rolled by and they hid between two houses. Citizens came out on their porches to watch, the rumble of so many vehicles a foreign sound.

Zach heard a woman ask what was happening from the porch next to them. "They're not Rangers," a man answered, speaking of the jeeps.

"Maybe from the new Irvington neighborhood?" she said.

"No." After the trucks had passed, the man said, "We need to see if we can find a Ranger. Right now."

Zach struggled with the moral obligation to warn them and a desire to disappear with his charge without a soul knowing. He pulled Renee to a crouch and they snuck in front of the house and continued on, keeping away from the street and ignoring any who called out to them.

At the corner there were gunshots and Zach raced Renee into an alley. This is civil war, he realized. Once the fighting started it would be difficult to end.

A loud *thwok* of a bullet impact sounded next to him. He realized with alarm they'd been spotted. He could not see any sign of attackers in the dark. They were using night vision goggles, he realized, of course they were. The night took on the menace of being stalked.

Zach yanked Renee forward and they ran half the length of the alley and then he doubled back and crept forward until they were stationed behind an old, tireless car.

He could hear the soft crunch of careful boots, heel to toe, as the Guardsman walked over a patch of gravel.

He brought Renee's ear to his mouth. "We can't outrun him," Zach whispered. "We have to jump him."

"No," Renee said.

"No choice," Zach said. "He's got goggles on. If we pull them off that will blind him."

They waited and tried to stifle the sound of their breathing.

Zach could feel the man's presence before he could see him, the sonic vibration of him just around the bumper. He crouched in a sprinter's stance and then leapt into him, getting his arms around the man's middle. There was a startled, quick *pok-pok* of automatic fire into the air as they fell. The man was stronger than Zach and though he held on, he could feel himself losing as they rolled back and forth on the ground, Zach's legs planted to keep from getting rolled over. The soldier was laden with gear and rattled as they fought, as if Zach wrestled a garbage can. Punches landed on his head and face and in the ribs, until finally he got the better of Zach and rolled him over. He drew back to hit Zach in the face and then there was a solid *whack* and the man collapsed to the side.

"With the lead pipe in the alley," Renee said, and he could hear a savagery in her voice.

"My god," Zach whispered. He struggled himself away from the Guardsman and tried to catch his breath. He felt the tenderness along his face and ribs for any lasting damage but found none. "You're supposed to ask if I'm OK."

"You'll get better," Renee said.

"Let's get his gear and get out of here."

They dragged the man behind the car.

"Should we kill him?" Renee said

"I don't know." Zach looked up and down the alley to see what attention their brawl had caused but heard only distant fighting. There was no way in hell he could imagine killing an unconscious man.

"He was hunting us," Zach said. "I doubt he knew it was you— he was hunting anybody, like sport. Unless—are you in Ranger's uniform?"

"Of course I'm in uniform. Let's kill him," Renee said.

"Please," the man groaned from the ground.

"Crap," Zach said. "Wait." Zach smashed in the driver's side window of the car with the acquired rifle and felt around until he found the trunk lever.

Zach prodded the soldier with the rifle. "Get in the trunk," Zach said.

"But—"

"Dude," Zach said. "I'm going to freak out. I am not good at this. I'm going to fucking kill you." Zach wasn't a hundred percent sure he knew how to operate the rifle so he just gave him a couple more hard jabs with it. The man grabbed the barrel of the gun and Renee kicked him in the head—now helmetless—and the man let go and curled up.

"Get in," Renee said.

The man got on all fours and said, "I recognize that voice."

"Yep," she said. She kicked him in the ribs and the man groaned and said he was going.

They closed the trunk and the Guardsman began banging from the inside.

"I always wanted to meet you," he said, his voice muffled.

"Holy christ, we're going to wake the neighborhood." Zach fumbled with the night vision goggles.

"Well, you met me," Renee said, feeling suddenly sick with herself. She leaned into a squat.

"How do you turn these fucking goggles on?" Zach's fingers shook as he tried to arrange them on his face.

"Like I'd tell you," the man said.

"I can turn off the emergency brake."

There was a silence from the trunk, then: "But we're not on a hill."

"Goddamnit, now I have the head strap tangled," Zach said.

"Let's go," Renee said.

"It's more of a monocle, really," Zach said, "unless, hey, were there two lenses?"

"It's a knob, on top," the man said.

"Oh, thanks. Sorry about the trunk."

Renee pulled Zach down the alley and the Guardsman began thumping against the trunk again.

"Maybe you should have asked him for the manual," Renee said.

Benjamin Parzybok

"I can see now," Zach said, but he wasn't sure he preferred this at all. The world was green and white and he saw shapes moving at the range of his vision, a ghost world. It was difficult to imagine they couldn't see him. It made him want to hunker down in someone's backyard until morning light came, but he suspected they would continue to search for her well into the night.

They padded down the alley. Though it was cleared up some since Sherwood, alleys were natural receptacles for trash and debris and the outgrowth of strange projects hidden from view. It was slow going and Zach frequently flipped the goggles on and off to navigate. *Off* to quell the graveyard fog of danger that lurked beyond his vision and to enhance his hearing, *On* to maneuver around some obstacle in front of them—burned debris or dead cars.

At 24th they crossed Prescott and headed toward Fremont. Renee led now, feeling the exhausted Maid Marian shell disintegrating in the adrenalin rush.

"What to do now?" she said.

"Hide, first—after, I have no idea. We need to see the city in the morning. If the Guard have it locked down then—I don't know— then we see what the press and the citizens do. We find out if we have any friends, and how many were killed. We get on the news. We control the story."

"I guess—" Renee said, pausing in the street.

Zach put on the goggles and turned, paranoid, but nothing moved in the scope. In the eerie ghost-glow he watched Renee put her hands over her face.

"*Goddamnit*," she said from behind her hands. "I don't want to be on the run."

"Come on." He pulled her up and turned her toward the tunnel. They passed a few more houses and then turned into the backyard where the tunnel had once entered Sherwood—when there was still a border there.

They stood over the camouflaged hole and wondered when they'd next be able to exit it.

"Well," Zach said.

She crouched down. "Oh shit," she said, the extent of what happened resurfacing, the message in their fate's eight ball floating up through the murkiness to declare *doom* before drifting back into obscurity again. She touched the inside of her forearm, a habit, where was writ: *There Is No End.*

Zach patted her shoulder and asked her to get in, looking about to see if they'd been noticed. On the corner lay Nevel's house, and he wondered how long it'd be before they searched it too. He could tell she was headed toward uselessness, burnt and empty and collapsed inside, like the nation. He snapped his fingers several times, more for himself than for her; he had to stay focused. If he could just keep her alive through the night, he thought. They would assess in the morning.

Once she'd gone down, he looked for a way to disguise the entrance. At the end of the driveway was a garage. Inside he found an old Mercedes. He imagined how lonely and wonderful it would feel to get in and drive away, just the two of them, were it not out of gas. He removed his shirt and padded the riflebutt with it and smashed the window in, finding pleasure in his second window smash of the night. Just to be sure, he checked the fuel gauge. Siphoned out by gas thieves long ago. With the car in neutral, he let down the emergency brake and slowly rolled it out of the garage toward the hole. Once the car was in motion he feared the hole would collapse with the weight, but it held.

With the car in place over the hole, he scooted himself under it until he could bend his legs into the hole. He lowered himself down until he touched the top of the stool, then he reached up and shot out the back tire. The sound was shocking and his ears rang, but the car sank until the tunnel was obscured.

When he came to the tunnel floor he called out to her. He flipped on his goggles and the dim shape of the tunnel materialized, the walls becoming clear to his left and right and the tunnel itself remaining a deep black hole in the center of his vision. There was no sign of her.

He edged forward and the dim black and green glow of the night vision gave him the creeps, like he was a character in the dungeon corridors of some stylized video game. At any second some beastly undead creature would appear.

Instead what he found was Renee, halfway up the tunnel, sitting on the ground with the wall to her back, slumped over. Her arms were wrapped around her chest and her neck bent at a pitiful angle.

The sight of her made his chest ache and he tried to imagine a future in which they were safe and happy and could just live. Maybe they'd make a journey for the east, he thought, and the thought brought a shudder of fear over him.

Zach stepped around her and went deeper into the tunnel. He explored each of the branches, many of them simple alcoves, some long, wandering offshoots that ended suddenly, as if the digger had grown bored or frustrated with the direction. At the end of one such branch he found what he was looking for—Nevel's water hoard. He fell to his knees in front of it, loving the man then. There were easily several hundred bottles, enough for them to stay for a long while, pending Nevel and Cora's generosity. The repressed thirst overtook him. He opened a bottle and drank until he felt sick, awash with it, a sea in his belly.

He took the remains of the bottle and set it beside Renee. "Drink some," he said but she didn't move.

Zach wandered to the edge of the basement. There in the middle of the room like some discarded mannequin, holding perfectly still and unaware of him in the night vision glow, Zach saw Nevel staring toward the tunnel entrance. He was dressed in a bathrobe, his hair askew. Zach stood for a moment waiting for the man to say something but then realized he couldn't see him. He was simply standing there in the dark. He must have some kind of sixth sense about his lair, Zach thought.

"Nevel," Zach said quietly, and Nevel jumped and flailed his arms in the air.

"Jesus fucking Christ, who's there?"

"Sorry, it's Zach."

Nevel bent over and breathed deeply, a landslide of curses issuing from him.

"Sorry for scaring you. We have a bit of trouble."

"I'll say!"

Zach told him about Sherwood and the Guard and Renee behind him in the dark.

"Oh god." Nevel fought back an urge to go check his children and his wife, as if the disaster were infectious. "Oh god. I thought—I thought she was winning."

Zach shrugged and knew his gesture was lost in the dark. "So, we're in your tunnel, Renee and I."

Nevel shifted his feet. Zach noted that he had what appeared to be rabbits—bunnies—on each of his slippers, made ominous and ghoulish by the light of the night vision. Zach studied him, the light making it like watching an old black-and-white television, the man's posture tilting a few degrees upon hearing the news that they were city property again and that his tunnel to paradise only housed fugitives now.

"What can we do?" Nevel said.

Zach asked if they could stay a while.

"Maid Marian is back there?"

"Yes."

"And what about that Amazon woman."

Zach shook his head no and then tried to keep his voice steady. "We don't know about any of them. There was an explosion."

"I'll tell Cora. Of course you can stay."

Nevel turned and padded up the stairs and Zach returned to the tunnel. He found Renee and switched off his goggles and sat in the dark listening to the sound of her breath and smelling the earth close about them. He fought a wave of claustrophobia and tried to set his mind to what was next, but every time he started to make plans, he realized that the foundation of all plans would be built on what the morning looked like. She would want to go back.

Just as he began to nod off, a light bounced down the tunnel from the direction of the basement.

"Hello?" said the disembodied voice in the black fabric behind the light. Zach's eyes stung. "Hello, are you safe? Come upstairs, we have a guest bed. He thinks of nothing."

"Hi, Cora," Renee said weakly.

"Maid Marian." Cora bent and embraced Renee's head. Zach could hear that she wept and they were silent for a while. "At least rest in a proper bed."

"If it's OK," Renee said, "I'd prefer to sleep down here; can we sleep down here?"

"If that's really what you prefer," Cora said, "but let me make it more comfortable. I know; I've slept in this tunnel."

Cora made a bed of sleeping bags and an air mattress in the cave where the water cache was. And there they lay down, the bottles glittering in the light of the candle she lit for them. Zach couldn't help but resent that water around him, even as he craved it, this wealth that had been the root of it all, the vital force they were intertwined with, their bodies built by and with it, and the cause of their suffering. It was water that had invented Maid Marian.

The air in this part of the cave felt different, as if in here the world did not consist of the inanimate, dried husks of things, but water-filled and enlivened, the very air lifelike.

Renee was catatonic and he stripped her of her Ranger uniform and lay next to her. "Have a drink at least, can't I get you a drink?"

She said nothing, her eyes open and unblinking.

"It'll be OK," he whispered. "It'll be OK," he said again, feeling fairly certain it would not be OK.

He felt her slipping into some icy state, a place where she might sleep down here forever, deactivated, her job over or failed. She was going to a still and shielded place in which she need not wonder if friends were dead or a country wrecked, or more likely, a place of her own making, to punish herself for those things. He felt like shaking her suddenly. Maybe she needed mouth-to-mouth resuscitation, maybe she needed those memories dislodged from her esophagus.

He felt he needed to evoke something, anything, so she didn't slip away into some coma. He kissed her and bit her shoulder but she did not move. "Renee," he said again, feeling desperate now, as if, unmoored, her soul would slip away if he didn't fight against the doom that pressed in on them. He leaned up and slapped her lightly across the face and her head turned where he'd slapped it and she said nothing.

"Please," he said.

He shook her shoulders but she was limp. "Please don't do this!" There was a thread of panic building up in him. He worried who she'd wake up as if he allowed emotional rigor mortis to set in overnight.

"Come on," he said. He put his ear up close to her face to listen for the sound of breathing. It was shallow and jagged, her mind no longer attentive to her faculties. He imagined her stuck reliving a single scene somewhere or just the barren echo of all the day's scenes. Her silence was foreboding, as if she'd already succumbed and he would wake to her dead beside him, the flesh beginning to rot, in sympathy with the country.

It seemed so small, such a tiny act, a mending thread of a life line thrown out, but next to her on the bed he whispered into her ear, weaving for her stories of what could be and what might be. Telling her how he loved her. Impossible outcomes, some so ridiculous he retracted, course corrected over his course corrections, until finally she moved, emitting a low groan or growl, and pulled him on top of her. He sighed into her neck and held on tight.

Jamal was speaking to his father about other potential neighborhoods that could add clout and resources to the territory. It had all been too easy. One day they were one size, and the next they'd ballooned, taking one of Portland's wealthier neighborhoods under their wing.

The neighborhood welcomed them. They were heroes.

"No more," Gregor said.

"But—" He imagined the entire city under their control—the stretches of farmland and resources they could plumb. Maybe the stabilization could spread past city limits. "Listen Pop, it's not about craving power, it's thinking about what we could do for the rest of the city. It's about how it's working here. The city should give up. We fit the new world. We are the government for what the world has become."

"It's power," Gregor said, "everything is only about power. This is an emergency government. We're a clan. Do you expect us to pave streets? To run sewage treatment?"

"Well, yes, of course. We've done everything else."

"We took the area by force. You don't think this is permanent, do you?"

Jamal started to speak, his mouth open. Of course he thought it permanent. They were efficient, they were loved, they were making change, it could go on forever.

Gregor poked him in the chest with his drink. "That we're here is a symbol of incompetence and chaos and corruption in the city. We're here because they let us, we're here because they fucked up. We've played a good game and helped a few people along the way, but the moment Maid Marian named Sherwood was the beginning of the end. What we should hope is that Sherwood sees us through to the other side, no more."

Jamal shook his head with disgust and scanned the party. He wasn't sure he wanted to be in this conversation. "You're such a fucking pessimist, listen to you." Jamal took a sip of his champagne and felt how woozy he was. Around them the map room had turned into a real party. Bea was asleep or passed out on the couch and people sat on the edge, mashing her in. Others were shouting and stumbling around. He realized his father was tapping him.

"I'm going to take a leak—hold my drink."

Jamal took the proffered champagne and saw that his father hadn't touched his drink yet.

After Gregor walked from the map room, Jamal drained his father's glass as well as his own. It was truly delicious having the sensation of champagne on his tongue. He'd been so dry, drunk nothing but water and tea endlessly and the distilled ration swill—something you drank for what it did to your head, not your tongue—and now here was the sweet and biting glory of champagne. His first sip brought with it a wave of nostalgia, from dozens of parties of the past.

He could feel his vision going unpredictable and he looked about the room for someone he wanted to talk to. There were Rangers and Going Street Brigade, neighborhood leaders from Irving who had long petitioned Maid Marian, a few water carriers and other Sherwood significants, but no one he felt compelled to slide over to. The map room was prettified up some—they'd taken down any secret data and the status indicators, but it was the same old map room, and he liked the idea of a party underneath the giant map. It made a sandwich of them, the drawing of the nation above, then them, the citizens, the meat of it, then the soil of the nation below. He watched citizens study the walls like tourists. He wondered what was taking his father so long. Perhaps the old fart had walked home to piss.

There was a soft touch on his shoulder and he turned to see the Ranger who had ridden him to the TV interview. He couldn't place her name. She handed him a drink and he juggled the cups in his hand to take it. "It appears the two you were holding dried up."

"What? Oh. Yes—thank you." He fitted the stems of the other glasses between his knuckles and sipped from his new drink. "I was supposed to be saving this for somebody."

"Oh," she said, and he could tell he'd not said the right thing. She turned at an angle and stared out toward the party. She looked lovely. Not in the dress he'd imagined her in, alas no, but government-worker-of-the-future pretty.

Then he understood. It was like they were at a high school mixer, and he'd forgotten how to do all this. "No, I mean it's for my father, the person's this was, was my father's," he said.

She tilted her head and smiled. "Cheers." She clinked her cup into his.

The cheers bumped a dollop of champagne out of his glass and onto his shoe and he looked down at it trying to keep his balance. He wished this were all done with, the chatting, the awkward, he wished they were in a quiet spot together, where he wouldn't have to try to barge any more words up the inebriated passage of his throat.

"Listen—I'd really like to sit down, got to sit down really soon here . . . want to find a place?" He turned toward the door, unable to wait for her answer, realizing with some suddenness that actually he *hated* champagne and the seasick, puke-in-the-mouth sensation it generated. He wanted to put his head against a pillow and let the room spin itself out. If he were there with an undressed woman, all the better, though the complications seemed too—*well*—complicated.

"You did a really great job on that interview," she said and miraculously she followed him as he moved toward the doorway. "I was worried for you. At first you looked so scattered and innocent. And then when you looked at the camera for a long time?"

"Yeah, people say I did that. I don't remember it." Jamal got his hand on the door frame and turned around to smile at her, to let her know he was still involved in the conversation before making his next foray.

Zach and Maid Marian passed them coming in. They looked as if they'd been fighting and Jamal idly wondered if that meant Maid Marian's room would be available. First Maid Marian and then Zach shouted out something but it was unintelligible to Jamal. He could barely understand the man when he was sober. Then the two hurried out past them.

"You catch that?" he said.

"No," she said and laughed.

"That guy's brain is a quackmire. Quagmire, I mean. They're dating, you know."

"Ooh, Sherwood gossip." She locked her arm through his and they turned toward the exit again, and he thought, is this all there was to it? Perhaps he'd been too daft to figure it out before, perhaps the whole nation was simply pairing up and saying they'd like to go off some place together and locking arms and *voilà*.

At the hallway he stared up the row of doors and tried to focus. It was wrong to sleep in Maid Marian's bed, but he remembered Bea had a bed in that room, and she was passed out on the couch. "You wouldn't think it too forward?" he said. "I've had a bit to drink and—"

She leaned in and kissed him and then the world erupted. There was a brief moment of consciousness as he inhaled dust and his hearing went static before he passed out. He was trapped under something heavy, still interlinked with the Ranger who'd kissed him, and where there'd been ceiling and party goers he now saw, through dust and a thousand Sherwood notes like snow in the air, stars.

———

Watching the party up in the map room from the backyard made Gregor feel uneasy. Celebrating a victory in such a manner was to be overly proud and oblivious. It was because his Rangers had been so afraid, he knew, and they had done well. He knew better than to interfere with such victory dances, and yet for himself, he enjoyed it rather more from the dust yard, it turned out, far away.

And then he heard the vehicles. He crouched to the ground and watched in horror in the dim light as the the soldiers quickly assembled and began to fire on Sherwood headquarters.

There was a terrific explosion and a section of the house fell away. Gregor sank to his knees as if a blow had been dealt him personally. So this is the end, he thought. There were screams coming from the house and people pouring out and the sound of gunfire.

Gregor had left without his gun and wore civilian clothes as usual. He eased back into the trees. This was not a battle he could win. There was no glory in this.

In the dark from deep in the backyard, on the other side of HQ's garden, he watched what he'd helped build destroyed. It was a familiar feeling. There were people in there he loved. A son, young and energetic and overly optimistic. There was Maid Marian, their temporary ruler and his strange and fascinating partner in this venture. He supposed in their short time together he'd begrudgingly come to love her. There was a government he'd helped create, and yet all along he'd known it was impossible, had he not?

"You bastards," he breathed out silently. They could not let it stand. People destroy things that work. Nothing lasts. Only him, apparently—in some better universe he would have been in the map room and taken that shell and died there in celebration with a sense that hope was possible. What a feeling that would have been. Instead, he was always the fucking survivor, left to battle his way through hell. Now, truly, there was nothing to live for.

He *had* felt hope, though, he realized suddenly, even as he anticipated its demise. He'd felt it here. He felt it come rushing around him like a deflating balloon, even as it was leaving, something he'd only vaguely known was there until now.

Another blast hit the house and the terrain was briefly illuminated. He exhaled and felt like his heart had been gouged out. How he was a hollow man once again. He could not fight this fight. A Ranger ran by him and Gregor reached out and caught his arm, his grip causing the man to cry out.

"Can you signal?" he said.

"General! They—"

"Signal immediately for all Rangers to shed their uniforms. Headquarters has been taken."

The Ranger was jittery and drunk and scared out of his mind and Gregor couldn't tell if he'd heard him.

"Understand?" Gregor shook the man.

The fighting was coming their way and a bullet decapitated the top of a corn stalk in the Sherwood garden a few feet from them. Gregor increased his grip on the man until he focused.

The Ranger nodded.

"And tell them everybody meets armed and on bicycle tomorrow at the old Safeway at noon. You got this?"

"But—" The man was a panicked animal, his eyes wild, and Gregor wasn't sure one message in his mind might not ricochet the other out.

"Go on, get out of here. Signal as many times as you can. Watch your back."

After the man ran off, Gregor turned and watched for a few more seconds. They were dragging people out of the house and cuffing them, jamming them into the back of a bus. The whole thing had been trivial. There was sporadic fire in the distance, but it had the feel of being over. They were not prepared for this—they'd never been prepared for this type of conflict. Gregor thought of the great water tanks beneath him, of the wealth lost. Of the garden in front of him, a sparkling jewel of green in a brown city. He wished they'd distributed it out to the people now. They should have been more generous while they could.

He turned and walked out the path Bea had made some time ago. Through fences and across other yards. There were people everywhere running, yelling amidst the gunshots. He walked without looking from side to side, he walked straight, the walk of the tin man, the purpose of a machine. The streets were chaotic at first, but within a dozen blocks he was back in the land of a sleeping populace, unaware that their country had changed overnight. That they would wake to city rule.

It was a long way home, some fifty blocks. Gregor picked up his pace.

———

At home Gregor paced through his household chores. He felt the moment he stopped moving he was at danger of turning to stone. Everything that bound him together was gone, and so he would rely on the inertia of routine to be the glue, that and revenge.

He had a unit gallon of water fresh from the morning's water carrier, when there was still Sherwood, and a meager stash of two more gallons. Everything else he'd stored away he'd given to the nation. He didn't know what would happen tomorrow. He could not show his face at a water distribution point. The city knew him. With a start he realized they would come look for him at his house, and being second in charge they would do so immediately. He was not thinking clearly.

Less dreaming, old man, more cunning, he told himself. He'd noticed himself slipping easily into reveries of late, thinking about the dead: his wife and other boy, the times he'd had when he was younger. Before Maid Marian had come to him, his life had been in contraction. He'd been winding things down. Thinking about the end of times, of quitting business, of enjoying ceremony and what few friends and family he had. What he wouldn't give for a cup of tea with someone quiet right now. His wife, for example.

He gathered a backpack. His load was uncomfortably heavy with his three unit gallons, a spare gun he kept for just this sort of circumstance, food and a few items. He slung his backpack on and exited through the back door. The night was a perfect summer night: stars and temperate and quiet. A vehicle pulled up to the front of his house. He shook his head in anger at himself, too close and too lucky. He wouldn't always be able to depend upon his luck like this. He was too old to run from them, carrying a heavy bag. He needed his wits to put him far ahead on the playing field. He was not a runner by nature, having, for one, grown a paunch, and two, always been of the mind that one does not flee one's troubles. He stood for a moment at the back fence of his yard. He steeled himself for a clumsy, rattly ascent over and then he said to hell with it and waved dismissively at the fence and that future of awkward flight. Why go against what you're best at?

He was a predator and he knew it. He was the eagle and the tiger, he was the tank, and trying to play the fat, aged field mouse would only get him killed sooner, or at least killed in a far less dignified way. He turned back toward his house, the only way to the street not over a fence, and trudged up the back steps, drawing his gun. It was loaded and ready. A predator is always ready.

Inside there was a racket like a rhino had been set loose. There were streaks of light as headlamp beams pulsed through the house, searching him out. Three or maybe four, he guessed, trying to shake off their fear by the noise they were making.

He entered the kitchen simultaneously with a Guardsman, but from opposite ends. The headlamp flooded light over him and he squinted against its brightness, the light like some alien tractor beam. The idiot was wearing no helmet, Gregor realized.

"Put the gun down!" the Guardsman yelled.

It angered him, seeing them in his own kitchen, after all they'd taken already. His only thought was to sweep the house clean of them, like some infestation that he was in charge of exterminating. This will be easy, Gregor thought, and put a hole through the center of the headlamp. The room immediately fell back into a peaceful darkness, and he squatted down while his eyes adjusted back to it. Just shoot the lights out. It's like being a kid all over again, removing street lamps one by one until whole neighborhoods lie under blankets of darkness. The man fell heavily to the floor, the light gone black. At once there was shouting from various locations in his house, all of them eager, apparently, to let him know where they were.

"Sorry!" Gregor hollered, "just an accident." Hunkered down next to the body he remembered the execution, and could see in his mind Jamal's face. The temptation loomed to simply tread through the house blinking off the lives of other men; the desire for revenge made this easy. But—and here Gregor allowed to seep into him some small kernel of emotion, for the fate of Jamal and the others. Much harder was avoiding that temptation. He would do what he could, he thought, to avoid this digression. Some settlement between the nature that came easy and that which came hard. He shucked his pack with a heavy thump and walked toward the front door. He could walk this house blind. They might as well put targets on their heads.

His hand closed over the doorknob. He heard someone upstairs, in the private lair of his family, and it irked him horribly to think of a man up there where his boys had grown up.

He sighed heavily, and climbed slowly to the top of the stairs. The glow of the man's light came from one of the rooms down the hall. "Robert, we need your help!" Gregor shouted down the hallway.

"There is no Robert," came the voice finally from Jamal's room.

Gregor leaned against the wall of the hallway and felt the wall-paper on his cheek in the dark. It was paisley, purple the dominant color, and he'd hated it since the moment his wife had installed it in 1994, a few years past a brief cultural foray into the design. He'd half-heartedly meant to update it. He'd gone through several purges of her stuff, conflicted over losing another physical manifestation of her, and yet wishing the items would decease in the haunting of him. But mostly, wallpaper was a hard thing to get around to.

"OK," Gregor said, "Billy, Danny, Jimmy, Whitey on the moon, I killed your buddy and now I've got nothing left to do. I don't care if you kill me or not, which leaves you, presumably, at a disadvantage, am I right?"

There was no answer, and on a whim Gregor licked the wallpaper, wishing for one last taste of his wife, her mouth, the salt of her, the way she tasted after a bath, but instead it was an aged, dried glue taste and he wished he'd refrained.

"I've got to go now, Robert. If I let you live you have to clean up the body. That's the deal. That's all I ask. I used to have a housekeeper, you know. Though she wasn't, you know, this committed. Can I get a confirmation?"

"Oh and hey," he said, "who's got the keys anyway?" The trou-blesome details of logistics. He was too tired to wait around for the young to make up their minds. "Are you in there pissing yourself or what?" He could do this. Just walk away, he told himself. Leave him here in the inside, in Jamal's room. He turned and walked toward the stairs. He didn't hear so much as feel someone enter the hallway behind him and Gregor reached his arm back behind him and fired, and the hallway went dark. It was no surprise to see he'd sent a bullet through this one's headlamp too. He had a highly developed spatial sense. The spatial sense had made him an accidental predator, in a time of guns, and only upon being thrust into it did his predator's mind finally form.

Gregor stepped over the dead soldier and went into Jamal's room and for a moment, breathing in the smell of his boy, he felt such an acute pain of loss that he stood thinking he'd wait them all out here, make his last stand where he stood. Stupid fuck-up, he thought, stu-pid party-going, idealistic sonofabitch. He slammed the butt of his gun into the wall, and put a two-inch-deep gouge in the plaster and paisley wallpaper.

He slid the barrel of his own pistol to his temple to try out the feel of it and after a while slowly removed it. He was always the last man standing, it was who he was. Too late to change that now.

He took a deep, last breath from his house, bullet smell and memory, and set out. He grabbed his pack from the kitchen and pondered where to go next. This house he could not stay in, full of the dead as it was. With his pack slung over his shoulder he paused at the front door, wondering if he wouldn't be better off with the fat bear escape over the back fence as he'd intended. But the bear had cleared out its prey, so he opened the front door and stepped through. A hot poker of pain stabbed through his leg. From behind a jeep, a man was shooting crazy at him, bouncing bullets off the side of the house.

"Shit!" Gregor said, gritting his teeth. He shot and then teetered over, unable to stand on his leg. There were people out on the street now, watching from their houses, friends and enemies. On the floor of the porch he held his leg and tried to get control of himself. He ratcheted himself up on one arm and then managed to come to a stand. The pain welled up an intense nausea in him. Grabbing the railing, he levered the top part of himself over the side of the porch and threw up. The wound was just above the knee and too much of a mess to know what was going on in there.

"Go home," he yelled. He didn't want to have to explain to any of these neighbors. Many would be happy to see him like this. He didn't want to tell them Sherwood was gone. He hobbled toward the stairs and lost control and tumbled down the two steps coming to a stop with his shoulder against the pavement. He fought to keep the blankness from veiling over his eyes, consciousness a feeble flame here amidst the pain. "Oh no," he said.

And then his neighbor from down the block, Maureen, stood over him. "Come on," she said urgently. She cupped his hand in hers and began to pull. "Hurry."

Gregor tried to say her name. They'd slept together twenty-five years ago and been found out. There had been few words in the intervening years for the brouhaha it had caused.

"I always knew this would happen to you, old man," she said.

"Maureen," he said finally and pointed to the jeep.

"All right," she said.

They managed to get him standing. He could feel the blood in his shoe and he felt his stomach going all weak on him again. "Hold on," he said, and with his hand on her shoulder, leaned over and waited to throw up again. When the feeling passed, he put his arm around her and hopped on the good leg, groaning, to the car.

At the jeep they paused. People hemmed in in the dark, curious neighbors and phantoms, ghosts of his past, people he'd drunk cocktails with, parents of children he'd commandeered at Sherwood, or those of children whose deaths he'd somehow had a part in. He could feel their presence. On the ground there was a dead city policeman, a black man. For a brief moment he wondered if he knew the man and then realized this was not the time for such memories. All the others had been Guardsmen.

He leaned against the jeep and Maureen said, "Well."

He understood her meaning. "I can drive," he said.

"You always did overestimate yourself."

Gregor wondered if the far reaches of Sherwood might still be operational. There was a clinic on 9th off Fremont. Or would they be expecting him there?

She sat him in the passenger seat and hurried around to the driver's side. They were both getting old, he thought, as he watched the way she got in, this type of hurry unnatural to her.

"You don't want to do this," he said.

"Yes I do. I know what you've been doing. I'm proud of you, Gregor. Besides, it's no different than caring for my grandchildren."

"Grandchildren?" He felt dizzy for a moment. "See. That's exactly why you don't want to get messed up in this."

"I'm driving you to the clinic. Don't you go being crazy."

Gregor smiled and closed his eyes and leaned his head back on the headrest. They pulled away from the curb and the dark mass of interested parties parted briefly to let them through.

"How are you, Maureen?" he managed after a while.

"Good, you?"

"Oh," he said, the sound of anguish erupted from him unexpectedly and then cut off. Never ask a question you don't want to answer yourself, he thought. He was setting his own goddamn traps.

He told her about the fate of Sherwood. She drove with the lights off, trolling cautiously along the streets, straining through her bifocal glasses to see what lay in the street in front of her and wary of the light of any other vehicle.

They drove in silence then, only speaking to point out objects in the road or to listen for the sound of gunfire and vehicles.

Santa Clara County Library District

408-293-2326

Checked Out Items 5/24/2016 13:37
XXXXXXXXXX8835

Item Title	Due Date
1. Memory of water : a novel / Emmi Itranta. 33305230708384	6/14/2016
2. Sherwood Nation : a novel / by Benjamin Parzybok. 33305234148843	6/14/2016

No of Items: 2

24/7 Telecirc: 800-471-0991
www.sccl.org
Thank you for visiting our library.

The clinic didn't know Sherwood was gone and Gregor did not bring it up. He did not explain the leg either. He was the general, he'd been in a gunfight. It was plausible enough and no more questions were asked. The clinic was in the home of a nurse, a high-ceilinged, early 1900s craftsman that had been cared for well.

The nurse made preparations for him to stay the night and he refused. She insisted, pointing out the seriousness of the wound. It sounded so good, to surrender into a bed, let the feeble painkillers gnaw away at the pain, wake up in a different country. As it was, at any moment he expected the National Guard to rap on the door. The bullet had gone through the flesh of his thigh and grazed the bone and then exited. He was lucky, she'd said, and he told her he was pretty sure there was no one less lucky. The luck was in all the wrong places.

She stitched him up and instructed him to keep the leg elevated and not to walk on it. He took a massive dose of ibuprofen and clenched his jaws.

The clinic had a single crutch and he took it, doing an awkward hobble and complaining act back to the jeep.

"You should go home now," he told Maureen, who waited for him.

"You could sleep at my place," she said.

"Where would we park the jeep? It's too close. I can't go near there."

She nodded. "I'll drop you near, then go park the jeep far away."

"All right."

He studied her face as she drove and knew that he had to let her go the first chance he could. It had been an unexpected kindness, and the way to repay that kindness would be to disassociate from her as quickly as possible. "You got somebody at home?"

"You don't know? My husband died in a car crash a few years back, at the beginning of the drought."

He nodded and said he was sorry and wished he'd stop asking questions. They drove in silence until they came close enough to her house to see the area bathed in the light of vehicles, a swarm of soldiers' silhouettes moving about in that light.

"We can't go back," she said.

Gregor swore and she turned down a side street. They drove looking for a safe driveway to pull into. In the end they pulled the jeep behind the dumpster space at the abandoned Safeway. Maureen fiddled with closing the top of the jeep. At least they would have shelter for the night.

"Thank you. I don't really know why you're doing this."

She shrugged and then hummed a few bars of Sherwood's anthem.

"Really?" he said. "No."

"No, not really."

Gregor picked up his hurt leg and propped it against the dashboard and gritted his teeth.

"Actually, yes."

"What?"

"Actually, yes," she said. "Everyone knew, or at least feared, it'd end some day. But I am doing it for Sherwood. I wish it had lasted."

Gregor nodded.

"You think there's any chance?" she said.

"No," he said quietly.

"Painkillers work?" she said.

He said he wasn't sure, meaning no, it was all he could do to talk through it. "We're going to need to sleep close to stay warm," he said.

"I've heard that before." She moved in close. He slouched in the seat to keep his leg elevated and she rested against his shoulder. "It'll be dawn soon," she said. "You rest."

Deep in the night Martin went and stood next to their captive's bed. He heard the booming of conflict outside and knew what it meant. Their Ranger would not forgive him now, she would never be family.

During the day they let her walk about the house, though they'd barred the exits. At night they still tied her to the bed. Her hands were splayed out and her feet roped down; she was sound asleep. He felt sick at himself.

He retrieved a knife from the kitchen and cut her bonds. She woke and in the dim light he could see her frightened expression.

"Something's happened," he said. He nodded toward the outside. As he did, a burst of gunfire could be heard some distance away. "You can go if you want. Or stay. Whatever." He realized he hadn't put down the knife yet. He gripped the blade and handed it to her, handle first. She took it warily. "Something's wrong out there."

"What is it?"

"I don't know," he said. "I doubt squealing on us is going to mean much now." Outside it sounded like a mass of trucks were rolling down Fremont, the busy street at the end of the block.

She got off the bed and walked to the front door and he followed behind. On the way he fetched the hammer from underneath his bed and pried the two-by-four off the front door.

"I don't have anything but Ranger clothes."

"I'll find something." He went and rummaged through Celestina's dead husband's clothes and came up with slacks and a white button down shirt. The man had worn no casual clothes. He found their captive on the front porch listening.

"You got people out there?" he said.

"Just friends, Rangers. Friends who are Rangers."

He wondered if they'd be dead by now, and if she had a sense of that or if he ought to tell her.

She dressed there on the front porch, shuffling into the slacks and shirt in a rush. Everything was slightly too large.

"Should have found you something dark." He took off his suit jacket and placed it over her shoulders. "There."

She struggled with keeping her pants up, so he removed his belt too and handed it to her and she cinched it around her waist. "You be careful out there," he said, awkward at this. "Come back here if you need to."

She scowled at him. "You're fucking crazy, do you know that? Something's wrong with you."

He shrugged.

"Tell Celestina good-bye." He watched her head out into the night, creeping along the front yards and staying off the street. When the dark enveloped her, his one eye stayed fixed on that space, listening to the fighting. A few people ran by, fugitives, he assumed. Trying the doors of houses, their breathing fast and scared.

After a while he went inside and nailed the two-by-four back over the door. Someone else had taken his revenge, after his own desire for revenge had melted away to more or less nothing, and he didn't know what to think about it.

He woke to a pounding at the front door. Looking out, he was amazed to see their captive was back. When he got the door open, she entered with her head bowed. She'd been crying—he didn't so much hear it as sense it. He pulled her to him briefly and said, there, OK.

Then he guided her through the house and she did not protest, went willingly to whatever fate he moved her toward. He steered her to Celestina's room. The old woman was awake; he could see the dark wells of her eyes in the room.

"Trust me," he said. "This is what you need. Por favor, Cele, Sherwood se murió." Without asking further Martin guided their captive into Celestina's bed, and she complied meekly.

Celestina folded the covers over their Ranger and put her hand on her arm. "Shh, duerma," Celestina said. *Sleep now.*

Martin went through the house then, testing locks and nailing boards back in place. There were the three of them. He had charges to protect. This was all he cared about now, he realized. He tucked his screwdrivers under the couch with the hammer, at the ready. He felt weirdly content, for the first time in a long time.

Zach and Renee sat in bed and stared into the utter dark of the tunnel and talked about what to do next.

They had gone through several cycles of sleeping and despair. Zach had tried to ply his brain for ideas, but nothing came. He felt stuffed full of sawdust. At each open of his mouth, all that came out was banality.

This was the end, he thought. The idea that they would live out the week—or even, would *want* to live out the week—felt unlikely. This was the time for madness, for doing that which was always held in check by the threat of consequences—by civilization. It was a dark but freeing feeling, though he had no idea how he might manifest this madness. Mostly, he wanted to go home.

They felt their way along the tunnel to the dim basement, and then across to the stairs. It was a treacherous and slow walk, full of shin bruisings and strange obstacles at head-height that they could not guess the nature of.

Up the stairs they listened to the basement door. There was a chaos of small feet on the other side. Of clonking and yelling and running. From the basement windows they could see that it was light out.

"Suppose it's close to broadcast? We slept through a day and a night?"

"No idea."

"Do we knock or?" Zach said.

"He's your boss."

Zach cleared his throat and tentatively knocked at a volume that would certainly be lost in whatever stampede was going on on the other side of the door. "He's not my boss," he said.

"OK, Zach," Renee said, "good work." She pushed him aside and opened the door. It was past dawn outside; the power would be on momentarily.

"Hello?" Renee called.

Nevel appeared at the door, dressed now, his hair indicating he'd slept with his head wedged in a vise, a gun tucked into his belt.

"What's going on?" Renee said. "Can we come up?"

"Sure. Fuck if I know. People are running helter-skelter in the streets. There's been gunfire. There were no water deliveries yesterday, and we decided not to go to distribution. News is on shortly."

Cora came and stood next to Nevel and her kids stood next to her, Luisa wrapping an arm around her leg. The whole family inspected them, their visitors from the basement. "Let them up, Nev."

"Thank you," Renee said, and felt sickened and grateful this family would take her in. "We won't stay here long."

Cora waved her hand. "I don't care any more," she said and they could see she was miserable and had been weeping. Her kids hovered close.

In the living room they waited.

Renee stood at the window and watched. It was nearing the hours of electricity and the few people on the street hurried toward their destinations. A jeep drove down Fremont and she instinctively crouched. It looked like her territory out there. She wanted desperately to walk back to HQ.

"Looks like nothing," she said. "They hit us with a tank and look at this. It's quiet out there."

"We heard a boom in the night—far off, but nobody knows what it was," Cora said. "I bet you're both starving—I'll cook when we have power."

The lights flickered on briefly, and then went out.

"Hey?" Nevel said. "Is that it?"

Zach held his breath. The news would mean everything.

Renee paced in front of the television. "They're going to leave us in the dark, literally."

"Renee?" Zach said.

"People need to know." She desperately wanted to break something and with great willpower managed not to stomp a Lego battleship that lay on the floor into oblivion.

She paced around the room once as if looking for an exit, and then sank into the couch. The little girl hovered close and stared, quiet, and Renee looked into her eyes and could fathom only a steadfast inspection. The name Maid Marian had been bandied about in this house, and this girl, she realized, now fixated on the materialization of that name. Here I am in the flesh, Renee thought, with self-hatred. This girl had lived her whole life in the drought. They stared at each other once more. The girl waited to see what the name did, and Renee couldn't think what that was anymore.

When she tried to talk to her refugee-hosting family, to this girl, to Zach, only the most microscopic portion of her was available for the task—the rest seethed in a mass of regret and rage. She wanted to see headquarters with her own eyes, pick through the rubble for some sign of hope, to look for those she'd lost. She tried not to think of their names.

"What?" she said, dimly aware that someone had spoken to her.

She saw Zach speak to her but the words didn't register. His mouth moved like a mannequin's, like something wrong and plastic. Her ears began to buzz and she stood up from where she sat and lurched toward the door. On the front porch she paced the length of it once, thinking that it was only air she needed, a respite from the emotional claustrophobia, but her feet turned down the stairs as if under their own hypnosis. At the street she moved to walk toward Sherwood but the rage in her won out and against all reasonable will to live she turned for downtown, only dimly hearing the calls from Nevel and Cora on the front porch, or the pleading of Zach, who gripped her arm now tightly, asking her to turn back, explaining how she'll be shot, as if this was something that ought to matter to her. She walked the old borderline of Sherwood toward the city.

At dawn, Gregor slowly disentangled himself from Maureen. He tucked her into the seat with the army-green wool blanket they'd found in the back and hobbled up the dumpster ramp out to the parking lot. At the top he stopped and leaned on his crutch, overcome with pain. He closed his eyes and waited to get a handle on it.

At the edge of the lot were the remnants of a border, but no Rangers or Guardsmen to watch over it. He wondered how others had fared in the night.

He sat on the curb before the entrance to the dead grocery store and waited for the others to arrive. His instinct was to fight. The war was not over until he was dead or the enemy was dead. In previous wars, it had always been the latter. But here the enemy sprawled. The city, the county, the state, and so on, like a fractal each iteration was enclosed by a larger iteration, and in the end his desire for revenge fizzled in the face of the size and unconcern his enemy showed him.

Perhaps then he could congeal the wrath he needed to exercise to a single person, and inevitably, he thought, that would have to be the mayor. Whether it was he who'd ordered the attack or simply stood by in acquiescence, the mayor felt right as a target.

He imagined shooting him in the face, perhaps, ending him quickly, marring him, or the stomach to watch him die slowly, while over him he would narrate the future the mayor had robbed them of.

He couldn't find a comfortable position for his leg. He tried to move as little as possible.

In the parking lot several wheelless cars lay like the bones of dinosaurs. They were painted prettily, brightly colored with flowers and trees. On one there was an idyllic scene of deer in a meadow; another had obviously been painted by children, with awkwardly shaped animals on one end and race cars on the other. All complements of the Sherwood volunteer force. Kids had played here as recently as yesterday, at home in their country, naive to the infinite greed of power.

The sun shone from the east, hot already. In the west there was a bank of clouds, a new dust storm coming in.

In his front pocket he found his pipe. He smoothed out the dirt on the ground in front of him, clearing a space to etch the plan he hoped would spring forth.

But the blank slate tired him. He put his pipe in his mouth and leaned back to wait.

He'd chosen the wrong side of the war to be on. A line of bicycles against tanks.

The first Rangers began arriving and Maureen joined him. They hunkered in the darkness of the store to avoid being seen as they gathered.

Gregor sat on a cash register counter and greeted each Ranger as he or she came in with an admixture of tiredness and grief and joy, that they'd come, that they lived. They looked lost and scared and in the end only a small crowd of about thirty amassed. They were motley, young and old, black and white, men and women. The perfect post-apocalyptic ragtag bunch of hangers-on, Gregor thought. These are the people I will lead to death. If there was something else that awaited them he couldn't think what. But in watching them, Gregor realized he wasn't sure he cared about the war anymore—these were his people, and like his own children, he just wanted the best for them.

They spread out and searched through the ransacked building, stepping over previous campsites and other areas where settlers had occupied the building. Being on the border and next to Woodlawn neighborhood, the building was in a gray area and never properly tended to by Sherwood HQ, and so it had stayed abandoned. There were signs of people having lived in the store, but none fresh. Sherwood had found homes for all who'd needed them. They circled about him and shared what news they had. He wished he had some golden offering for them, some shining gem of hope. They talked about Maid Marian and whether she'd died or not, about who else was missing and who had made it.

"Has anyone seen Jamal?" he asked, but no one had.

Gregor asked who had children or parents to take care of, and the six who raised their hands he sent home.

He sat and watched them pack up their bicycles and pedal away, relieved and frustrated to be dismissed. "We can't have you knowing the plan." Gregor smiled, covering up, he hoped, the empty room in his mind where a plan should be lodged.

When it came time for him to speak, he bowed his head and stared at the bandage on his leg. He was silent until he could hear them fidget, until they wondered if the old man had gone to sleep.

"This is the end of one road," Gregor said, "and from here we must decide onto which road we will continue.

"On the one hand, we are defeated. The little dream of Sherwood is dead." He looked around the room to make sure all had registered this. "I don't want you to think of Sherwood again—we will not be able to go back there. We have only two choices, two slim, miserable paths from which to choose."

He recognized many of Jamal's Going Street Brigade, their faces hardened by extra training, and he wished his son were among them.

"We can allow those who control this city to define us. We can attempt to fit in, find ways to hide ourselves, merge back into the city, integrate in disguise. We can bow to that which is imposed on us and suffer under their deceit and muddled management and careless disregard. Times are hard. We hear less and less from the world and one begins to wonder if the world has given up on us. And so the city will continue to flail along, squeezing us until the end, when chaos overwhelms all.

"I don't want to live that way." Gregor put both hands over his face, pausing in the speech for emphasis and to give himself time. There was grit and he tasted salt and wondered when the last time he'd bathed was, when the last time he'd fully immersed himself in water. He held a dim memory of pouring a cold ration in a dirty bathtub on a hot day. A year ago? Two years?

"Our other choice is to impose our own rule. I like to win and this is a war that, in some fashion, we can still win. We know we can do better, right? We have already done better." Gregor realized every single one of them would be thinking about Maid Marian then, and wondering what could be done without her at their head.

"We will do what she did," he said, "but we will not make her mistakes."

"Don't say that," someone called out.

Gregor nodded and took note and put his hands in the air to still them. "We would not all be here were it not for Maid Marian, and by here I mean united toward a common goal."

There was chattering then, all comparing notes again of the last time they'd seen her and if she was dead and if she wasn't dead what then?

"We cannot wait to find her. That none of us have heard means she fled or, I'm sorry to say, was killed. If she fled, we can only hope our actions are a beacon to bring her back.

"To topple a government is easy," Gregor said and he could see that he held their attention. They were all his. Despite losing Renee he'd been their general, and they were his for the leading. "All you do is remove the head. You secure the support of those whose support is necessary, and you move faster than your opposition. They did it to us, right?

"We are criminals. By staying in this room, we are targets waiting for punishment by the powers that be. But though we are small, we are fast. If we take out the head, within a few hours from now *we* can be the powers that be." It was such an impossibly ambitious statement that that he could only grin after saying it, and knew that it appeared as a mad confidence.

There was commotion again then, and a pitch of fear rose up, and he realized he must hurry to keep them.

"It's a sad maxim, but winners write history, and as far as I'm concerned, the blank page awaits. And so, my brave soldiers," he raised his voice, "load your guns! Holster them to your cycles. We ride to city hall in fifteen minutes. For Sherwood!"

They echoed his last sentence then and seemed to take heart and he turned away and began to prepare, letting them know he was finished. He could hear them move with speed, his words had worked. Perhaps they would take the city back, perhaps they could do some good, but in his mind he knew, at the moment, his only lust was to kill.

They pooled water and drank, and then stashed what they had left under a pile of garbage. They didn't know when they'd be coming back.

Gregor took Maureen's arm and limped back to the jeep. He would lead them by Jeep, now that he could no longer ride.

"I'll take you back to your place," he said and squeezed across her shoulders. "It'll be cleared out now."

She nodded. "You could come too."

He smiled at her. "I'd like that. Very much. Maybe when this is over, but not yet. Someday I would very much like to fade away."

Gregor had not been outside of Northeast Portland for nearly two months and he was chagrined at how the other neighborhoods had continued to degrade. Their strange parade, a jeep followed by twenty-six bikes, was watched by serious, hollow-eyed citizens as they passed. A rotten smell of smoke blew along with them, of something burning that should not burn. They came to Fremont and Mississippi, the end of the neighborhoods, with its vantage over a confusion of freeway and office buildings and the city beyond, and Gregor paused. He traced prospective routes from where they'd stopped down the hill to city hall and allowed his mind a moment to wander, to trace out alternate courses of action, to change his mind and let go, set his people free of this death duty. He could return to Maureen's house. He could show up sheepishly knocking on her door, ask her what she was going to do for the next fifteen years, if she minded having someone around to get old with. Fifteen years? Is that what he had left? Without a family it felt like a marathon of time to chew through.

The Rangers on their bikes swarmed around the jeep and waited, silent, knowing they were headed into entanglement, afraid and anxious and ready to follow their general into the pit.

Gregor put the jeep in first gear, wincing as he pressed the clutch with his damaged leg, and rolled down the hill with a small army of cyclists behind. He looked back at them in his rearview mirror and saw again what in a previous life he'd never expected to see: former art students, waitresses, a couple of nappy-haired Jefferson grads barely into their twenties, Iraq war veterans, a mother and father whose child had died, former carpenters, schoolteachers, all of them drought-hardened and trained as Rangers, ready now to follow an old black dog down to city hall to take control of the city or die trying. It was an emotional sight and he had to quickly eject it from his mind or lose confidence in the project all over again.

There were no checkpoints. They passed a couple of police who looked up from their duties and stared at them, wondering what entity might be riding by them in a National Guard jeep and an entourage of bicycles, but all of the action and chaos was in Sherwood, and they wore no uniforms and were not detained.

They rode along the east side of what once was called the river but for which now a new name needed coining.

At the Hawthorne bridge they pointed themselves toward the Portland skyline across the river and paused again.

"This is a simple plan," he said, "it's a desperado's plan. What you must do to clear your mind, do so now. There will be battle." It's a simple speech, too, Gregor thought, wishing he had some charm to give them or a tea ceremony to perform. He looked each of them in the eyes and felt grateful they'd followed him this far. He hoped it was not for nothing.

He waved his hand forward and drove and they followed over the bridge.

On the other side they went the three blocks to city hall, driving hard. Two guards were coming out of the building and Gregor skipped the curb and accelerated into them. He crushed one, and winged the other, whom he shot when the guard pulled his gun.

"Strip their weapons," he yelled, and then he backed up and accelerated his jeep through the front glass doors of city hall.

There were six more guards at the security gate inside the doors and Gregor crouched down in the jeep as gunfire peeled about him from all directions. He heard the clatter of bicycles dropping and Rangers pouring in behind him and then the gunfire was over. He lifted his head to see the bodies of the guards being relieved of their guns. Three Rangers were on the floor.

He wrangled with the door of the crashed jeep until he realized it would not pry open. He crawled over the top with the help of the Rangers, calling out in pain when his leg bumped.

Two of his Rangers on the floor were already dead; the last lay still and whimpered and he could see from the quantity of blood that she would die in the next few minutes. He put his hand on her head and talked to her, resisting the urge for a mercy killing, which would not be understood.

"Upstairs, everybody—we can't hold the door when they come." He called over one Ranger he knew to be a weak shot and told him to stay with the dying Ranger on the floor until first sight of anyone, and then to follow. Gregor called four Rangers to him and stepped into the antique glass elevator that was at the center of the open building. The doors closed.

"They have power," a lanky, serious Ranger named Barbara said.

"Of course," Gregor said. "This is city hall."

Through the glass of the elevator he watched the rest of the Rangers swarm up the three flights of stairs into the large foyer and felt proud. By the time the elevator door opened there was another gun battle. A pane of glass next to his head shattered and they crowded out of the elevator and took cover behind a pillar. Guards—city police— were stationed behind other pillars leading up to the entranceway of the mayor's suites.

In a show of bravado Gregor hobbled into the fray. He stepped into view and his gun was stripped from him by a bullet gone wide. It spooked him and he ducked behind a pillar. Though uninjured, his hand stung from the blow. One of the Rangers kicked the gun back to him and he saw where it'd been hit, a notch above the grip where he'd held it. He decided to desist from impulsive idiocy.

Another of the guards was taken out, and two more Rangers were laid out on the floor, one of them screaming and the sound made him sick and mad.

He could sense the mayor inside. He felt the eagerness of revenge and became impatient.

Behind them forces would come soon—they'd storm up the stairs just as he had. He needed to finish this and be inside. In a lull between useless gunfire—the guards were under excellent cover and their bullets found no mark either—Gregor borrowed a second gun, one for each hand, and stepped into the hallway again. It was quiet for a moment. The screaming had stopped. Those who'd been dying had died or stopped their howling. All he could hear was his old man's shuffle, the awkward hobble of an overweight man with a bullet wound in his leg. It was a lonely feeling. For a moment it felt like he was the only one there, as if he were limping down the marbled corridors of a nursing home or hospital, seeking out the nurse's attention, a catheter in one hand, a *Playboy* magazine in the other.

"You are outnumbered. We will not go away. You know how this play ends." In each hand he held a pistol, and longed for the crutch he'd left behind in the jeep. The leg would not swing forward like he wished. "Give in and live." Hadn't he just a moment ago opted against idiocy? Here he was, he nodded wryly, uncaring if this was where he finally fell.

The guard on the left peeked from behind his pillar and shot wide, and Gregor shot back, his left hand nearly as tuned as his right. The shots echoed loud in the quieted chamber and he felt sick about the needless elimination of men who certainly had very little blame in all this. He braced himself for pain or death, his urgency for revenge making him stupid again. "OK," he said, after the sound of the body slumping to the floor had all etched itself into their minds. "I am lowering my pistols. Give in now, gentlemen. Slide your weapons to the center of the hallway."

A moment later a rifle skittered across the marble floor. Two handguns followed shortly after. He accepted their surrender and thanked them. He instructed a Ranger to cuff them with their own cuffs.

Adrenalin was coursing through him and his leg was feeling better, and now that he'd started, he wanted more. He made for the mayor's door without looking back, knowing that behind, his forces had been awed. He could hear a few of the weaker ones lean over and be sick from the violence, as blood spread slick on the floor, the ex-soldiers now more loyal than dogs. With the gun in his right hand he waved them forward toward the door. He very much looked forward to speaking with the mayor.

The door to the mayor's office opened a crack and Gregor froze, real-izing he'd left himself open. If there was a big weapon back there he was finished. A voice called out.

"Hello?"

"We're still here," Gregor said.

"Hello, Gregor. We are not armed inside."

"Who am I talking to?"

"This is Christopher. You don't know me."

"I know who you are," Gregor said, the photograph he'd taped to the wall of the map room of the mayor and his partner clear in his mind. "How do you know me?"

"General of Sherwood Rangers? Wasn't that hard to deduce, hon-estly."

"Is the mayor here?"

Christopher hesitated. "Yes, he's here. What do you want?"

Gregor wasn't sure how to answer the question. The want went deep, carved a ravine down the center of him. There was a dead wife and two boys, a neighborhood crushed by poverty, and a country that he wanted to phoenix. All of these things were unobtainable, and so what could be exchanged? "We want your heads."

There was a long pause from the doorway. Gregor signaled his Rangers to get in position around the door and at ready.

After a while Christopher replied, "Obviously we'd prefer a dif-ferent arrangement. Can we make an agreement that there will be no bloodshed while we talk this out?"

"We're coming in," Gregor said. "Line up inside the door."

"No bloodshed?" Christopher said.

"All right, no bloodshed while we talk," Gregor said easily, the words meaningless to him.

"If you kill us," Christopher said, "then you have no leverage, and no protection against the National Guard."

"We have nothing already," Gregor said. "We have no country to return to."

"No bloodshed," Christopher said.

"Goddamnit, you are in no position to ask such a thing." They had little time—they ought to be under protection of the mayor's office already. He walked forward and with the tip of his gun pushed the door wide. Christopher stood on the other side. He looked tired. He had aged significantly since the picture on his wall. He wore a white, collared shirt and blue slacks, both of which were cleaner than the clothes Gregor could remember seeing on anyone for quite some time. He smiled, as if it were standard operating procedure to welcome in a load of militants. There was a reasonableness to him, a quality of honesty, and Gregor wished momentarily that this were the mayor in front of him, that he could lay out a list of demands and that they could talk it out without bullshit.

"Well, this is uncomfortable," Christopher said.

"Where is he?"

"They're all in there." He pointed to a big oak door behind them.

Gregor pushed Christopher in front of him and they all filed into a large conference room that had been made into the living room of the mayor's quarters. With guns drawn they hurried in and spread out, covering the five people there. Gregor sent ten Rangers to seal and guard as much of the way as possible.

At the end of the conference room was a wall of glass with glass doors leading out onto a balcony. He could see the smoke signal of what was left of Sherwood HQ, a line of smoke that tied the earth and sky together.

"Everybody lie down," Gregor said.

He directed that the mayor and his team be searched. They looked scared and, considering that smoke signal out the window and how his leg felt and how tired he was suddenly, he thought they had good reason to be. He wondered if he could shoot them all and then just *pretend* he had a hostage situation. So much easier than keeping real, live hostages. He stared out the window over the city while his people searched the prisoners.

"You got shot," the mayor said.

"Yep."

They were lying in front of the couch next to a giant TV which played the demo for a WWII video game. He recognized it. Jamal had roped him into playing it with him at one time.

"Who shot you?"

Gregor grimaced at the shiny-haired, bruised-eyed dude on the floor, the living symbol, in his mind, of the drought, the TV personality mayor, the crusher of Sherwood. Gregor sat on the plush leather couch with his boots a couple of inches from the mayor's face. He leaned over so he could get a look at him. He felt hot and wondered if the leg had taken infection. He had not slept or eaten and he still wasn't entirely sure why he was here.

"You have a kitchen here?"

"I could make you all sandwiches," Christopher said.

Gregor looked over at the immaculately dressed Christopher lying on the floor and felt a surge of gratefulness toward the man, and a little guilt for having him, who must have fought arduously to keep such a nice outfit in these times, lie on the floor.

"Please," Gregor said.

"They're turkey. I have chips and soda too."

There was a wave of murmuring that went through the Rangers at this news.

Gregor turned and pointed at two Rangers. "Help Christopher."

Gregor looked down at the mayor again. "You play that?" He gestured toward the video game on TV.

"You?" the mayor said.

"Krauts or allied forces?"

"Both."

He was looking for reasons to hurt him, he knew that. Any answer the mayor gave was going to piss him off; merely the sound of his voice invoked a desire for violence.

He got up and limped over to the window where he could see Sherwood's smoke column. The pain in his leg was severe now, with the adrenalin that had gotten him here spent. The red stain in the bandage had grown large and wet. He wondered if they were having trouble putting the fire out or if the intent was to burn the block down.

"How many were arrested and how many were killed?"

The mayor started to get up and Gregor yelled at him to stay down.

"I need you to answer questions, Brandon," he said, putting extra weight on the name. "Heartless Bartlett," he tried, leaning into the syllables, "without any extra shit attached to them."

"We arrested twenty-eight."

"That's it?"

"We found forty-one bodies."

Gregor gritted his teeth. He watched the Rangers go tense, some overcome by the number. "Back down," he said, waving at a few who'd stood, their faces contorted by emotion. "I want the twenty-eight released."

"And then you'll let us go?"

"Very unlikely. But we're talking. I said I'd talk first."

"Eighteen of the arrested are in the hospital, including your son and his girlfriend."

Gregor said nothing.

"You didn't know he was alive?" The mayor sat up again. "He's wounded. We could trade."

"For what? You think I'm going to let you go? Get back on the floor," Gregor said, as if he was speaking to an idiot child. Gregor limped over to the couch with his gun raised.

"I would prefer not to lie down."

"You would prefer not to? What is wrong with you?" Gregor gestured to the gun in his own hand, as if to say, see? We're not alone here.

"You're not going to shoot me," the mayor said, "I'm your only bargaining chip."

That, Gregor realized, was a logical point, though to which he had no attachment. He wanted his son back, and bargaining with this man might allow for that to happen. At the same time, shooting Mayor Bartlett outright would give him such an amount of satisfaction that in this particular moment he couldn't be sure which he wished for more, and so he put a bullet in the mayor's thigh exactly where his own bullet wound was.

"Now we match," Gregor said as the mayor hollered and cussed and writhed on the floor. He didn't feel like he'd lessened his bargaining power any, either. Gregor sat on the edge of the couch and watched.

"You fucker!" the mayor screamed. "You'll never see your son again!"

"It's got more bullets," Gregor said, gesturing again to his gun.

Several of the mayor's advisers were weeping, their faces pressed into the floor. He looked up and saw Christopher, whose expression had darkened. He regretted setting the mood in the room then, and again found the emotional complications of hostages wearying.

"Ah hell," he said. "First aid?"

"In the bathroom," an adviser said. The mayor had gone white and was breathing heavily and leaking blood onto the wood floor.

Gregor fetched the first-aid kit himself from the small bathroom off the main room. He checked the faucet out of habit and found running water, which made him feel like putting a bullet in the mayor's other leg. He turned it on and let it dribble over his hand. A miraculous thing, an order of wastefulness out of this time. The stream was weak but steady.

He leaned out of the bathroom. "How is this possible?"

"Water line hooked up to a tank." Christopher shrugged. "It gets refilled."

"There's running water," he said to his Rangers as he went to attend to the mayor. "One minute each, take turns, don't waste."

The kit was good. He laid it out next to the mayor and had two Rangers hold him down. "What a bloody mess," Gregor said. There was a great pool of stickiness and already he couldn't remember what he'd shot him for. All that and the bullet had gone to one side, tearing a chunk of flesh out as it passed, an inch and a half from missing altogether. He felt old. He tore open access to the wound and began to dress it as best he could, applying layers of gauze wrapped tightly around his leg. "Maid Marian," he said.

The mayor's teeth were clamped and his back arched against the pain. "Where is she?" the mayor said.

Gregor stopped to inspect the mayor. "You don't know! Interesting," he said. "She's a wily one. Thought you might have got her. We really fucked up your pants." He pointed to his own, where they matched. "Can't help you with that."

Gregor called for some wet towels. "I like bandaging wounds. Sometimes my men used to get shot up, and if it was necessary we'd get them hospital ready. You wouldn't believe how often that saves a man. It's kind of like plumbing. You're stopping the leak. We're just systems of pipes. You made a terrible mess on your floor here, but since you bastards have running water here we can get this cleaned up. Going to scar pretty good, though."

Gregor finished and groaned with the effort of standing up. He'd been on his knees and his own dirty bandage had blossomed a deeper red. "Give him this—" Gregor pulled six ibuprofen from the kit and handed them to a Ranger, then took six for himself. "You can stand up now if you like," Gregor said, but the mayor's eyes were closed and he wasn't acknowledging him.

The Rangers were taking turns at the bathroom sink, drinking their fill of water, washing their faces, pleasuring in watching a small stream of water splash over their hands, like kids at a fountain.

Christopher offered him a sandwich from a tray, his face rigidly held blank, a wax carving of himself.

Gregor tried not to gulp down the sandwich but his hunger made his mouth work like a bear trap and he couldn't help himself. Then he set his mind on doing what they'd come to do. He pulled the mayor to a stand on one leg, his eyes watering and his teeth clenched. "Come on, we got to release those prisoners. I'll help you hobble. Between us we've got two good legs."

The mayor used the police radio to talk to the chief. He called for the release of the prisoners and pardoned those who were hospitalized so that they would go free when they were out of the hospital and as he did so Gregor wondered what kind of a mayor he'd make himself. He remembered that, given control of Sherwood, within twenty-four hours he'd formed an execution line and he thought perhaps that was his answer.

"See, think what we've done to your reputation already, letting them go like that."

"I did not order the tank."

"Oh?" Gregor said. "I suppose it was the pope?"

"I would never have killed so many."

"Listen, you did though. And we're going to even up the score a little today."

The mayor blanched. "It was the National Guard."

"Don't buy it." There was no sign that the rest of the city even knew that they'd taken over the mayor's office and he wondered what the hell was going on out there. Surely one of the policemen had a chance to radio off something?

He could see the appeal of the job. This office, with the advisers and the power, commanding respect at the top. In theory, he liked the idea of school budgets and business development programs, but in practice he suspected his drug lord days, and Sherwood days, were more pleasurable. The neighborhood projects he'd supported felt more like flying in on the back of an eagle with a bag of cash. No proposal, no argument, no hassle. You're a savior and then you're done.

Perhaps he could plant one of his Rangers here as mayor. He looked around the room for a likely candidate and, seeing no possibilities, realized it would have to be him. He wished Maid Marian were here for this coup d'état. And it occurred to him then that it was an absurd little fantasy. No coup was possible without her. She could have rallied the police force, he thought, quelled the Guard, ridden her reputation into change. As general, he could only expect bloodshed.

He steered the mayor back to the couch, where he stared sullenly at the ground and asked for the release of his advisers.

"Good man," Gregor said. He signaled that the advisors could get up and pointed to chairs where they were to sit. He wondered how long they were going to have to wait for the mayor's rescue team to show up. The Rangers were jittery; having sated themselves on sandwiches and running water, they were fiddling with their guns and looking for signs out the windows. The revenge they wanted could be had at any time. Gregor toyed with how much more they might yield from the situation. He hoped that she would materialize out there somewhere in the city, the news radioed into the mayor's office. He decided to stall, to see if a course of action would come to him.

"All right," Gregor said, picking up a controller and offering the mayor the other.

"You don't want to play me," the mayor said.

"What else are we going to do?" Gregor laughed. "Talk? We've got a lot to say to each other?"

The mayor stared at the floor.

"We're going to be here for hours, Bartlett. We may be spending the rest of our lives together, short as they may be," Gregor said, "Or oh—wait, I *understand*—you're *worried* about my performance?" Gregor smiled, felt himself acting it up a little, taking up the dead air on the stage he'd planted them on. "You're worried you'll beat me. That's sweet of you. But you're all slowed down with leg wounds, and I'm a good shot," Gregor said. "Plus I've got this." He held up his gun.

"You'll shoot me if I win?"

"Haven't decided yet."

The mayor tossed the controller to the floor. "You're a crazy sonofabitch."

Gregor chuckled and enjoyed the idea both that his reputation might allow someone to think he would shoot them over a video game, and also at the idea of shooting someone over a video game.

"Anyway, we're going to play. While we do, maybe you can help me understand what we're going to do with this city, and how we're all going to get off this island without dying."

"Who all?"

"Me all."

"Goddamnit," the mayor said and took the offered controller. "My leg hurts." He rapidly flipped through the startup screens and when he came to the screen where he had to decide whether to play Axis or Allies he hesitated and then chose Allies, then he leaned back into the couch and closed his eyes.

"Whoa whoa whoa," Gregor said. "Get back there, go back, you're playing Axis."

"You invaded my office, I get to be Allies."

"No way, not after that blitzkrieg you performed last night—my office is destroyed. You're playing Axis."

"Point blank executions? That sound like the Allies to you? What, are you going to play them ironically?"

Gregor chuckled and looked up toward the rest of the onlookers, and he could see that no one in the room was having as much fun as he was. "I'm beginning to like this guy," he said to no one in particular. "But you're choosing Axis."

The mayor sat and obstinately stared somewhere to the left of the television.

Gregor exhaled in disgust and gripped his gun and stared at the ceiling and thought through his options, of which the primary was shooting the man's other leg. "All right," he said after a while, "play your pansy-assed Allies. I'll be the krauts. I speak German, und du wirst heute sterben, du saumäßiger soldat!"

"Seriously?" The mayor looked across the room until his eyes met Christopher's and they exchanged a look.

Gregor shrugged. "My dad was stationed in Munich. I spent eight years of childhood there."

Gregor was grinning like a madman now that the game was about to start. He admired his white kraut, breathing patiently into the screen, tidy and rigid and vacant. Gregor was excited to shoot the piss out of everything. "Losgehen!"

He was vaguely aware that he had to capture some flag but the whole thing was over frustratingly fast. The mayor had obviously devoted a good deal of his term to the pursuit.

They played again but Gregor became dispirited—despite the chorus of encouragement he was receiving from the Rangers gathered around the couch now.

They finished and Gregor handed his controls and the mayor's over to a couple of the young Rangers behind him, eager and obviously more experienced at this type of thing than he was. "Invite those guys too." Gregor pointed at the mayor's people, feeling as though they might all be a big happy family while they waited for the bloodbath, that what they might need most of all is a diversion. The mayor's aides moved where they were directed with all the speed of drying dung.

"Come on, my führer, let's see why your rescue is taking so damn long. It's hard to make demands for your life if no one is intent on saving it." He pulled the mayor to a stand and the mayor cried out. "Let's go look at our city." He grabbed the mayor by the shoulder and steadied him as he hopped and shuffled and complained out onto the balcony. "Maybe everybody gave up and we're suddenly in power?"

"Roger is going to be in no hurry to help me. Probably hopes for the opposite outcome."

"Who the hell is Roger?"

"Major General Aachen, National Guard."

"Oh. But he's going to look like an asshole if he leaves you here with the terrorists."

The mayor shrugged. On the balcony they stared out into the city. Gregor nodded toward the pillar of smoke, acknowledging it as if it were an entity under whose service he now performed. He balled his fist and brought his right knuckle to his lips and kissed. A prayer, a recognition, an apology.

"Still burning," the mayor said.

As Gregor turned to the mayor to make some threat or joke or caustic remark, a hole was born in the mayor's chest. A repulsive sound ripped through the air, of rending flesh, and glass breaking behind them. The mayor jerked backwards and then was in a heap on the floor of the balcony.

"Jesus Christ!" Gregor dropped to one knee, favoring his hurt leg, and peeked over the concrete balcony but could see nothing. He looked back into the room to make sure one of his Rangers hadn't gone rogue, even as he knew the bullet had come from elsewhere. He waited for the barrage to hit them, and watched the mayor's life dim. He laid him out and ripped at the shirt as Rangers crawled toward the balcony.

"First aid!" he yelled into the room. They had made a terrible mistake, he thought, a horribly unlucky miss. His habit of being the last one standing felt supernatural under such odds. And then he tried to imagine how such a miss could have taken place, between a tall white man and an old black bear. Christopher was on the balcony with him then, holding the mayor's head, his own face pressed against his ear, whispering.

Gregor risked another look over the balcony but could see nothing. The city was lifeless. Inside, the video game console—which had continued to war even as the Rangers stood and gaped—went suddenly dark.

"The radio," Gregor yelled, "try the radio!" but it too was dead.

It was not a poor shot, Gregor realized. The likely scenario came to him with sickening dread. This was not his coup.

A terrible boom sounded above them, an echoing terror, and Gregor ducked at whatever new devilry was coming down on them. Some fantastic, fucking artillery.

"Pop," a Ranger said, crouched in the doorway to the balcony. "It's thunder."

Gregor looked up into the sky to see a blue vein of lightning come down onto a building not far from them. The thunder sounded again and despite his inner warnings he stood and leaned against the wall to get a better sense of what was happening.

The sky boiled darkly, and as he watched, with the sound of Christopher's hysteria in the background, it thundered again, this time farther off. On the balcony he felt as though he could reach up and touch whatever happened there, whatever cloud god warred in the turmoil. He wished he could grab ahold of a leg and give him an angry shake. The sky lit up and another blast of thunder rolled over them. It was so loud and consuming that Gregor leaned out into the balcony, forgetting whatever sniper menace. Dust blew in a gust around him, circling the balcony, giving everything a quick coating of grit.

With the mayor's shirt torn away he tried to focus. He wiped away a portion of the blood with a wet towel and saw that they'd shot high, several inches above the heart. He exchanged looks with Christopher.

"I didn't do this," Gregor said.

Christopher asked him to hurry. Blood welled up in the hole. Gregor ripped another bandage from the first aid kit, smeared it with a glob of Vaseline and taped it hard against his chest. He felt the mayor breathing but his eyes did not open. He did the same for the wound on his back, where the bullet had exited.

A drop of rain hit him square in the forehead, a great powerful drop, as if he'd been prodded by an index finger. It melted across his forehead and he whispered rain and stared up and waited for another drop, but the sky did nothing.

"Come on, you cocktease sonofabitch!" he yelled into the sky and shook his fist, but there was no answer.

Gregor turned angrily on the crowd of Rangers and advisers behind him who crowded at the edge of the balcony in a dumb state of spectating. "You." He pointed at a blond-haired, suit-jacketed man who looked like he was riding out some ambitious career ladder. "Get a car! He needs to be at the hospital."

A kid Ranger in her twenties, having stared at the mayor too long, rushed past him and threw up her sandwich over the edge. Thunder sounded again.

"Let's go!" he shouted across the balcony but it was lost in a great peal of thunder. He wondered if they'd be allowed to escape or if the way was trapped. "Let's go!" he yelled again and waved his Rangers off the balcony.

"Christopher," Gregor said, putting his hand on the man's bowed shoulder, "I'm sorry."

Christopher nodded.

"We'll be blamed for this, whether he—whether he passes or not—and you're a witness. They'll want to shut you up."

"Yes."

"You could come with us."

"No. Thank you, I will stay with him."

Gregor rode the glass elevator to the basement with the mayor. Christopher was under one of they mayor's shoulders, and a big, hunky advisor under the other, their faces ashen. "This chat's not over," he told the mayor, but he had long ago lost consciousness. Through the elevator glass he watched his Rangers take the stairs by twos in a hurry to get outside. He'd instructed them to carry their dead to the front door where he would pick them up.

The cars were beautiful black Lincoln Town Cars. He helped the mayor and Christopher off in the first one and watched it accelerate out of the basement. After they'd left, he stood next to the car he would steal from the city and sighed. He felt a certain loneliness, an insignificance in learning that someone else's coup had won out. He was just an old man who needed to find a place to sleep tonight.

Inside his car, he inhaled deeply of the leather luxury, and then inspected the dashboard. It was immaculate and lacked nothing. Gregor drove out of the basement parking garage and into the open and stopped to let the Rangers load their dead in. Three in the back-seat strapped in with seat belts, another strapped in the passenger seat, her head slumped over to the glove box. The smell of blood was thick in the car. He had known each of them.

A dirty, sporadic, sprinkling rain obscured the windshield and for a while he drove along with his Rangers. As they biked he saw their foolish grins, their relief. Alive, and the miracle of a little water from the sky. He watched their faces through windshield glaze and it made him happy. They were like puppies, cycling manically and grinning like fools, the grief in them like wadded pieces of paper deep in pockets, to ignore now and unravel later. As with every fickle rain, they considered the possibility that this changed everything. That this was the end. Maybe it was, he thought, but he suspected it was not.

Again, he thought of Maid Marian: holed up or in flight or dead somewhere.

His leg ached with a nauseating pain. There seemed a certain rightfulness to his driving away with the mayor's car. He patted the steering wheel thoughtfully and tried to decipher what might happen were the mayor to live or die. The National Guard saw the opportunity and took it.

He was tired. He turned off of Martin Luther King Boulevard and headed east toward the cemetery. He would bury the dead. They were his to care for. He knew the Sherwood gravediggers and along the way he would find them, if they were still alive. Then he'd drive to Maureen's to help her put out catchment for the rain, if there was rain to catch, and then he would put his leg up and rest and wait for what was to come.

Zach tried to get through to her but it was like talking to the living dead. Not even a blink of registration. He would go with her, then. The fear of the impending moment rang in him, a bees' nest as he walked behind her, watching for her body to jerk with the blow of shrapnel, launched from the next National Guard jeep that might happen along.

After a while he realized he wasn't alone. Behind him Nevel held his daughter Luisa and Cora and Jason walked hand in hand. Zach turned and tried to shoo them. "Go home," he whispered urgently, "what are you doing?"

"We're coming with her," Cora said.

He told them she would be shot. They could all be shot.

"She came for us," Cora said. Cora leaned down and spoke to the boy's ear and then he took off running ahead. Zach watched him run up porches and pound on doors and then run to the next house. People came out and watched Renee walk in the middle of the street. She made her way down Fremont, her face hard and impassive, like the bow of a ship in the ocean.

Many left their porches at the sight. Behind them, the smoke from Sherwood HQ rose like a beacon. Many had believed her dead. They fell into place around and behind them, leaving Maid Marian at the front.

As they walked the crowd grew. Jason came back to them after a few blocks, panting and ecstatic, and other kids took up his job.

By the time they reached Martin Luther King Boulevard they were nearly a hundred strong. Maid Marian continued to burn in front of them, and they were the tail of her comet. Overhead the clouds were thick and tumultuous, a churning blackness in them. On the ground the dust was still and the streets were quiet. They said nothing as they walked. The only sound was that of hundreds of footsteps.

Zach watched the back of Renee's head and knew she could not be talked to or persuaded. He checked the streets left and right for Guard jeeps or city vehicles as he marched. Beside him Nevel and Cora and Jason and Luisa walked holding hands, Luisa quick-stepping to keep up, even her chirp quieted by the moment. What were they marching for, Zach wondered, but he felt it too. This was their ship. Without it they were sunk.

By the time they reached Broadway, bicyclists and skateboarders had joined, and many more marchers, so that they were a swarm, flying straight to the center. They numbered into the many hundreds, perhaps thousands.

Maid Marian turned west to cross the bridge, which would lead them through Chinatown to the center of the city.

The National Guard had constructed an impromptu blockade in the middle of the bridge, having by now been forewarned.

The crowd followed Maid Marian to the edge of the bridge, and she kept walking. A string of the crowd, an arm of it, reached out with her, followed her onto the bridge toward the blockade. Tear gas canisters were launched, and Maid Marian walked in smoke.

At the front of the Guard, directly in line with the trajectory of Maid Marian's path, was a young soldier named Daniel Curant. He was twenty-one years old and had joined the National Guard because he wanted to be noble and good.

He loved Maid Marian.

All night he thought of her as he lay on the top bunk in the barracks, wishing now he could work for her as a Green Ranger. In his mind the Rangers had risen in his esteem idealistically, so that it surpassed, even, the calling of the Guard. He kept a newspaper picture of her tucked into his pillowcase. He knew his chances, but even still he couldn't help but imagine them together, with a little farmhouse perhaps, like the one his grandparents had had on Sauvie Island. Dogs would run and play at the river's edge while they walked through the fields, and there would be a glow about her. And as she walked, he would observe that her feet scarcely touched the ground.

She seemed to be walking straight for him now through a mist of tear gas and he was having trouble concentrating on much else but the hypnotizing appearance of her glory. She shone, her black hair like a blaze around her, her figure pronounced against the dark dust storm coming in behind her. He could not yet see but clearly imagined the freckles across the bridge of her nose that he'd studied as if he were trying to decipher a foreign language. A message written just for him.

He watched the sway of her hips as she approached, unsettled by seeing in the flesh one with whom he'd shared such imagined intimacy, as if at any moment she might recognize him from his own fantasies or, terrifyingly, know what experiences he'd played out for them in his mind. Her face was stony and grim and it made him anxious.

The Guards around him shuffled nervously. She came closer, unflinching in her stride, focused straight ahead, on him, it seemed. She was going to walk into his embrace.

The man to his right, PFC Connor, said something about how when that bitch is finally gone their jobs would be a lot easier, and with alarm Daniel realized she was going to die. That unless she stopped and turned back some asshole was going to shoot her. His skin went haywire, sweat glistened across him as he panicked. He glanced up and down the line and with all his being he knew he must save her. Could he stop them? Take one out before they shot? His face tightened into a grimace of fear as he looked out at her over his shield. It came to him what he must do. He drew his own gun and pulled it up. He'd always been a little to the left. He aimed for her shoulder and tried to account for his deficiencies. If he could just wing her, clip her like a bird, stop her trajectory. Maybe he could save her. He would save her and he'd tell her that and she would smile and thank him. *She* would understand.

He was jostled—several Guards called out when his gun came up—but he knew it had to be him. He watched her as he pulled the trigger, sending with it a wish, everything in his mind emptied into that bullet, the dogs on the river and the farm and the taste of strawberries and lying under clean sheets and hope, so that it might envelope her, that it might be the bullet that saved her. She spun around, as if she were a dancer, performing for him on stage, and then she was on the ground. He hadn't seen where he'd hit her.

There was a terrific cry from the crowd who waited at the edge of the bridge. As one they rushed forward. Chaos broke loose among the Guards and someone knocked him from behind and he fell and someone else was on top of him, holding him down.

He could see her for a moment through the legs of others. He'd aimed for her left shoulder. They could fix a shoulder.

It felt like a string connected them. Lying on the ground, from the crown of one head to the crown of the other. A rumbling blast cascaded through the air and he smelled tear gas. Perhaps this is it, he thought, they were passing on, one shot, the other trampled in riot, connected by their fragile mortality. Joy sprang into him then; they were to be wedded by their synchronous passing. The chaos swayed over him and then back, like lying in ocean surf. Then his view of her was blocked by fields of boots.

The crowd rushed the soldiers and more tear gas was fired and guns were pulled. Another ear-splitting boom sounded, like God's own angry voice, rattling the bridge. Daniel felt the bridge shake down to its very foundation. A drop of water moistened his cheek.

After. After the clash and the blood trickled in the gutters of the bridge, and what little rain drizzled it wetly from there onto the banks of the dry river, after he, Zach, had struggled to reach her, and after he'd been beaten down and tread upon, a kick to his back that sprawled him out on the ground, after the people were arrested or dissipated or too injured to walk away, and after her body was removed, limp—he'd seen only an instant's image of an arm swinging lifeless over the side of an ambulance's stretcher—Zach walked up Broadway.

He had not been arrested. Weirdly ignored as he walked away from the chaotic scene, in slow pursuit of the ambulance, his mind focused only on her.

At the hospital he was told she had died. When the ambulance pulled in, she was already gone. A constant inflow of patients arrived and the nurse was at first kind and then increasingly short with him.

Outside, standing a few paces from the hospital entrance, he felt insubstantial, as if his body were made of layers of old burlap. He stood there and swayed as people rushed around him, and then he continued toward home.

He walked in the middle of the street. By now the freak rain had darkened it, the big drops falling sparsely. He turned at 20th and walked the bridge that spanned the freeway and watched I-84 below as the thoroughfare bore the military vehicles returning to base. His skin was numb, though the rain kept working at him, each one a surprise, chipping away the exoskeletons he'd piled on top, fashioned of fear and longing and necessity. His mind was numb too, a robotic insistency propelling him homeward.

At 21st and Flanders he stood transfixed as a large family scattered every dish they owned in the yard to catch the rain. They had flower vases, teacups, overturned drums, buckets, frying pans, sheets of plastic laid across cardboard boxes, and as the six of them streamed to and from the house, each time with some new vessel, they laughed and shouted at each other with glee. In the pans were mere drops.

They would not net but a few cups, but he stood transfixed by their joy all the same.

The air was fresh and electric.

As he walked blindly toward his building, his shoes slapped into a tiny dirty puddle that had formed. It was a tactile sensation that bore repetition, and for a moment, upon first being cognizant of it, he stood where he was and tapped the same foot in and out of the puddle. Each time was a small pleasure.

At home, he paced his building. It became his new occupation, and he practiced it for days. Tamping down each floorboard with his footsteps like a blacksmith works a sword. Tempering them in his search to rest his mind. The news talked about Maid Marian's death endlessly, and this required an infinite amount of pacing, of climbing the building's stairs, of looping around his roof, leaving only for rations when need became dire.

In this way, for some time, his building became an island. Walked persistently by the castaway for no other reason than the act of standing still invited pain. A week passed, or perhaps two, lost in the meanderings of his building.

In this failing city run now by a semi-hostile National Guard, the future yawned uninviting and endless in front of him, and so he thought of it little. He only walked.

He watched as much news as he could manage each night, sharp slivers of it entering him before he was compelled to turn it off. With the mayor hospitalized, Commander Aachen appeared regularly in his stead to read in monotone, devoid of any of Mayor Bartlett's charm, joyless in his delivery, until it was clear, but never stated, the mayor would not be coming back.

Zach studied the face of the older man as it filled the frame of his television set, his blond hair like bits of old hay. He was a dull reader. He seemed to believe that the intricate order he set up post–city council was somehow a bootcamp for the city that would quell its desires and set it straight. He wanted it, Zach saw, being on the television and in charge. He was not their accidental guardian. The newscasters appeared lifeless, changed since the city had changed, and he suspected they were under censor. They had heard little to no news from the outside world. The city slept on in a post–Maid Marian coma.

Guard jeeps coursed up and down its veins, redirecting and taming and quashing.

Zach slept twelve and fourteen hours at a stretch, going to sleep at sundown and waking midday the next. It was a sickness, he told himself, that he was trying to sleep out. Many times he pondered infinite sleep as a cure to what ailed him, and he considered the various ways to obtain it. When he awoke there was little he could think to do but begin pacing again.

After some weeks, in a vacant stride through his office, he passed his desk. Upon it there was a clean, white sheet of paper and a pencil, untouched for some time. He continued circling around the building, and each time he landed back at the desk, with the blank paper there and its implied question, the paper a window to climb through. Outside a large, National Guard truck rumbled past and stirred up a cloud of dust.

Dear Sherwood Nation, he wrote.

Zach tried to think of a way to pivot off the first line. He felt like he owed everyone a last word to hang on, or an apology, the guilt of his silence weighing on him. But there was so much to say and he could think of no way to say it. *Long time no see. How's your family? Do you miss Maid Marian? Do you ever think about . . .* He stood from the desk and for two more days he paced, avoiding the blank page.

No, he realized, there was nothing to say.

Instead, he would go there. He would go talk to them. He would find the others, the water carriers and the volunteer leaders and the Rangers, he would find everyone who remained.

He folded the paper into his pocket. He would use it yet. And then he left his building and walked north.

Commander Roger Aachen of the National Guard, protectorate of the city-state of Portland, sat in his office in Big Pink, the namesake-tinted US Bancorp Tower that overshadowed the northern edge of downtown. On the thirtieth floor there'd once been a restaurant, and there he had set up office, in one of the booths with its sweeping view. Below him were the dead river, all of Northeastern Portland, the former site of Sherwood, and several bald, brown mountains beyond.

At the moment, he was busy removing staples from a series of reports, with a sad disappointment for and frustration in his report-preparer, Major August Gonzalez, who he was coming to realize could not properly grasp—much less learn for himself—the proper way to staple a pile of papers.

"You see, Major? How upon opening?" Here the commander vigorously opened and closed the top sheet of the report several times, eyeing the major who stood before him. "The paper begins to tear if you've stapled it parallel with the top edge?" He paused to see if Major Gonzalez offered some defense for himself but none was forthcoming. "Think about the natural fold one makes when browsing a report. Think about the arc and reach of a human arm." Here the commander mimed turning the page of a stapled report, first away from himself, as if he were throwing a gut punch, and then at an angle to the left, in the manner of a Frisbee toss. "You see how much more natural that is? How the arm does not spring, but pivots, rotates? The staple at an angle is stronger, with its deeper bite into the paper's flesh."

"Yes, sir, I'm sorry sir."

Roger stared at the major and was not convinced the young man understood. He needed to signal his comprehension more forcefully, if so. Did he realize he was giving him—*handing it to him*—a metaphor for how one might approach anything? A strategy, if you will, for life.

The major was a handsome man, the commander observed distantly, and despite the incident here, he continued to *look like* what the commander felt a military man ought to look like. Pressed and clean, with a sharp jaw, and just the hint of having been hard at work.

Major August Gonzalez cleared his throat. "As to the content of that one, sir," he pointed to the one the commander was removing a staple from presently, with not a little difficulty, "we might discuss the new—with your permission, we're calling them micro-nations?"

"Shit," Roger said. He'd accidentally torn the entire corner from the paper in attempting to remove the previous staple and held his hands open over the disaster, looking up at the major to show that this was the younger man's doing. "We can't have a discussion about content with the shape these reports are in! You see? Now what? It cannot be reattached."

Major August Gonzalez took on the stoic look of one who has come to retreat early and regularly into the solace of an internal mantra.

Were the commander to ask him to return and redo the reports, as he expected he would, it would not be the first time. He began to suspect the commander might be stalling in his inspection of the reports. The previous reports had detailed National Guard defections, which happened after the US Government stopped supplying rations for the Guard to distribute, after the commander was officially discharged from the National Guard, after he, Commander Aachen, disbanded the city council.

Now, Major August Gonzalez felt confused about whom he actually worked for. It *felt* like the National Guard, but the National Guard had lopped them off, like a gangrenous leg.

"This one talks about Richmond . . . the micro-nation."

"A particularly inept name, is it not? *Richmond*." The commander pronounced it in a shrill French accent, the sound more akin to the squeal of tires. "But hardly rich, these people."

"Yes, sir."

"Optimistic thinking, maybe."

"Probably, sir."

"These reports," Roger gathered the now staple-free stacks together into a large heap and handed them back to the major, "will have to be redone."

"I have paper clips, sir, if they can make do?"

Roger stared at the major with a sad look, and wondered if the man would ever do anything great in his life, or if his trajectory was dead set on a repeating cycle of middling successes. The thought depressed him.

"What is your father like, Major?"

"He's dead, sir."

"Ah," Roger said.

"If I may, sir, these micro-nations, Richmond in the southeast and now Sherwood again, sir? Which appears to be regenerating—and I'm afraid there are signs of others—their resources and techniques are more sophisticated than we've seen. With the Russian water tanker—we believe the brain-trust of the former micro-nation and a portion of AWOL Guardsmen—"

The commander was waving him away. "Please. *Please*, come back when these are human-readable. And a glass of water, if you will."

After Major Gonzalez had attended to the commander's needs he took the stack of paper to the twenty-seventh floor, using the stairs, where an enormous array of cubicles surrounded office machinery from some long-gone corporation. There he sat in his cubicle, put his feet up on the desk, leaned back in the chair and stared at the ceiling. He liked it in here, this abandoned hive-like place now partially repopulated by the National Guard, with its labyrinth of desk-boxes. The stack of paper, with their torn corners weighed heavily on his hands, the product of a man who preferred excessive and excessively organized data in order to move forward in life. A man, he thought, who intended to play his chess game no matter that the board had long ago been scrapped and burnt by a citizenry who needed to keep their hands warm on a cold evening. *Citizenry*, Major August Gonzalez repeated in his mind. It was an apt mantra. Its many-syllabled rhythm calmed; it sounded like something wonderfully, mystically foreign. Sitta *Zen*ree, Sitta *Zen*ree.

He wondered why he was still here. Many of his fellow Guardsmen had simply vanished. Gone on an errand—say, the restapling of reports—and not returned, their uniforms left in unceremonious heaps in the elevator when it hit the ground floor. Major Gonzalez did not like to think of himself as a quitter, and in fact quitting came with great difficulty to him. He was an excellent cog, he knew, a perfectly functioning piece of machinery required in the building of something great. A cog that did not lack for insight or perception or raw smarts. In time, he would have ambitions, as they fit into the scope of the organization. And that was key. He loved the Guard. With the comfort of its structure and the numbing pleasantness of its rigmarole and the sense that he was part of a greater good. To protect, to shield, to watch over.

He rifled through the reports on various individuals, or what they could learn of them. Bea Gallagher, deceased; Leroy Wallace, deceased; Zachary Jefferson, location unknown; Jamal Perkins, Sherwood M.N.; Gregor Perkins, location unknown; Brandon Bartlett, house arrest; Renee Gorski aka Maid Marian, deceased. Really, these reports no longer mattered, he thought, in light of the new, more pressing issues. Still, it was important to process and to learn from what happened.

Major Gonzalez carried his laptop to the big printer, set it on top, and connected it directly with a USB cable. He reprinted everything: water status, past and future micro-nations, supply situation, Guard relations. When the print job was finished he found the heavy-duty stapler and angled it in the manner the commander had instructed.

He enjoyed stapling, with its decisive *chunk* through a stack of paper. And each time he did so, he inspected the job through the scrutinizing gaze of the commander to see if he could find fault with it.

"What're you doing, Auggie?"

Major William and he had trained and risen up the ranks together. An ugly, flat-faced black man whose sense of humor and easy nature made him welcome company wherever he went, his ability to execute had guaranteed his rising through the ranks on par with himself. He had a duffel bag over his shoulder and hovered at the edge of the big printer.

August waved his hand at the reports and attempted to reply straight-faced. "Stapling," he said, "what else is there?" He braced himself for a little teasing.

"That old man," William whispered and did not smile.

"Not the first time on these," August said.

William patted him on the shoulder.

"You?" August said.

"Taking my team on desalination inspection."

Major Gonzalez continued stapling but was aware that William did not move on. There were half a dozen or so other National Guard higher-ups in the office working on various projects.

"So?" he said finally.

"Heading back up to see the chief?" William said.

"Momentarily."

August compiled the reports into a neat, newly stapled stack and headed to the stairs. Major William tagged along behind.

"Come on, take the elevator, buddy!" William said and steered him. "Disrespectful not to. City's got no power. It's like leaving food on your plate when there's kids starving out there."

August chuckled uncomfortably. "If you say so."

William held the door for him, and then shifted in front of the elevator buttons before August had time to punch one. He felt the elevator suddenly begin to descend.

"—Oops!" William said easily. "It's a sign! Maybe you see me on down instead?"

"Got no choice now, do I?"

William went serious. "Lots of choices, Auggie."

August watched the digital counter. 24, 23, 22.

"What do you mean."

"Mmm." William shrugged. "Speaking generally." He dropped his duffel to the ground, unzipped it, and pulled out a set of clothes. He shook these out and eyed August. Then he began stripping out of his uniform.

"Willy!" August said, suddenly alarmed.

"Just wanted to say good-bye. Pull that for me, would you?" He nodded at the elevator force-stop.

August reached up and punched the emergency button. Floor 14, he noted. A most terrible wrenching fear had dug into his gut, and he couldn't believe he was standing in front of his friend as he shed the career they'd been mutually working on for years. Major William was no minor player. In his hands he straightened the paper edge of the reports and could not find words to speak.

William put on a set of blue jeans and a black polo shirt, and, as per training, folded his uniform into a neat bundle and put it back in the duffel bag. "Got two sets in here."

"Of what?"

"Clothes, genius-man. Attire. Civilian-style."

August slid to the floor of the elevator and clutched the reports, careful not to sully them.

William kicked the duffel across the floor of the elevator. "Go ahead, put them on then."

Major August Gonzalez closed his eyes and leaned his head back against the elevator wall. He thought of the number of people he would disappoint, his mother and uncles, his brother José, stationed in New Orleans, other friends in the Guard, Commander Aachen. "You look funny in street clothes," he said.

"That's where you are wrong," William said. He adjusted his collar and August could see his friend, whom he could not remember ever being nervous, transformed. "No one has ever looked so good." He snapped his fingers.

"Just like that?" August continued to grip the reports.

"Some would call this fashionably late."

August snorted and with his right hand held the bridge of his nose. "Lot to throw away," he said.

"Lot to gain! Don't need to tell you that. A decision needs to be imminent, here."

"Years of training and et cetera."

"What are those reports telling you? Were you a gambling man, which I know you are not, where's the odds?"

"Ah, Willy, shit hell."

"Which side is right?"

"Not as simple as that."

"Simple as you want to make it. The clothes, comrade."

August squinted across the elevator for a moment and imagined them both walking from the building together as civilians and found it surprisingly easy to manage. "Alright." Cross-legged, he stripped his shirt off and did not bother to fold it. Inside he found a red flannel lumberjack shirt. He held it up at William. "Really?"

William chuckled with pleasure. "Make it snappy."

August did not change pants. He stood, put the reports in the duffel bag, and handed it back to his friend.

William pointed at the control panel. "Monsieur?"

"Yes, sir," August said. He released the emergency stop. The elevator descended. "What do you think we'll do there?"

"Everybody has a need for bright individuals what can take initiative, and has a little information besides. Richmond and the others, Sherwood even, they accept—you know—our kind."

"Defectors?"

"Ugly word."

"It is."

As they approached the second floor August reached out and grabbed hold of the elevator force-stop and paused. Then gave it a yank.

"I hope this is just last words?" William asked.

"I can't do it, Willy. Damn it." He stood there immobilized with fear, the elevator just ten feet away from exposing him as a traitor. August unbuttoned the red flannel shirt and this he folded neatly and handed back to William, and waited with his hand outstretched until the other man dug in his duffel bag for the major's uniform.

"Auggie?"

"Don't say it, alright?"

"Goddamnit. I'm going to watch for you."

"Please don't say any more."

"I'm going to wait for you. Going to watch for you."

"Willy."

William forked two fingers and pointed them at his own eyes then at August. "Right? You watch your back with that old fucker. When your mind is right, get out fast."

August nodded.

The elevator descended to the first floor and Major August Gonzalez watched his friend exit into the empty lobby and walk out, with a loping, non-uniformed stride. Then the doors closed and the elevator started back up. Quietly he mouthed "Sitta *Zen*ree, Sitta *Zen*ree."

During the elevator's ascent, he realized he'd just deposited several months' worth of intelligence into Willy-the-defector's duffel bag and he had a long, sad chuckle. He was surprised to find he had very little remorse.

He could print more, and staple as many as were required.

EPILOGUE

Hey Boyfriend.
So like, Canada, eh? Is there really any other way I can start such a letter?

I made it.

It's amazing how much time one can spend on like each sentence. The "I made it," written just there, one line's worth away, took about a day to compose. Anxiously, hard-worked-at, and then an unbelievable effort with little to show for it in the space after its period. This letter sitting here abandoned hour after hour on this small painted-wood desk. A child's desk, I think, with its colorful drawers, or perhaps that of a quirky old woman, looking to add a little more color to her life.

Now look, another day's gone by and already I don't have the desk to talk about any more, used up as a topic as it is. How can there be so much to tell and yet it cost so much to say?

I am, quite obviously if you're reading this, a-live, as it were, such as it is. Turns out you do something bold, you make friends and enemies everywhere. You become divisive to ambulance drivers. Your fate debated by nurses. Even army dudes can't make up their minds among them. In the twisty route from ambulance to hospital to prison I drew a lucky route, and then that route was dusted over.

I wasn't able to do much for myself for some time. There's a wicked ache in my shoulder now off and on, just above the heart, and many a time I tell myself it's the ache for another's heart, too far away. It's not a pretty wound, even you wouldn't think so. i.e. one must try hard to look in the mirror and not say eww . . .

I try to fill my days with something other than remorse, but that's a difficult thing to do, being the rich game that it is. Sometimes when I sleep, I cycle through the faces, some whose fates I know, and some I don't. Ach, hope. In this little household up north I have chores, simple things we do to stay alive. Aspects of Sherwood here, adopted from, and talked about much, and for that, in my anonymous little way, I am happy. Though did it really need to cost this many lives to spread these simple things (fuckfuckfuck).

There is some news I have to share.

Damn it. There it is again, a week this time spent in toil in the space after that period above.

Not only am I alive, I'm pregnant.

Surprise!

There. See how easy that is to say? (Not really, I'm sweating bullets here + other salty water-droplet like things from other sources, etc, with no little amount of precipitation). So 2x alive, I guess you could say, which in one letter is probably about 10x too much to reveal to poor you all at once, my sweet. To give you some idea of its origin, we're estimating I'm about eight months (no small lithe creature am I), and so do your own math there.

Honestly, the remorse and regret thing? It's the like fifty-something foot wall I'd have to climb prior to hoping to ever speak words to you like: We should meet up! We should totally hang out!

Much less: Do you think she looks more like you or me?

But needless to say, I have been thinking about you a great deal.

Next to this letter here, I've put another blank sheet, at the top written: Hey Boyfriend!

You know, get a jump on episode #2.

Bit by bit. Spoonfuls of sand. That's the best she can do.

yrs,

-r

p.s. Vancouver East Nation, c/o Ariel Boat Builders Residence.

p.p.s. believe me, it was no small feat of endurance to scrawl out that address above. This anonymity a certain—not pleasure, more like the absence of pain. Lost in a connectionless whirlpool, no one to injure but herself. And since delivery of this is in no way certain, I will wait long without expectations. Forever if need be.

This heartrending and inspiring book is about the tragic events that led to the modern concept of community nations, so called for their micro size, and their ability to thrive much more ably under extreme duress. Told to us by Brandon Bartlett, who, before becoming a historian and spokesperson for this new model of government, brought down Sherwood Nation with the help of the National Guard, and then fought a coup d'etat of his own. Read about the historic journey of Maid Marian, and learn about the successes and failures of community nations in the changed landscape of the west.

"What Christopher and Brandon Bartlett (yes, that Bartlett, former mayor of Portland) have done here is nothing short of remarkable. While perfectly depicting the rise of what we now commonly know as the Community Nation, they enrich the reader with a series of guides for making sure your community nation is sustainable and highly functional. I highly enjoyed and unreservedly recommend this book."—*Zachary Jefferson, inventor of the Unit Gallon and former chief statistician for Sherwood Nation*

ACKNOWLEDGMENTS

This book started in the anarchic favelas of Rio de Janeiro and finished at a crossroads town in rural Washington state, and many people helped along the way. Were I to be a part of a secession movement, I would certainly want all of the following people along, who were a great help in putting this book together. Members of my writing group who slogged through the earliest versions: Lisa Hoashi, Becky Kluth, Karen Munro, Tammy Lynne Stoner, Laura Larsell, Victoria Blake, and an especial thanks to David Naimon, who provided a sane ear for a truckload of book-anxiety, or mercilessly teased me out of it. John Metta helped me to understand that a drought of this scale is practically impossible in the region I set it, though I pig-headedly continued on anyway. Mel Favara, Jenni Fallein, Melanie Hudson, Marisa Anderson, Andrea Dunne, Bronwyn Barrick, Jan Parzybok, and Ezra Parzybok all helped tremendously by reading drafts of the book. I'm very grateful to my publisher, Gavin J. Grant, for believing in me, and for the enormous number of times he has read and worked on the book, easily winning the prize for the most work put in. The same goes for my agent, Eddie Schneider. A very early beginning was read by the good people of Rio Hondo Writer's Workshop, and of particular help were Kristin Livdahl, Maureen F. McHugh, and Karen Joy Fowler. Roy and Dottie Moulton were vital, providing space on their land for me to work and trusting I was not frittering away in there playing games on my phone, because I totally wasn't. Lastly: Laura Moulton, as always, as a co-conspirator, co-adventurer, and for braving that awful granite hunk of a first draft, and my kids, Coen and Sylvie, for indulging me in this madness.

Benjamin Parzybok is the author of the novel *Couch* and a number of short stories. He has been the creator/co-creator of many other projects, including *Gumball Poetry* (literary journal published in capsule machines), the Black Magic Insurance Agency (city-wide, one-night alternate reality game), and Project Hamad (an effort to free a Guantanamo inmate and shed light on habeas corpus). He lives in Portland with the artist Laura Moulton and their two kids. Find him online at levinofearth.com.

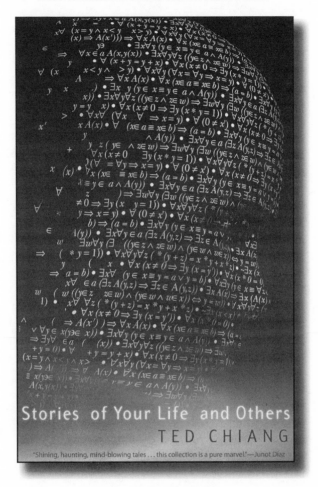

Stories of Your Life and Others
TED CHIANG

"Shining, haunting, mind-blowing tales . . . this collection is a pure marvel."—Junot Díaz

Ted Chiang's debut collection has been widely hailed as one of the best in recent memory. The eight stories in this book have received the Nebula, Hayakawa, Seiun, Sturgeon, Hugo, Locus, and Sidewise awards.

"Shining, haunting, mind-blowing tales . . . this collection is a pure marvel. Chiang is so exhilarating so original so stylish he just leaves you speechless."—Junot Díaz (author of *The Brief Wondrous Life of Oscar Wao*)

paper · $16 · 9781931520720 | ebook · $9.95 · 9781931520898

Shirley Jackson Award winner · *Publishers Weekly* Top 10 Best Books of the Year · io9 Best SF&F Books of the Year · Story Prize Notable Book · Tiptree Award Honor List · Philip K. Dick Award finalist

"Each tale is a beautifully written character study. . . . McHugh's great talent is in reminding us that the future could never be weirder — or sadder — than what lurks in the human psyche. This is definitely one of the best works of science fiction you'll read this year, or any thereafter."—Annalee Newitz, NPR

paper · $16 · 9781931520294 | ebook · $9.95 · 9781931520355

"A lot of people are looking for magic in the world today, but only Benjamin Parzybok thought to check the sofa, which is, I think, the place it's most likely to be found. *Couch* is a slacker epic: a gentle, funny book that ambles merrily from Coupland to Tolkien, and gives couch-surfing (among other things) a whole new meaning."
—Paul La Farge, author of *Haussmann, or The Distinction*

COUCH

benjamin parzybok

A novel. An odyssey. An epic furniture removal. A road trip. An exuberant and hilarious debut in which an episode of furniture moving gone awry becomes an impromptu quest of self-discovery, secret histories, and unexpected revelations.

"The essential message of *Couch* appears to be that the world and our lives would be better if we all got off our couches (literal and metaphorical) a bit more often."—*The Zone*

paper · $16 · 9781931520546 | ebook · $9.95 · 9781931520973